Princeless
RAVEN
THE PIRATE PRINCESS

Year Two:
Love and Revenge

Chapter Five:
The Kiss

Written By: Jeremy Whitley

Art By: Christine Hipp

Colors By: Xenia Pamfil

Lettered By: Justin Birch

Edited By: Nicole D'Andria

Cover By: Christine Hipp

Cover Colors By: Xenia Pamfil

Bryan Seaton: Publisher/ CEO - Shawn Gabborin: Editor In Chief - Jason Martin: Publisher-Danger Zone
Nicole D'Andria: Marketing Director/Editor - Danielle Davison: Executive Administrator
Chad Cicconi: Deck Swabber - Shawn Pryor: President of Creator Relations

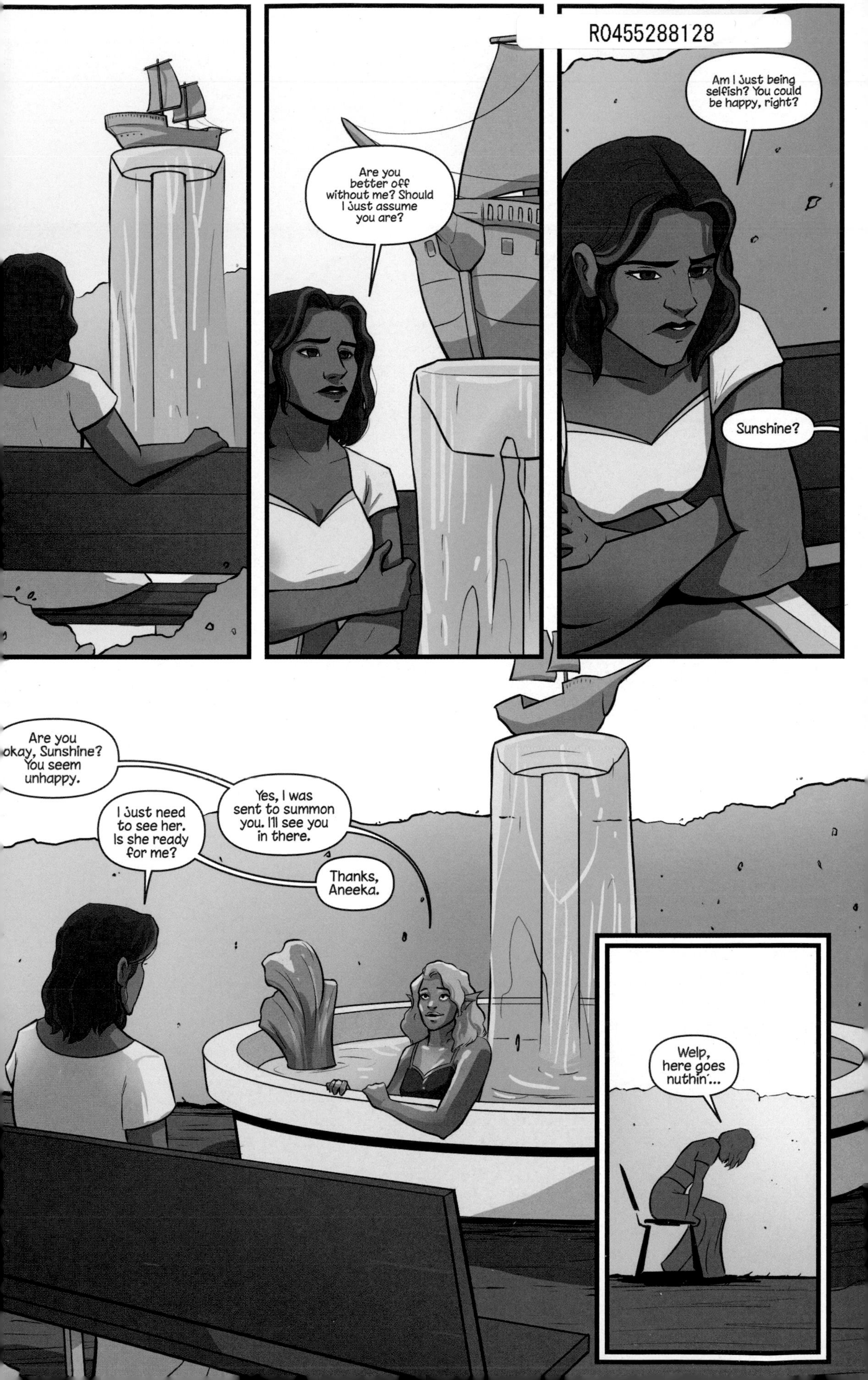
Are you better off without me? Should I just assume you are?
Am I just being selfish? You could be happy, right?
Sunshine?
Are you okay, Sunshine? You seem unhappy.
I just need to see her. Is she ready for me?
Yes, I was sent to summon you. I'll see you in there.
Thanks, Aneeka.
Welp, here goes nuthin'...

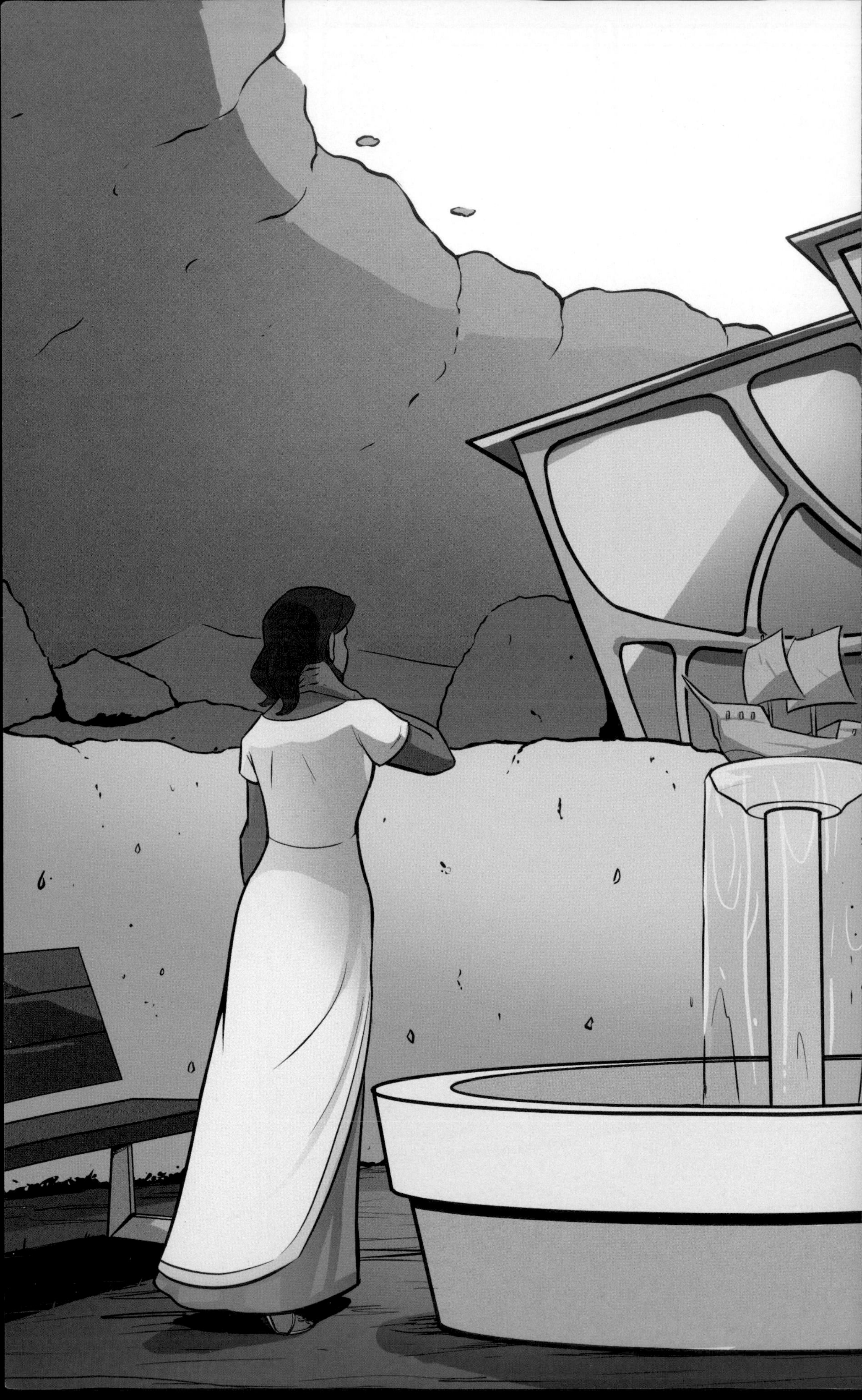

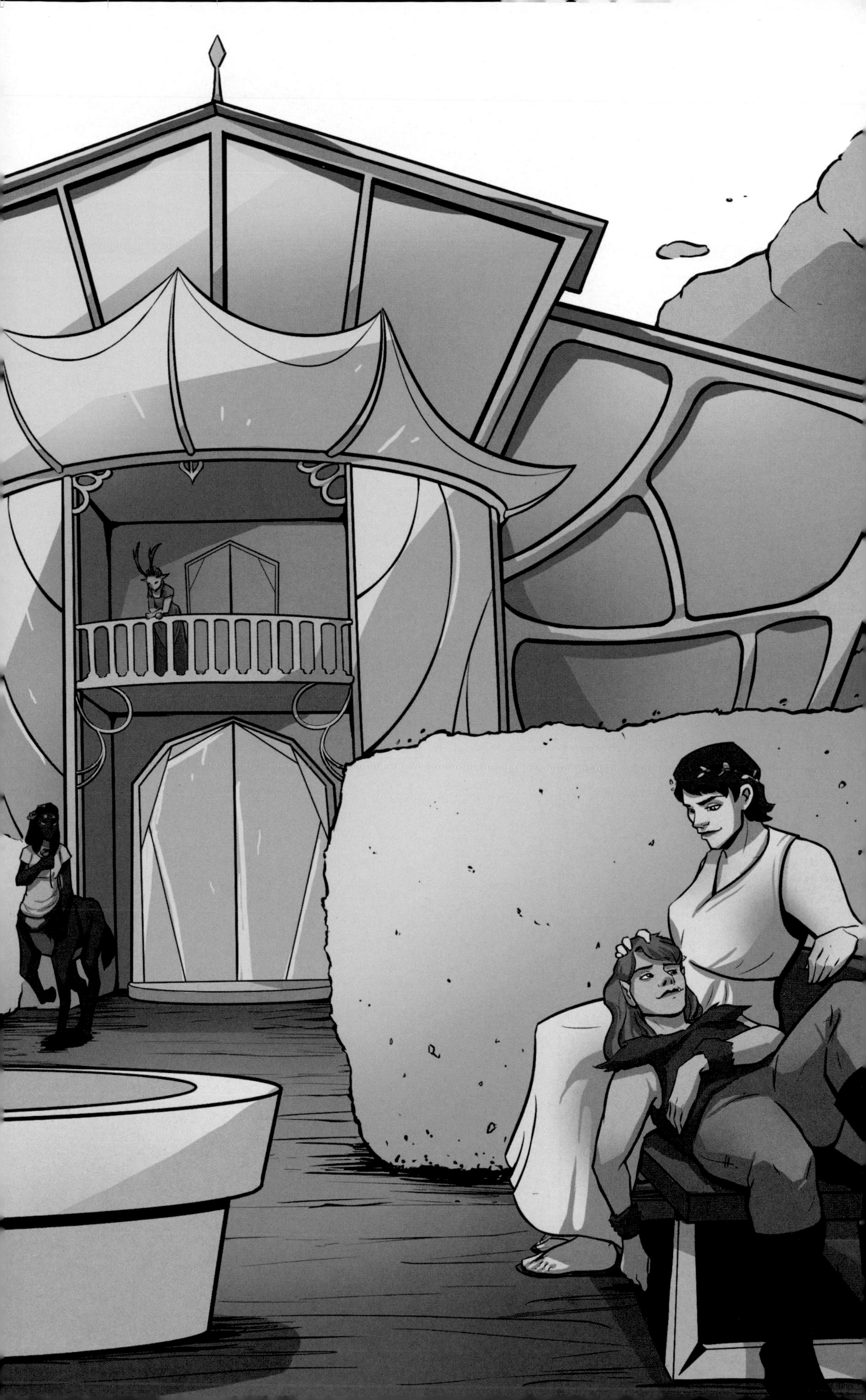

Melancholy still?

I'm afraid so, my liege. She seems unable to enjoy this place as the others have.

A shame. She is so beautiful when she smiles. I wish—

And here she is now.

Queen Pavarti. I am sorry to trouble you.

Nonsense, Sunshine! If you wish to speak with the Queen of the Sea, I wish to hear from you.

Thank you. Your highness, it's been a month since I arrived here.

I remember it well. One of my loyal subjects saved you from a watery grave.

Yes, highness, and I am very grateful.

But?

You said that if at the end of a month I still wanted to see my friends, you would let me see them.

I see. And now you wish to see them?

I do. I'm worried about them.

And if you see that they are well, will it calm your mind?

Yes, your highness.

Very well. Come to m[y] scrying poo[l]

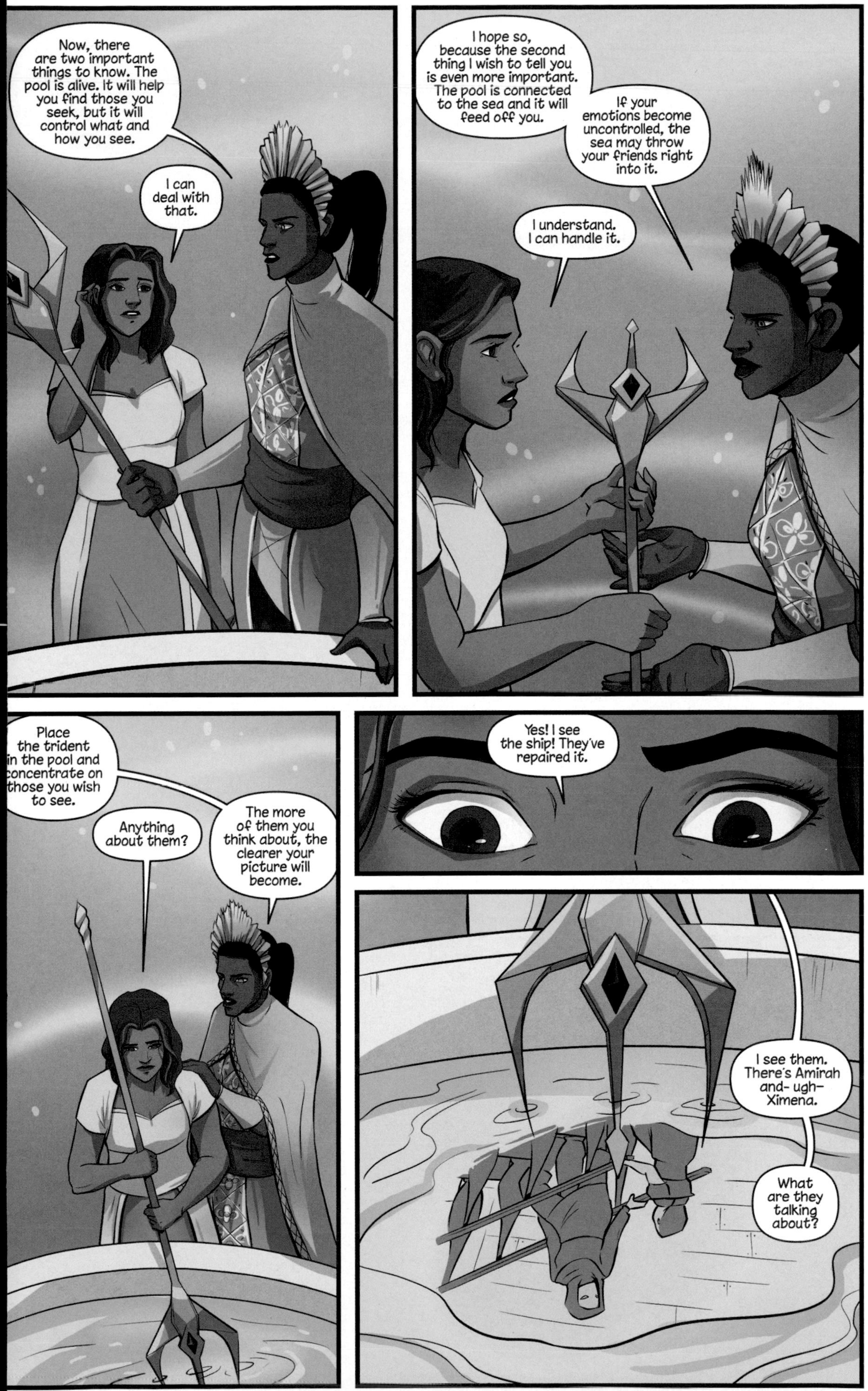
Now, there are two important things to know. The pool is alive. It will help you find those you seek, but it will control what and how you see.
I can deal with that.
I hope so, because the second thing I wish to tell you is even more important. The pool is connected to the sea and it will feed off you.
If your emotions become uncontrolled, the sea may throw your friends right into it.
I understand. I can handle it.
Place the trident in the pool and concentrate on those you wish to see.
Anything about them?
The more of them you think about, the clearer your picture will become.
Yes! I see the ship! They've repaired it.
I see them. There's Amirah and- ugh- Ximena.
What are they talking about?

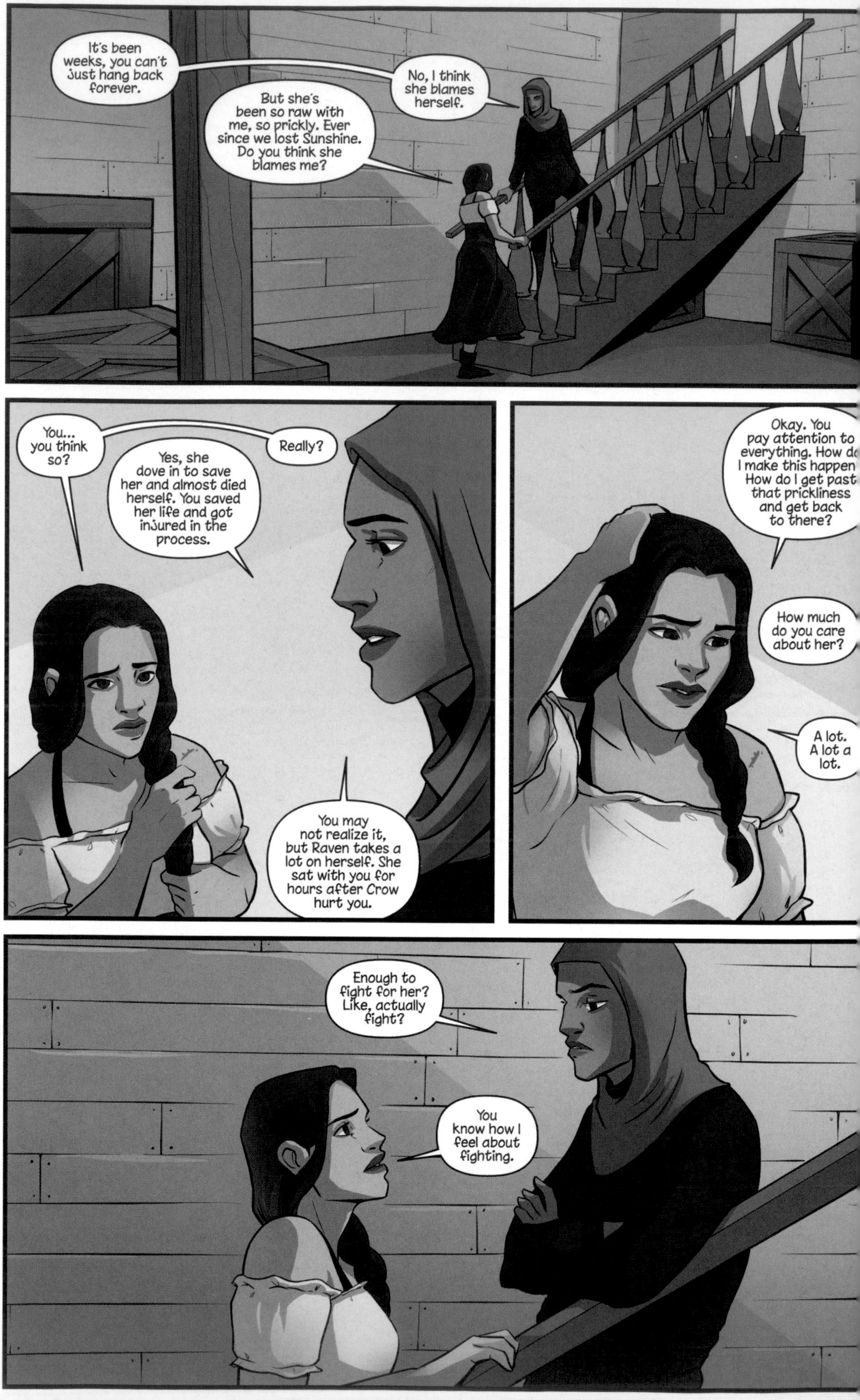
It's been weeks, you can't just hang back forever.
But she's been so raw with me, so prickly. Ever since we lost Sunshine. Do you think she blames me?
No, I think she blames herself.
You... you think so?
Really?
Yes, she dove in to save her and almost died herself. You saved her life and got injured in the process.
You may not realize it, but Raven takes a lot on herself. She sat with you for hours after Crow hurt you.
Okay. You pay attention to everything. How d
I make this happen
How do I get past that prickliness and get back to there?
How much do you care about her?
A lot. A lot a lot.
Enough to fight for her? Like, actually fight?
You know how I feel about fighting.

And I know how Raven feels. Raven feels that if you love something, you fight for it.

Is that—

Yes, that's why she raided an island and took on a small army for you.

Guh, just the thought of that make me lightheaded.

Oh, hey guys.

Hello, Zoe.

Hi.

Okay, so, I'm just gonna pretend like you guys didn't just completely stop talking the moment I got close to you.

And just...

Yeah, okay.

I'm just saying, if you want Raven to pay attention to you, ask her to teach you to fight.

Whew, I'm not sure if I'm ready for that.

You're not sure you're ready for an exercise that guarantees she'll spend hours with you, will certainly involve physical contact, and you know makes her happy?

I just—

Well... does that help you make up your mind?

Oh yeah.

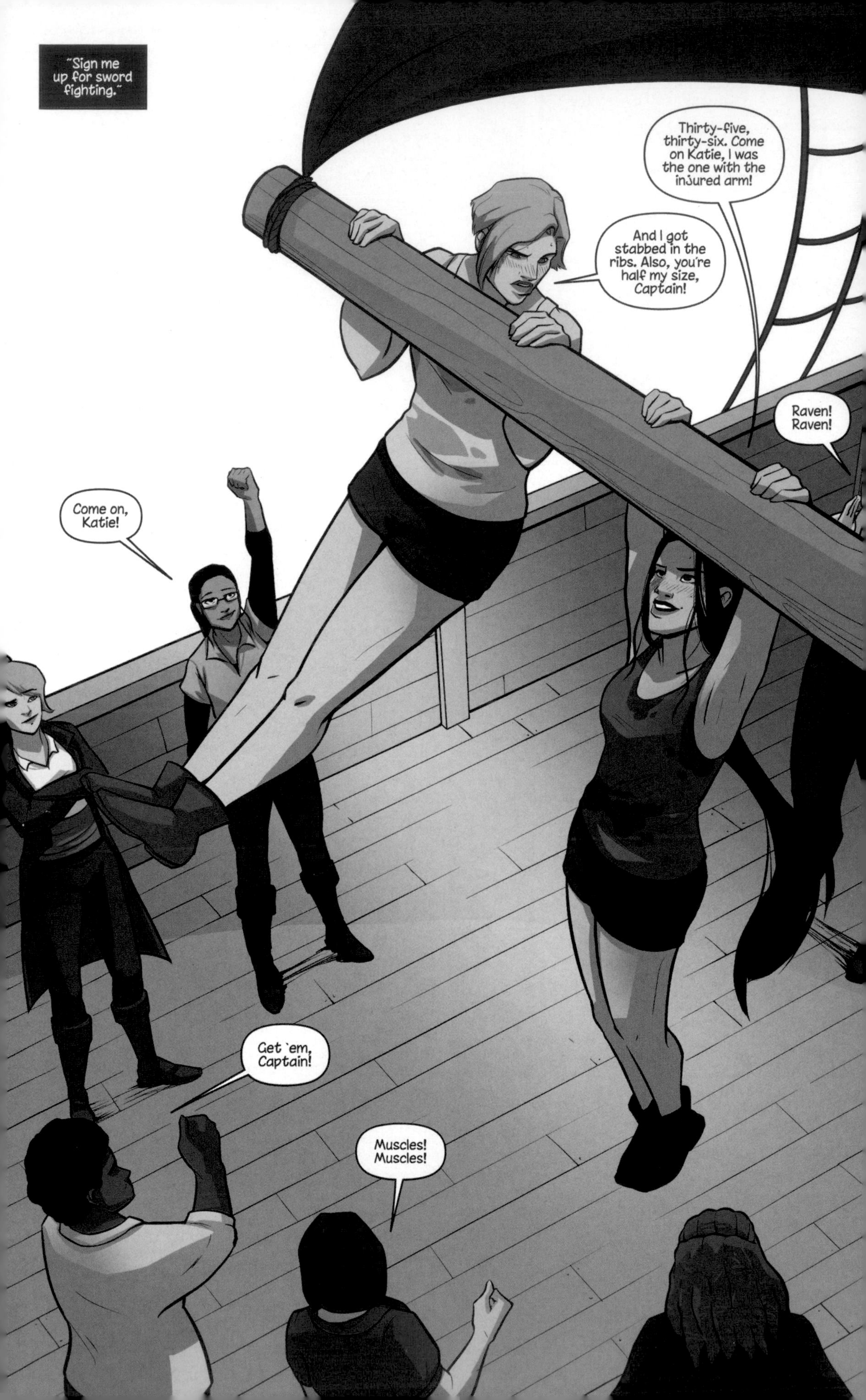
"Sign me up for sword fighting."
Thirty-five, thirty-six. Come on Katie, I was the one with the injured arm!
And I got stabbed in the ribs. Also, you're half my size, Captain!
Raven! Raven!
Come on, Katie!
Get 'em, Captain!
Muscles! Muscles!

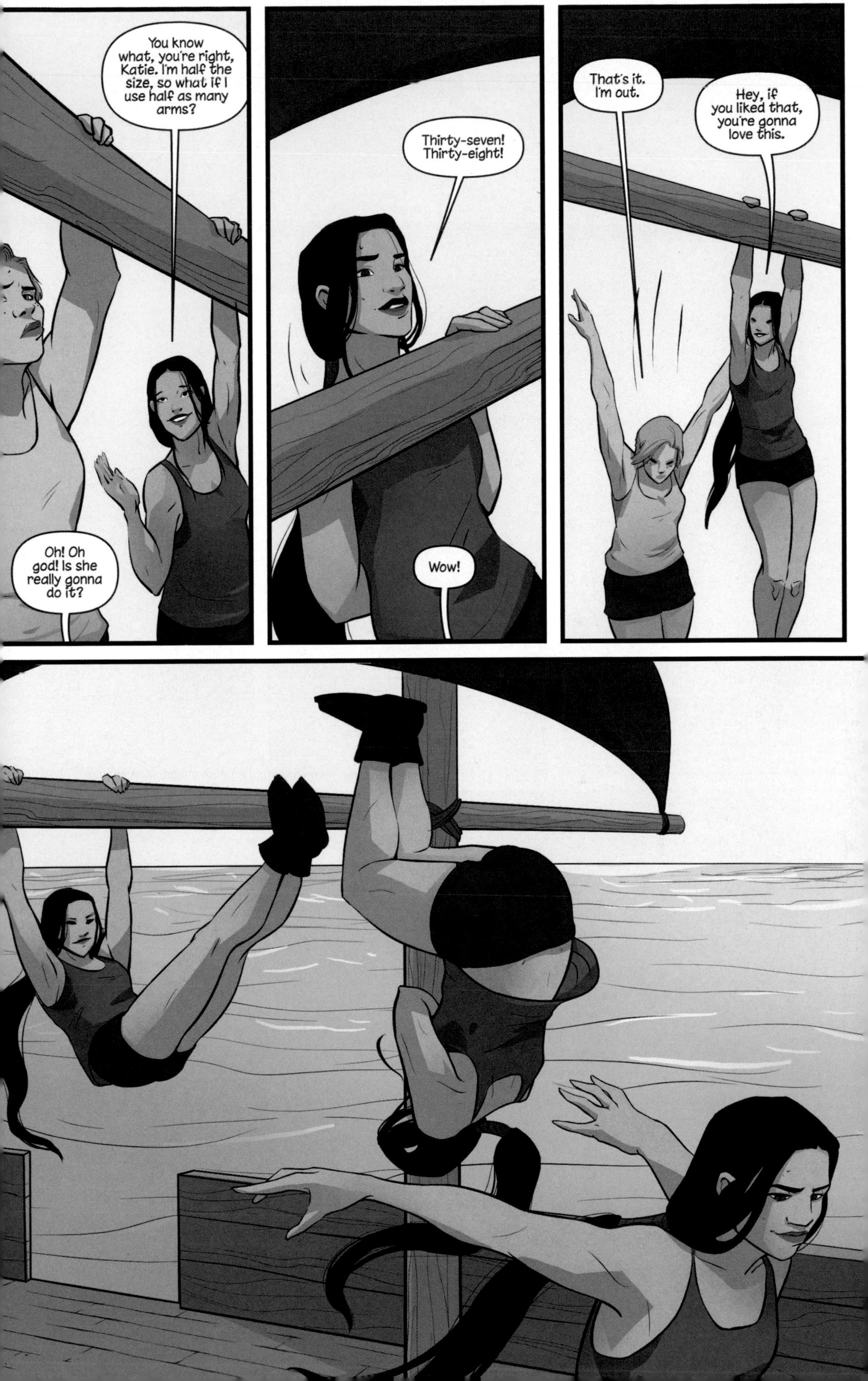
You know what, you're right, Katie. I'm half the size, so what if I use half as many arms?
Oh! Oh god! Is she really gonna do it?
Thirty-seven! Thirty-eight!
Wow!
That's it. I'm out.
Hey, if you liked that, you're gonna love this.

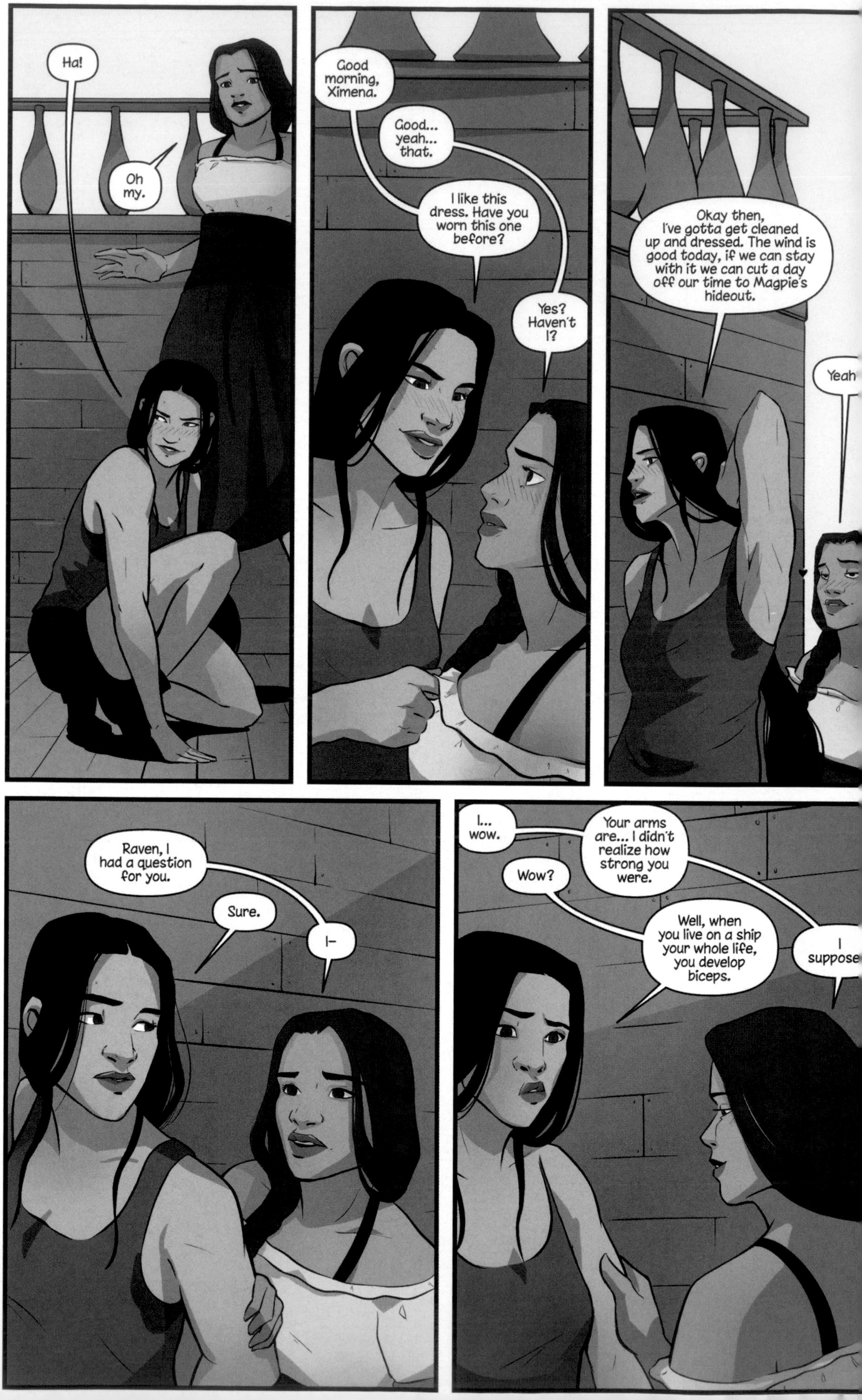
Ha!
Oh my.
Good morning, Ximena.
Good... yeah... that.
I like this dress. Have you worn this one before?
Yes? Haven't I?
Okay then, I've gotta get cleaned up and dressed. The wind is good today, if we can stay with it we can cut a day off our time to Magpie's hideout.
Yeah
Raven, I had a question for you.
Sure.
I–
I... wow.
Your arms are... I didn't realize how strong you were.
Wow?
Well, when you live on a ship your whole life, you develop biceps.
I suppose

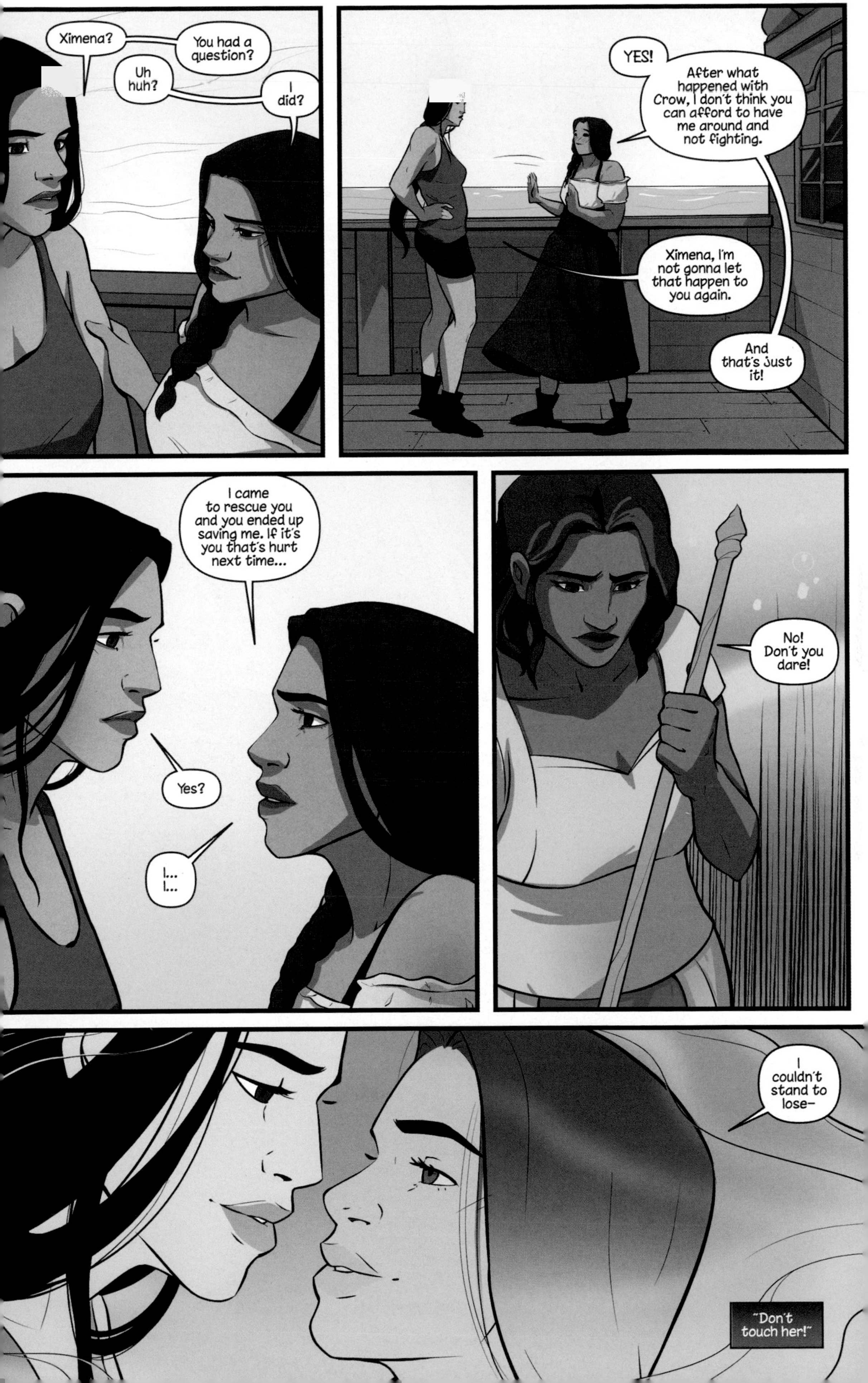
Ximena?
You had a question?
Uh huh?
I did?
YES!
After what happened with Crow, I don't think you can afford to have me around and not fighting.
Ximena, I'm not gonna let that happen to you again.
And that's just it!
I came to rescue you and you ended up saving me. If it's you that's hurt next time...
Yes?
I... I...
No! Don't you dare!
I couldn't stand to lose—
"Don't touch her!"

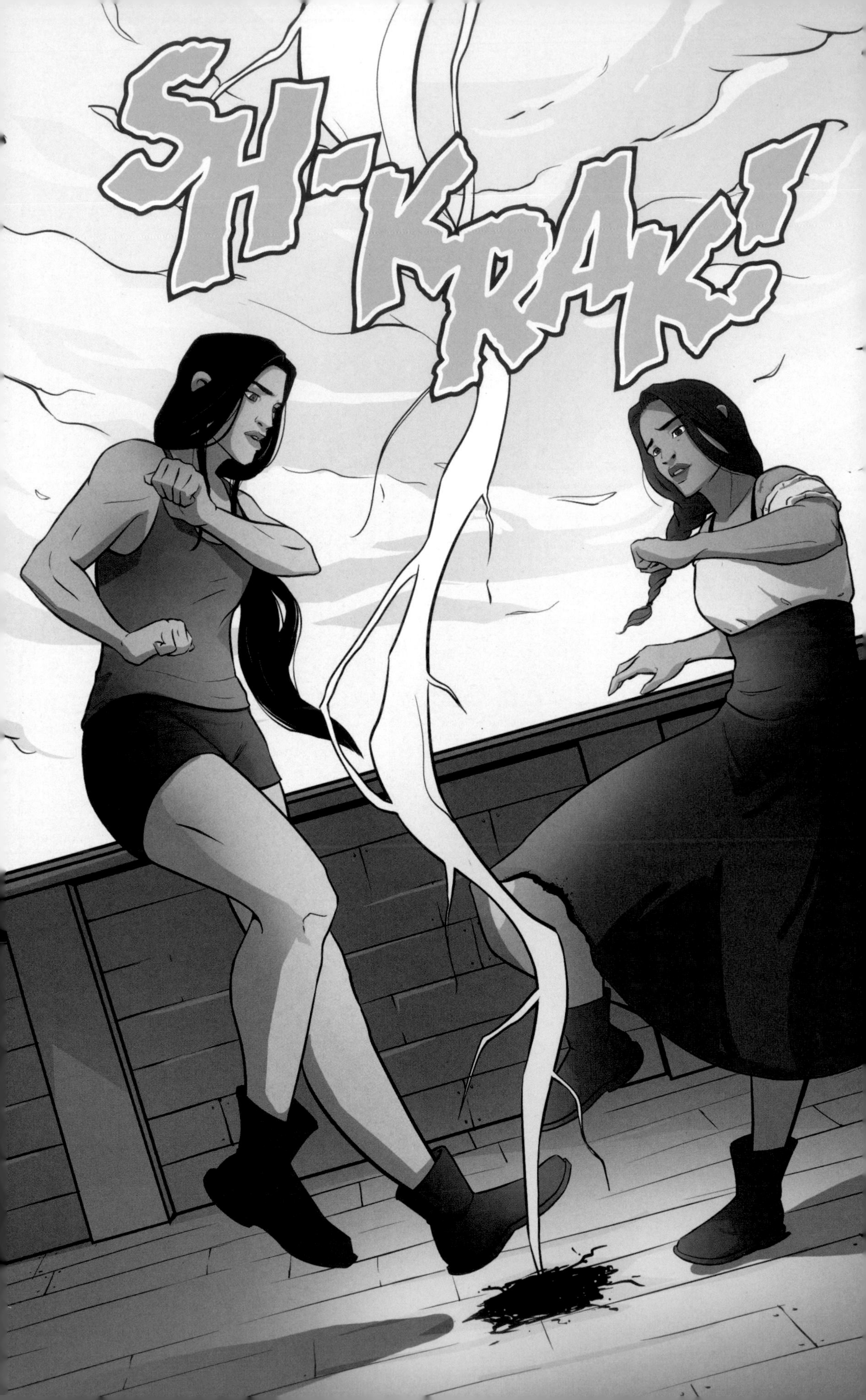
SH-KRAK!

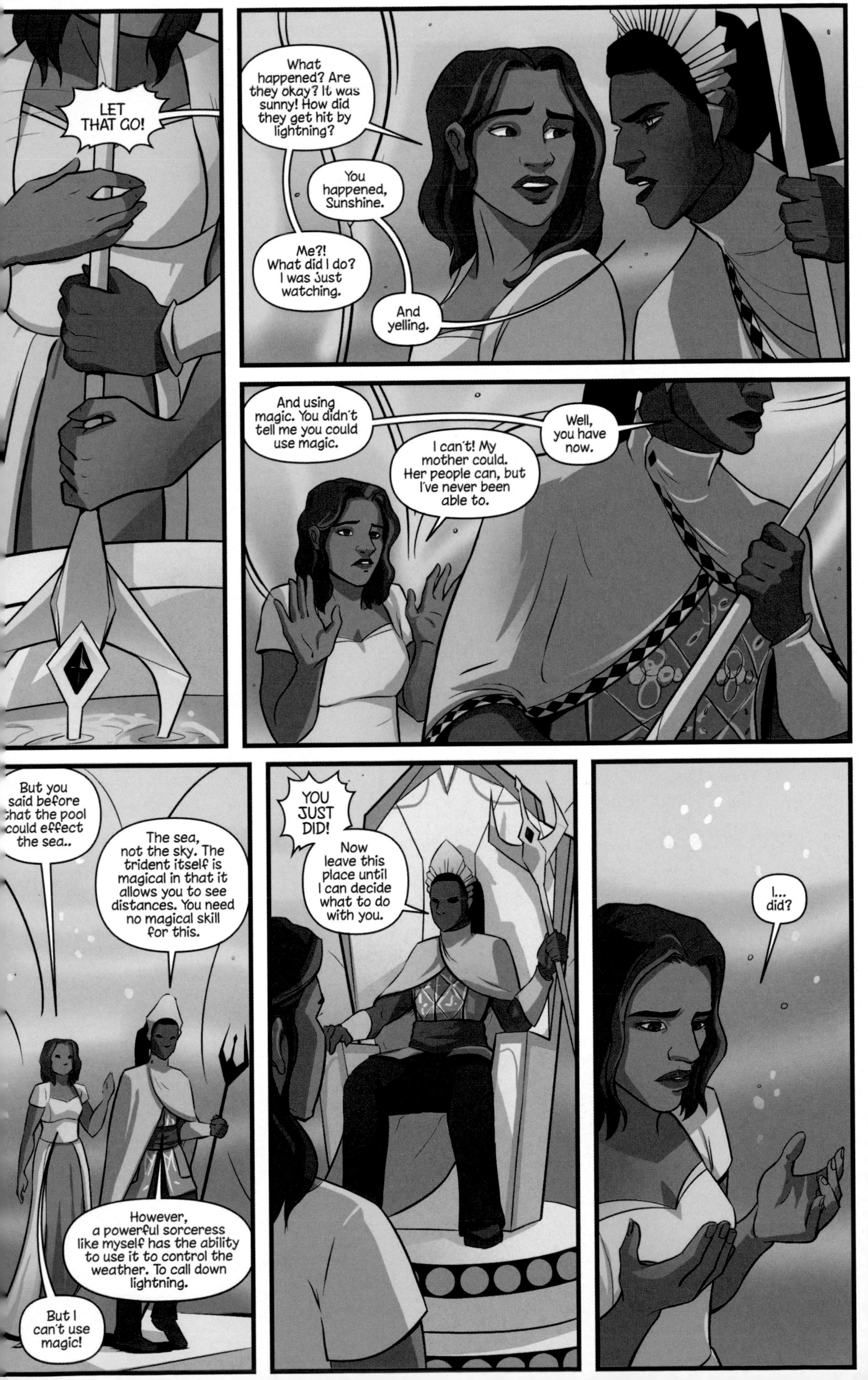
LET THAT GO!
What happened? Are they okay? It was sunny! How did they get hit by lightning?
You happened, Sunshine.
Me?! What did I do? I was just watching.
And yelling.
And using magic. You didn't tell me you could use magic.
Well, you have now.
I can't! My mother could. Her people can, but I've never been able to.
But you said before that the pool could effect the sea..
The sea, not the sky. The trident itself is magical in that it allows you to see distances. You need no magical skill for this.
However, a powerful sorceress like myself has the ability to use it to control the weather. To call down lightning.
But I can't use magic!
YOU JUST DID!
Now leave this place until I can decide what to do with you.
I... did?

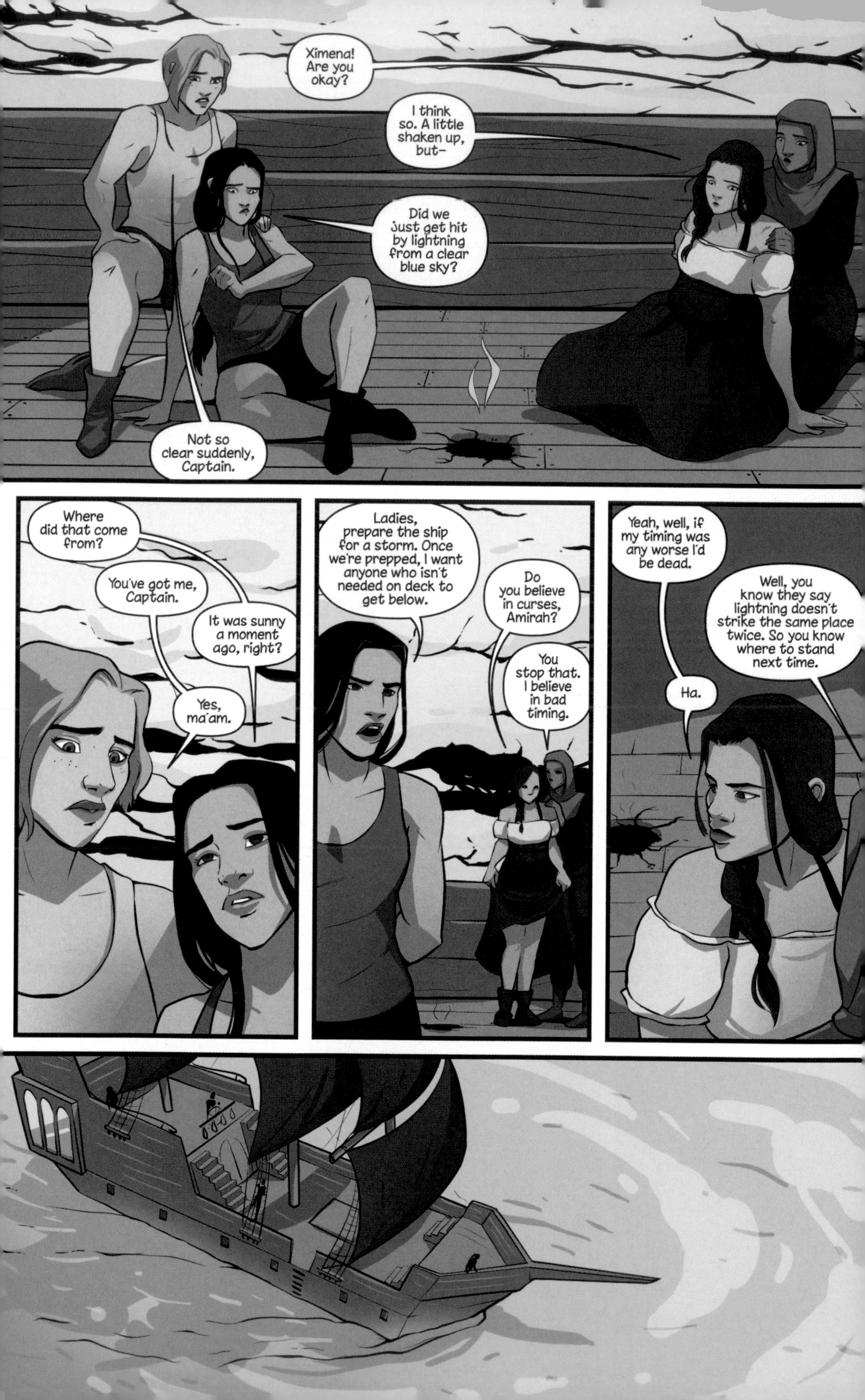
Ximena! Are you okay?
I think so. A little shaken up, but–
Did we just get hit by lightning from a clear blue sky?
Not so clear suddenly, Captain.
Where did that come from?
You've got me, Captain.
It was sunny a moment ago, right?
Yes, ma'am.
Ladies, prepare the ship for a storm. Once we're prepped, I want anyone who isn't needed on deck to get below.
Do you believe in curses, Amirah?
You stop that. I believe in bad timing.
Yeah, well, if my timing was any worse I'd be dead.
Well, you know they say lightning doesn't strike the same place twice. So you know where to stand next time.
Ha.

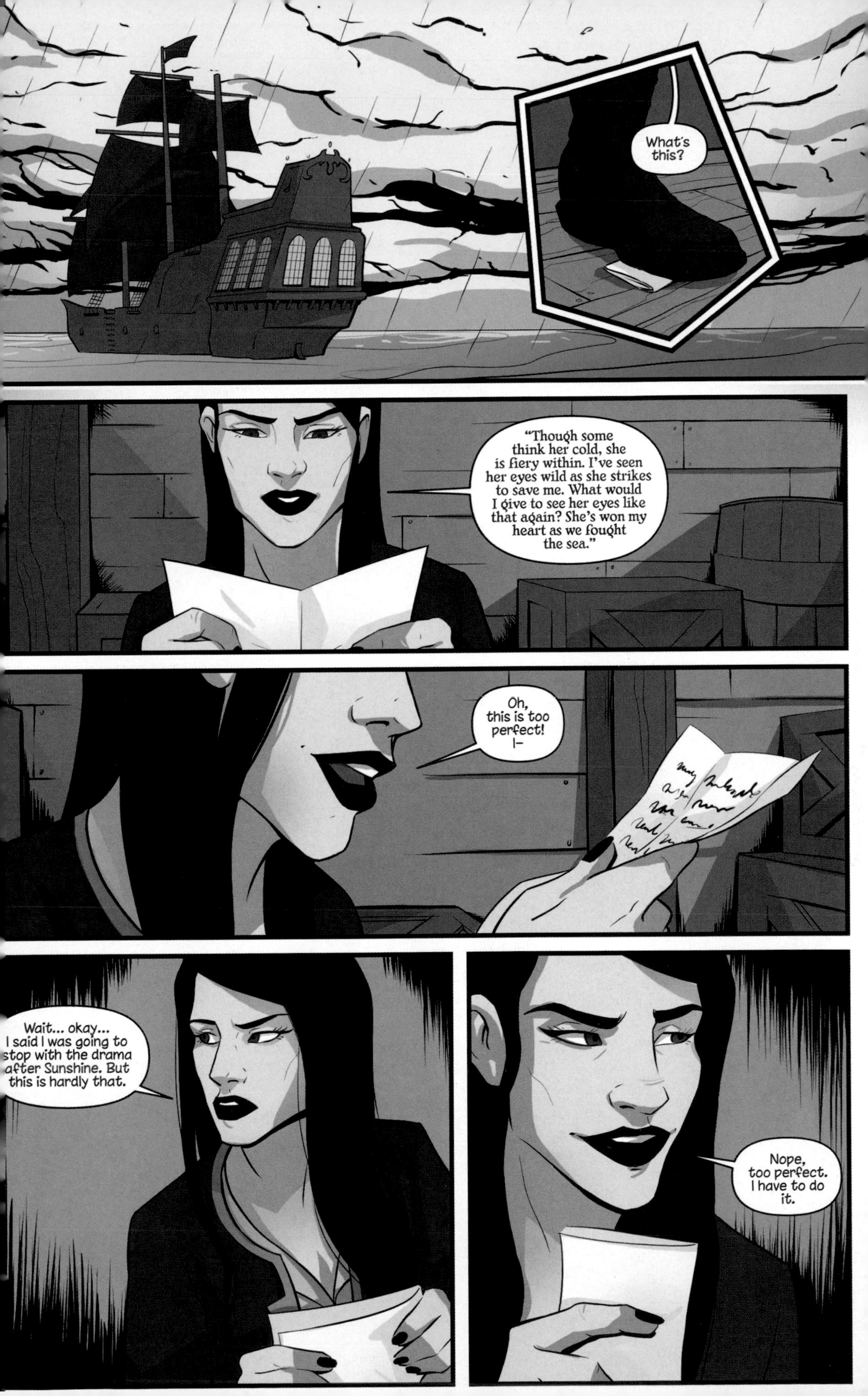
What's this?
"Though some think her cold, she is fiery within. I've seen her eyes wild as she strikes to save me. What would I give to see her eyes like that again? She's won my heart as we fought the sea."
Oh, this is too perfect! I–
Wait... okay... I said I was going to stop with the drama after Sunshine. But this is hardly that.
Nope, too perfect. I have to do it.

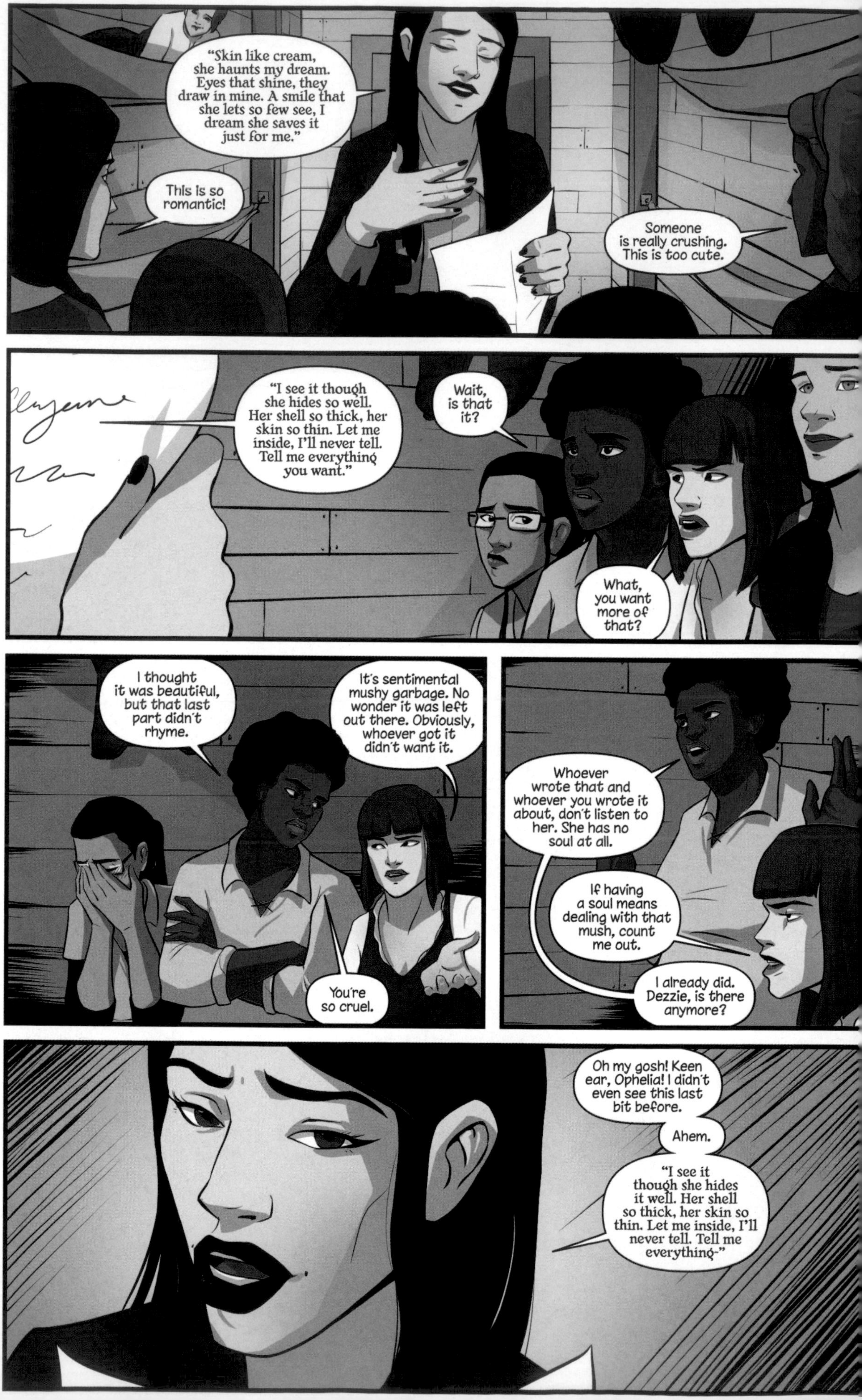
"Skin like cream, she haunts my dream. Eyes that shine, they draw in mine. A smile that she lets so few see, I dream she saves it just for me."
This is so romantic!
Someone is really crushing. This is too cute.
"I see it though she hides so well. Her shell so thick, her skin so thin. Let me inside, I'll never tell. Tell me everything you want."
Wait, is that it?
What, you want more of that?
I thought it was beautiful, but that last part didn't rhyme.
It's sentimental mushy garbage. No wonder it was left out there. Obviously, whoever got it didn't want it.
You're so cruel.
Whoever wrote that and whoever you wrote it about, don't listen to her. She has no soul at all.
If having a soul means dealing with that mush, count me out.
I already did. Dezzie, is there anymore?
Oh my gosh! Keen ear, Ophelia! I didn't even see this last bit before.
Ahem.
"I see it though she hides it well. Her shell so thick, her skin so thin. Let me inside, I'll never tell. Tell me everything-"

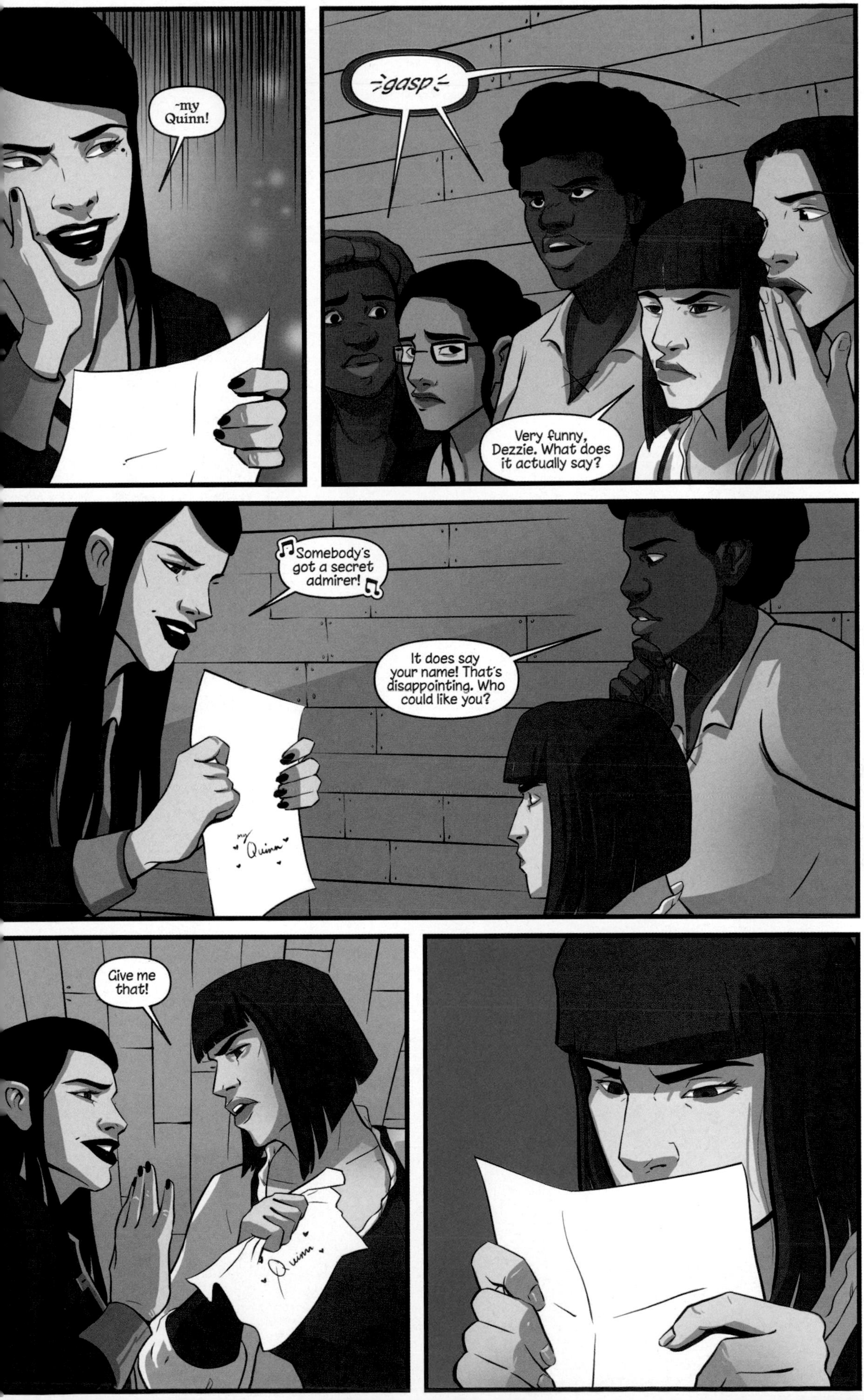

-my Quinn!
gasp
Very funny, Dezzie. What does it actually say?
Somebody's got a secret admirer!
my Quinn
It does say your name! That's disappointing. Who could like you?
Give me that!
Quinn

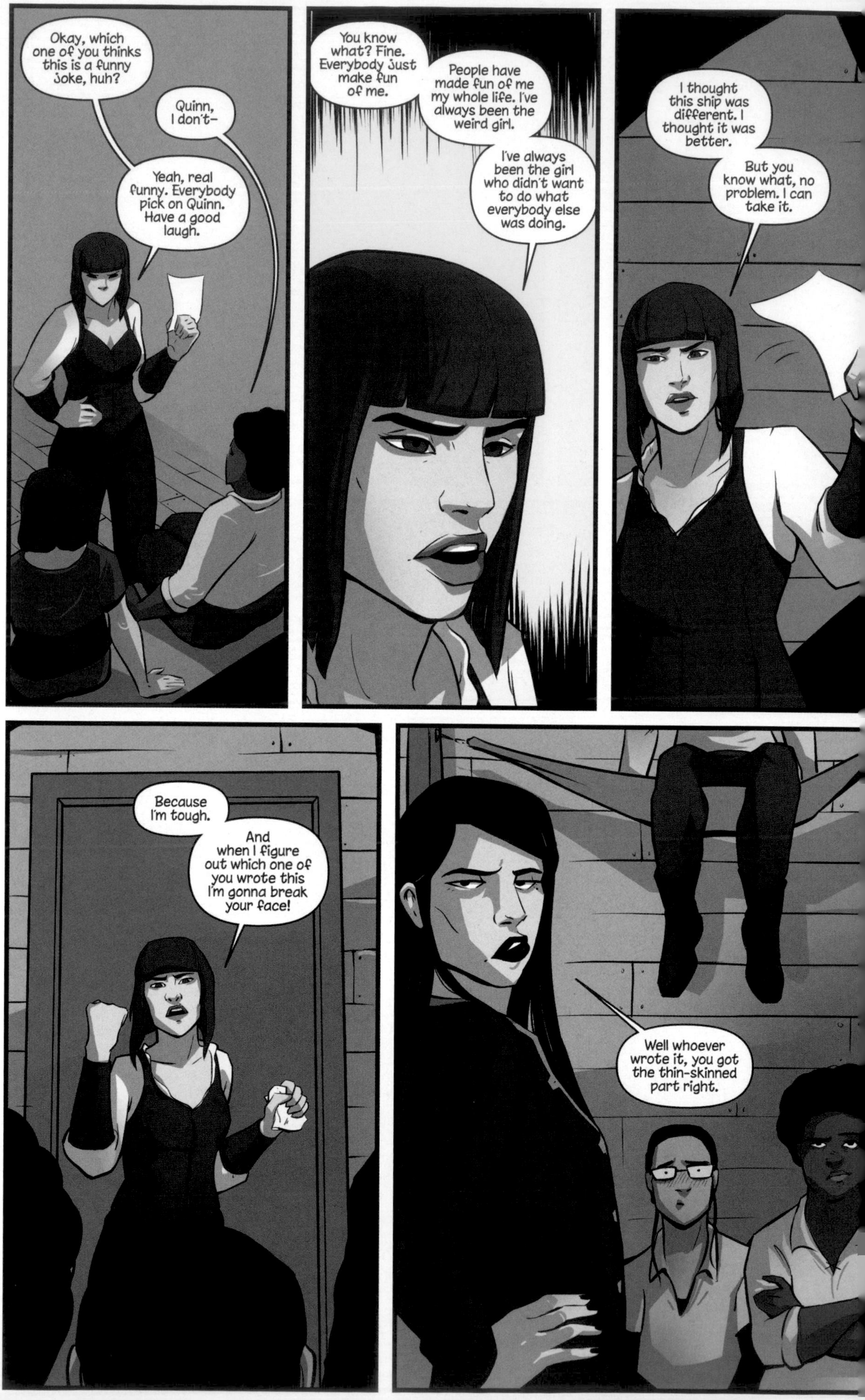

Okay, which one of you thinks this is a funny joke, huh?
Quinn, I don't-
Yeah, real funny. Everybody pick on Quinn. Have a good laugh.
You know what? Fine. Everybody just make fun of me.
People have made fun of me my whole life. I've always been the weird girl.
I've always been the girl who didn't want to do what everybody else was doing.
I thought this ship was different. I thought it was better.
But you know what, no problem. I can take it.
Because I'm tough.
And when I figure out which one of you wrote this I'm gonna break your face!
Well whoever wrote it, you got the thin-skinned part right.

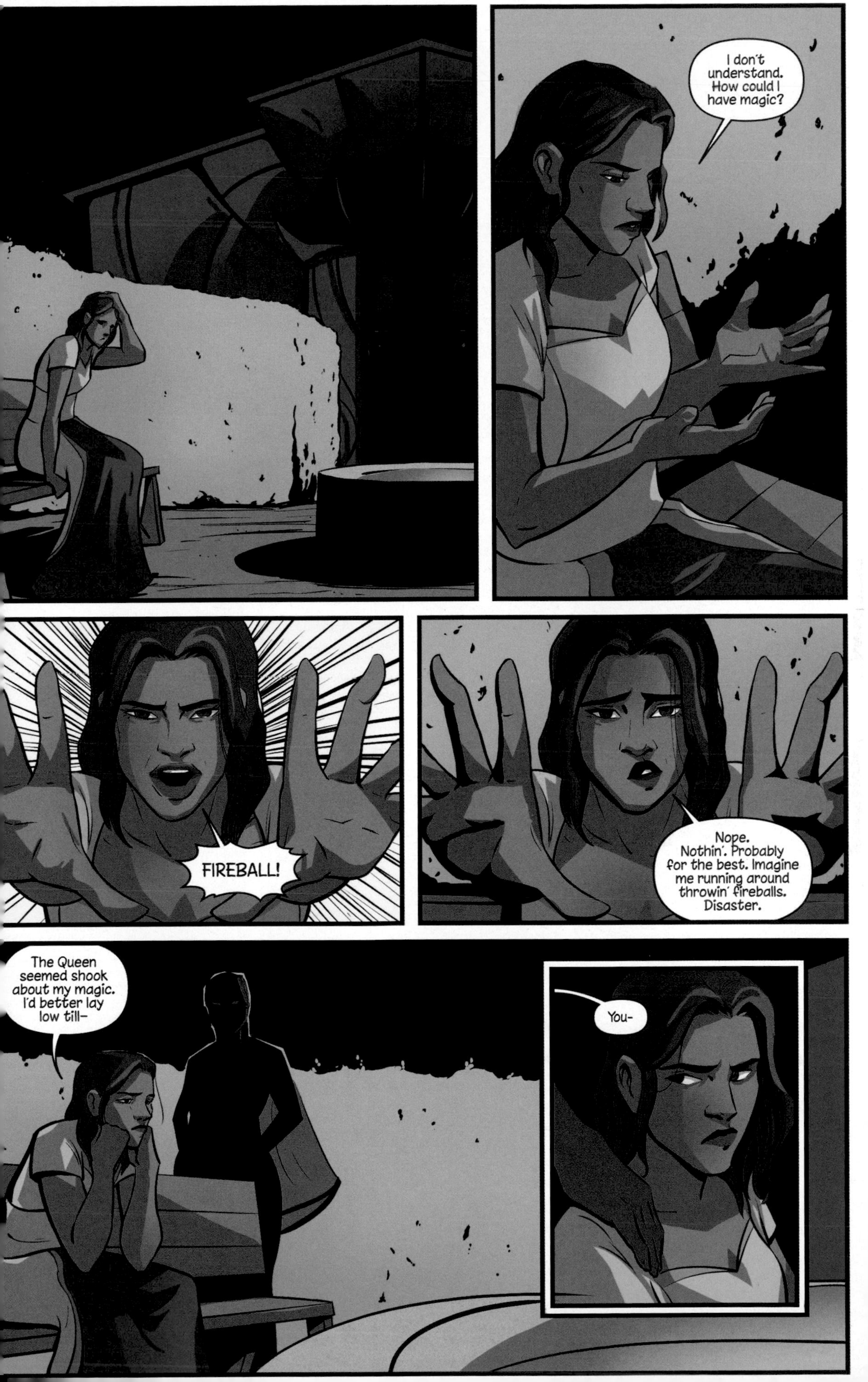
I don't understand. How could I have magic?
FIREBALL!
Nope. Nothin'. Probably for the best. Imagine me running around throwin' fireballs. Disaster.
The Queen seemed shook about my magic. I'd better lay low till–
You–

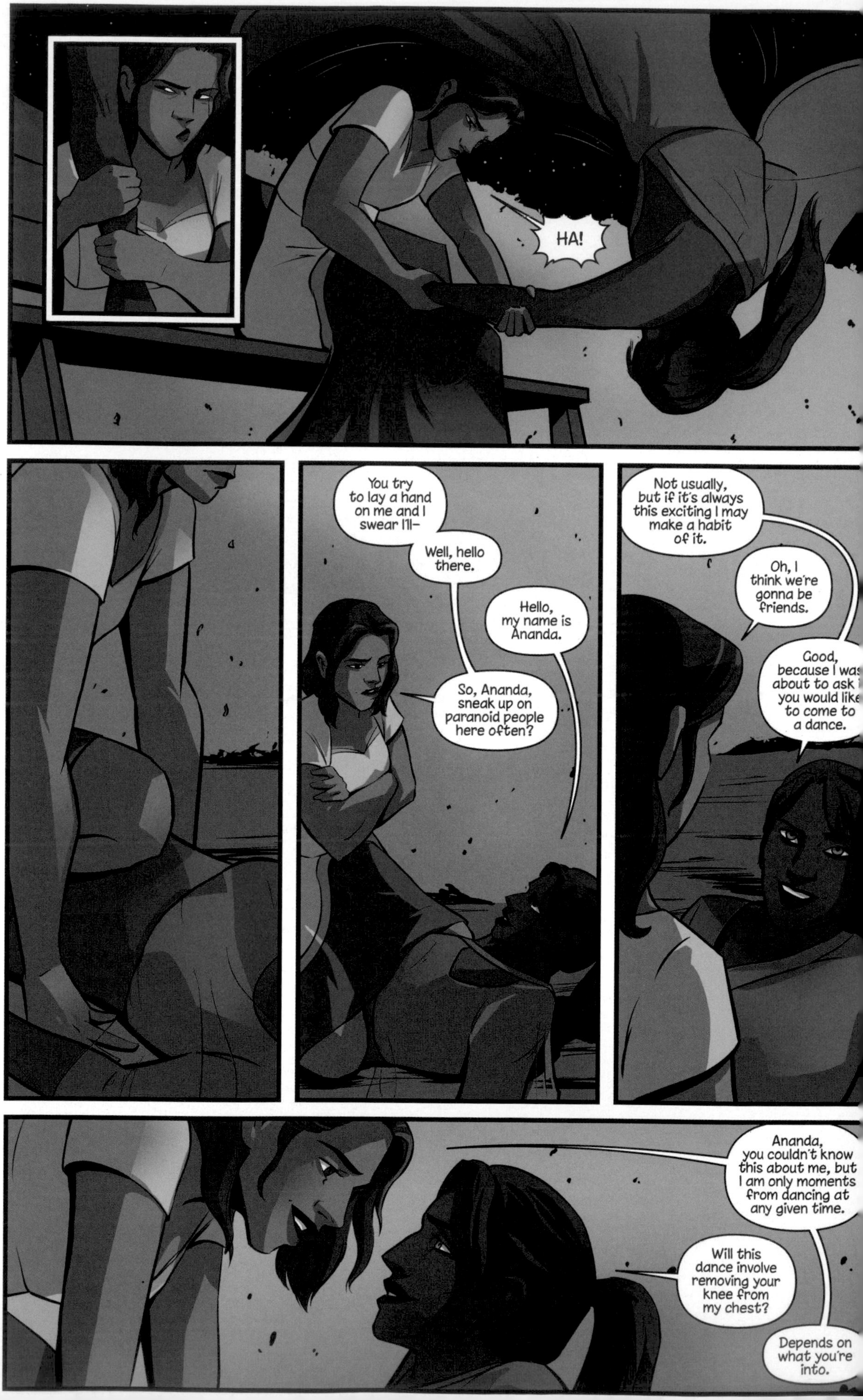
HA!
You try to lay a hand on me and I swear I'll–
Well, hello there.
Hello, my name is Ananda.
So, Ananda, sneak up on paranoid people here often?
Not usually, but if it's always this exciting I may make a habit of it.
Oh, I think we're gonna be friends.
Good, because I was about to ask if you would like to come to a dance.
Ananda, you couldn't know this about me, but I am only moments from dancing at any given time.
Will this dance involve removing your knee from my chest?
Depends on what you're into.

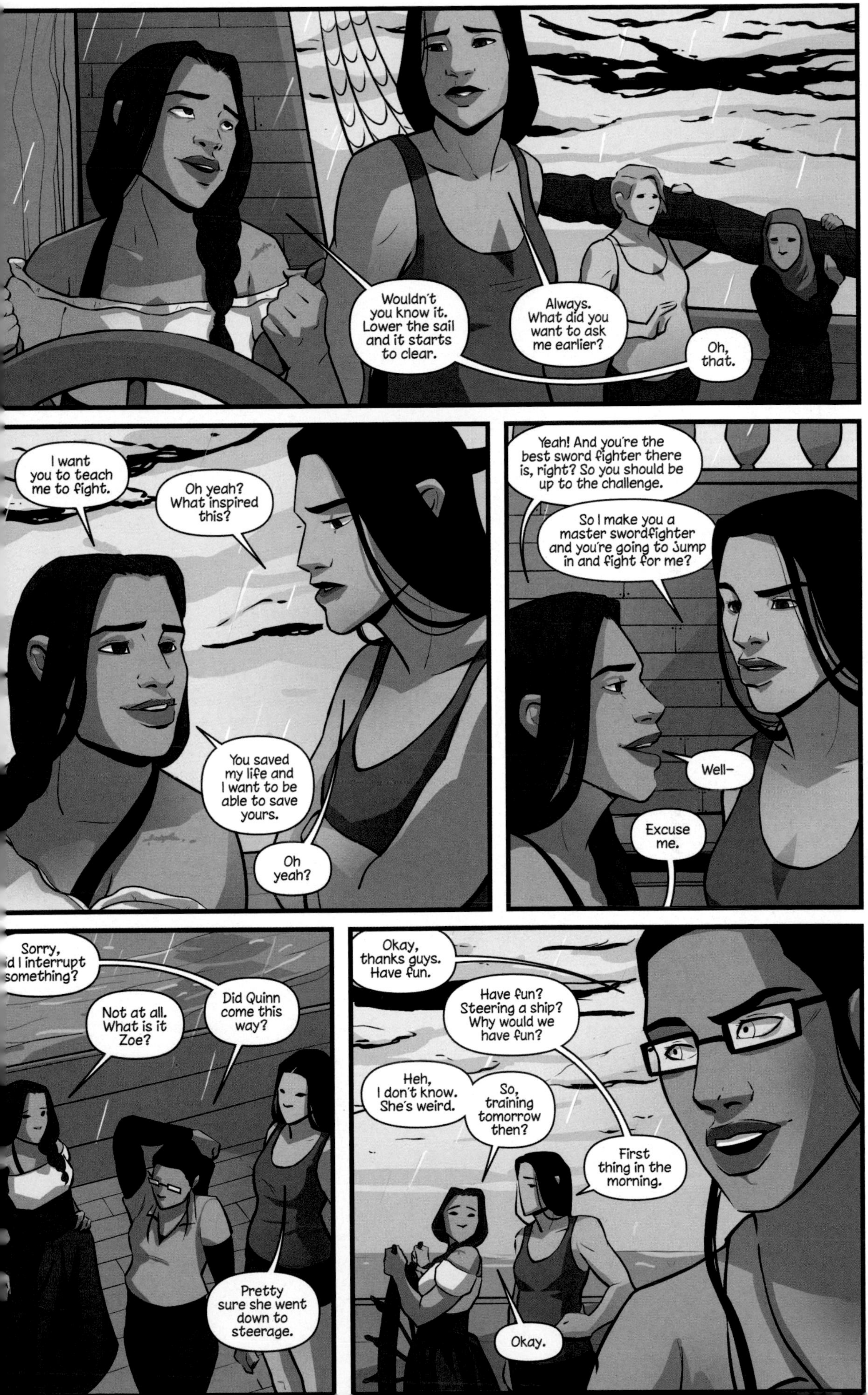
Wouldn't you know it. Lower the sail and it starts to clear.
Always. What did you want to ask me earlier?
Oh, that.
I want you to teach me to fight.
Oh yeah? What inspired this?
You saved my life and I want to be able to save yours.
Oh yeah?
Yeah! And you're the best sword fighter there is, right? So you should be up to the challenge.
So I make you a master swordfighter and you're going to jump in and fight for me?
Well-
Excuse me.
Sorry, id I interrupt something?
Not at all. What is it Zoe?
Did Quinn come this way?
Pretty sure she went down to steerage.
Okay, thanks guys. Have fun.
Have fun? Steering a ship? Why would we have fun?
Heh, I don't know. She's weird.
So, training tomorrow then?
First thing in the morning.
Okay.

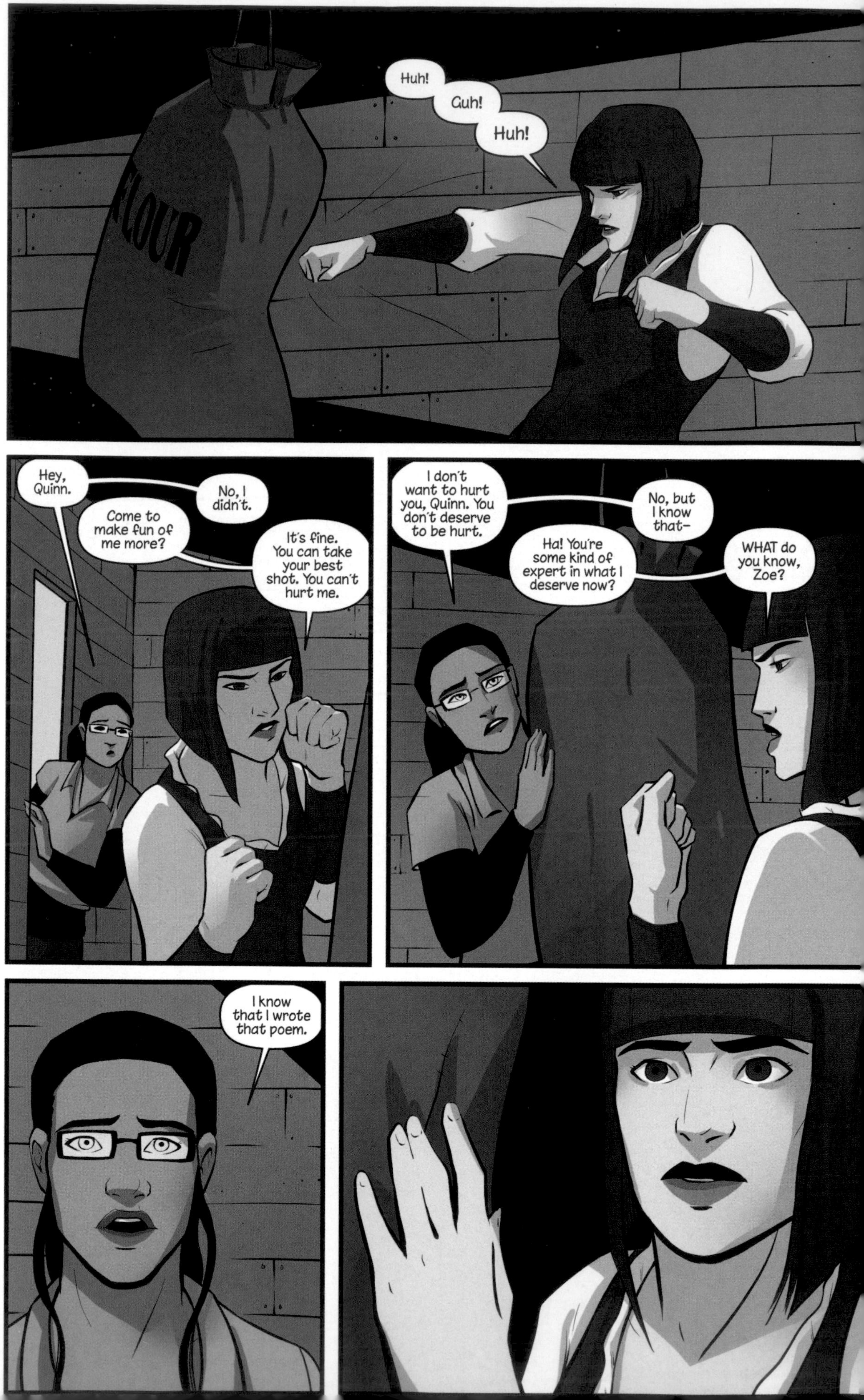
Huh!
Guh!
Huh!
FLOUR
Hey, Quinn.
Come to make fun of me more?
No, I didn't.
It's fine. You can take your best shot. You can't hurt me.
I don't want to hurt you, Quinn. You don't deserve to be hurt.
Ha! You're some kind of expert in what I deserve now?
No, but I know that-
WHAT do you know, Zoe?
I know that I wrote that poem.

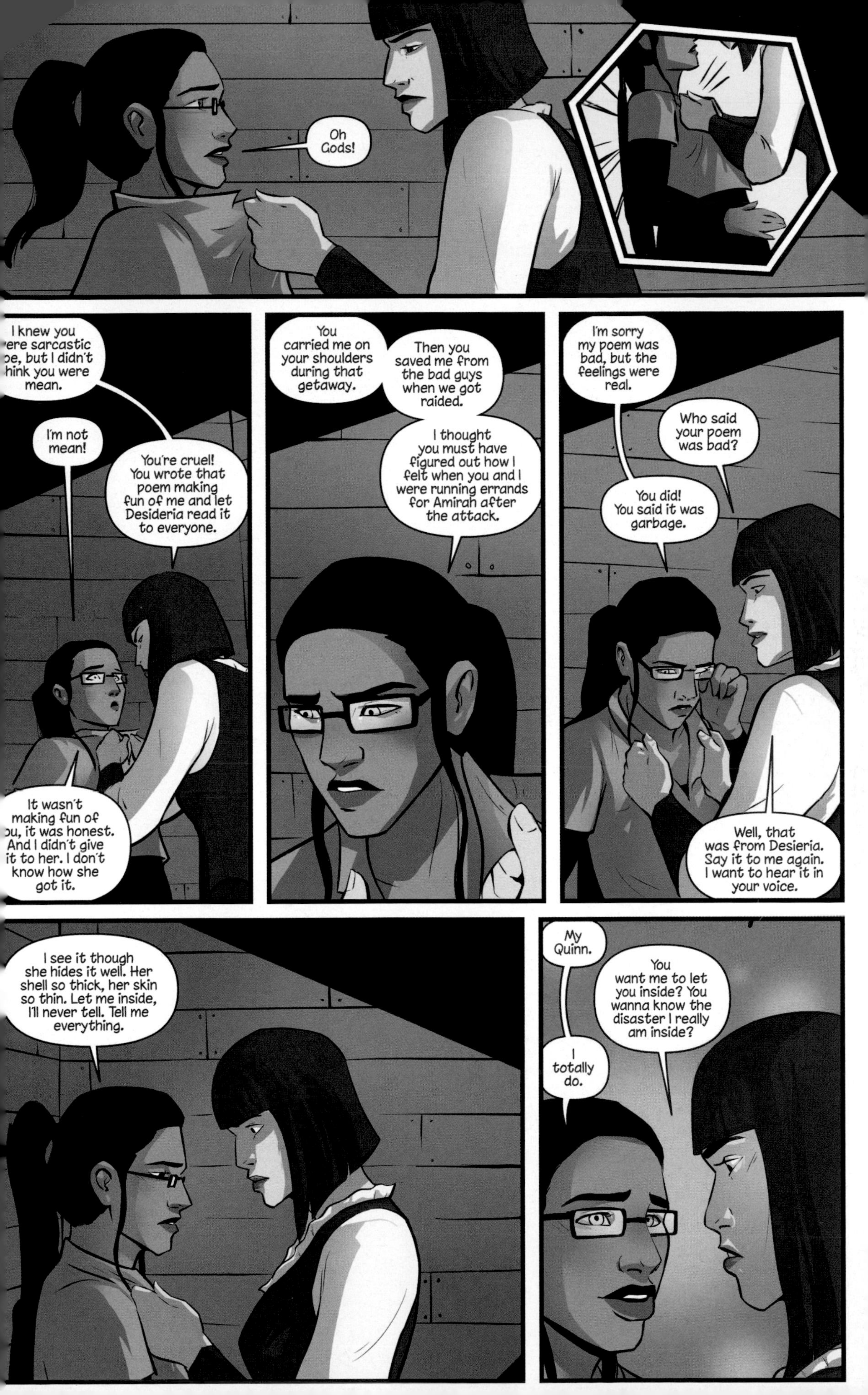
Oh Gods!
I knew you ere sarcastic oe, but I didn't hink you were mean.
I'm not mean!
You're cruel! You wrote that poem making fun of me and let Desideria read it to everyone.
It wasn't making fun of ou, it was honest. And I didn't give it to her. I don't know how she got it.
You carried me on your shoulders during that getaway.
Then you saved me from the bad guys when we got raided.
I thought you must have figured out how I felt when you and I were running errands for Amirah after the attack.
I'm sorry my poem was bad, but the feelings were real.
Who said your poem was bad?
You did! You said it was garbage.
Well, that was from Desieria. Say it to me again. I want to hear it in your voice.
I see it though she hides it well. Her shell so thick, her skin so thin. Let me inside, I'll never tell. Tell me everything.
My Quinn.
You want me to let you inside? You wanna know the disaster I really am inside?
I totally do.

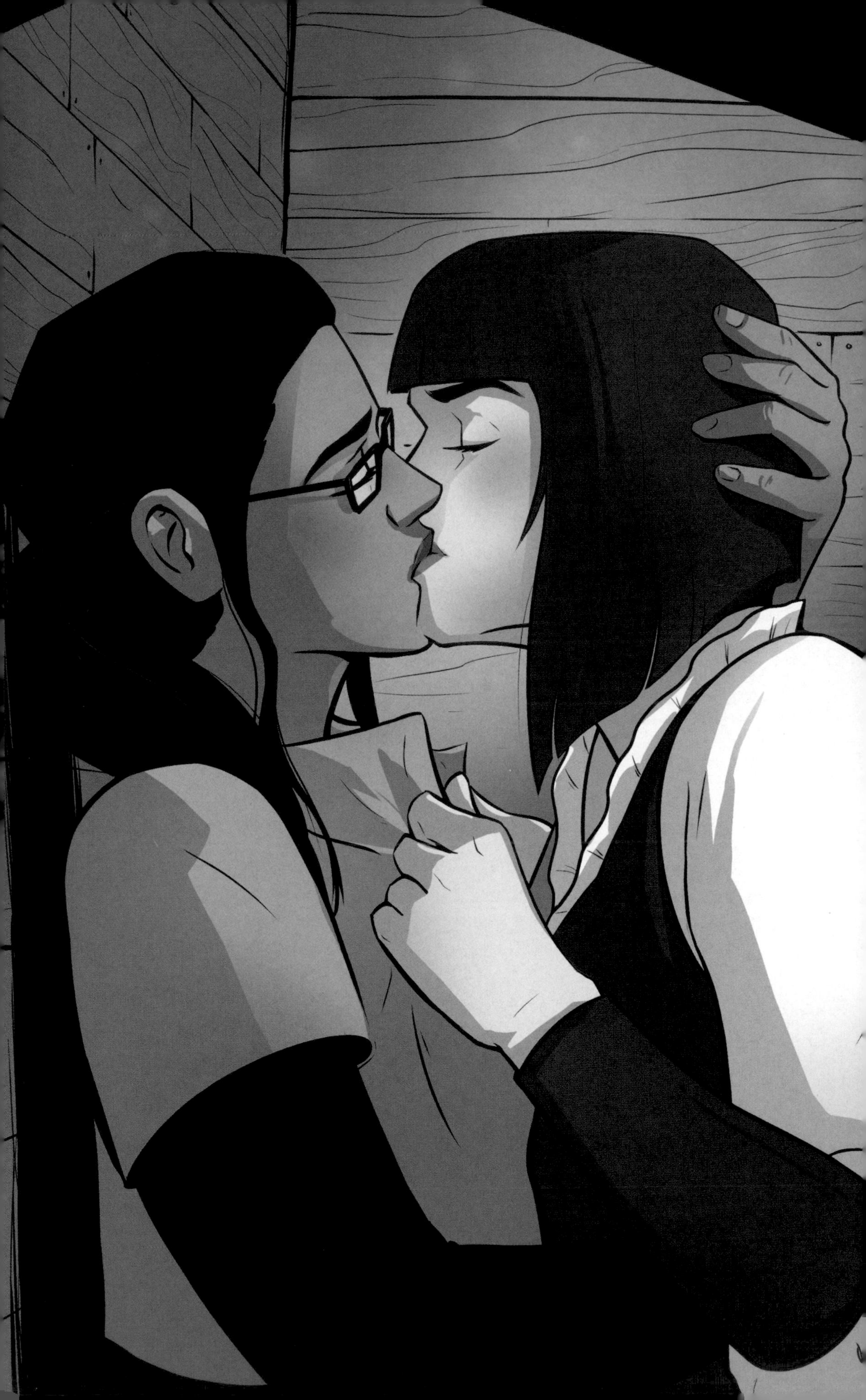

Cover thumbnails by Christine

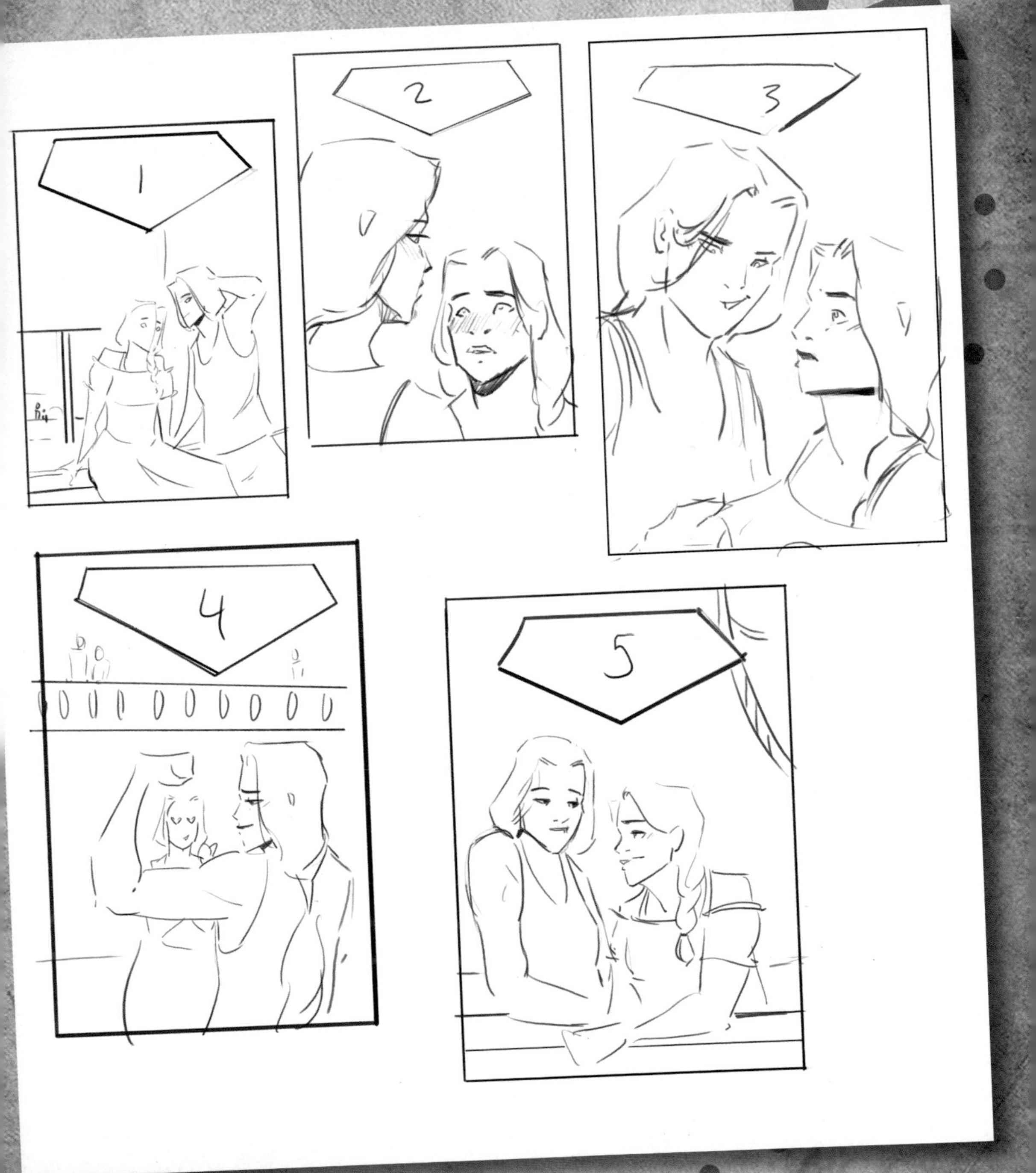
1
2
3
4
5

Character sketches by Christine

Clothing designs for Pavarti, Queen of the Sea

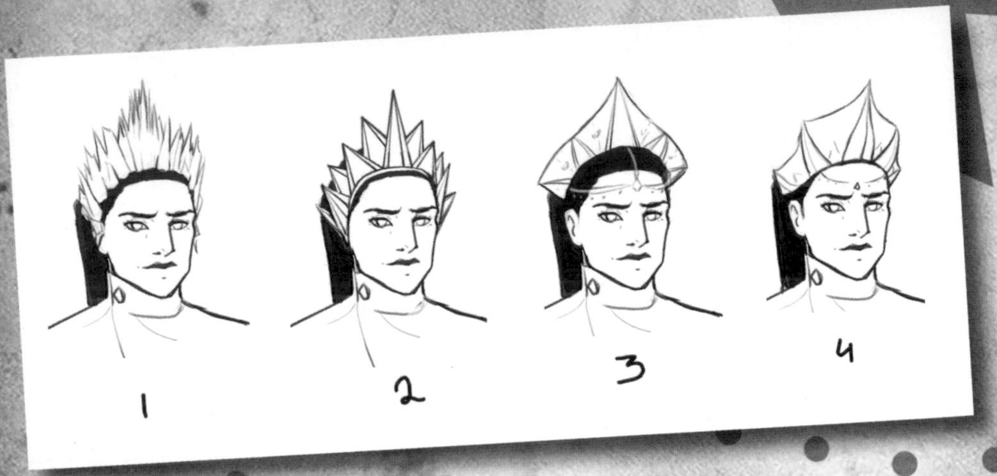
1
2
3
4

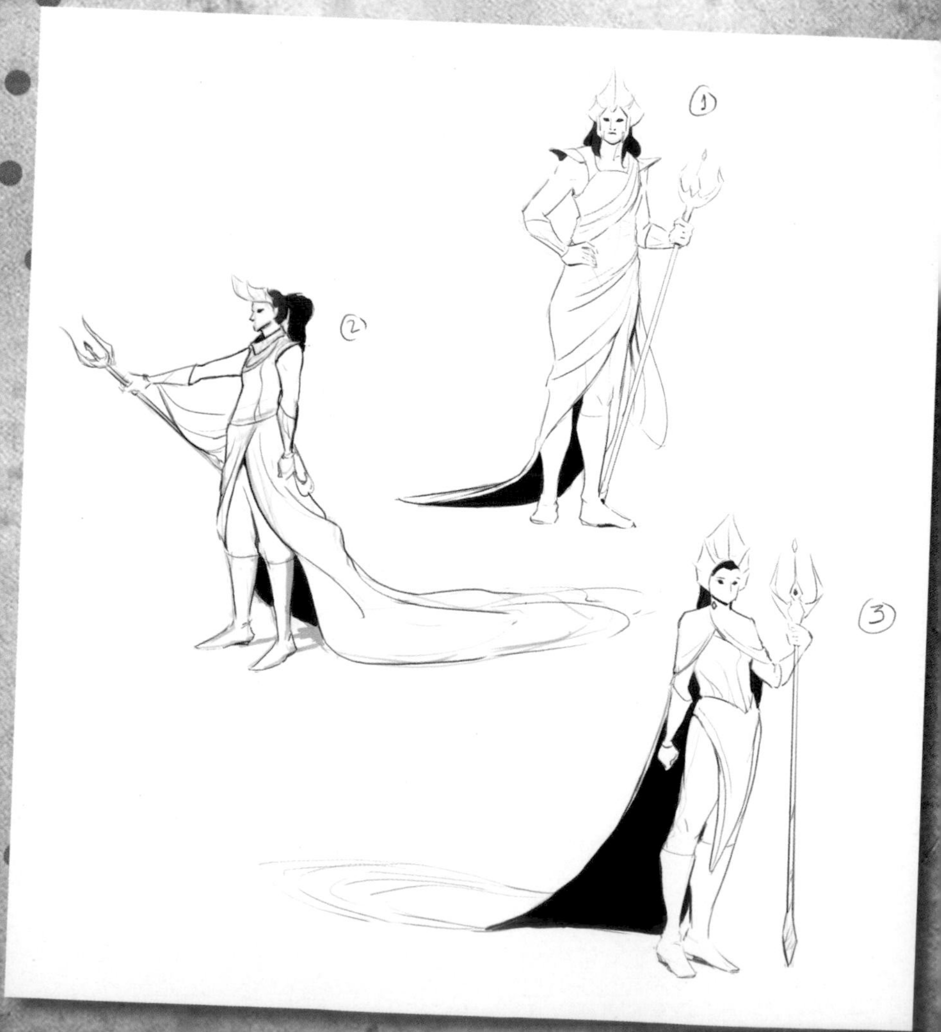
1
2
3

Page 9 Progression

Page 9:

Panel 1: Raven takes one of her arms off the sail and hangs by only her right arm.

RAVEN
You know what, you're right Katie. I'm half the size, so what if I use half as many arms?

CREW
Oh! Oh god! Is she really gonna do it.

Panel 2: Raven does a one armed pull up.

RAVEN
Thirty-seven! Thirty-eight!

CREW
Wow!

Panel 3: Katie drops off the sail onto the deck. Raven laughs from the sail in the background, she is swinging back and forth.

KATIE
That's it. I'm out.

RAVEN
Hey, if you liked that, you're gonna love this.

Panel 4: Raven flips off the sail, spinning through the air over the gathered crew.

Page 9 Inks

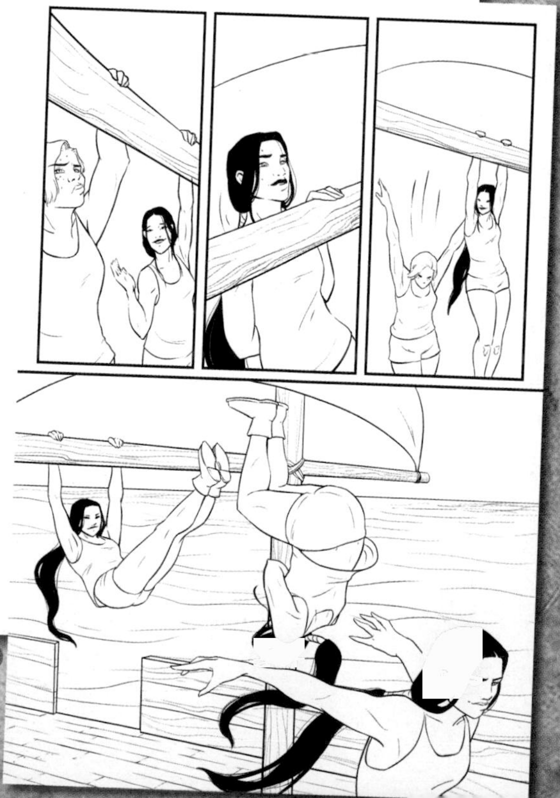

Page 9 Pencils

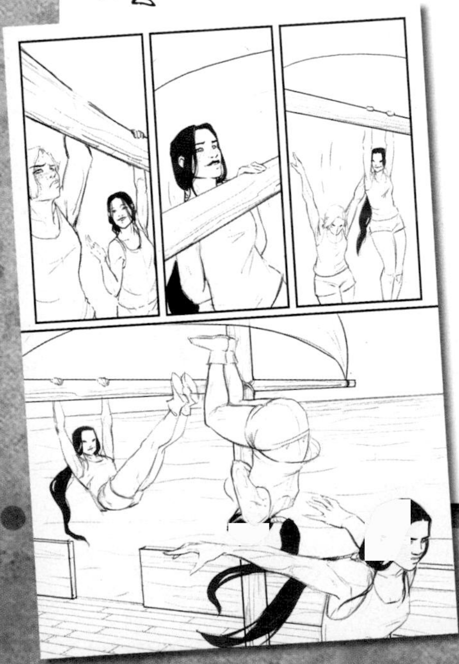

Page 9 Progression

Page 9 Colors

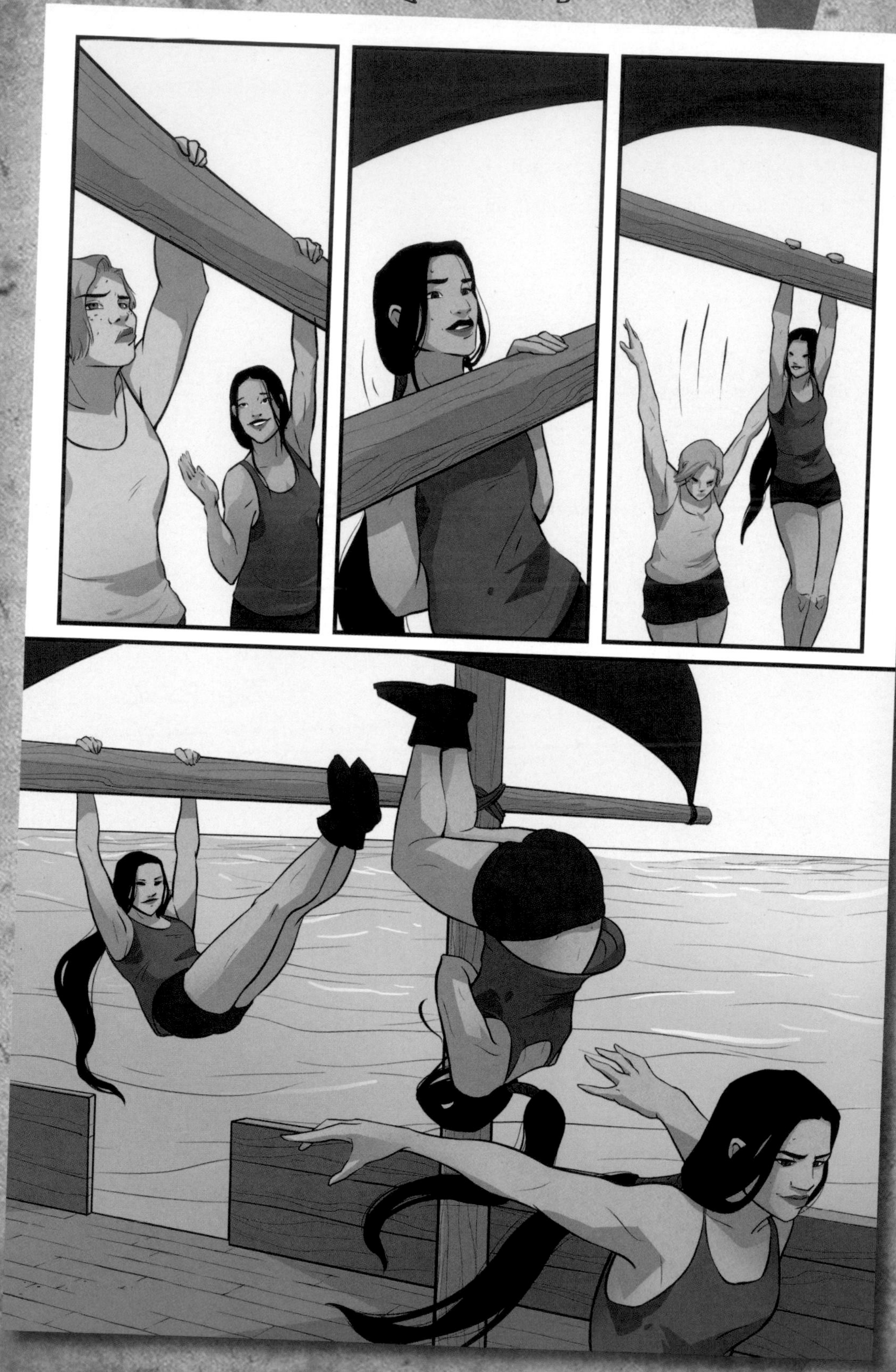

Page 20 Progression

Page 20:

Panel 1: Sunshine grabs the arm instinctively.

Panel 2: Sunshine flips the figure onto the ground in front of her.

Panel 3: Sunshine kneels down on the chest of the figure, holding the person in place.

Panel 4: Sunshine discovers she's face to face with a beautiful young woman who appears to be about the same age as her and of Indian descent. She has long black hair and wears a dress with some elements of sari in it. Preferably not something that's a straight up sari, but with Indian influences. This is Ananda.

SUNSHINE
You try to lay a hand on me and I swear I'll—

SUNSHINE
Well, hello there.

ANANDA
Hello, my name is Ananda.

SUNSHINE
So, Ananda, sneak up on paranoid people here often?

Panel 5: Ananda smiles at Sunshine.

ANANDA
Not usually, but if it's always this exciting I may make a habit of it.

SUNSHINE
Oh, I think we're gonna be friends.

ANANDA
Good, because I was about to ask if you would like to come to a dance.

Panel 6: Sunshine leans down over Ananda.

SUNSHINE
Ananda, you couldn't know this about me, but I am only moments from dancing at any given time.

ANANDA
Will this dance involve removing your knee from my chest?

SUNSHINE
Depends what you're into.

Page 20 Inks

Page 20 Pencils

Page 20 Progression

Page 20 Colors

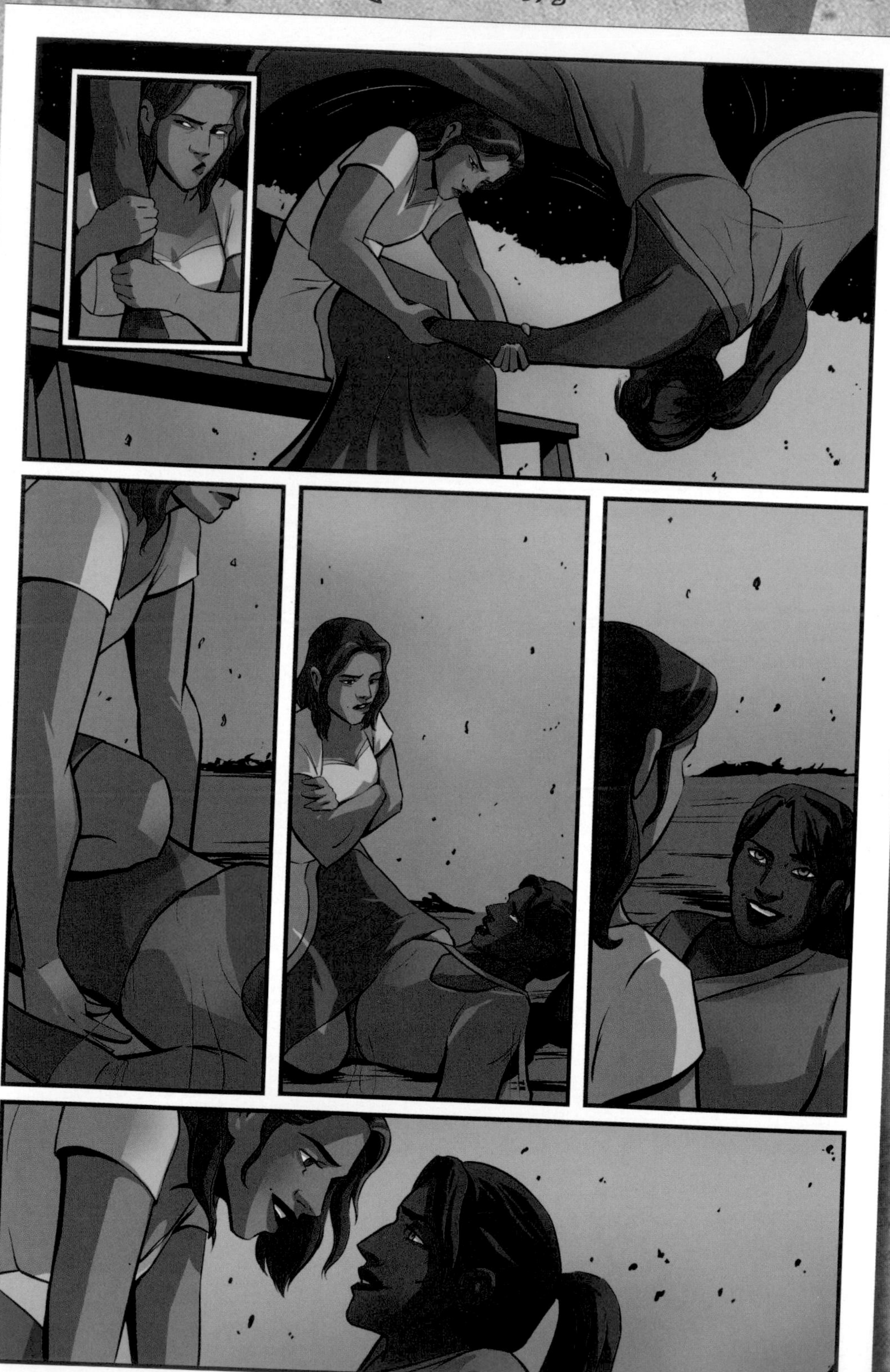

Princeless

Raven

The Pirate Princess

Year Two: Love and Revenge

Chapter Six: The Heart of the Sea

Written By: Jeremy Whitley

Art By: Christine Hipp

Colors By: Xenia Pamfil

Lettered By: Justin Birch

Edited By: Nicole D'Andria

Cover By: Christine Hipp

Cover Colors By: Xenia Pamfil

Bryan Seaton: Publisher/ CEO - Shawn Gabborin: Editor In Chief - Jason Martin: Publisher-Danger Zone
Nicole D'Andria: Marketing Director/Editor - Danielle Davison: Executive Administrator
Chad Cicconi: Deck Swabber - Shawn Pryor: President of Creator Relations

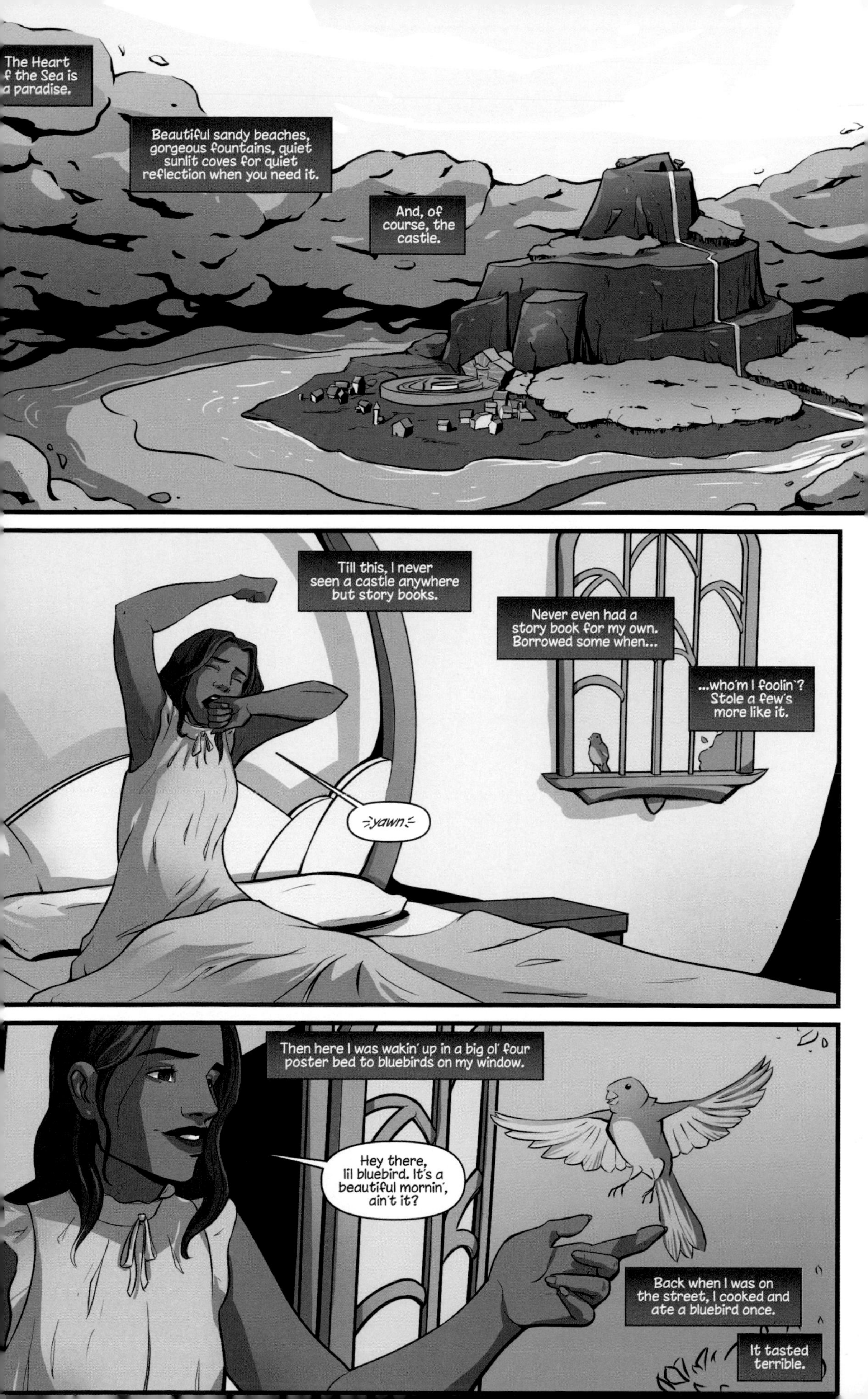
The Heart f the Sea is a paradise.
Beautiful sandy beaches, gorgeous fountains, quiet sunlit coves for quiet reflection when you need it.
And, of course, the castle.
Till this, I never seen a castle anywhere but story books.
Never even had a story book for my own. Borrowed some when...
...who'm I foolin'? Stole a few's more like it.
yawn
Then here I was wakin' up in a big ol' four poster bed to bluebirds on my window.
Hey there, lil bluebird. It's a beautiful mornin', ain't it?
Back when I was on the street, I cooked and ate a bluebird once.
It tasted terrible.

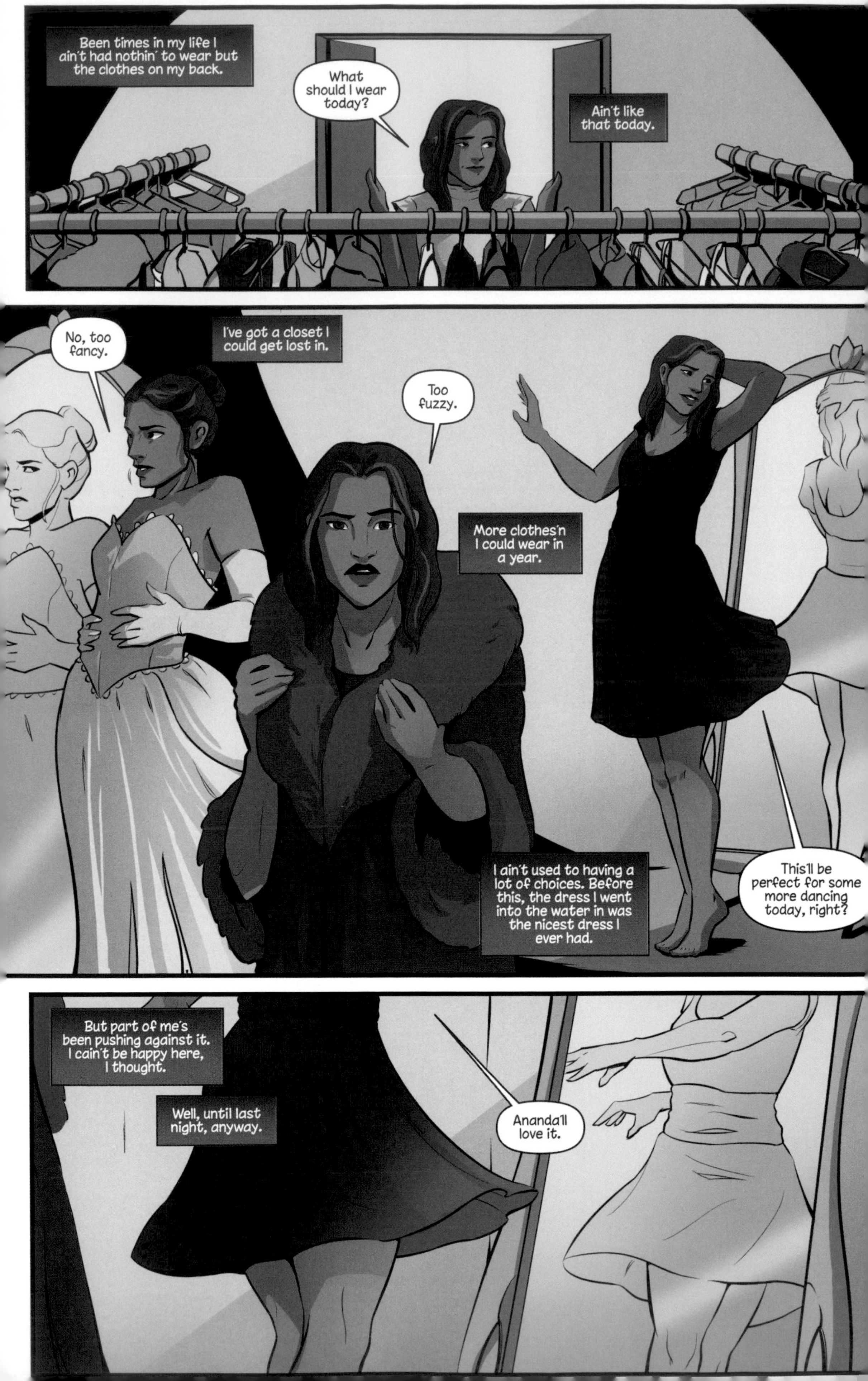
Been times in my life I ain't had nothin' to wear but the clothes on my back.
What should I wear today?
Ain't like that today.
No, too fancy.
I've got a closet I could get lost in.
Too fuzzy.
More clothes'n I could wear in a year.
I ain't used to having a lot of choices. Before this, the dress I went into the water in was the nicest dress I ever had.
This'll be perfect for some more dancing today, right?
But part of me's been pushing against it. I cain't be happy here, I thought.
Well, until last night, anyway.
Ananda'll love it.

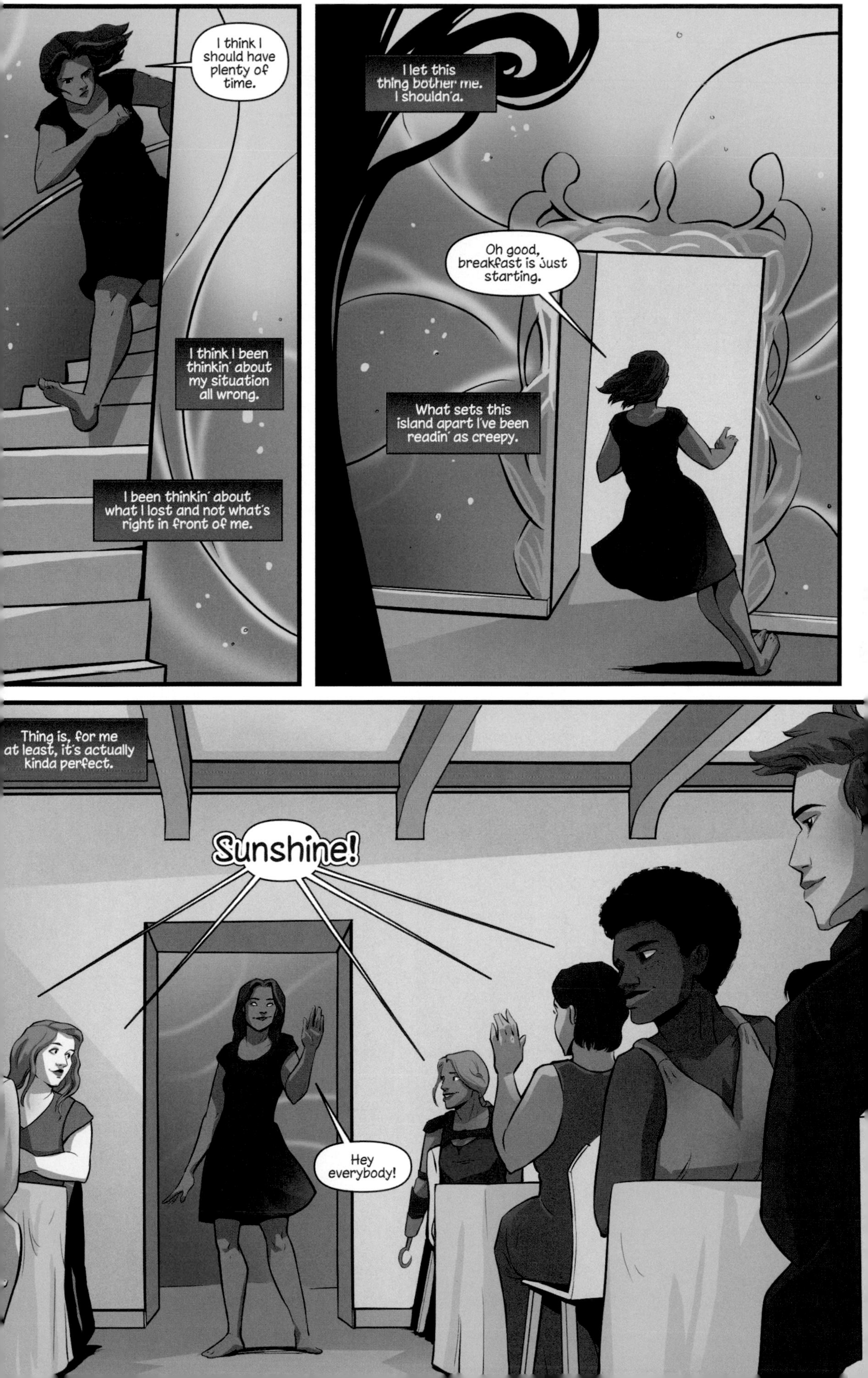

I think I should have plenty of time.
I think I been thinkin' about my situation all wrong.
I been thinkin' about what I lost and not what's right in front of me.
I let this thing bother me. I shouldn'a.
Oh good, breakfast is just starting.
What sets this island apart I've been readin' as creepy.
Thing is, for me at least, it's actually kinda perfect.
Sunshine!
Hey everybody!

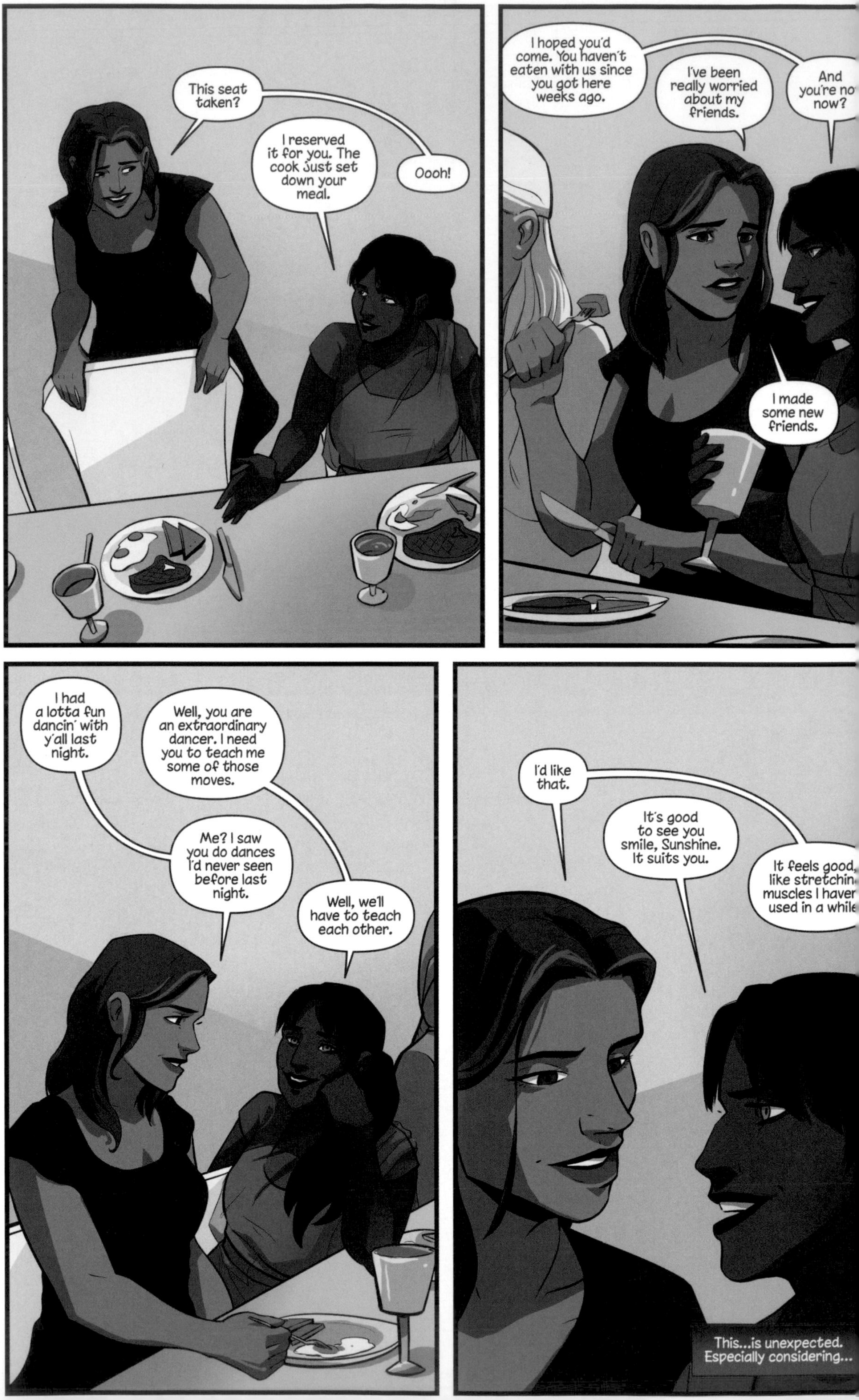
This seat taken?
I reserved it for you. The cook just set down your meal.
Oooh!
I hoped you'd come. You haven't eaten with us since you got here weeks ago.
I've been really worried about my friends.
And you're no now?
I made some new friends.
I had a lotta fun dancin' with y'all last night.
Well, you are an extraordinary dancer. I need you to teach me some of those moves.
Me? I saw you do dances I'd never seen before last night.
Well, we'll have to teach each other.
I'd like that.
It's good to see you smile, Sunshine. It suits you.
It feels good, like stretchin muscles I haver used in a whil
This...is unexpected. Especially considering...

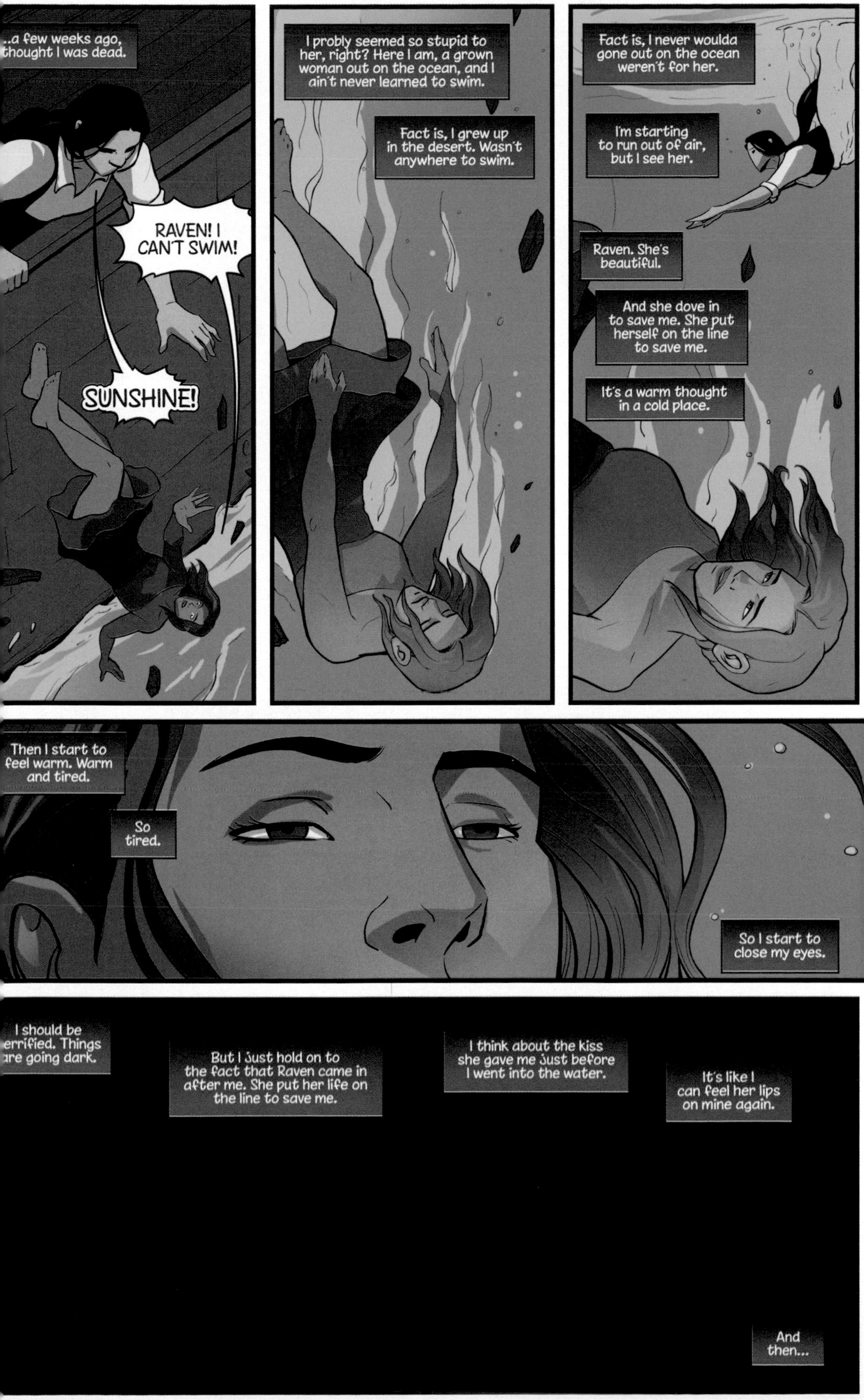
..a few weeks ago, thought I was dead.
RAVEN! I CAN'T SWIM!
SUNSHINE!
I probly seemed so stupid to her, right? Here I am, a grown woman out on the ocean, and I ain't never learned to swim.
Fact is, I grew up in the desert. Wasn't anywhere to swim.
Fact is, I never woulda gone out on the ocean weren't for her.
I'm starting to run out of air, but I see her.
Raven. She's beautiful.
And she dove in to save me. She put herself on the line to save me.
It's a warm thought in a cold place.
Then I start to feel warm. Warm and tired.
So tired.
So I start to close my eyes.
I should be errified. Things are going dark.
But I just hold on to the fact that Raven came in after me. She put her life on the line to save me.
I think about the kiss she gave me just before I went into the water.
It's like I can feel her lips on mine again.
And then...

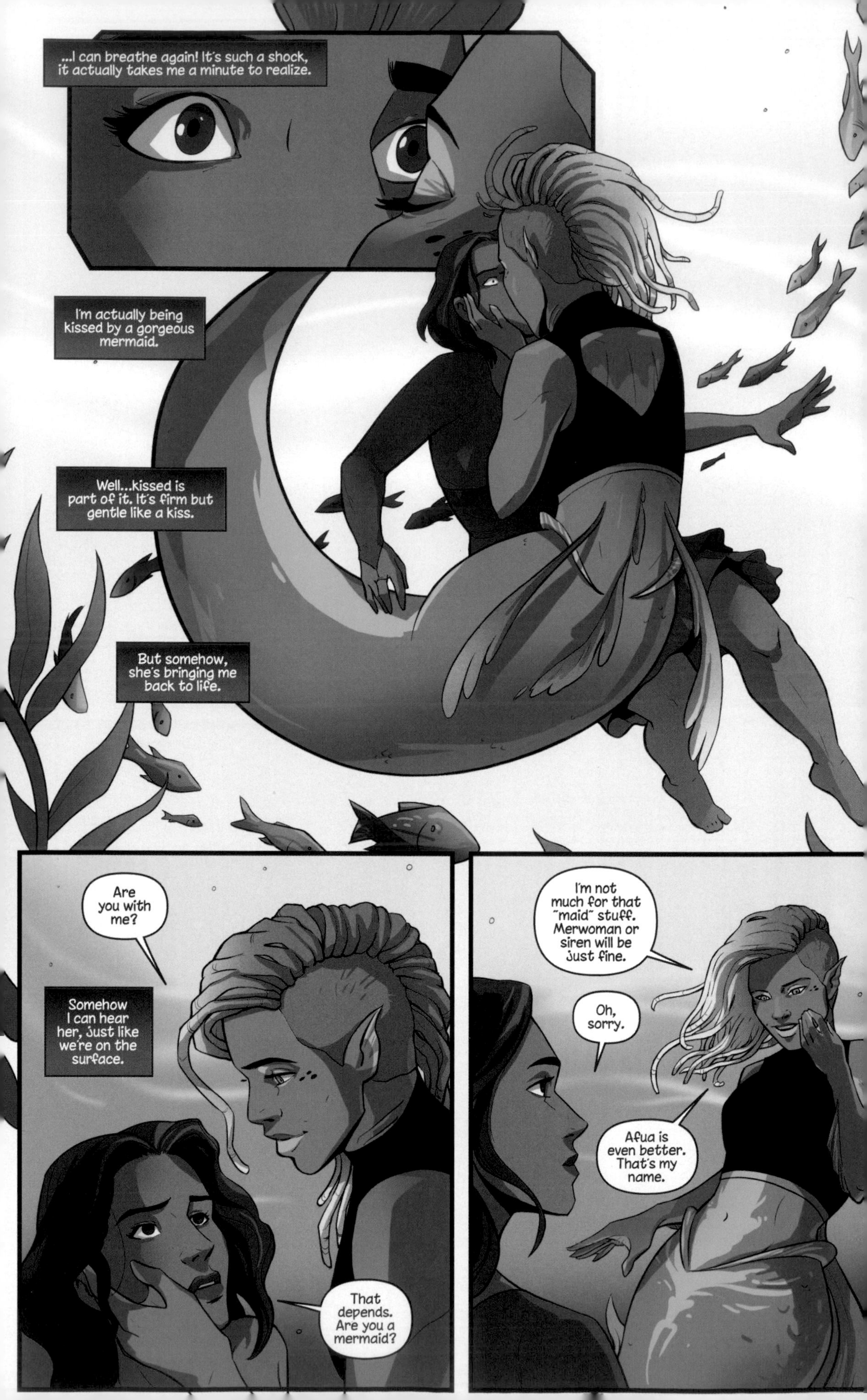
...I can breathe again! It's such a shock, it actually takes me a minute to realize.
I'm actually being kissed by a gorgeous mermaid.
Well...kissed is part of it. It's firm but gentle like a kiss.
But somehow, she's bringing me back to life.
Are you with me?
Somehow I can hear her, just like we're on the surface.
That depends. Are you a mermaid?
I'm not much for that "maid" stuff. Merwoman or siren will be just fine.
Oh, sorry.
Afua is even better. That's my name.

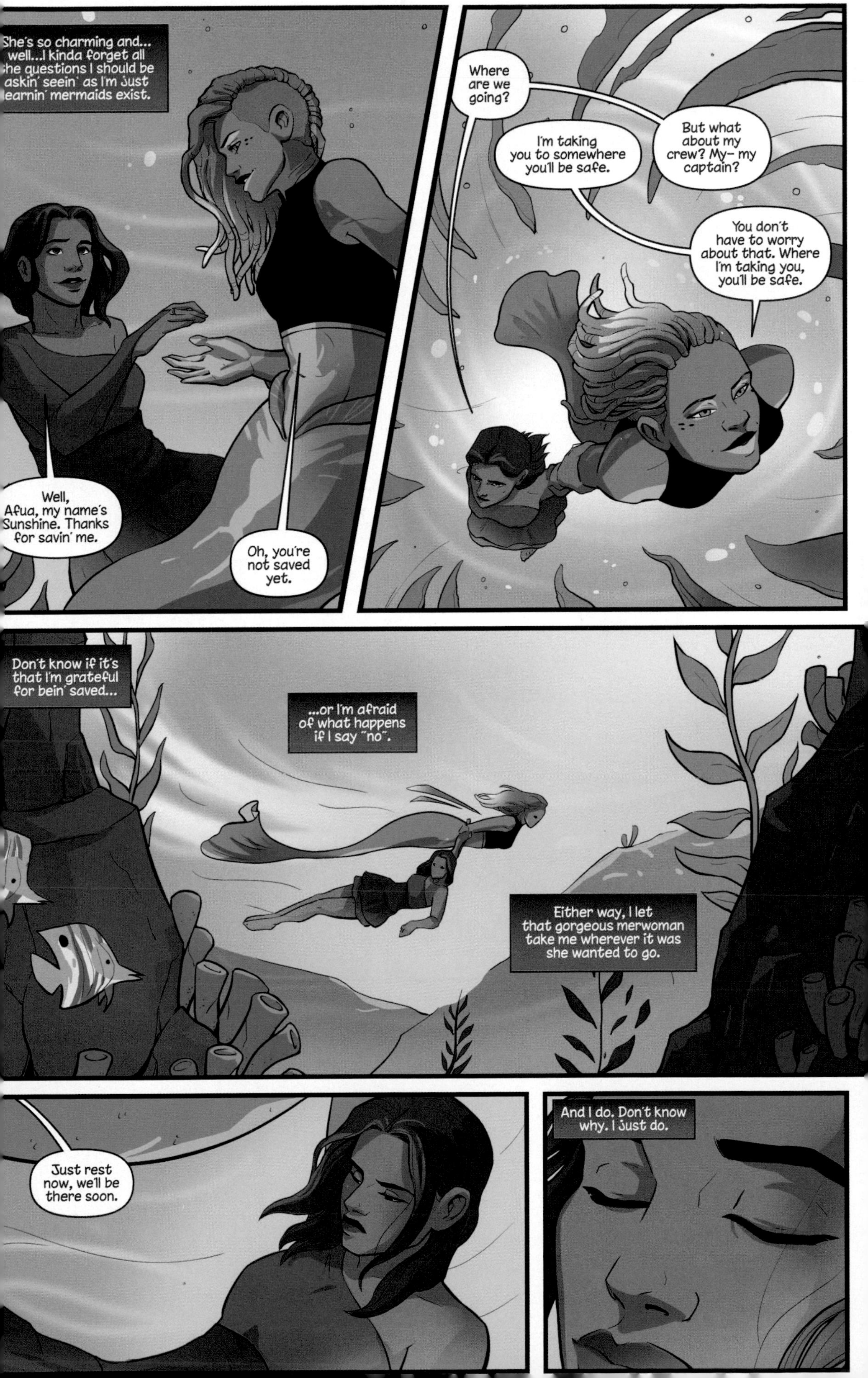
She's so charming and... well...I kinda forget all the questions I should be askin' seein' as I'm just learnin' mermaids exist.
Well, Afua, my name's Sunshine. Thanks for savin' me.
Oh, you're not saved yet.
Where are we going?
I'm taking you to somewhere you'll be safe.
But what about my crew? My– my captain?
You don't have to worry about that. Where I'm taking you, you'll be safe.
Don't know if it's that I'm grateful for bein' saved...
...or I'm afraid of what happens if I say "no".
Either way, I let that gorgeous merwoman take me wherever it was she wanted to go.
Just rest now, we'll be there soon.
And I do. Don't know why. I just do.

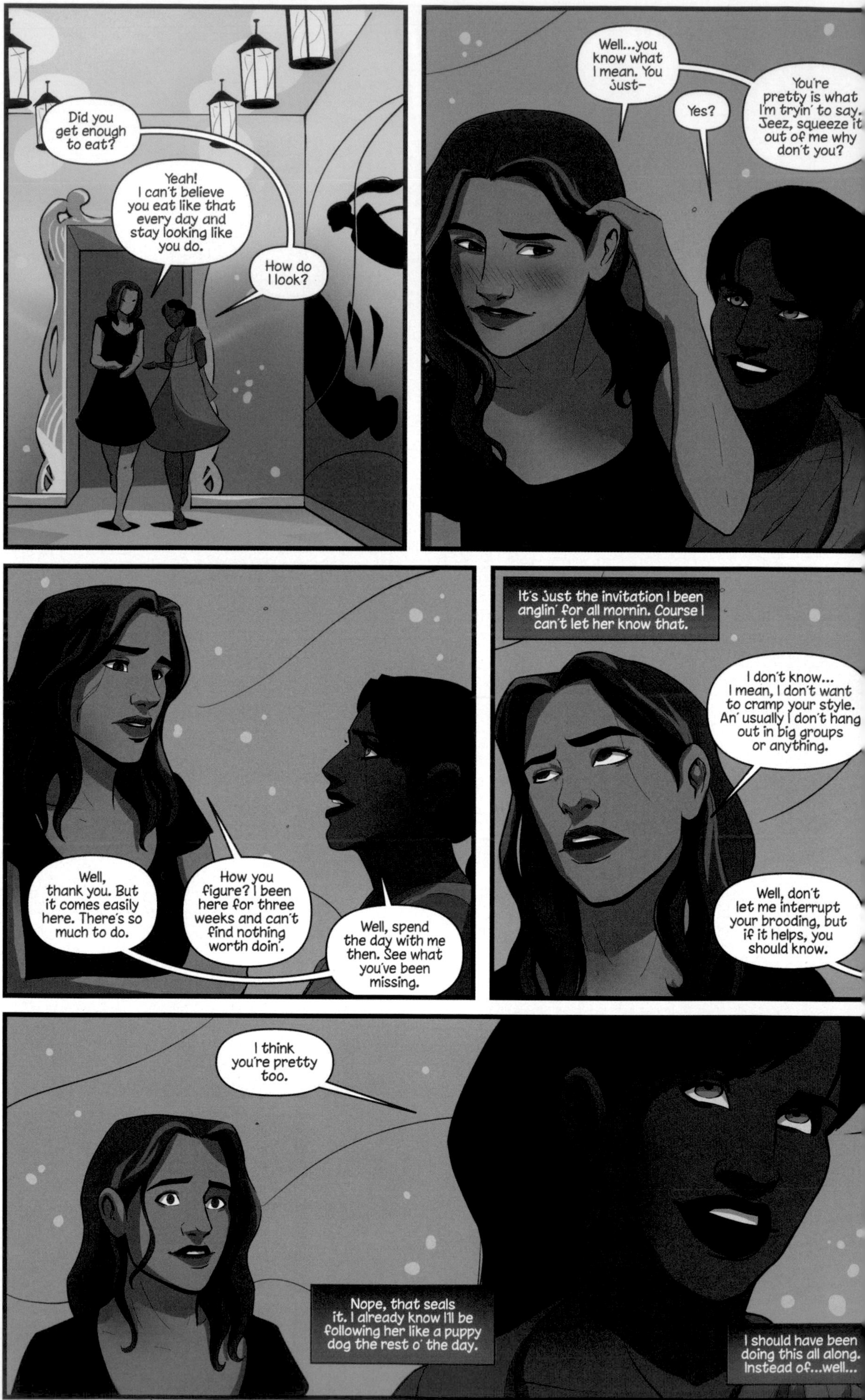
Did you get enough to eat?
Yeah! I can't believe you eat like that every day and stay looking like you do.
How do I look?
Well...you know what I mean. You just-
Yes?
You're pretty is what I'm tryin' to say. Jeez, squeeze it out of me why don't you?
Well, thank you. But it comes easily here. There's so much to do.
How you figure? I been here for three weeks and can't find nothing worth doin'.
Well, spend the day with me then. See what you've been missing.
It's Just the invitation I been anglin' for all mornin. Course I can't let her know that.
I don't know... I mean, I don't want to cramp your style. An' usually I don't hang out in big groups or anything.
Well, don't let me interrupt your brooding, but if it helps, you should know.
I think you're pretty too.
Nope, that seals it. I already know I'll be following her like a puppy dog the rest o' the day.
I should have been doing this all along. Instead of...well...

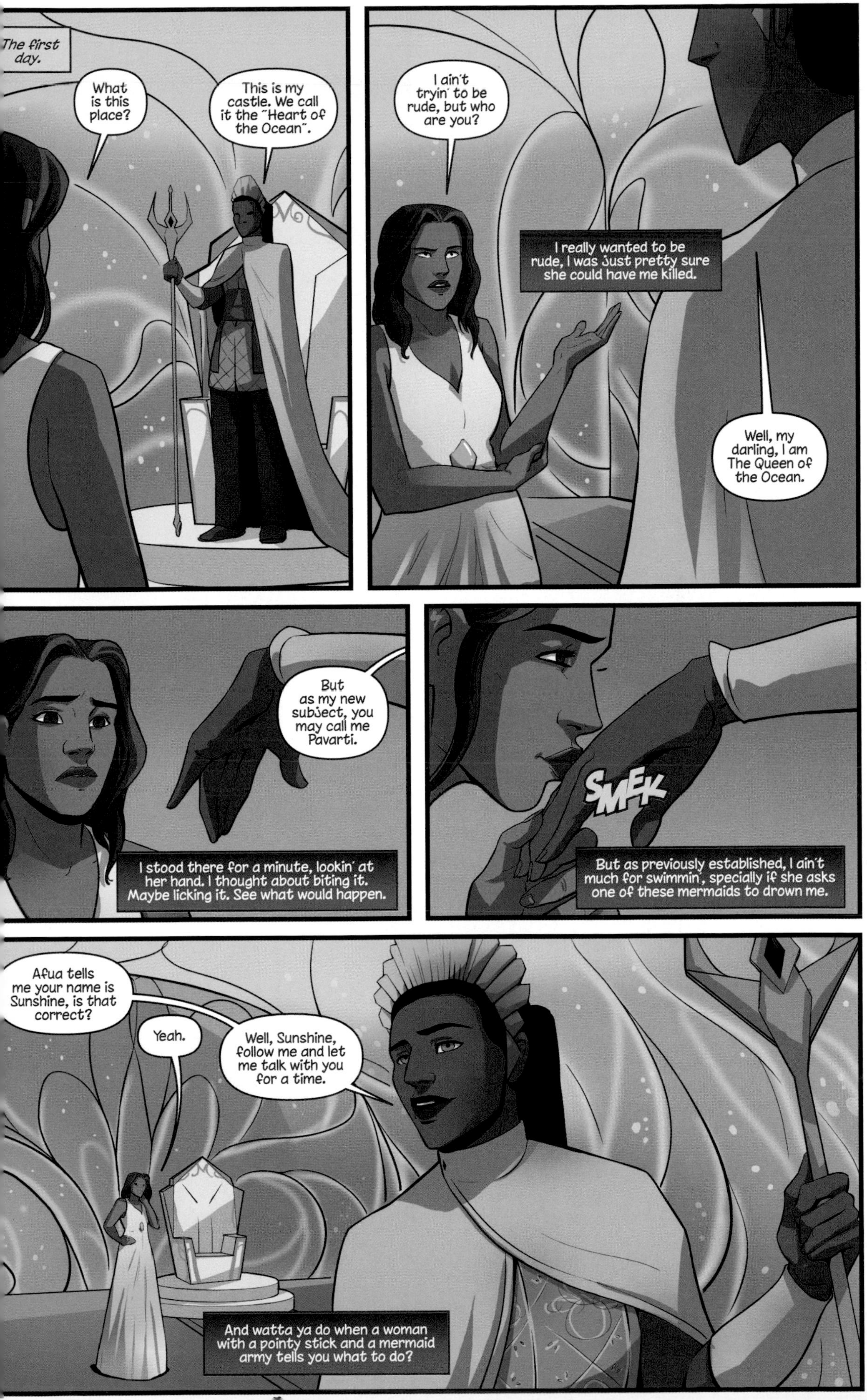
The first day.
What is this place?
This is my castle. We call it the "Heart of the Ocean".
I ain't tryin' to be rude, but who are you?
I really wanted to be rude, I was just pretty sure she could have me killed.
Well, my darling, I am The Queen of the Ocean.
But as my new subject, you may call me Pavarti.
I stood there for a minute, lookin' at her hand. I thought about biting it. Maybe licking it. See what would happen.
SMEK
But as previously established, I ain't much for swimmin', specially if she asks one of these mermaids to drown me.
Afua tells me your name is Sunshine, is that correct?
Yeah.
Well, Sunshine, follow me and let me talk with you for a time.
And watta ya do when a woman with a pointy stick and a mermaid army tells you what to do?

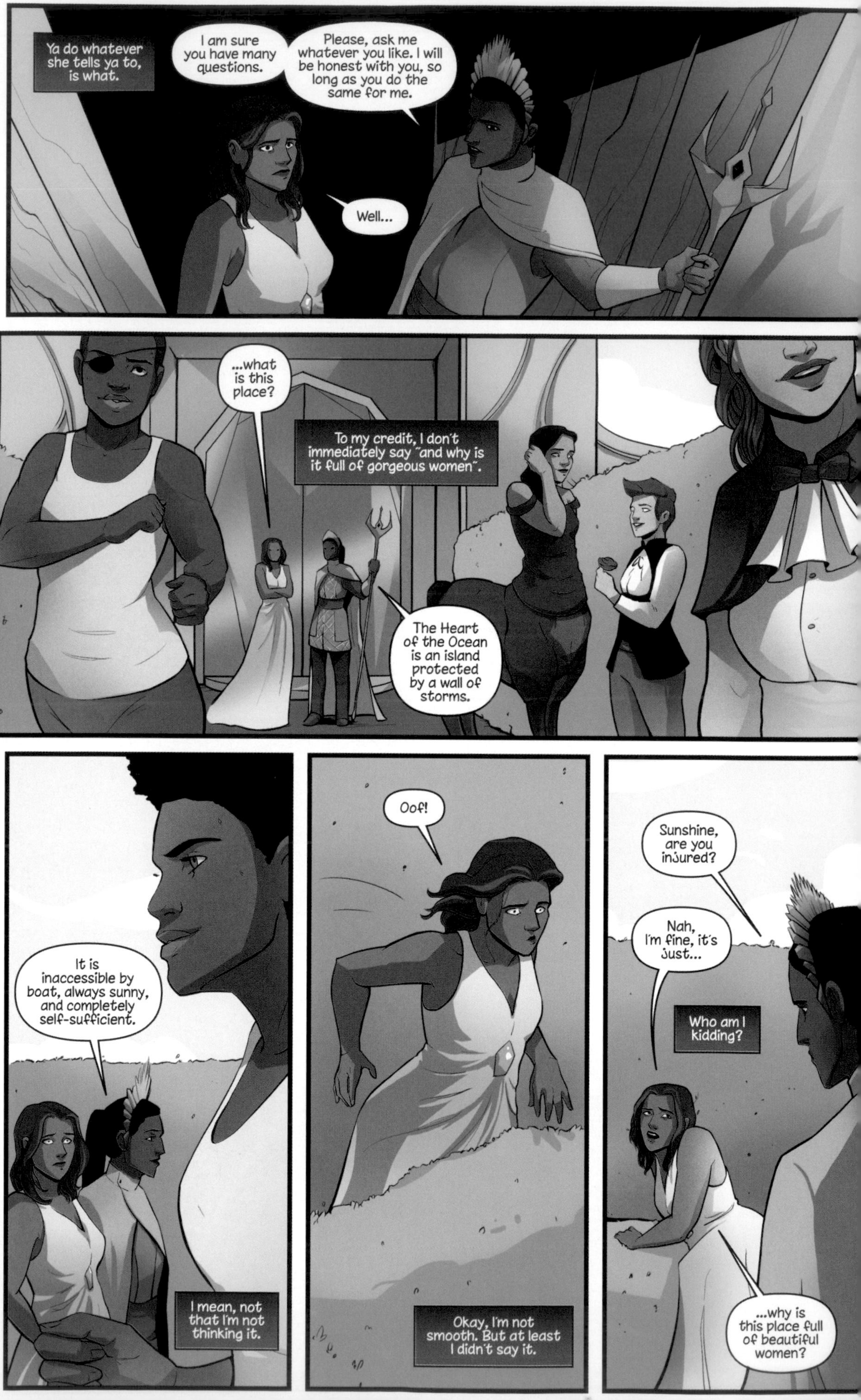
Ya do whatever she tells ya to, is what.
I am sure you have many questions.
Please, ask me whatever you like. I will be honest with you, so long as you do the same for me.
Well...
...what is this place?
To my credit, I don't immediately say "and why is it full of gorgeous women".
The Heart of the Ocean is an island protected by a wall of storms.
It is inaccessible by boat, always sunny, and completely self-sufficient.
I mean, not that I'm not thinking it.
Oof!
Okay, I'm not smooth. But at least I didn't say it.
Sunshine, are you injured?
Nah, I'm fine, it's just...
Who am I kidding?
...why is this place full of beautiful women?

They are my collection.

Come again?

The sea is a cruel place for women and often they find themselves cast into the ocean.

Cold, alone, drowning, uncared for.

Like you.

Now you hold on just a minute there! Raven—

Ahem.

My captain tried to come in after me. She dove right in.

Afua said you were alone.

Well, I couldn't swim and—

And the captain of a ship couldn't swim well enough to save you?

We were under attack!

I think...

Oh Sunshine, what makes you so certain this captain of yours would abandon her ship and crew to save you?

Because we kissed. It was amazing. It meant something.

If she had been with you, I'm sure Afua would have brought her too. But there were no others.

But that is the way with all of these women here.

Dying or near death my mermaids have plucked them from the sea.

When others had abandoned them, I saved them. I saved you.

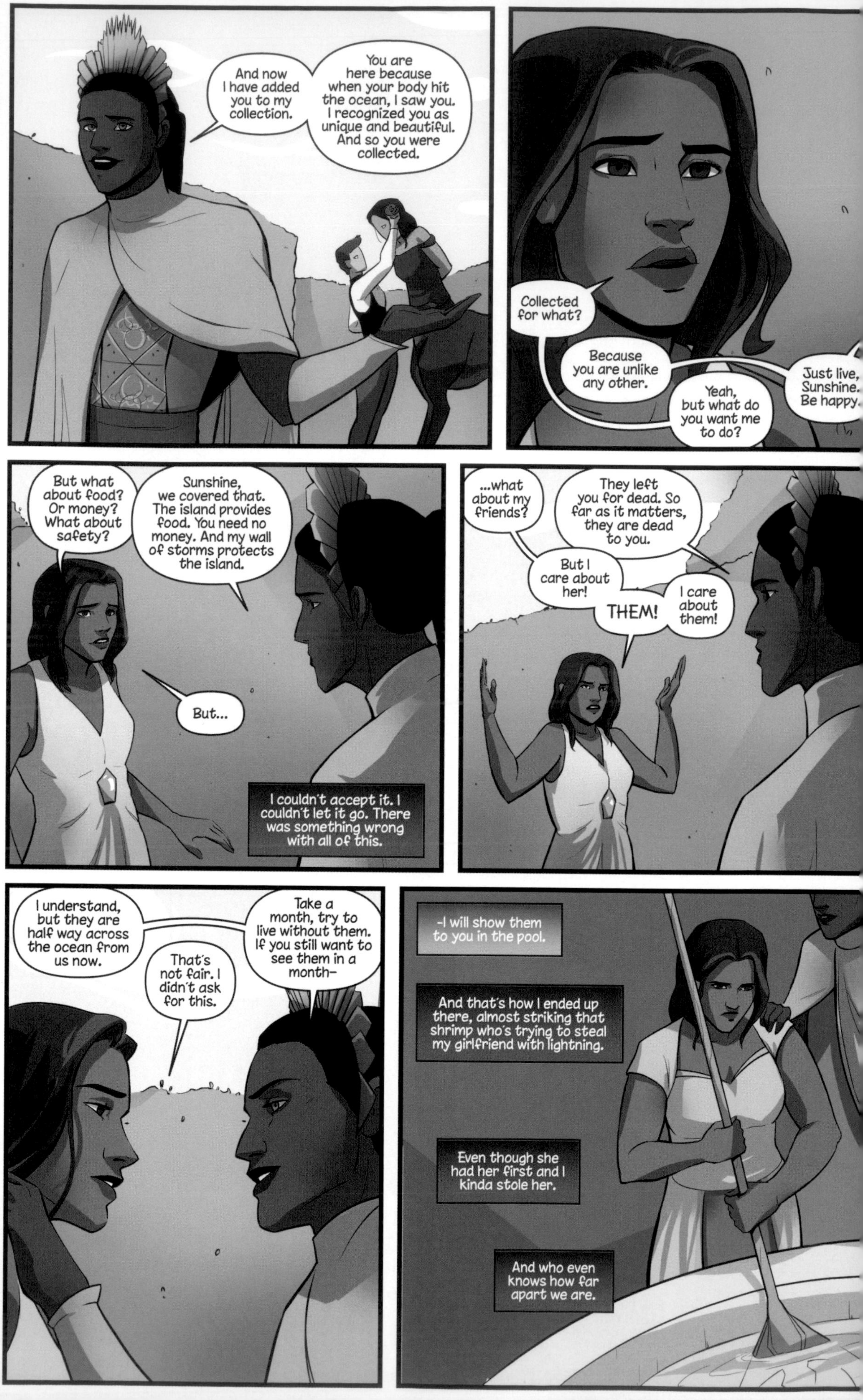
And now I have added you to my collection.
You are here because when your body hit the ocean, I saw you. I recognized you as unique and beautiful. And so you were collected.
Collected for what?
Because you are unlike any other.
Yeah, but what do you want me to do?
Just live, Sunshine. Be happy.
But what about food? Or money? What about safety?
Sunshine, we covered that. The island provides food. You need no money. And my wall of storms protects the island.
But...
I couldn't accept it. I couldn't let it go. There was something wrong with all of this.
...what about my friends?
They left you for dead. So far as it matters, they are dead to you.
But I care about her!
THEM!
I care about them!
I understand, but they are half way across the ocean from us now.
Take a month, try to live without them. If you still want to see them in a month-
That's not fair. I didn't ask for this.
-I will show them to you in the pool.
And that's how I ended up there, almost striking that shrimp who's trying to steal my girlfriend with lightning.
Even though she had her first and I kinda stole her.
And who even knows how far apart we are.

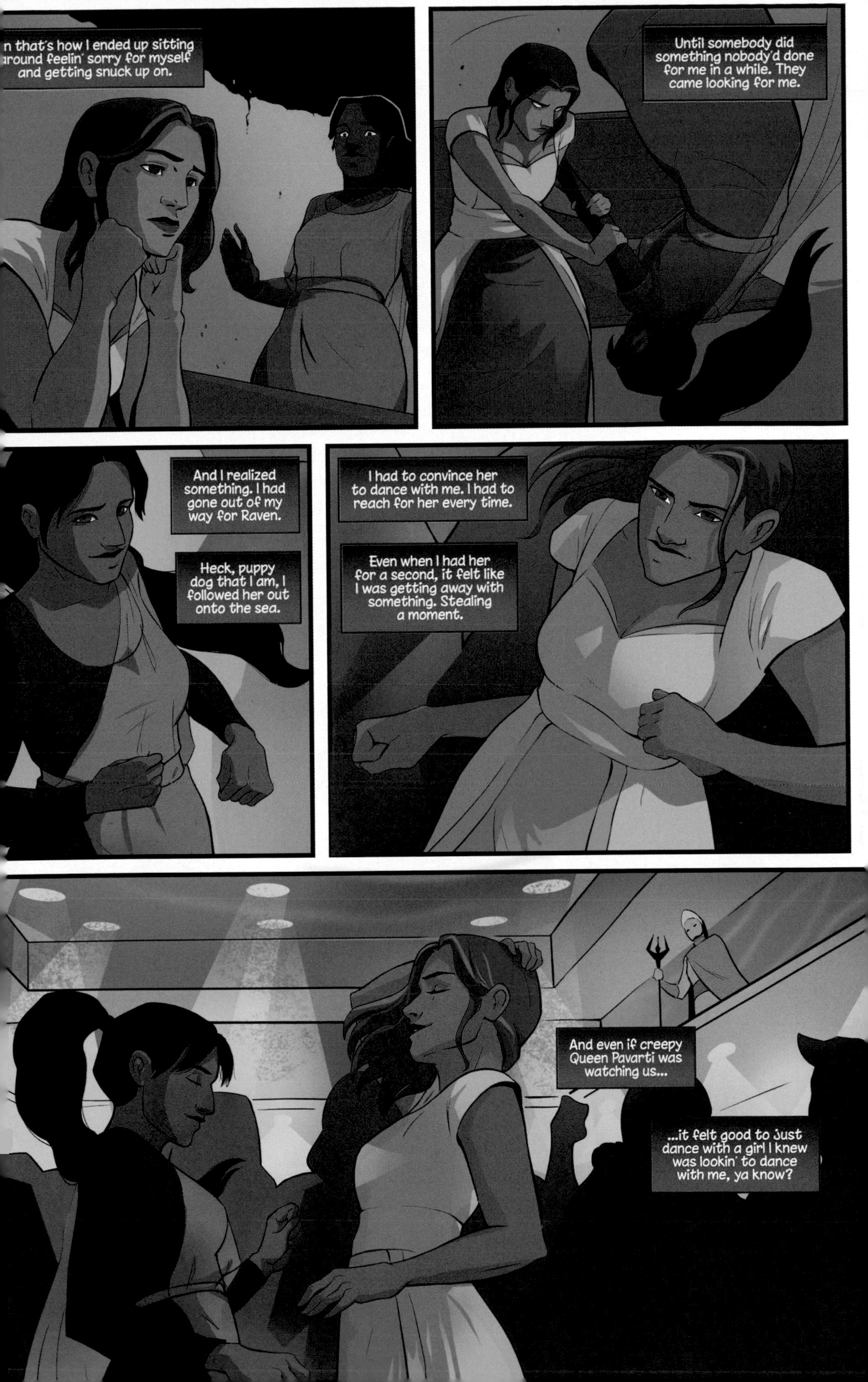

n that's how I ended up sitting around feelin' sorry for myself and getting snuck up on.
Until somebody did something nobody'd done for me in a while. They came looking for me.
And I realized something. I had gone out of my way for Raven.
Heck, puppy dog that I am, I followed her out onto the sea.
I had to convince her to dance with me. I had to reach for her every time.
Even when I had her for a second, it felt like I was getting away with something. Stealing a moment.
And even if creepy Queen Pavarti was watching us...
...it felt good to just dance with a girl I knew was lookin' to dance with me, ya know?

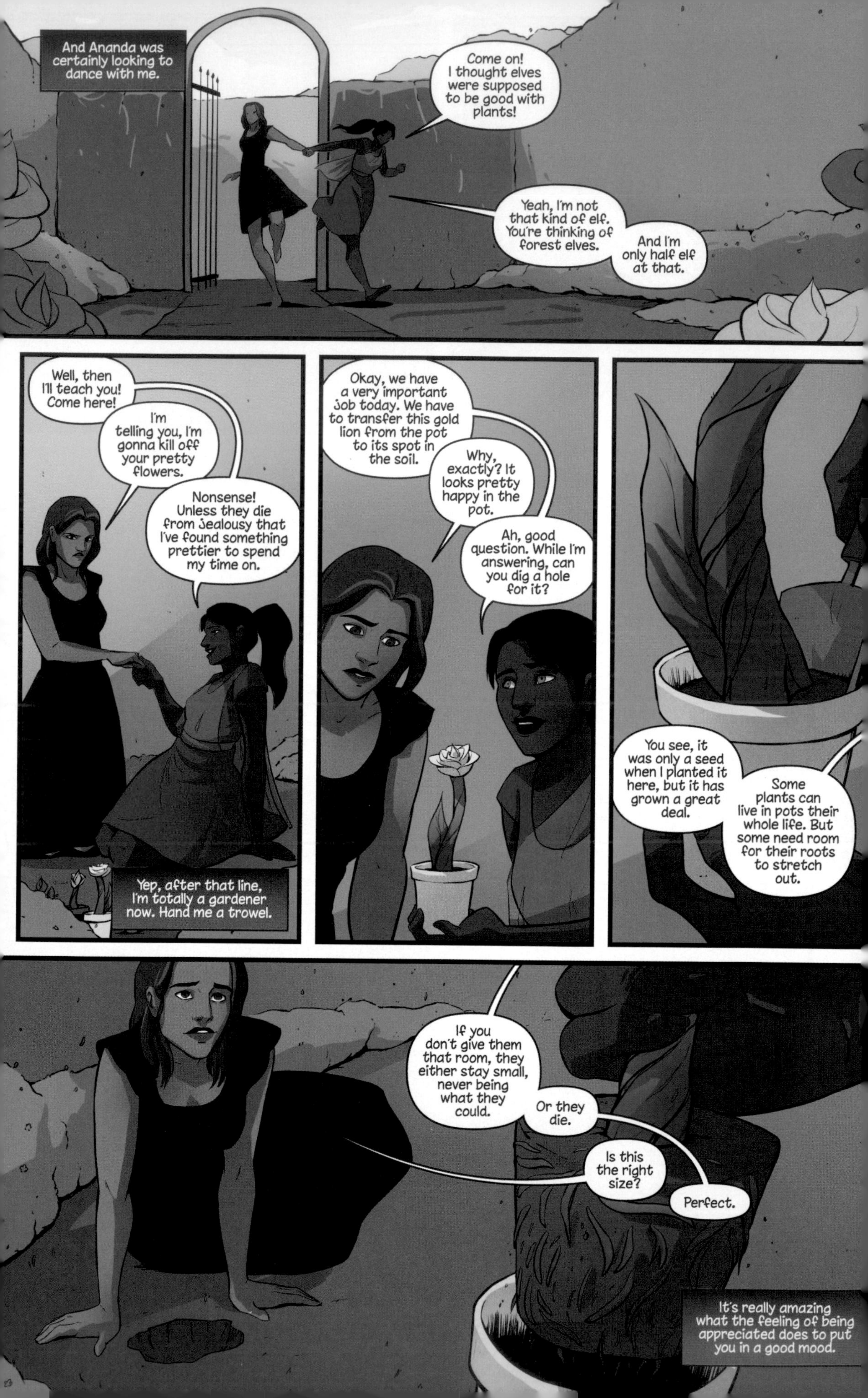

And Ananda was certainly looking to dance with me.
Come on! I thought elves were supposed to be good with plants!
Yeah, I'm not that kind of elf. You're thinking of forest elves.
And I'm only half elf at that.
Well, then I'll teach you! Come here!
I'm telling you, I'm gonna kill off your pretty flowers.
Nonsense! Unless they die from jealousy that I've found something prettier to spend my time on.
Yep, after that line, I'm totally a gardener now. Hand me a trowel.
Okay, we have a very important job today. We have to transfer this gold lion from the pot to its spot in the soil.
Why, exactly? It looks pretty happy in the pot.
Ah, good question. While I'm answering, can you dig a hole for it?
You see, it was only a seed when I planted it here, but it has grown a great deal.
Some plants can live in pots their whole life. But some need room for their roots to stretch out.
If you don't give them that room, they either stay small, never being what they could.
Or they die.
Is this the right size?
Perfect.
It's really amazing what the feeling of being appreciated does to put you in a good mood.

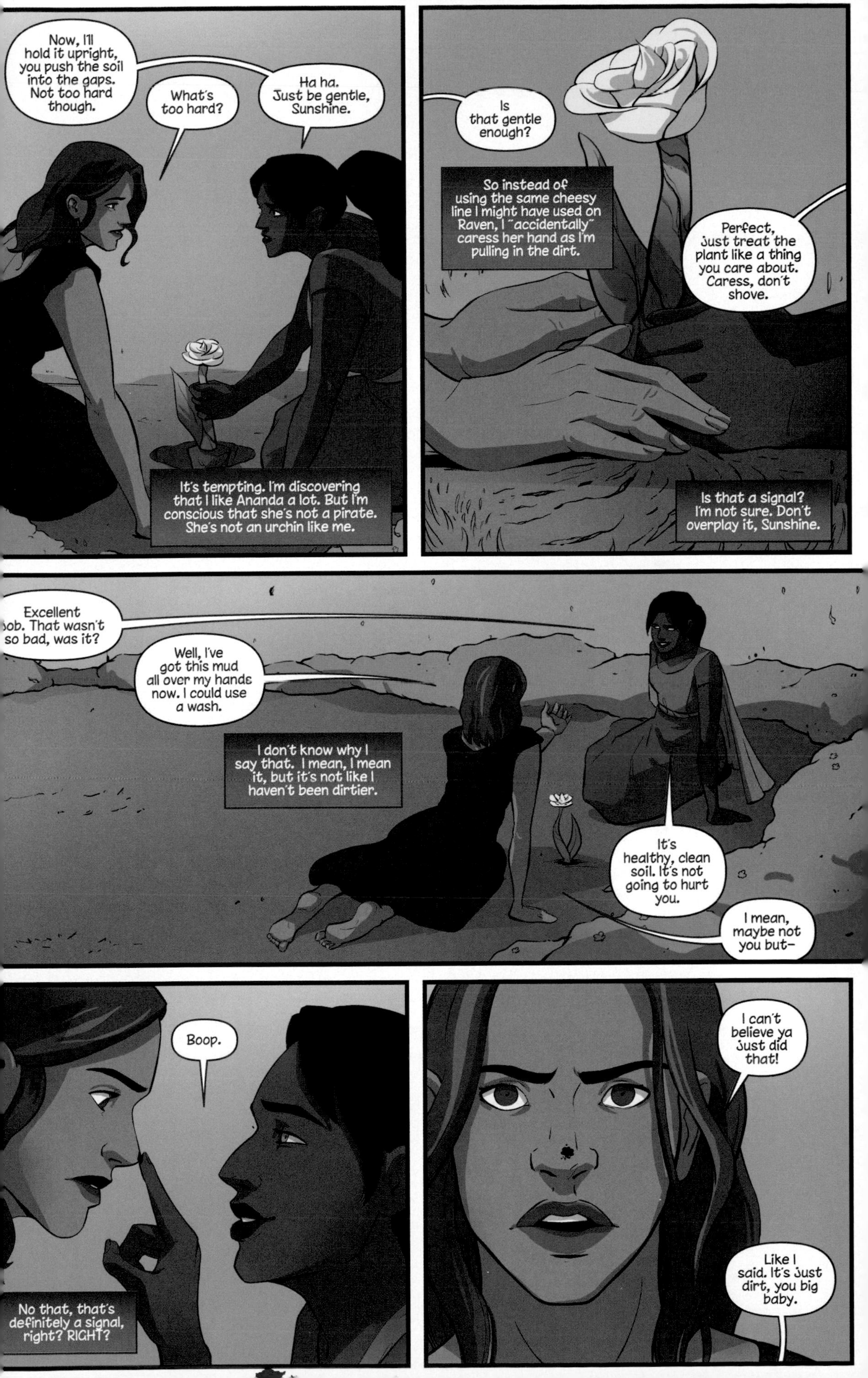
Now, I'll hold it upright, you push the soil into the gaps. Not too hard though.
What's too hard?
Ha ha. Just be gentle, Sunshine.
It's tempting. I'm discovering that I like Ananda a lot. But I'm conscious that she's not a pirate. She's not an urchin like me.
Is that gentle enough?
So instead of using the same cheesy line I might have used on Raven, I "accidentally" caress her hand as I'm pulling in the dirt.
Perfect, Just treat the plant like a thing you care about. Caress, don't shove.
Is that a signal? I'm not sure. Don't overplay it, Sunshine.
Excellent job. That wasn't so bad, was it?
Well, I've got this mud all over my hands now. I could use a wash.
I don't know why I say that. I mean, I mean it, but it's not like I haven't been dirtier.
It's healthy, clean soil. It's not going to hurt you.
I mean, maybe not you but–
Boop.
No that, that's definitely a signal, right? RIGHT?
I can't believe ya just did that!
Like I said. It's just dirt, you big baby.

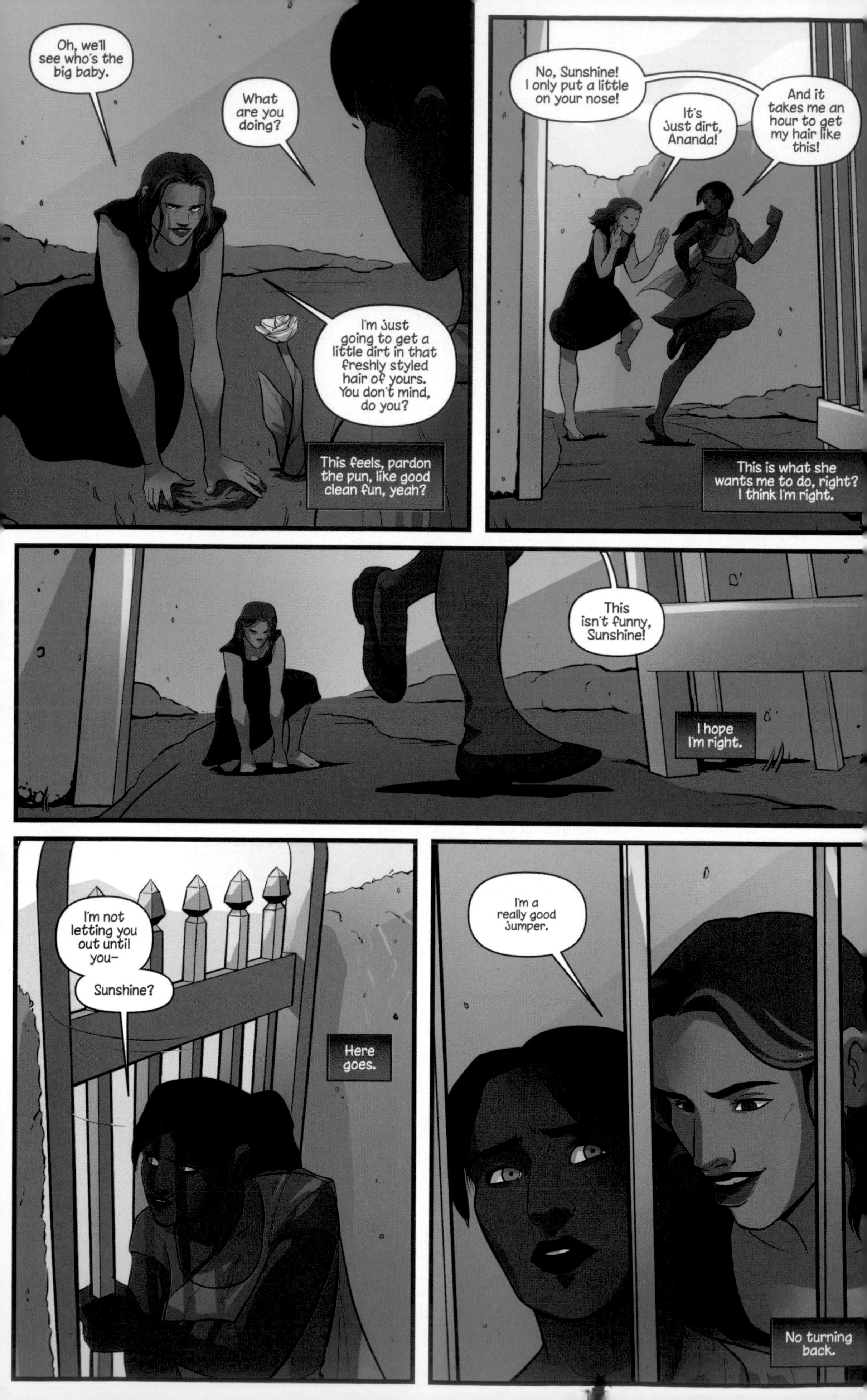
Oh, we'll see who's the big baby.
What are you doing?
I'm just going to get a little dirt in that freshly styled hair of yours. You don't mind, do you?
This feels, pardon the pun, like good clean fun, yeah?
No, Sunshine! I only put a little on your nose!
It's just dirt, Ananda!
And it takes me an hour to get my hair like this!
This is what she wants me to do, right? I think I'm right.
This isn't funny, Sunshine!
I hope I'm right.
I'm not letting you out until you–
Sunshine?
Here goes.
I'm a really good jumper.
No turning back.

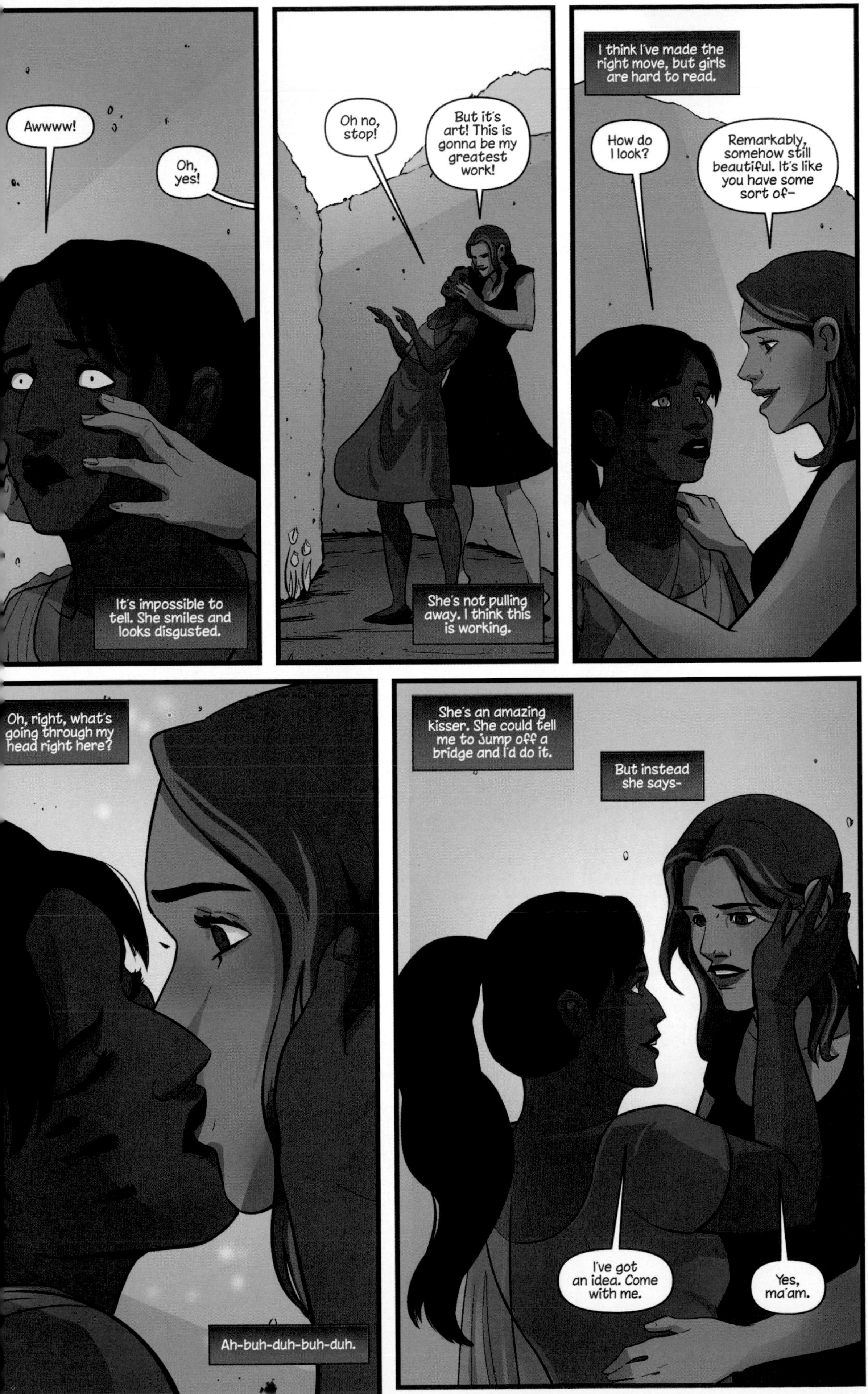
Awwww!
Oh, yes!
It's impossible to tell. She smiles and looks disgusted.
Oh no, stop!
But it's art! This is gonna be my greatest work!
She's not pulling away. I think this is working.
I think I've made the right move, but girls are hard to read.
How do I look?
Remarkably, somehow still beautiful. It's like you have some sort of–
Oh, right, what's going through my head right here?
Ah-buh-duh-buh-duh.
She's an amazing kisser. She could tell me to jump off a bridge and I'd do it.
But instead she says–
I've got an idea. Come with me.
Yes, ma'am.

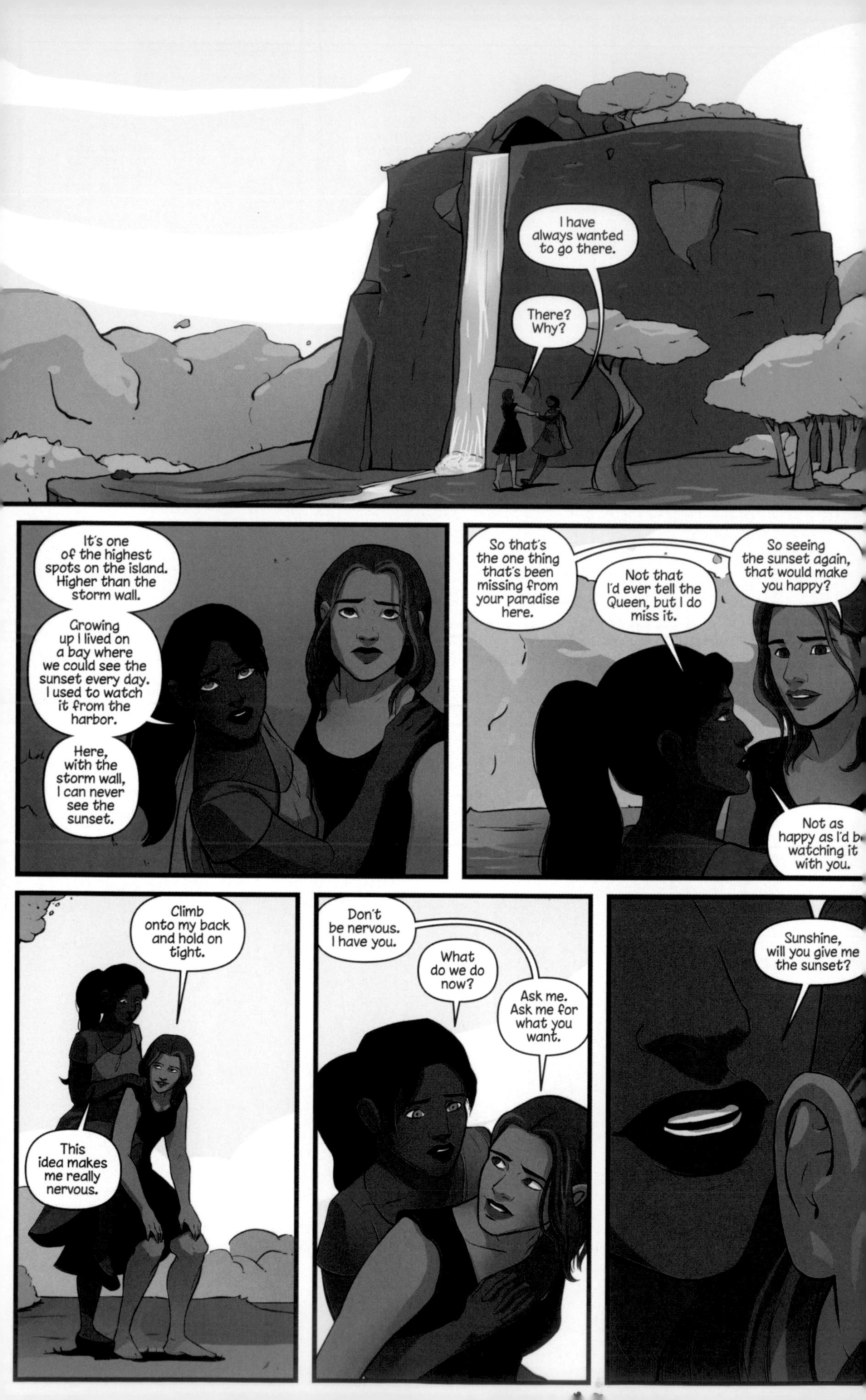

I have always wanted to go there.
There? Why?
It's one of the highest spots on the island. Higher than the storm wall.
Growing up I lived on a bay where we could see the sunset every day. I used to watch it from the harbor.
Here, with the storm wall, I can never see the sunset.
So that's the one thing that's been missing from your paradise here.
Not that I'd ever tell the Queen, but I do miss it.
So seeing the sunset again, that would make you happy?
Not as happy as I'd b
watching it with you.
Climb onto my back and hold on tight.
This idea makes me really nervous.
Don't be nervous. I have you.
What do we do now?
Ask me. Ask me for what you want.
Sunshine, will you give me the sunset?

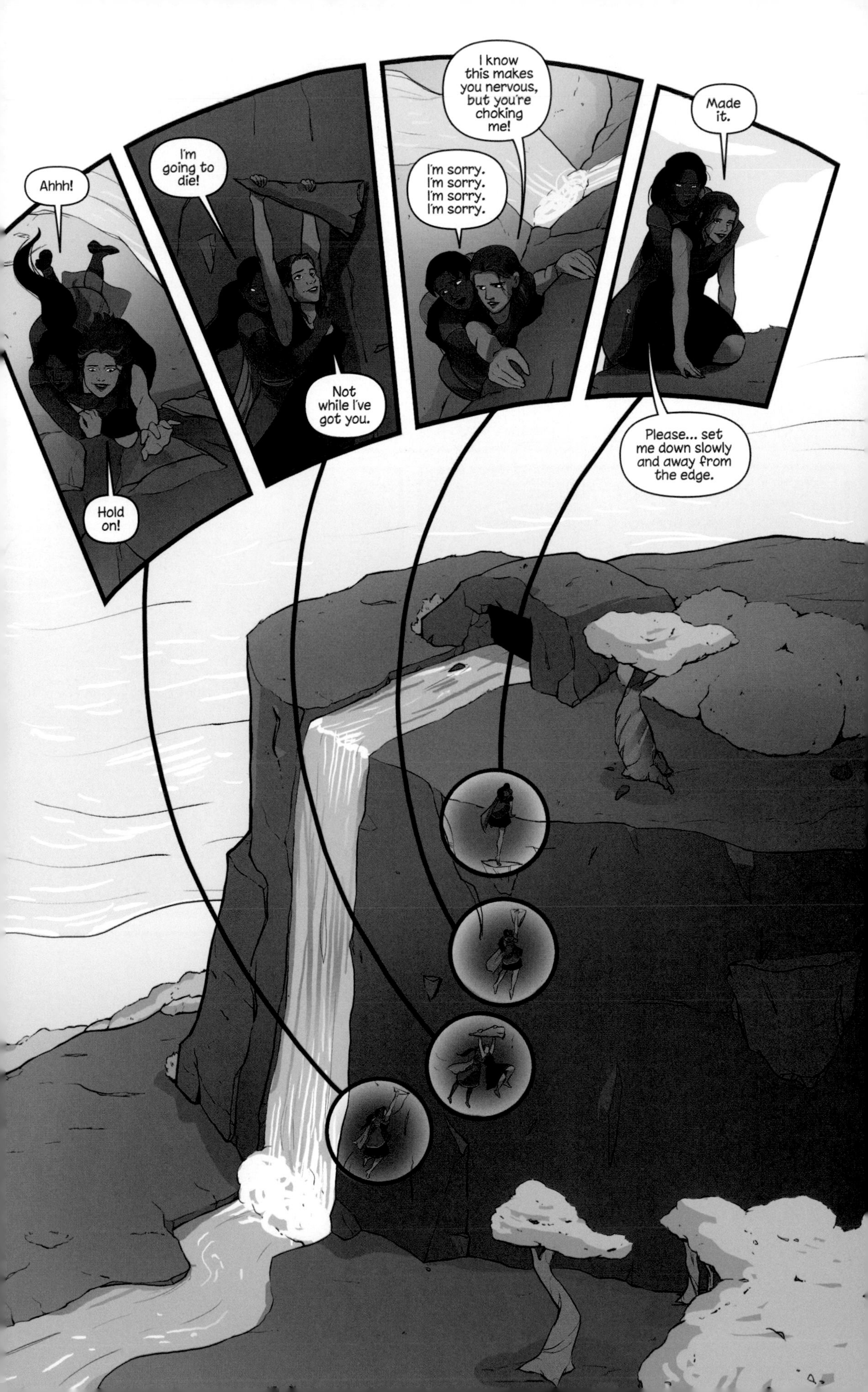
Ahhh!
Hold on!
I'm going to die!
Not while I've got you.
I know this makes you nervous, but you're choking me!
I'm sorry. I'm sorry. I'm sorry. I'm sorry.
Made it.
Please... set me down slowly and away from the edge.

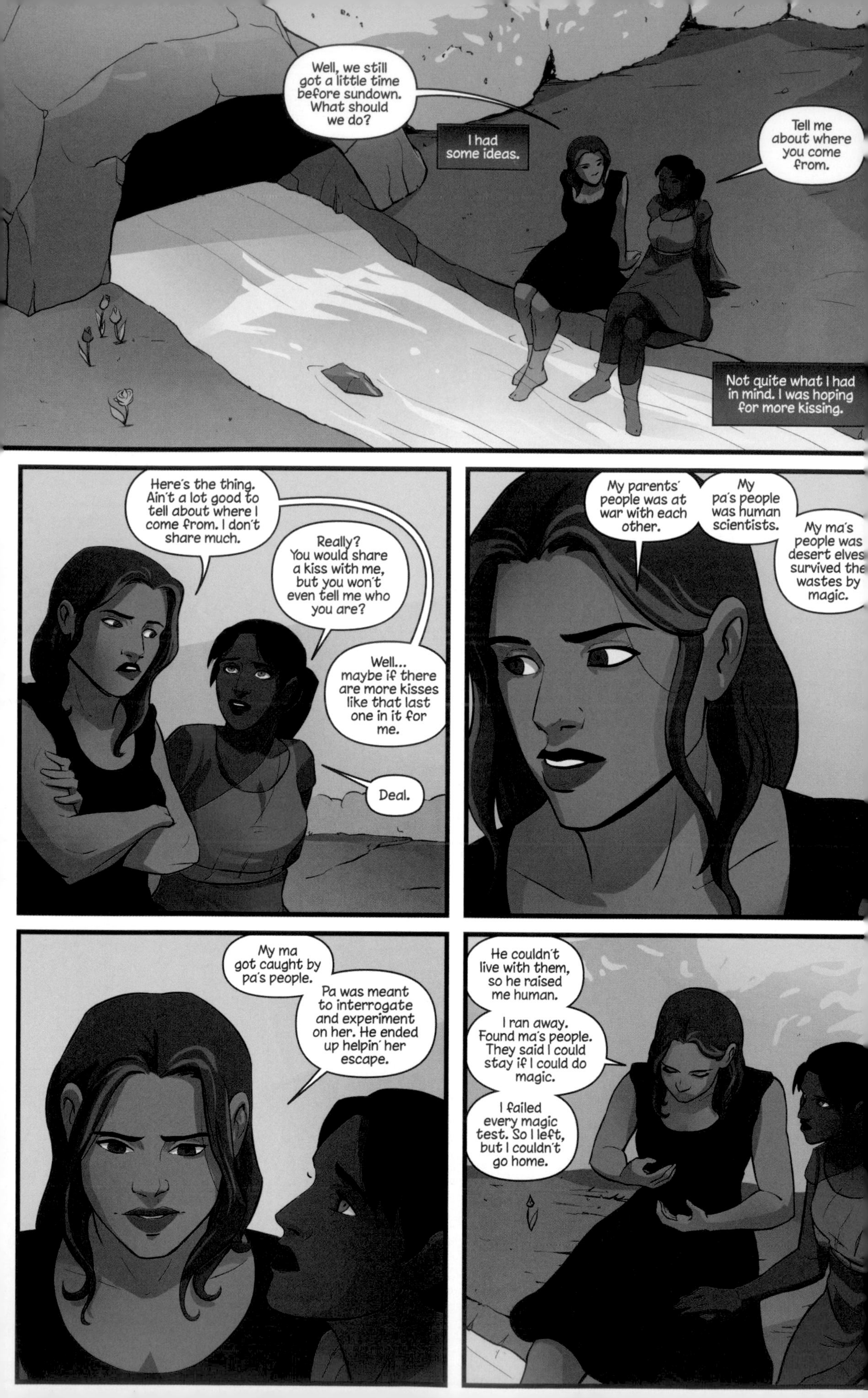
Well, we still got a little time before sundown. What should we do?
I had some ideas.
Tell me about where you come from.
Not quite what I had in mind. I was hoping for more kissing.
Here's the thing. Ain't a lot good to tell about where I come from. I don't share much.
Really? You would share a kiss with me, but you won't even tell me who you are?
Well... maybe if there are more kisses like that last one in it for me.
Deal.
My parents' people was at war with each other.
My pa's people was human scientists.
My ma's people was desert elves survived the wastes by magic.
My ma got caught by pa's people.
Pa was meant to interrogate and experiment on her. He ended up helpin' her escape.
He couldn't live with them, so he raised me human.
I ran away. Found ma's people. They said I could stay if I could do magic.
I failed every magic test. So I left, but I couldn't go home.

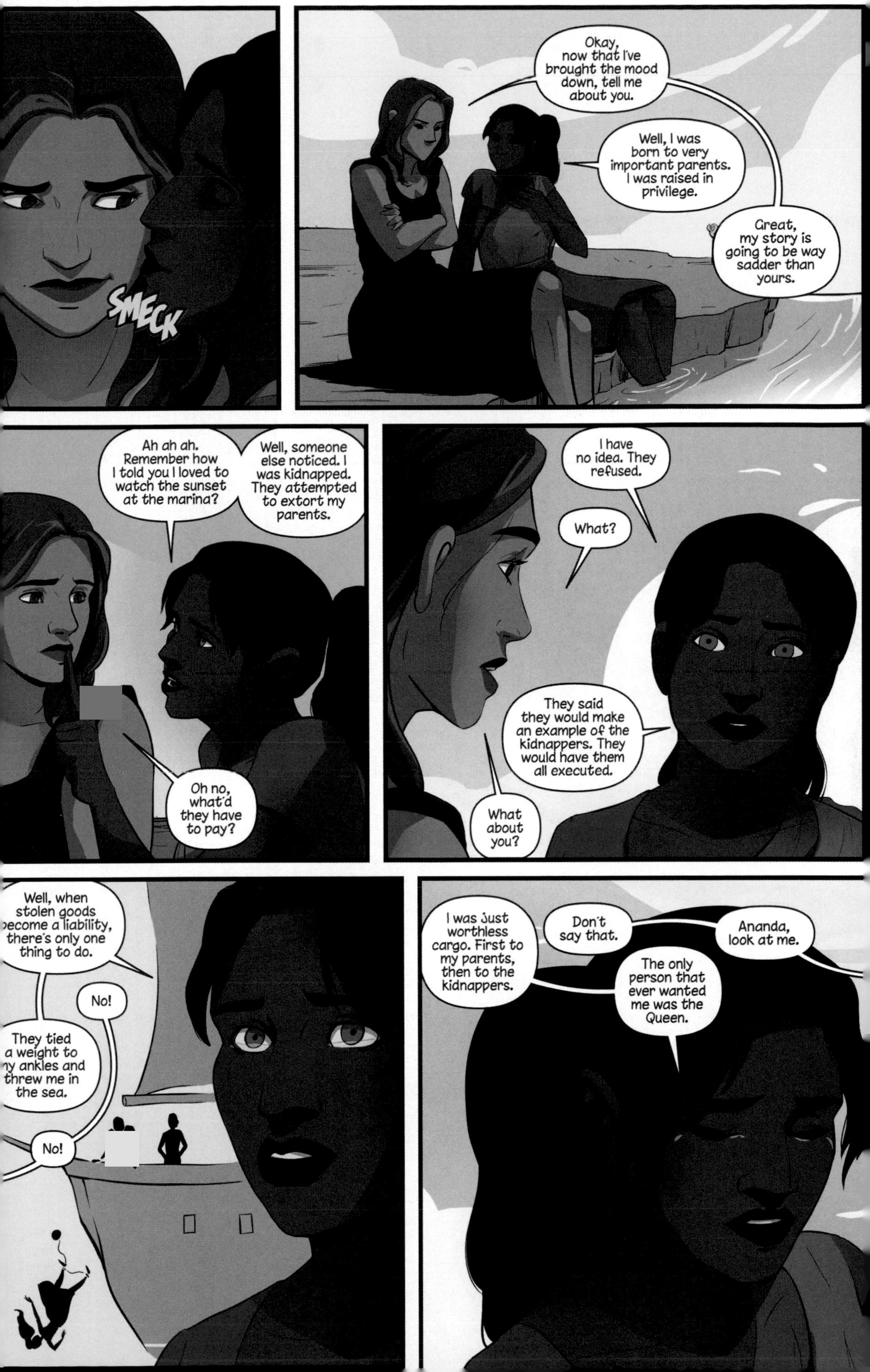
SMECK
Okay, now that I've brought the mood down, tell me about you.
Well, I was born to very important parents. I was raised in privilege.
Great, my story is going to be way sadder than yours.
Ah ah ah. Remember how I told you I loved to watch the sunset at the marina?
Well, someone else noticed. I was kidnapped. They attempted to extort my parents.
Oh no, what'd they have to pay?
I have no idea. They refused.
What?
They said they would make an example of the kidnappers. They would have them all executed.
What about you?
Well, when stolen goods ecome a liability, there's only one thing to do.
No!
They tied a weight to ny ankles and threw me in the sea.
No!
I was just worthless cargo. First to my parents, then to the kidnappers.
Don't say that.
Ananda, look at me.
The only person that ever wanted me was the Queen.

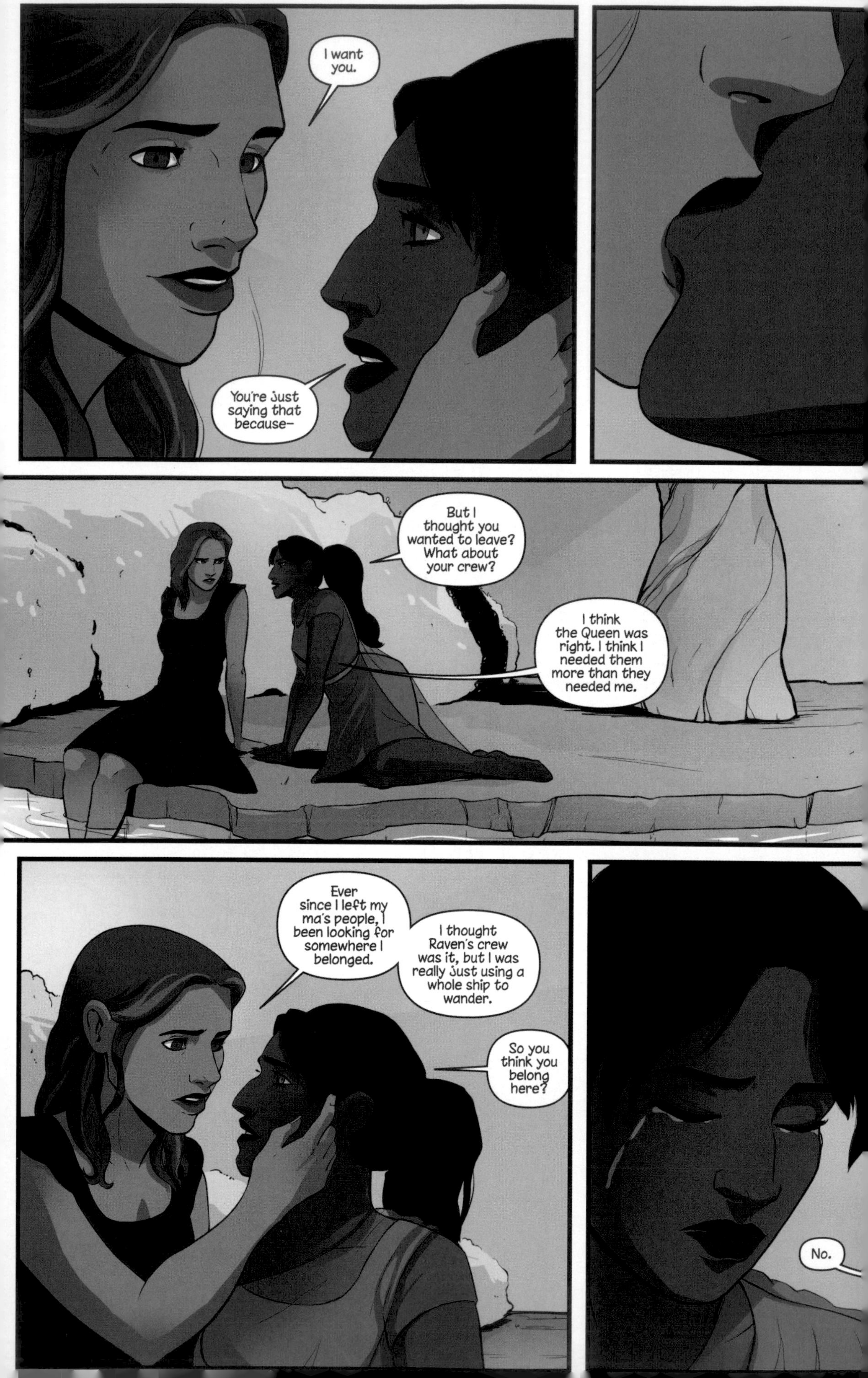
I want you.
You're just saying that because-
But I thought you wanted to leave? What about your crew?
I think the Queen was right. I think I needed them more than they needed me.
Ever since I left my ma's people, I been looking for somewhere I belonged.
I thought Raven's crew was it, but I was really just using a whole ship to wander.
So you think you belong here?
No.

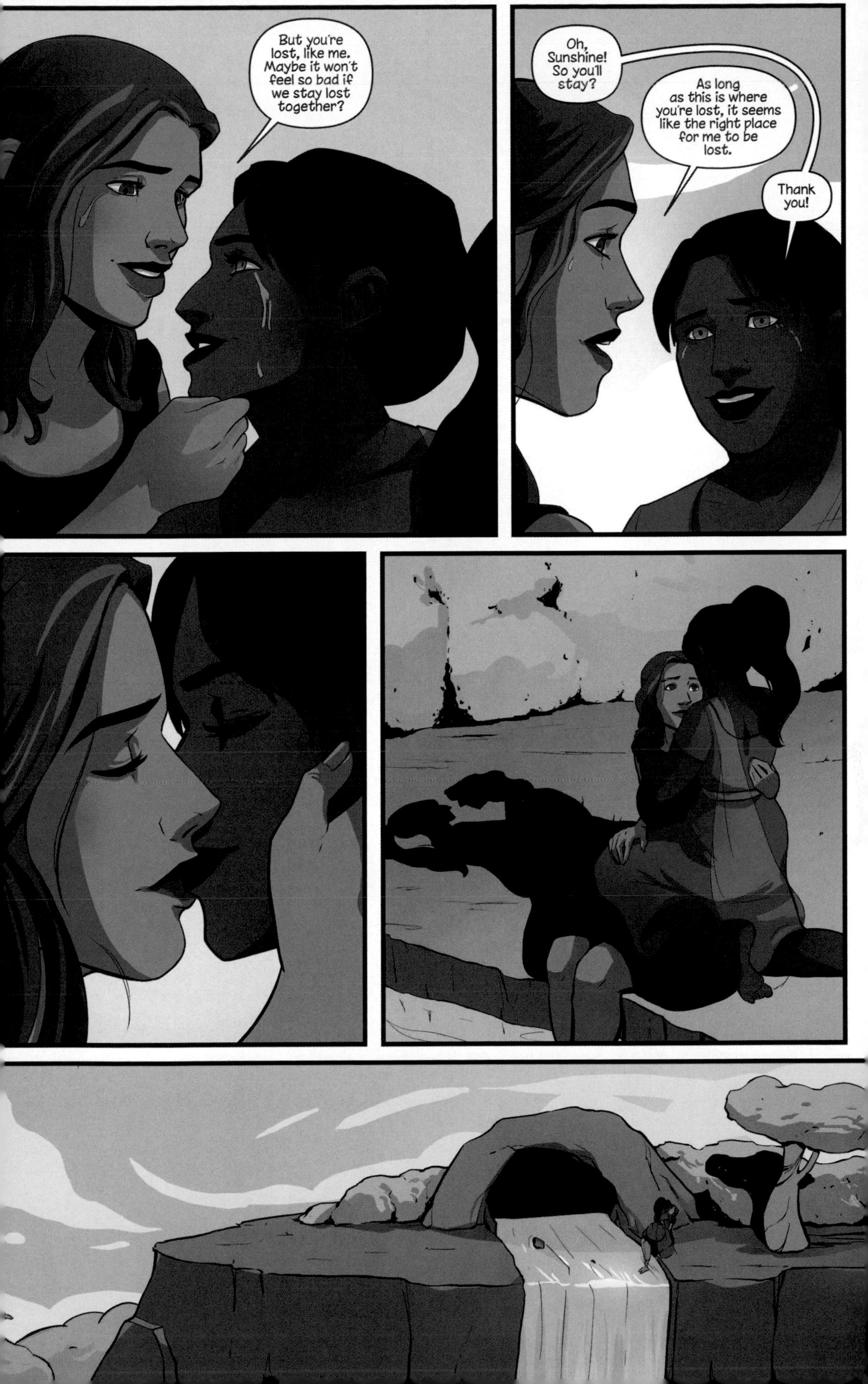
But you're lost, like me. Maybe it won't feel so bad if we stay lost together?
Oh, Sunshine! So you'll stay?
As long as this is where you're lost, it seems like the right place for me to be lost.
Thank you!

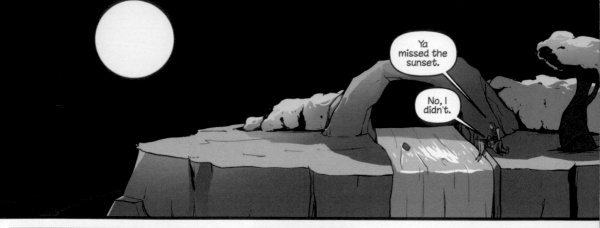

Ya missed the sunset.

No, I didn't.

I'll have more chances to see it, right?

I'll bring you here anytime you like.

Anytime. I like that word. It sounds permanent.

You don't say "anytime" to any old person. No, not just... whoever.

Girl, you're fallin' asleep. Startin' not to make sense.

You keep rubbing my hair like that and I'll be asleep.

The Queen will be so happy.

Oh yeah, why's that?

Well, she suggested I should go and find you the other night.

Huh?

She was afraid you'd try to... I don't know, run away somehow.

Was she?

Yeah, she said that she thought we'd get along. That I should get to know you.

So I wouldn't leave?

Well, yeah, probably. But also to, you know, make us both happy.

Happy, huh?

Character sketches by Christine

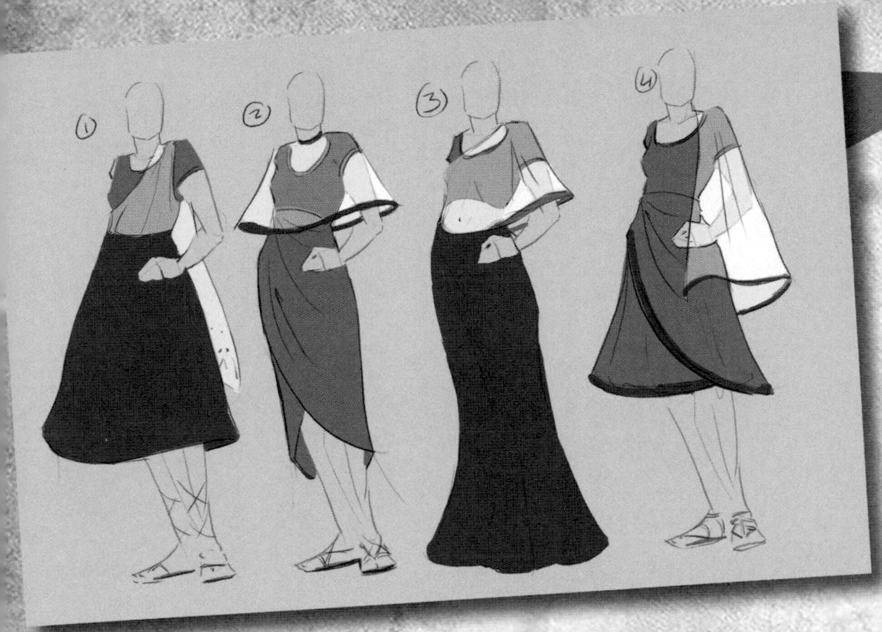

1
2
3
4

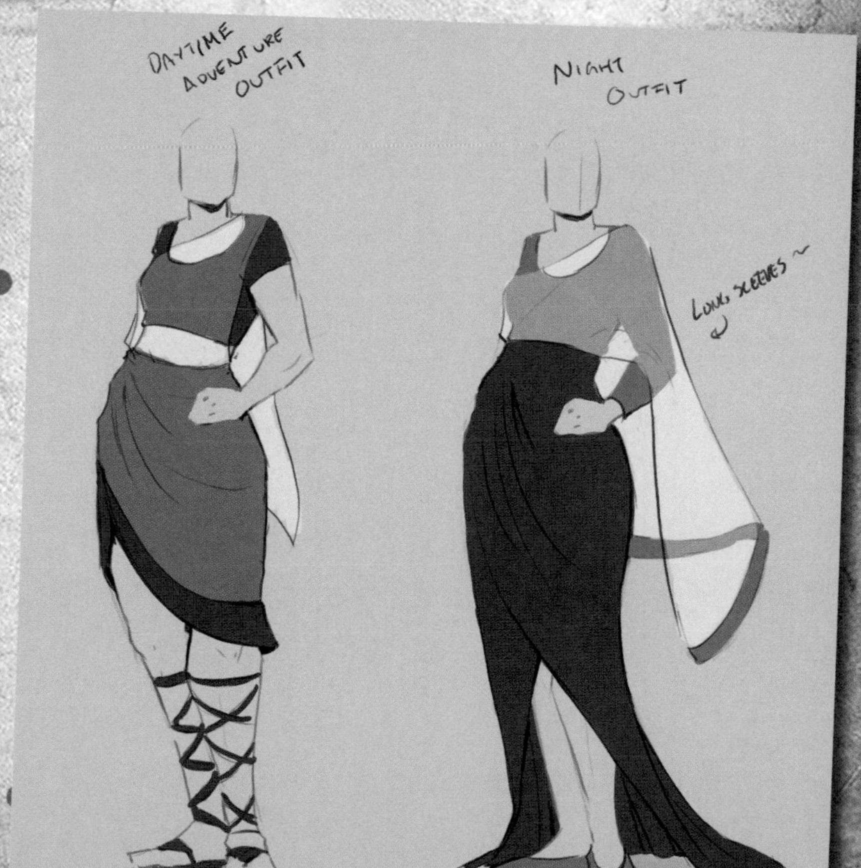

DAYTIME ADVENTURE OUTFIT
NIGHT OUTFIT
LONG SLEEVES ~

Character sketches by Christine

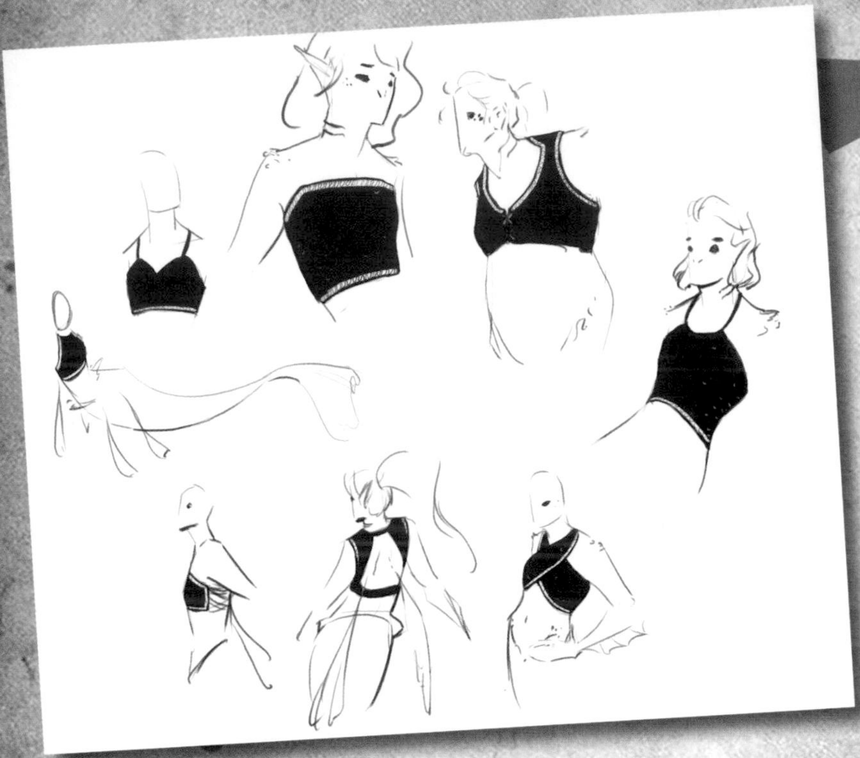

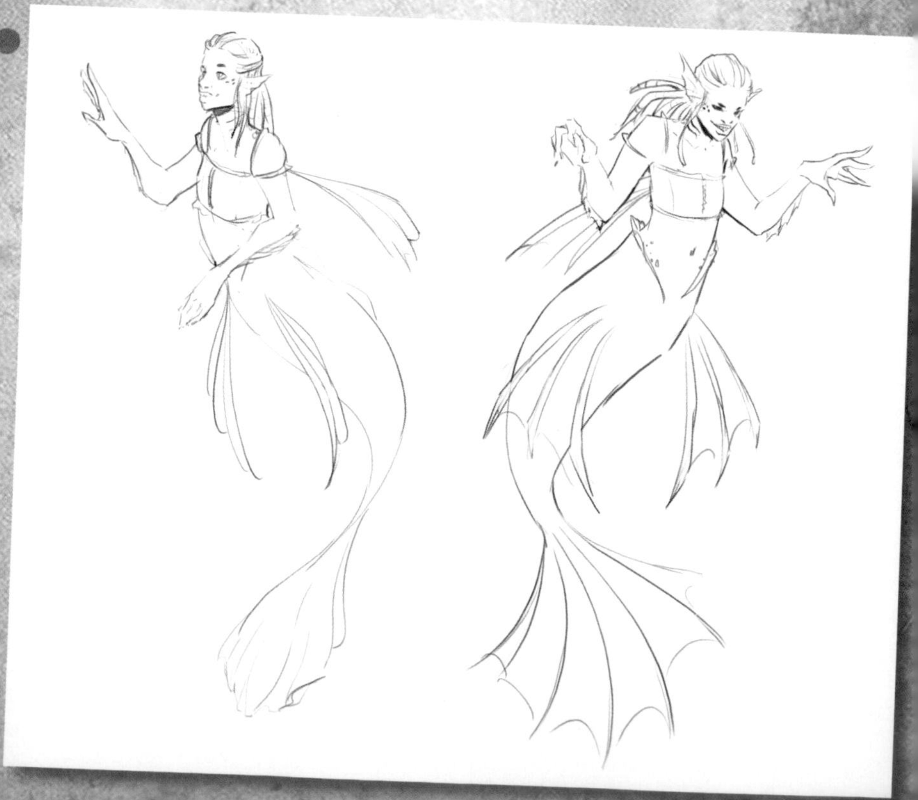

Page 6 Progression

Page 6:

Panel 1: Sunshine's eyes open.

SUNSHINE (CAPTION)
I can breathe again! It's such a shock, it actually takes me a minute to realize.

Panel 2: Zoom out. Sunshine is being kissed by a mermaid. The human half of the mermaid is a black woman with dreadlocks. I'll let you figure out the clothing on the top half.

SUNSHINE (CAPTION)
I'm actually being kissed by a gorgeous mermaid.

SUNSHINE (CAPTION)
Well…kissed is part of it. It's firm but gentle like a kiss.

SUNSHINE (CAPTION)
But somehow, she's bringing me back to life.

Panel 3: Sunshine looks awed as the mermaid pulls back.

MERMAID
Are you with me?

SUNSHINE (CAPTION)
Somehow I can hear her, just like we're on the surface.

SUNSHINE
That depends. Are you a mermaid?

Panel 4: The mermaid laughs.

MERMAID
Hahaha.

MERMAID
I'm not much for that "maid" stuff. Merwoman or Siren will be just fine.

SUNSHINE
Oh, sorry.

MERMAID
Afua is even better. That's my name.

Page 6 Inks

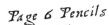

Page 6 Pencils

Page 6 Progression

Page 6 Colors

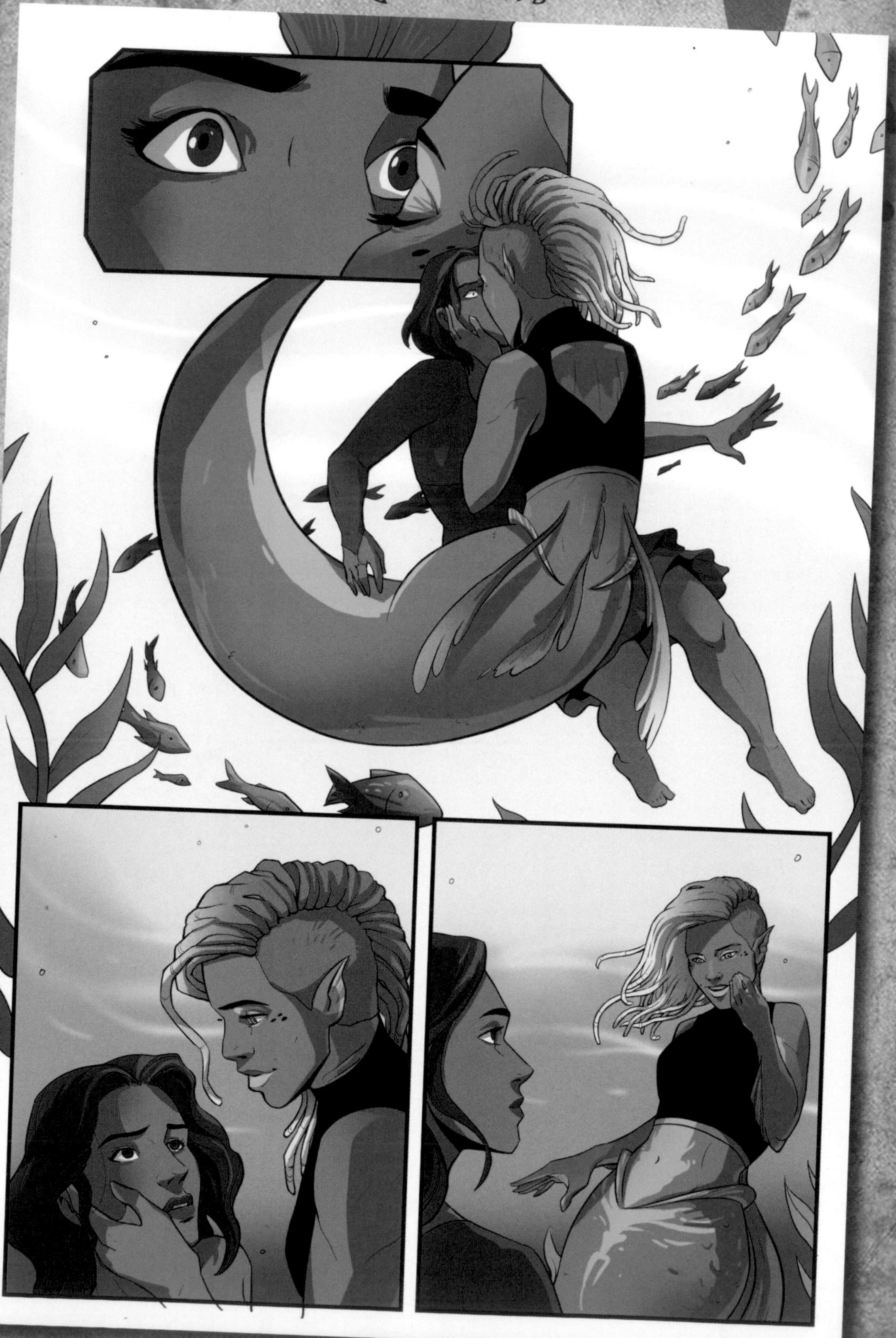

Page 19 Progression

Page 19: I picture this image as being a sort of overlay of the rock face with smaller images pulled out.

Panel 1: Sunshine leaps up to a lower outcropping.

ANANDA
Ahhh!

SUNSHINE
Hold on!

Panel 2: Sunshine hold onto a stalactite type outcropping, swinging from it.

ANANDA
I'm going to die!

SUNSHINE
Not while I've got you.

Panel 3: Sunshine climbs the wall in another spot, Ananda holding very tightly to her.

SUNSHINE
I know this makes you nervous, but you're choking me!

ANANDA
I'm sorry. I'm sorry. I'm sorry. I'm sorry.

Panel 4: Sunshine lands in the entrance to the cave on a shelf of rock that moves alongside the river.

SUNSHINE
Made it.

ANANDA
Please…set me down slowly and away from the edge.

Page 19 Inks

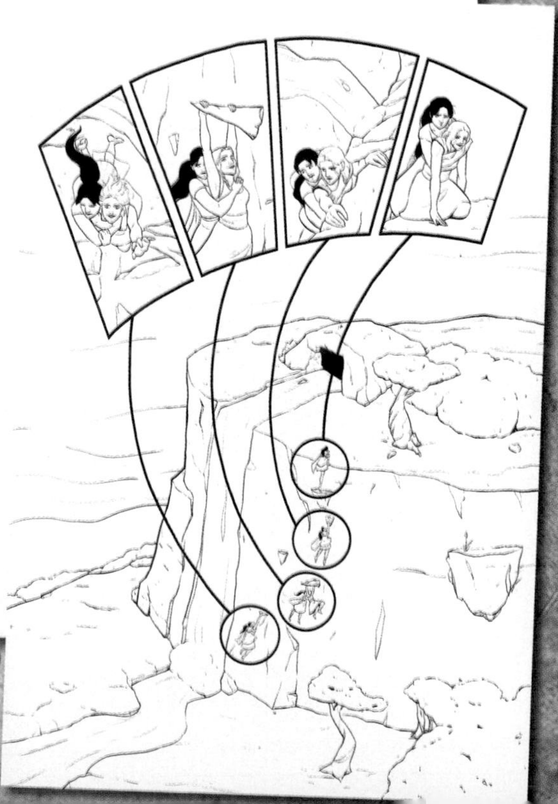

Page 19 Progression

Page 19 Colors

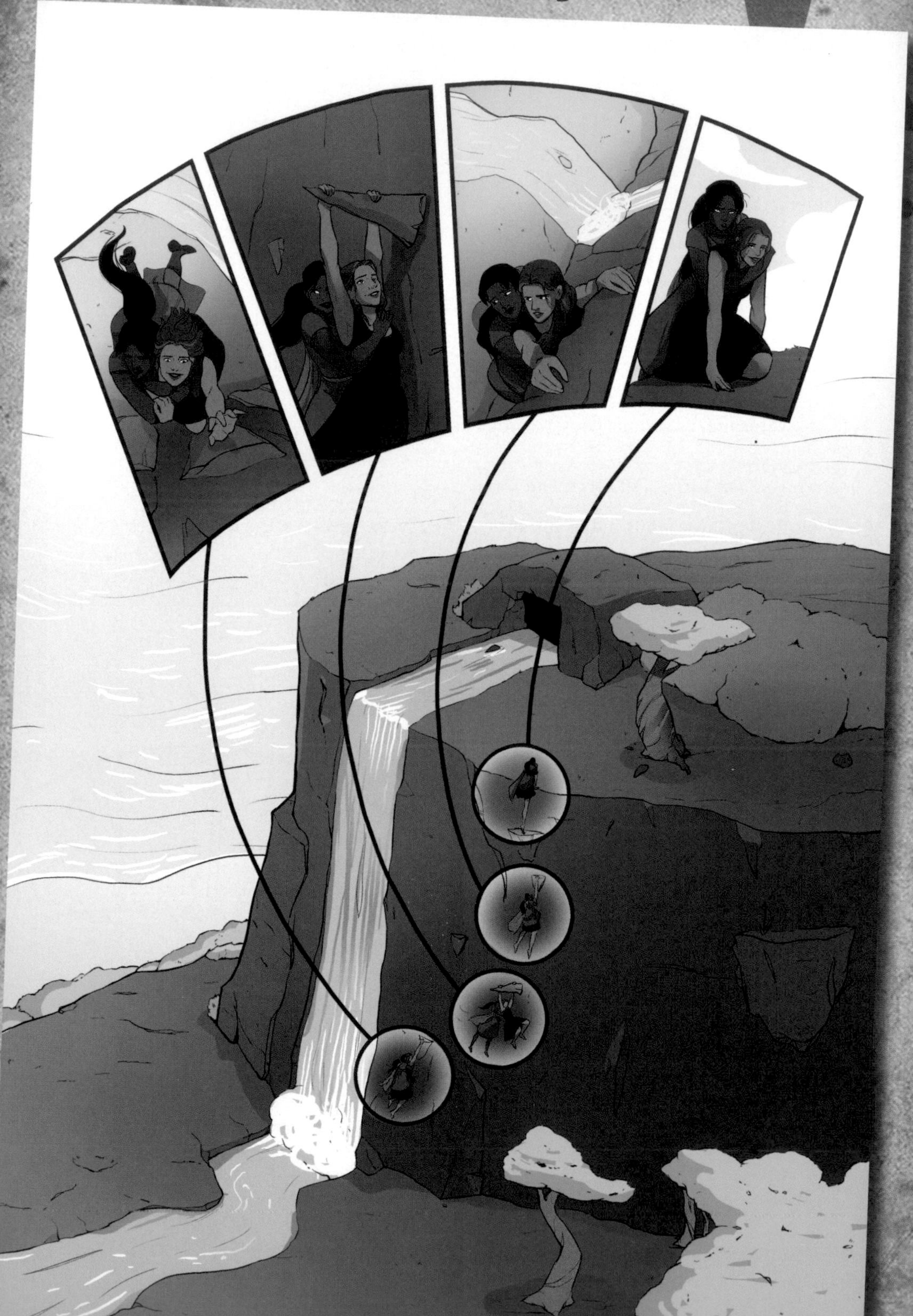

Princess Raven: The Pirate Princess

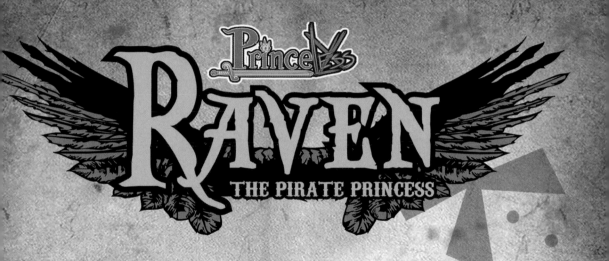

Year Two: Love and Revenge

Chapter Seven: The Dreaded Pairing Off

Written By: Jeremy Whitley

Art By: Christine Hipp

Colors By: Xenia Pamfil

Lettered By: Justin Birch

Edited By: Nicole D'Andria

Cover By: Christine Hipp

Cover Colors By: Xenia Pamfil

Bryan Seaton: Publisher/ CEO - Shawn Gabborin: Editor In Chief - Jason Martin: Publisher-Danger Zone
Nicole D'Andria: Marketing Director/Editor - Danielle Davison: Executive Administrator
Chad Cicconi: Deck Swabber - Shawn Pryor: President of Creator Relations

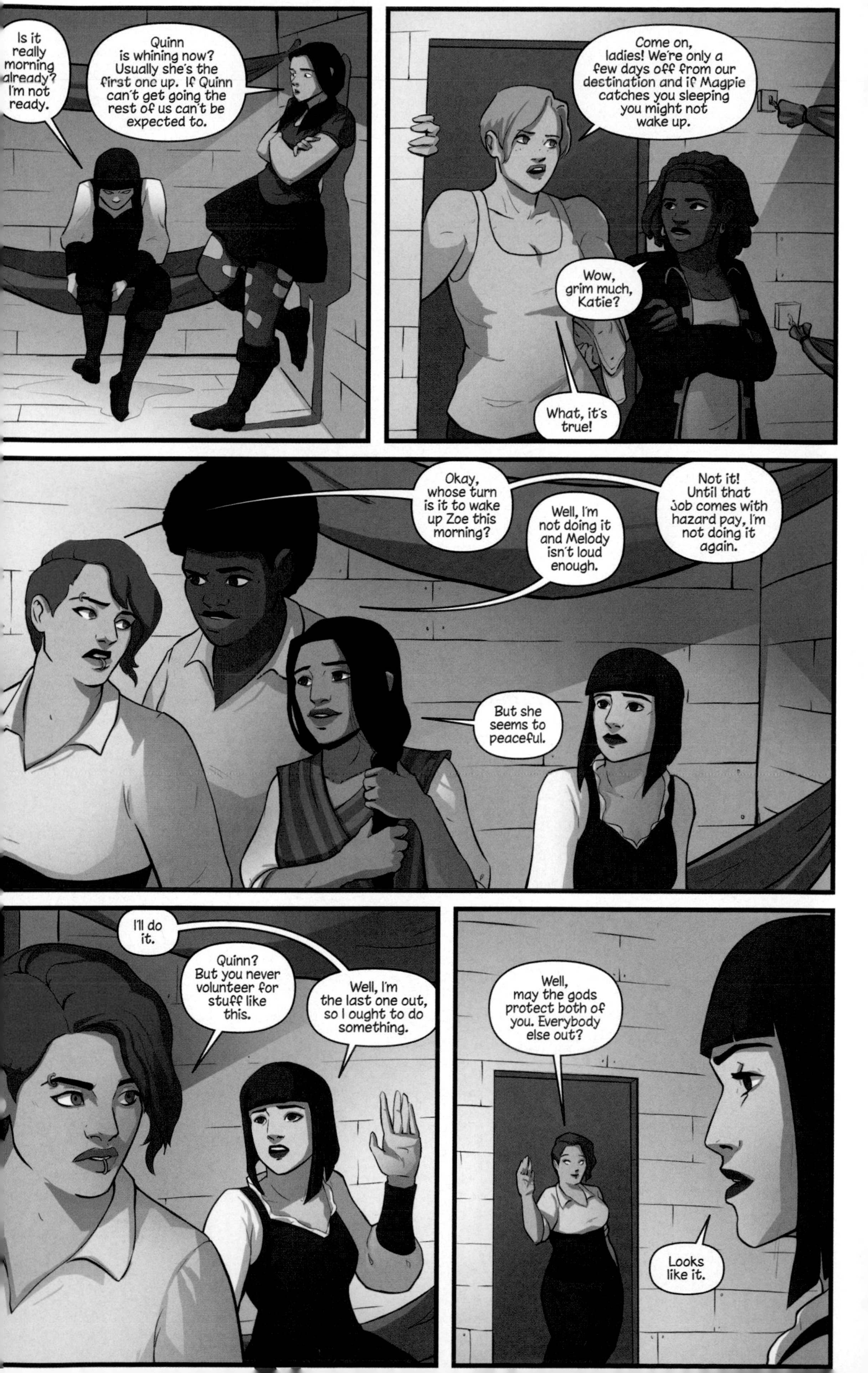
Is it really morning already? I'm not ready.
Quinn is whining now? Usually she's the first one up. If Quinn can't get going the rest of us can't be expected to.
Come on, ladies! We're only a few days off from our destination and if Magpie catches you sleeping you might not wake up.
Wow, grim much, Katie?
What, it's true!
Okay, whose turn is it to wake up Zoe this morning?
Well, I'm not doing it and Melody isn't loud enough.
Not it! Until that job comes with hazard pay, I'm not doing it again.
But she seems to peaceful.
I'll do it.
Quinn? But you never volunteer for stuff like this.
Well, I'm the last one out, so I ought to do something.
Well, may the gods protect both of you. Everybody else out?
Looks like it.

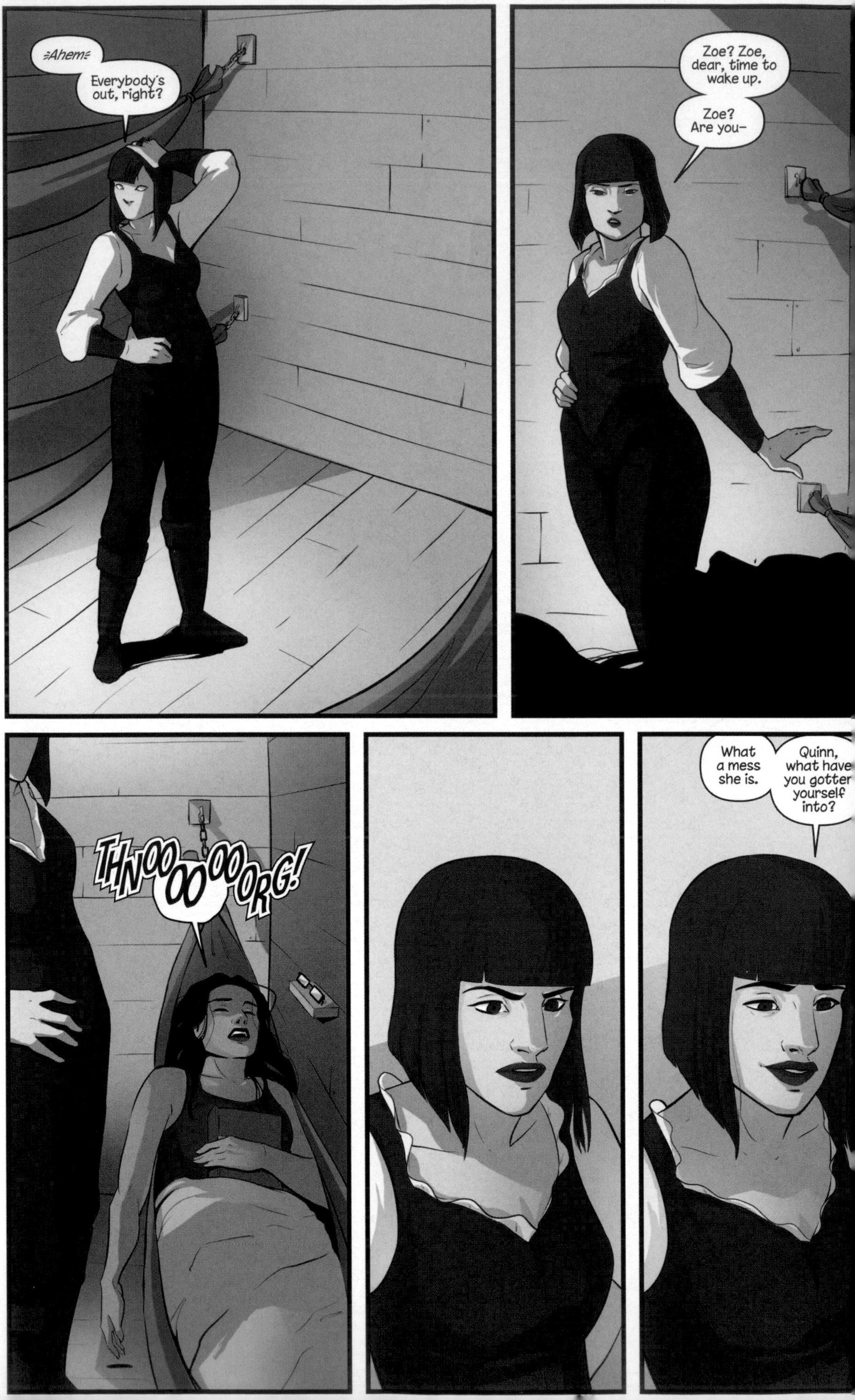

=Ahem=
Everybody's out, right?
Zoe? Zoe, dear, time to wake up.
Zoe? Are you-
THNOOOOOOORG!
What a mess she is.
Quinn, what have you gotten yourself into?

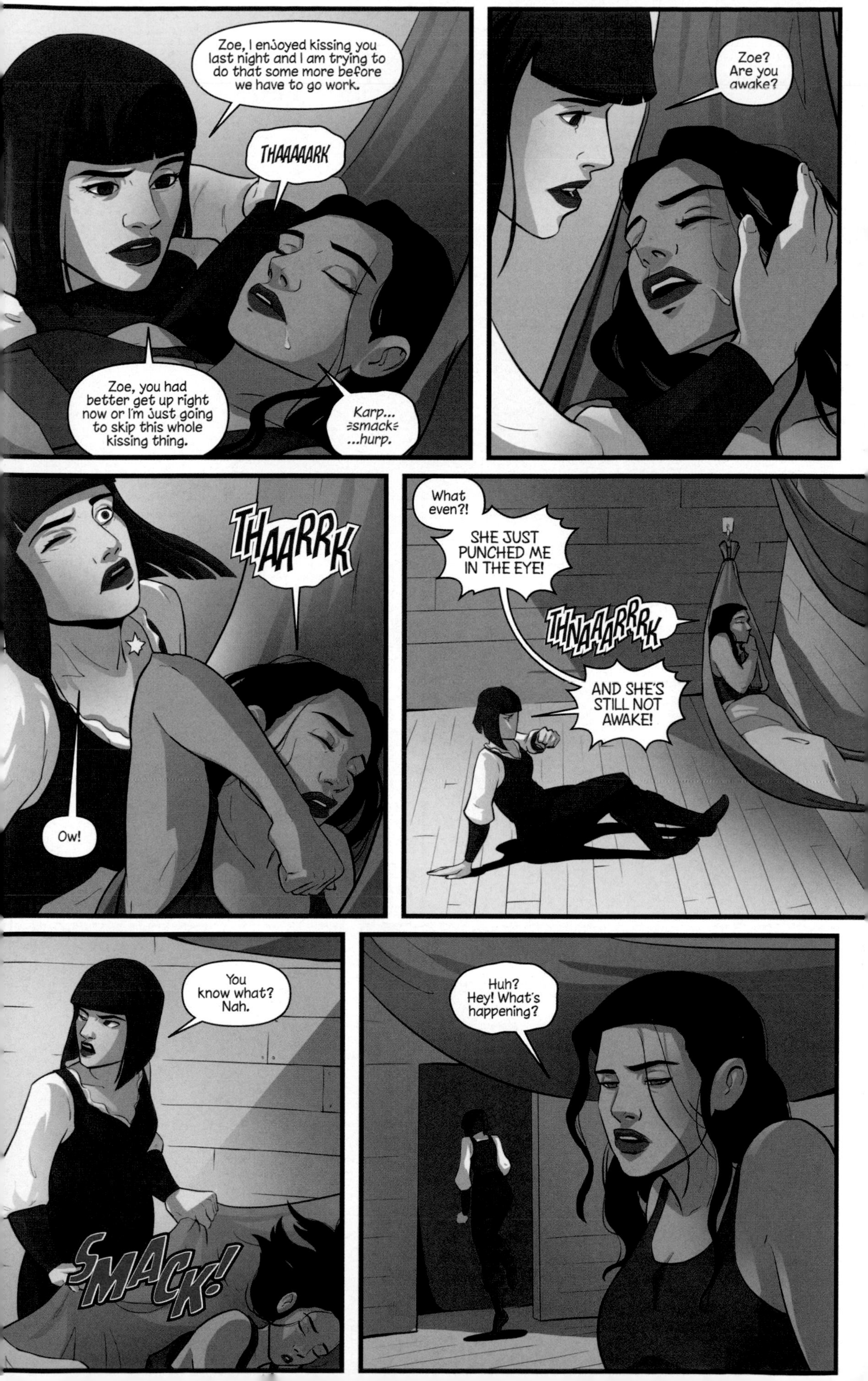
Zoe, I enjoyed kissing you last night and I am trying to do that some more before we have to go work.
THAAAAARK
Zoe, you had better get up right now or I'm just going to skip this whole kissing thing.
Karp... ≈smack≈ ...hurp.
Zoe? Are you awake?
THAARRRK
Ow!
What even?!
SHE JUST PUNCHED ME IN THE EYE!
THNAAARRRK
AND SHE'S STILL NOT AWAKE!
You know what? Nah.
SMACK!
Huh? Hey! What's happening?

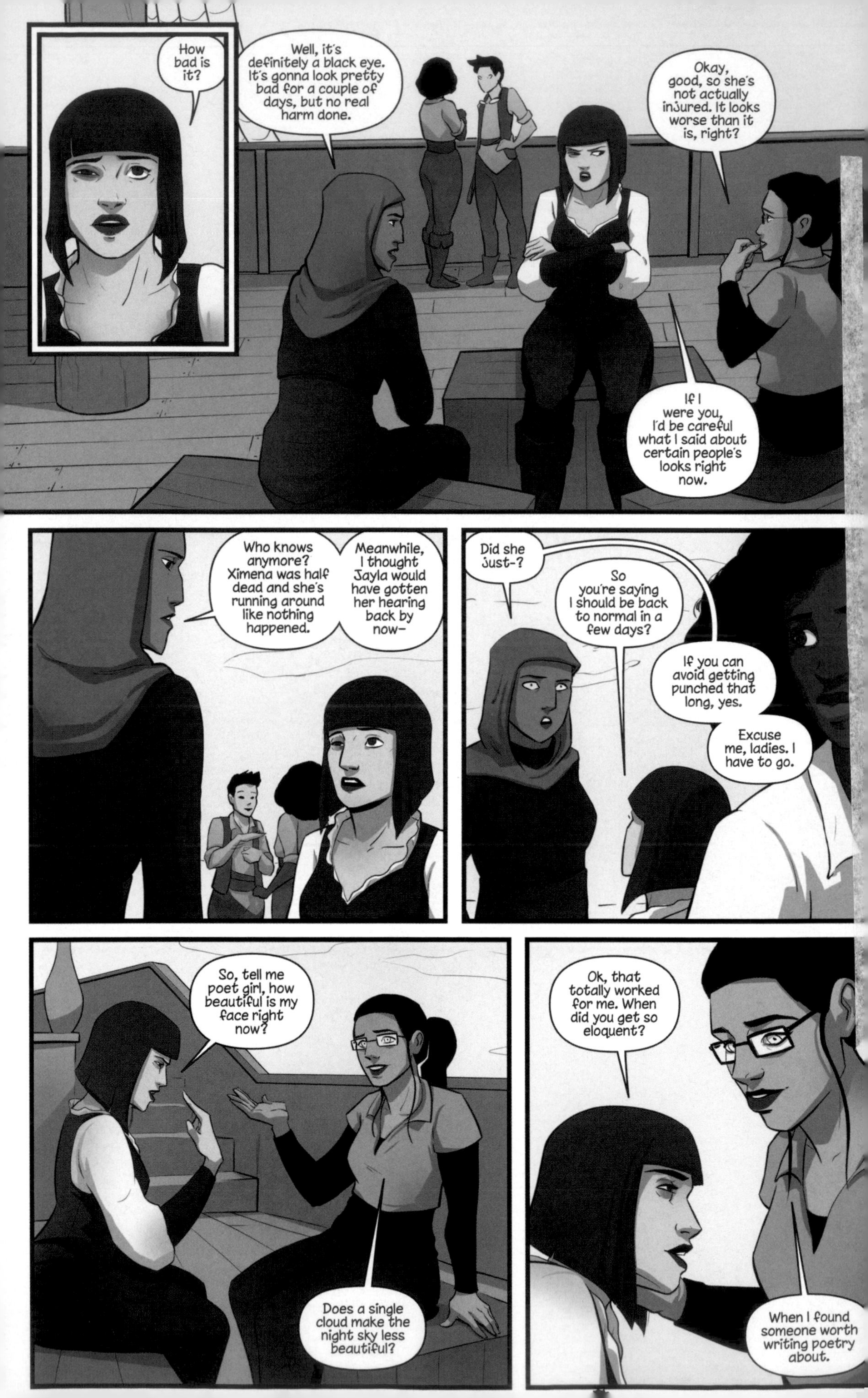
How bad is it?
Well, it's definitely a black eye. It's gonna look pretty bad for a couple of days, but no real harm done.
Okay, good, so she's not actually injured. It looks worse than it is, right?
If I were you, I'd be careful what I said about certain people's looks right now.
Who knows anymore? Ximena was half dead and she's running around like nothing happened.
Meanwhile, I thought Jayla would have gotten her hearing back by now–
Did she just–?
So you're saying I should be back to normal in a few days?
If you can avoid getting punched that long, yes.
Excuse me, ladies. I have to go.
So, tell me poet girl, how beautiful is my face right now?
Does a single cloud make the night sky less beautiful?
Ok, that totally worked for me. When did you get so eloquent?
When I found someone worth writing poetry about.

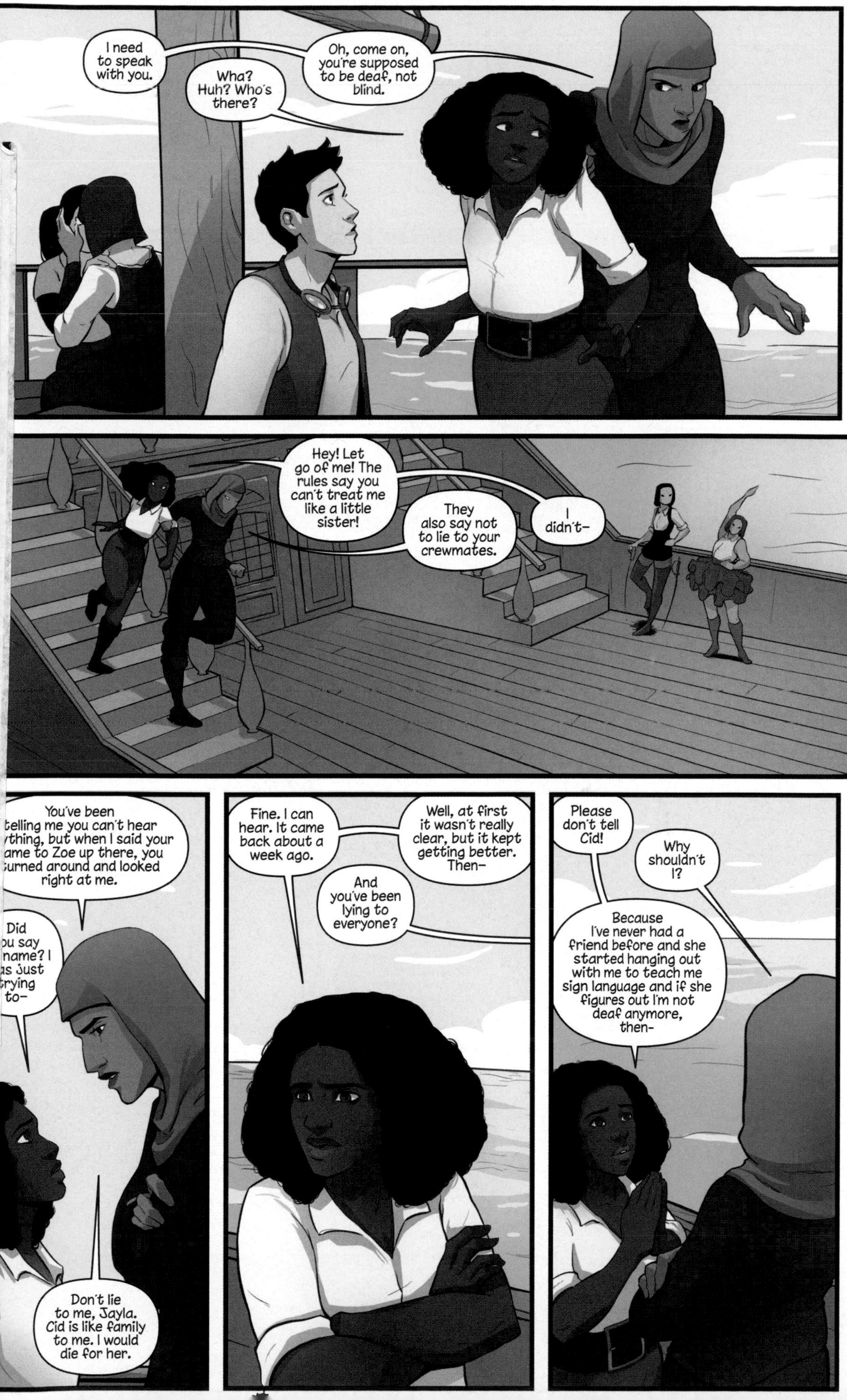
I need to speak with you.
Wha? Huh? Who's there?
Oh, come on, you're supposed to be deaf, not blind.
Hey! Let go of me! The rules say you can't treat me like a little sister!
They also say not to lie to your crewmates.
I didn't-
You've been telling me you can't hear ything, but when I said your ame to Zoe up there, you turned around and looked right at me.
Did ou say name? I as just trying to-
Don't lie to me, Jayla. Cid is like family to me. I would die for her.
Fine. I can hear. It came back about a week ago.
And you've been lying to everyone?
Well, at first it wasn't really clear, but it kept getting better. Then-
Please don't tell Cid!
Why shouldn't I?
Because I've never had a friend before and she started hanging out with me to teach me sign language and if she figures out I'm not deaf anymore, then-

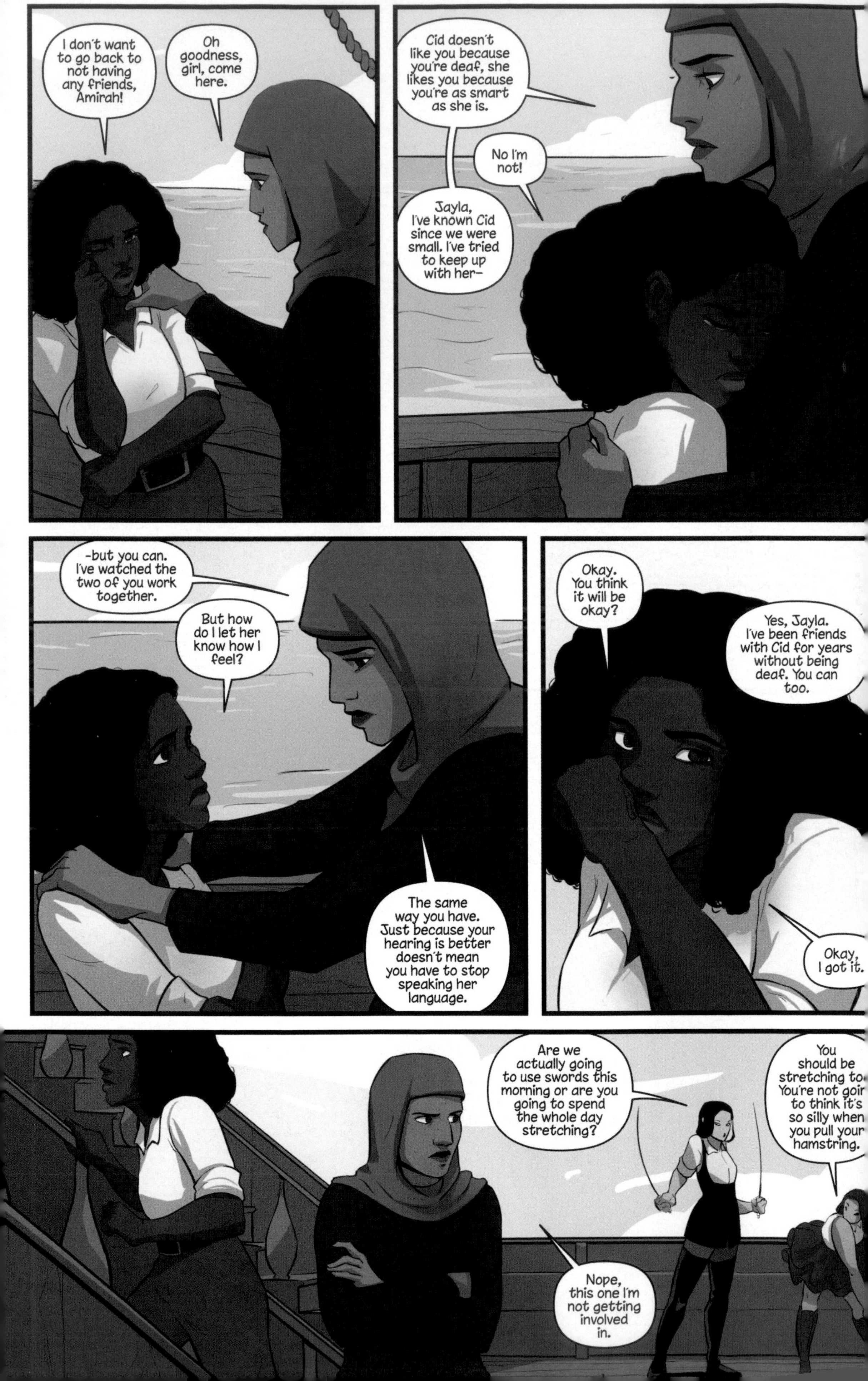
I don't want to go back to not having any friends, Amirah!
Oh goodness, girl, come here.
Cid doesn't like you because you're deaf, she likes you because you're as smart as she is.
No I'm not!
Jayla, I've known Cid since we were small. I've tried to keep up with her–
-but you can. I've watched the two of you work together.
But how do I let her know how I feel?
The same way you have. Just because your hearing is better doesn't mean you have to stop speaking her language.
Okay. You think it will be okay?
Yes, Jayla. I've been friends with Cid for years without being deaf. You can too.
Okay, I got it.
Are we actually going to use swords this morning or are you going to spend the whole day stretching?
You should be stretching to You're not goir to think it's so silly when you pull your hamstring.
Nope, this one I'm not getting involved in.

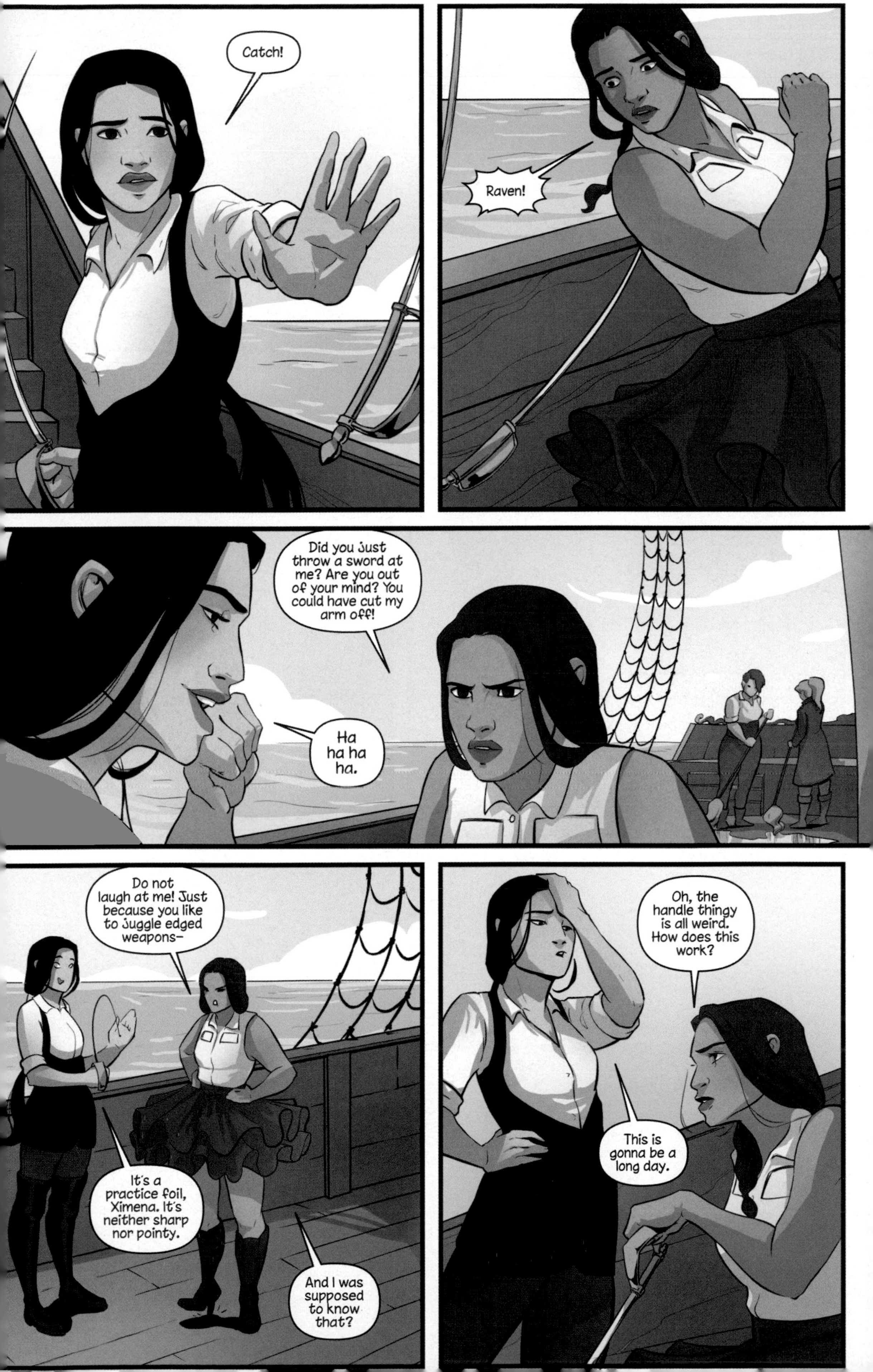
Catch!
Raven!
Did you just throw a sword at me? Are you out of your mind? You could have cut my arm off!
Ha ha ha ha.
Do not laugh at me! Just because you like to juggle edged weapons–
It's a practice foil, Ximena. It's neither sharp nor pointy.
And I was supposed to know that?
Oh, the handle thingy is all weird. How does this work?
This is gonna be a long day.

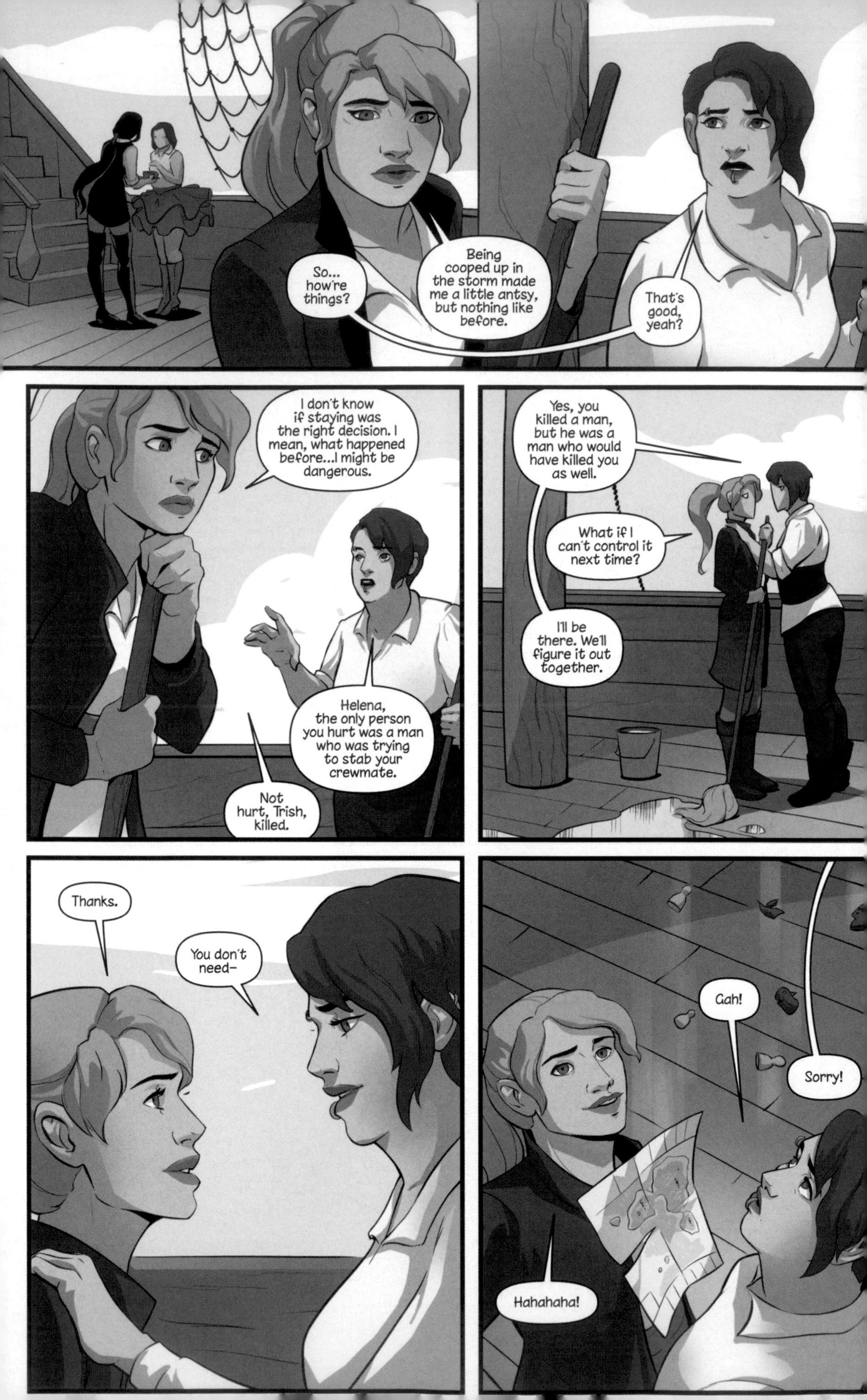
So... how're things?
Being cooped up in the storm made me a little antsy, but nothing like before.
That's good, yeah?
I don't know if staying was the right decision. I mean, what happened before...I might be dangerous.
Helena, the only person you hurt was a man who was trying to stab your crewmate.
Not hurt, Trish, killed.
Yes, you killed a man, but he was a man who would have killed you as well.
What if I can't control it next time?
I'll be there. We'll figure it out together.
Thanks.
You don't need–
Gah!
Sorry!
Hahahaha!

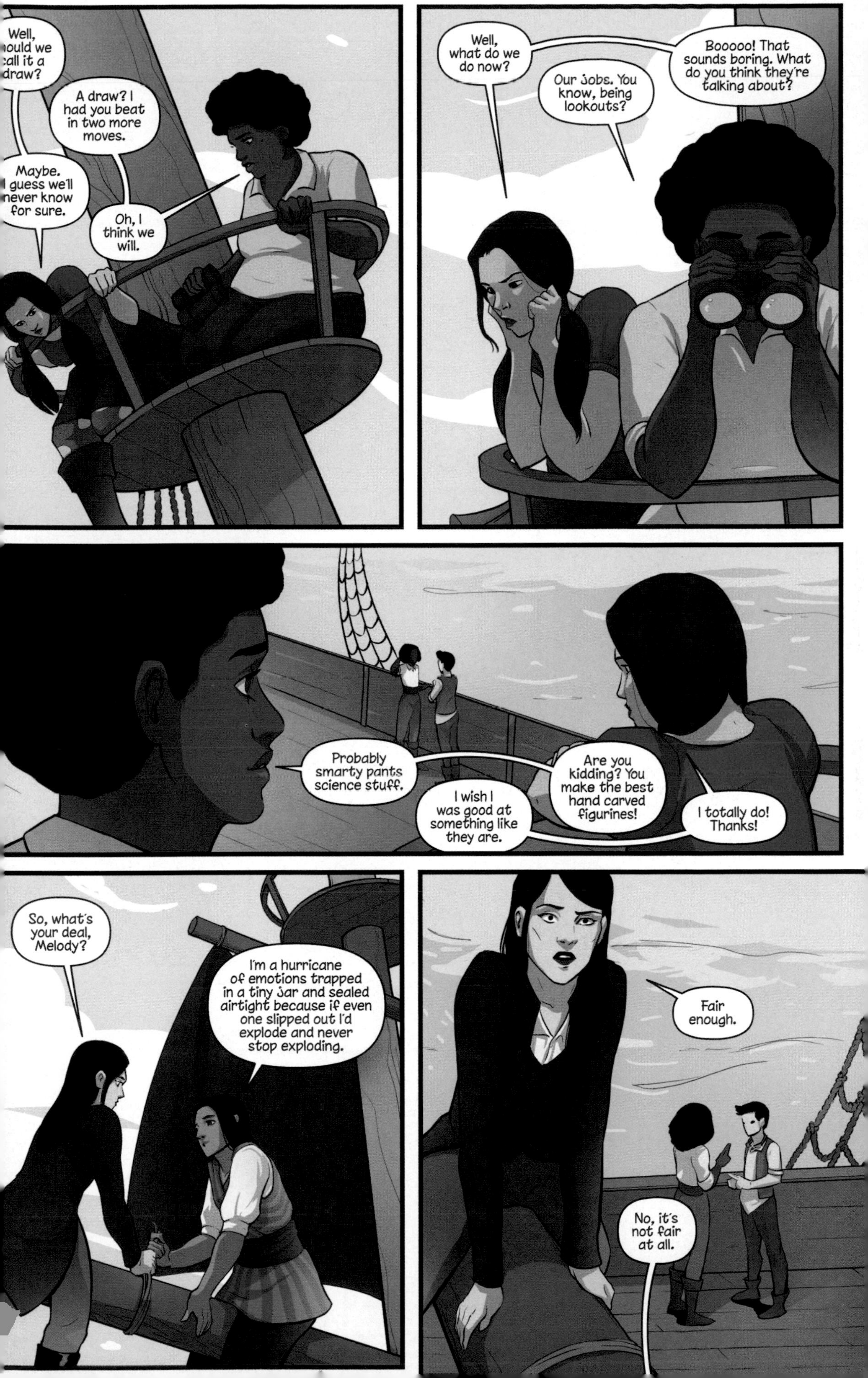

Well, ould we all it a draw?
A draw? I had you beat in two more moves.
Maybe. I guess we'll never know for sure.
Oh, I think we will.
Well, what do we do now?
Our jobs. You know, being lookouts?
Booooo! That sounds boring. What do you think they're talking about?
Probably smarty pants science stuff.
I wish I was good at something like they are.
Are you kidding? You make the best hand carved figurines!
I totally do! Thanks!
So, what's your deal, Melody?
I'm a hurricane of emotions trapped in a tiny jar and sealed airtight because if even one slipped out I'd explode and never stop exploding.
Fair enough.
No, it's not fair at all.

Here goes.

"I"

"can"

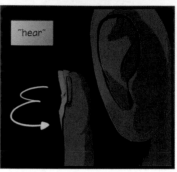

"hear"

"again."

"Yay!"

"Still"

"friends?"

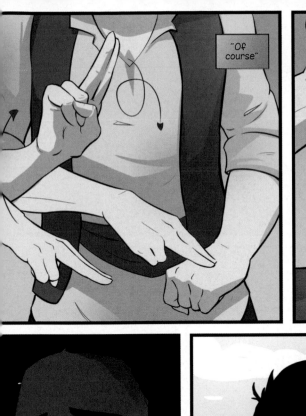

"Of course"

"stupid."

Ha ha ha ha.

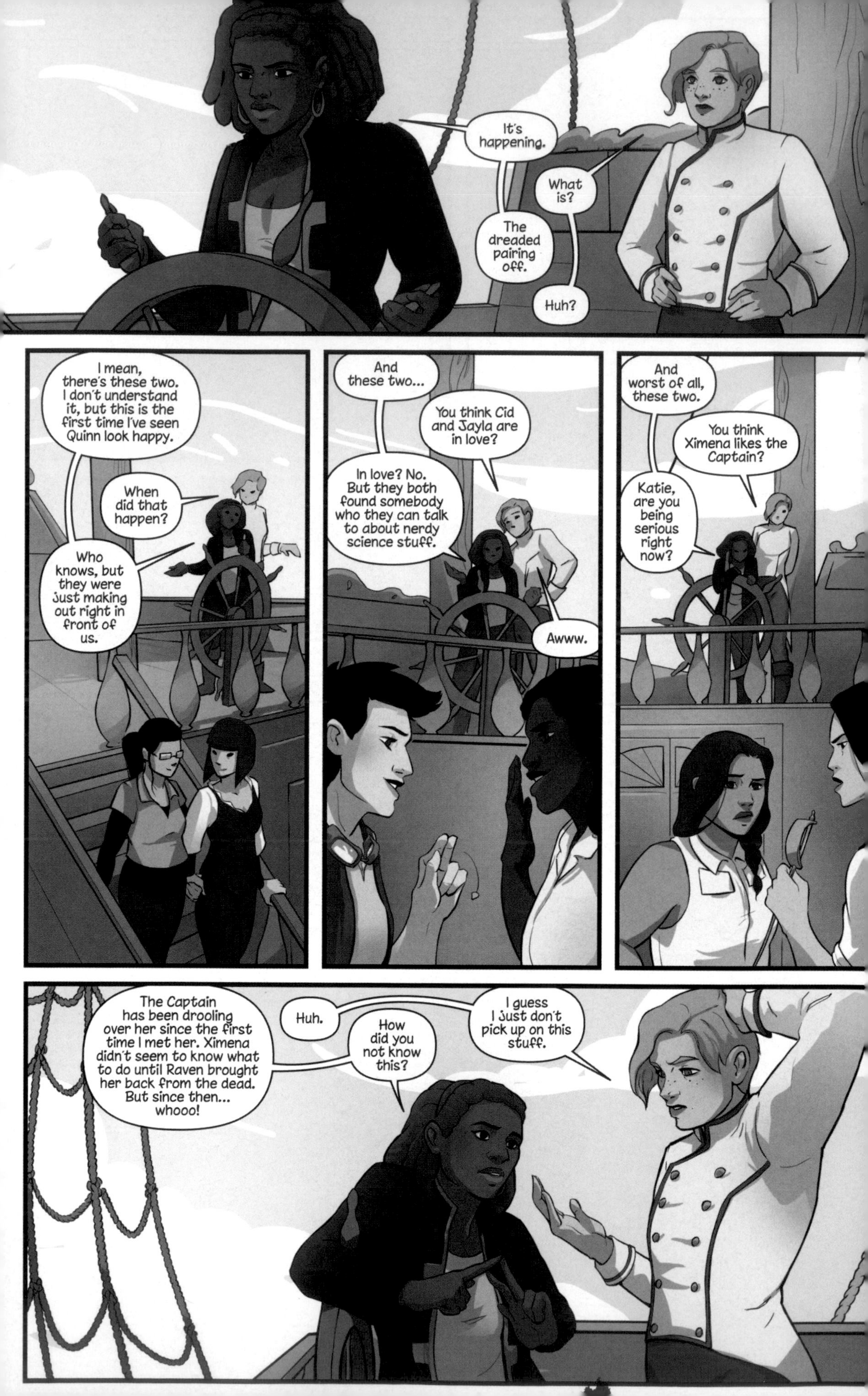
It's happening.
What is?
The dreaded pairing off.
Huh?
I mean, there's these two. I don't understand it, but this is the first time I've seen Quinn look happy.
When did that happen?
Who knows, but they were just making out right in front of us.
And these two...
You think Cid and Jayla are in love?
In love? No. But they both found somebody who they can talk to about nerdy science stuff.
Awww.
And worst of all, these two.
You think Ximena likes the Captain?
Katie, are you being serious right now?
The Captain has been drooling over her since the first time I met her. Ximena didn't seem to know what to do until Raven brought her back from the dead. But since then... whooo!
Huh.
How did you not know this?
I guess I just don't pick up on this stuff.

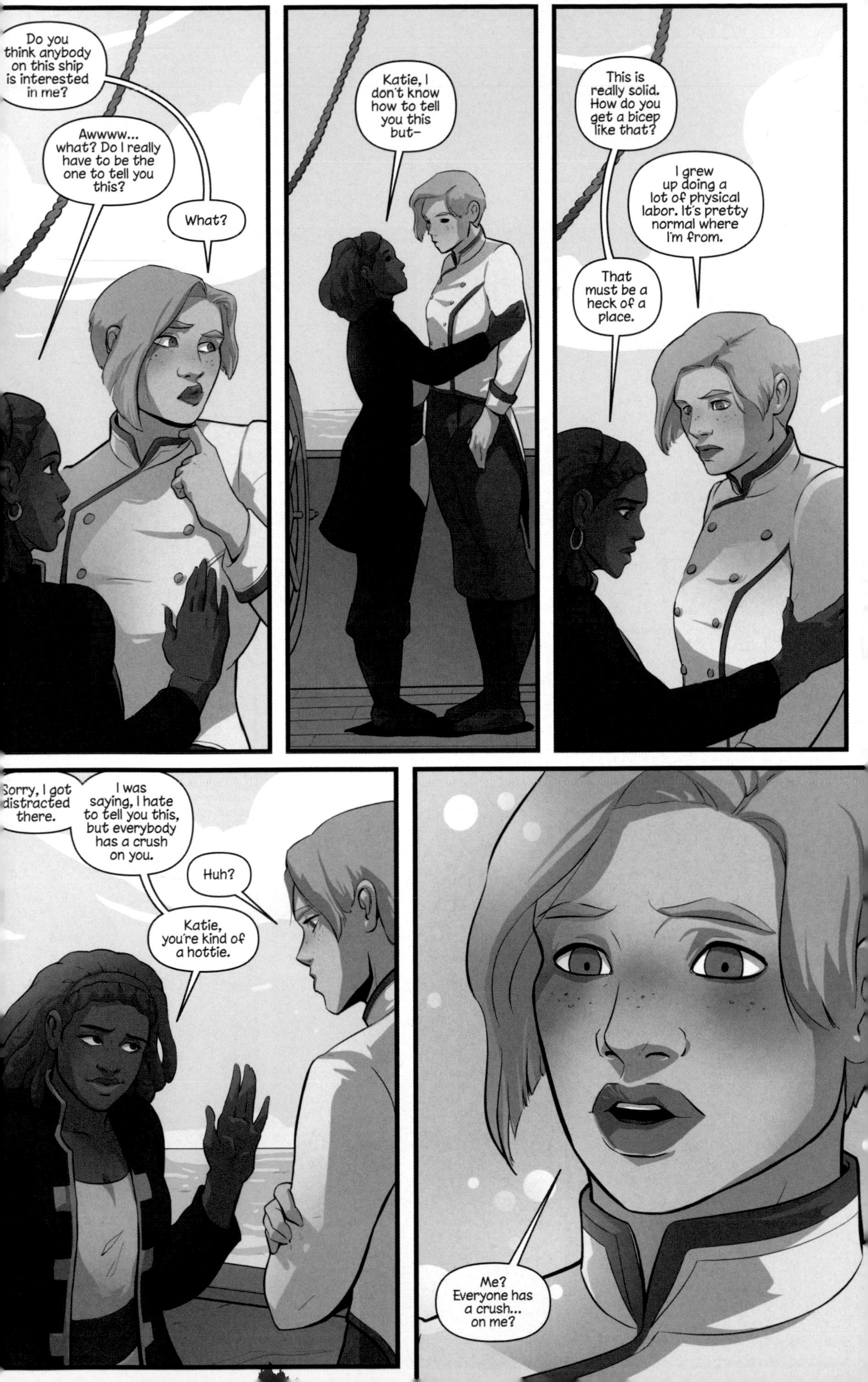

Do you think anybody on this ship is interested in me?
Awwww... what? Do I really have to be the one to tell you this?
What?
Katie, I don't know how to tell you this but-
This is really solid. How do you get a bicep like that?
I grew up doing a lot of physical labor. It's pretty normal where I'm from.
That must be a heck of a place.
Sorry, I got distracted there.
I was saying, I hate to tell you this, but everybody has a crush on you.
Huh?
Katie, you're kind of a hottie.
Me? Everyone has a crush... on me?

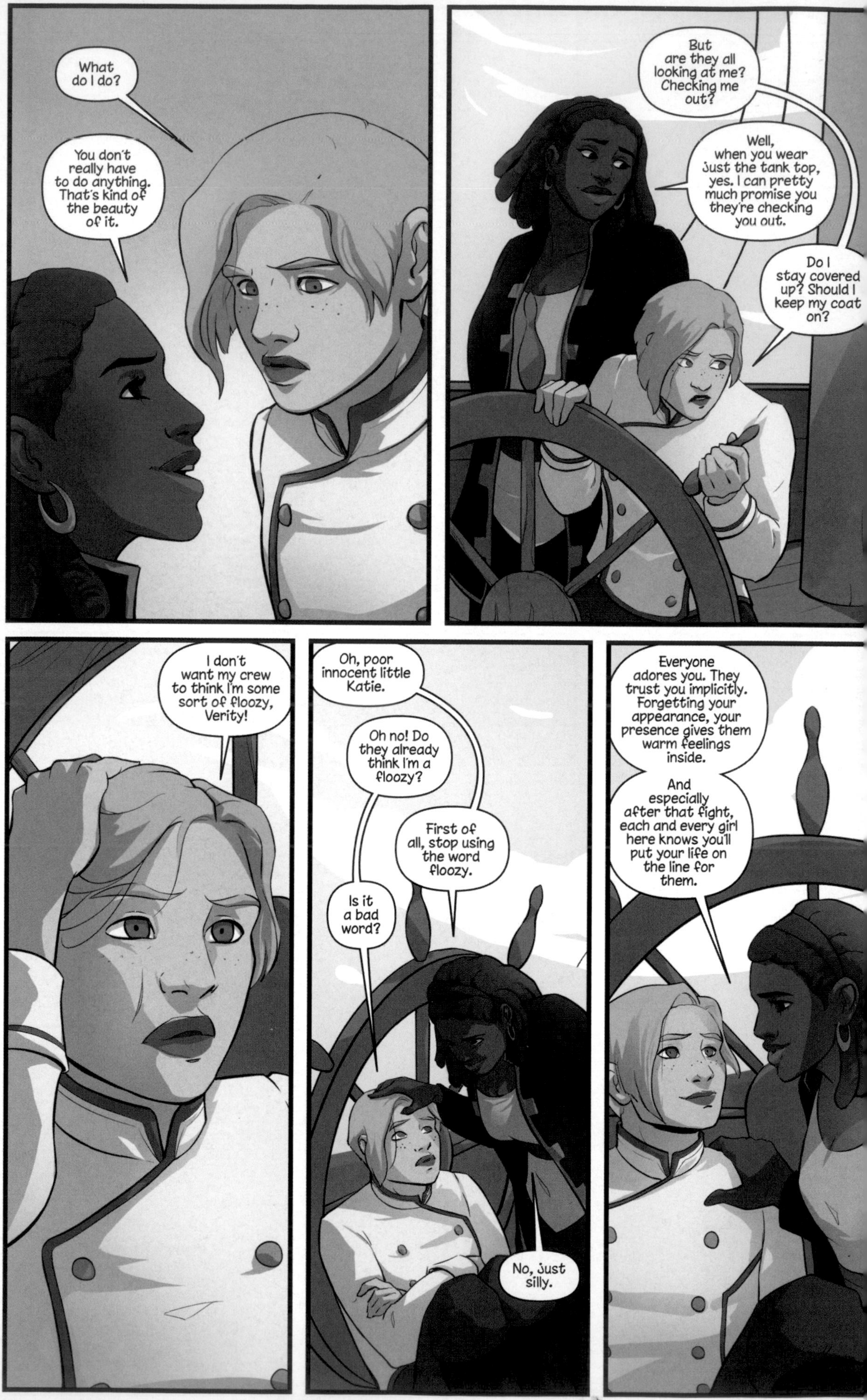
What do I do?
You don't really have to do anything. That's kind of the beauty of it.
But are they all looking at me? Checking me out?
Well, when you wear just the tank top, yes. I can pretty much promise you they're checking you out.
Do I stay covered up? Should I keep my coat on?
I don't want my crew to think I'm some sort of floozy, Verity!
Oh, poor innocent little Katie.
Oh no! Do they already think I'm a floozy?
First of all, stop using the word floozy.
Is it a bad word?
No, just silly.
Everyone adores you. They trust you implicitly. Forgetting your appearance, your presence gives them warm feelings inside.
And especially after that fight, each and every girl here knows you'll put your life on the line for them.

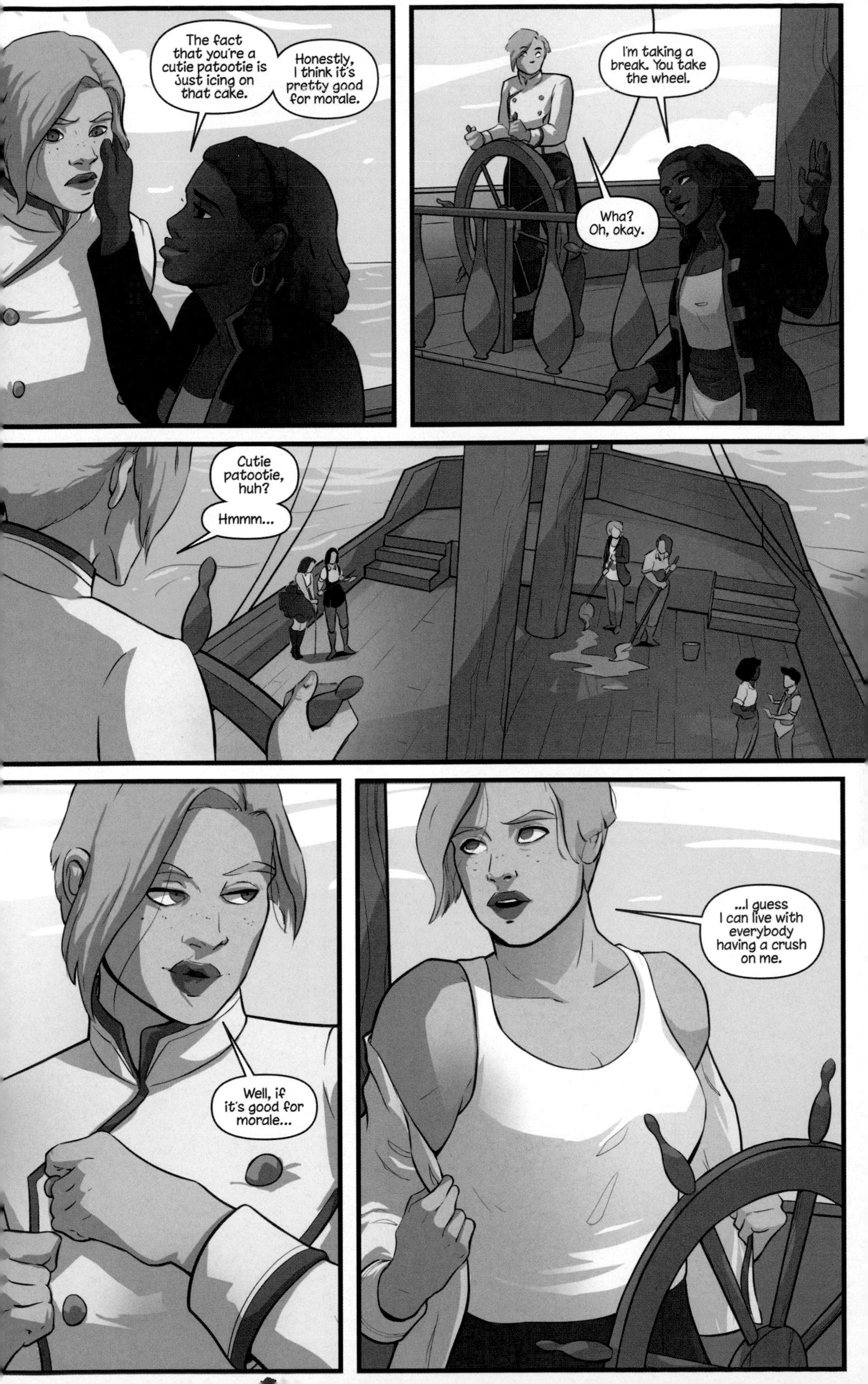
The fact that you're a cutie patootie is just icing on that cake.
Honestly, I think it's pretty good for morale.
I'm taking a break. You take the wheel.
Wha? Oh, okay.
Cutie patootie, huh?
Hmmm...
Well, if it's good for morale...
...I guess I can live with everybody having a crush on me.

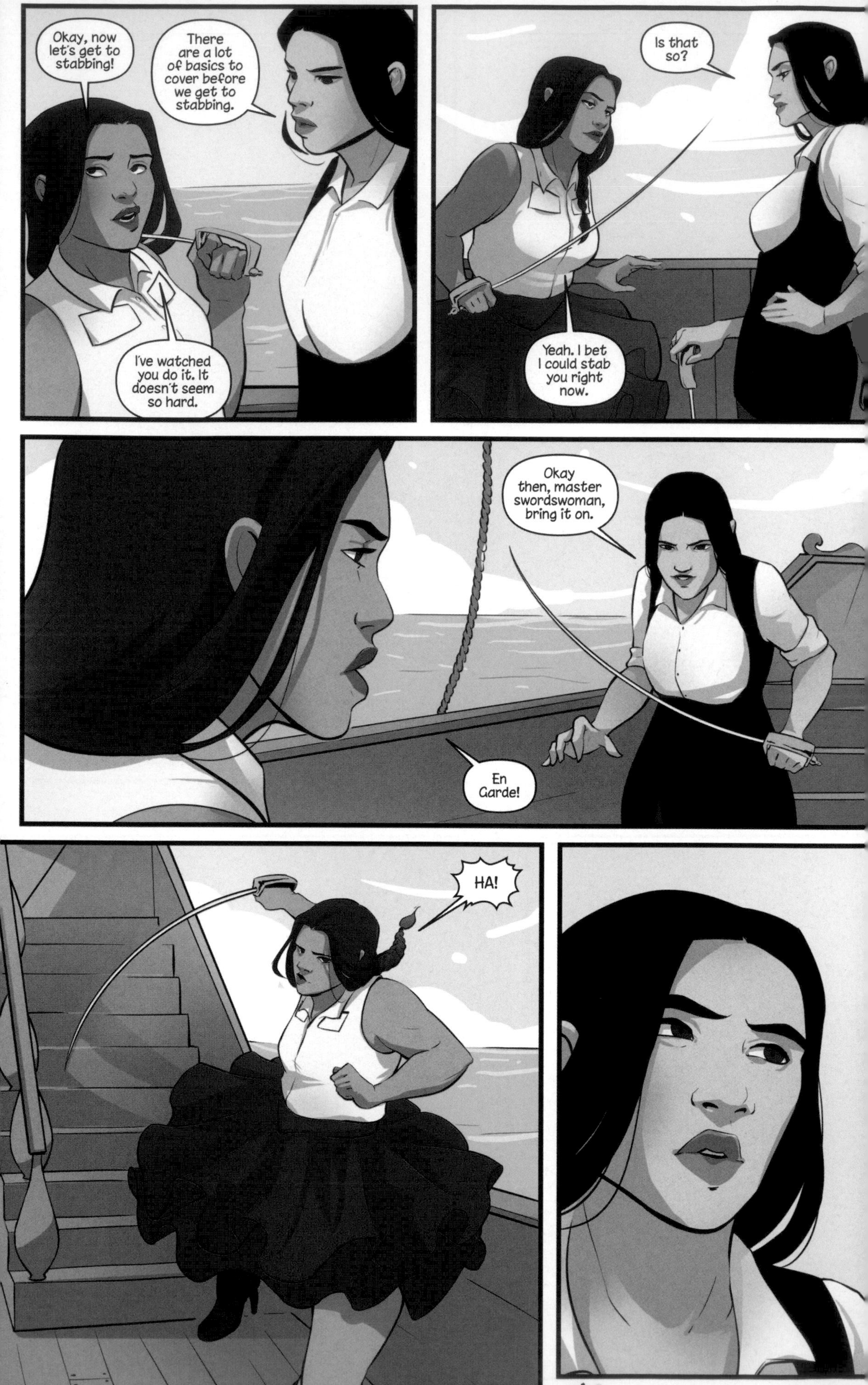
Okay, now let's get to stabbing!
There are a lot of basics to cover before we get to stabbing.
I've watched you do it. It doesn't seem so hard.
Is that so?
Yeah. I bet I could stab you right now.
Okay then, master swordswoman, bring it on.
En Garde!
HA!

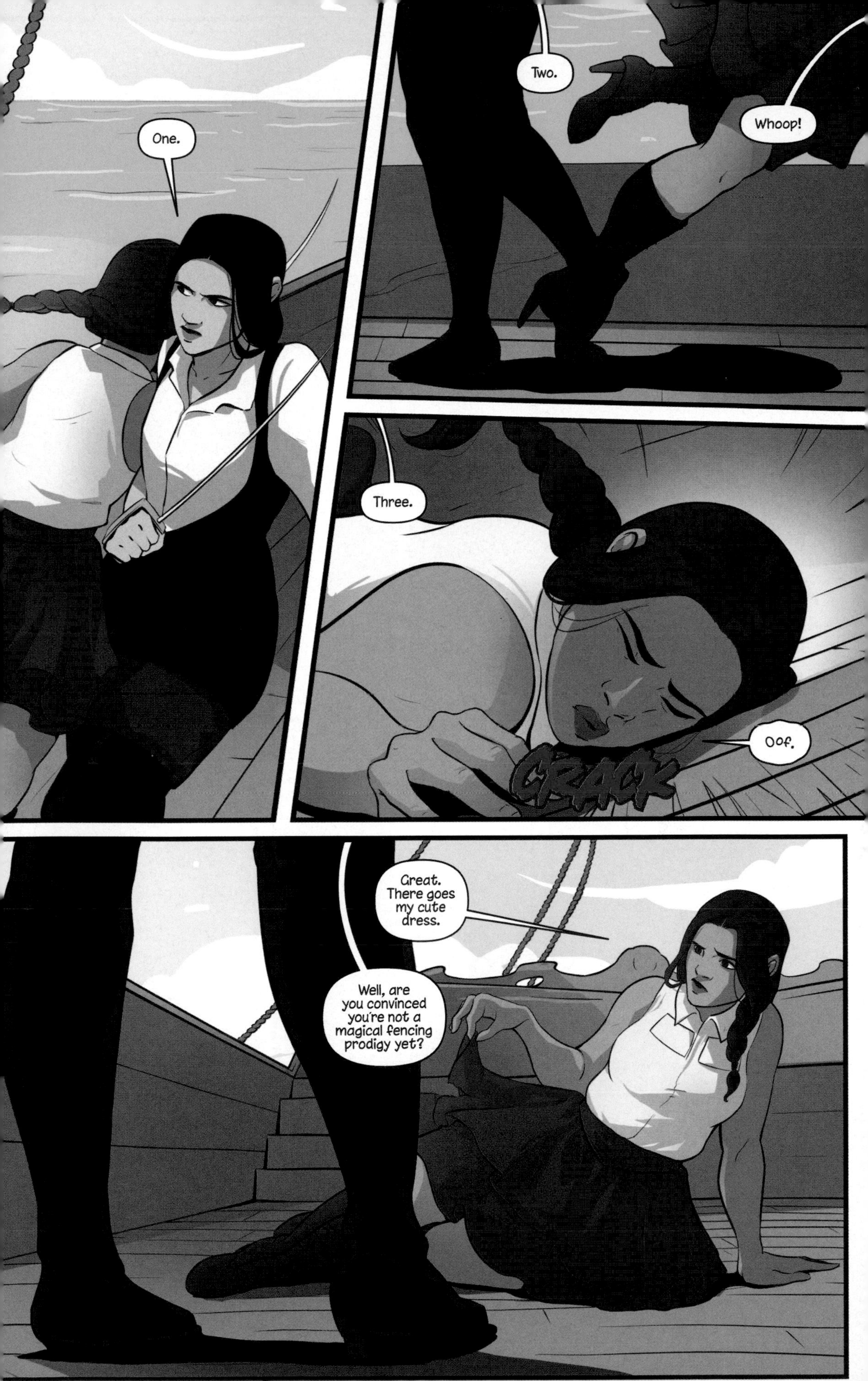
One.
Two.
Whoop!
Three.
CRACK
Oof.
Great. There goes my cute dress.
Well, are you convinced you're not a magical fencing prodigy yet?

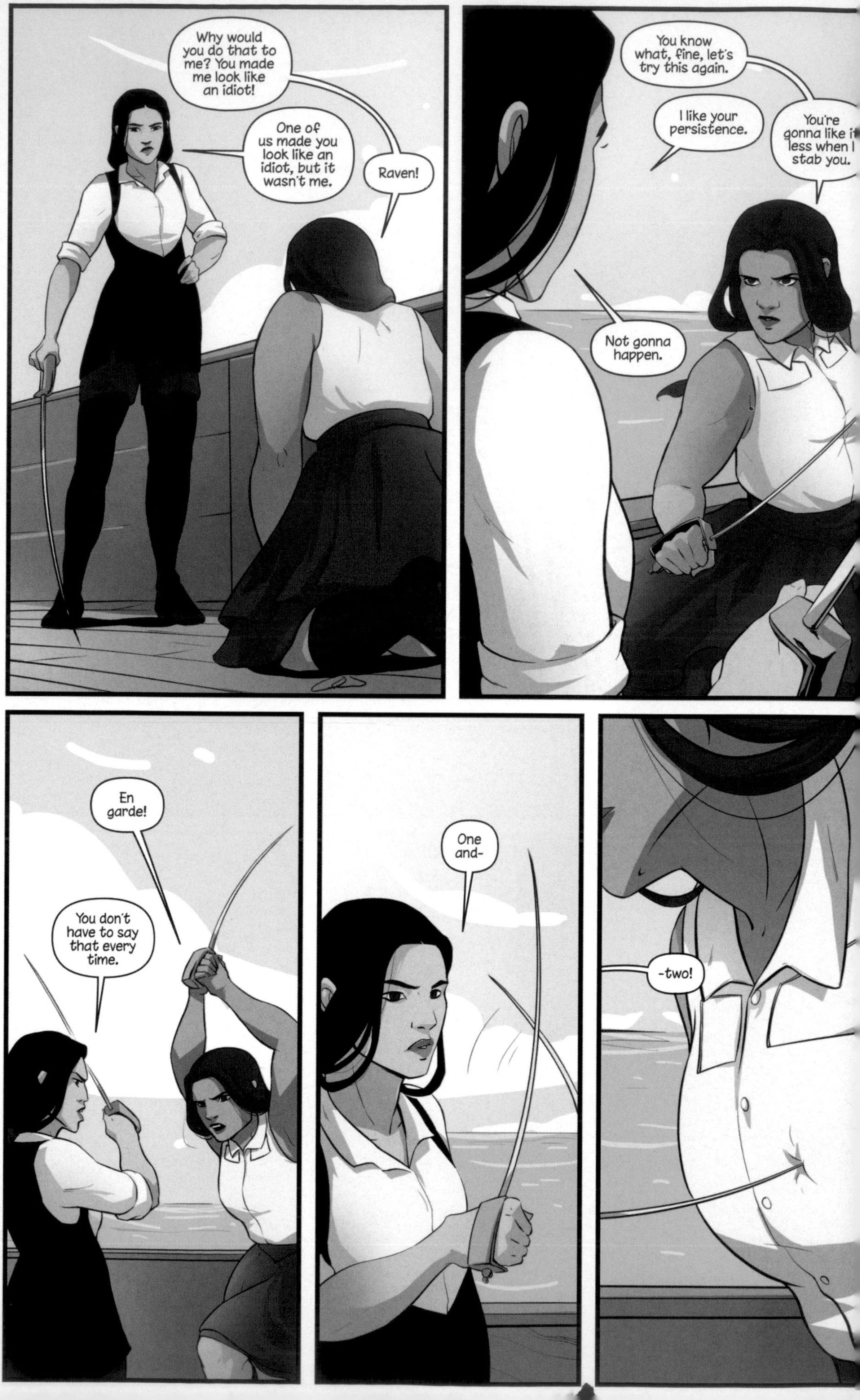
Why would you do that to me? You made me look like an idiot!
One of us made you look like an idiot, but it wasn't me.
Raven!
You know what, fine, let's try this again.
I like your persistence.
You're gonna like it less when I stab you.
Not gonna happen.
En garde!
You don't have to say that every time.
One and-
-two!

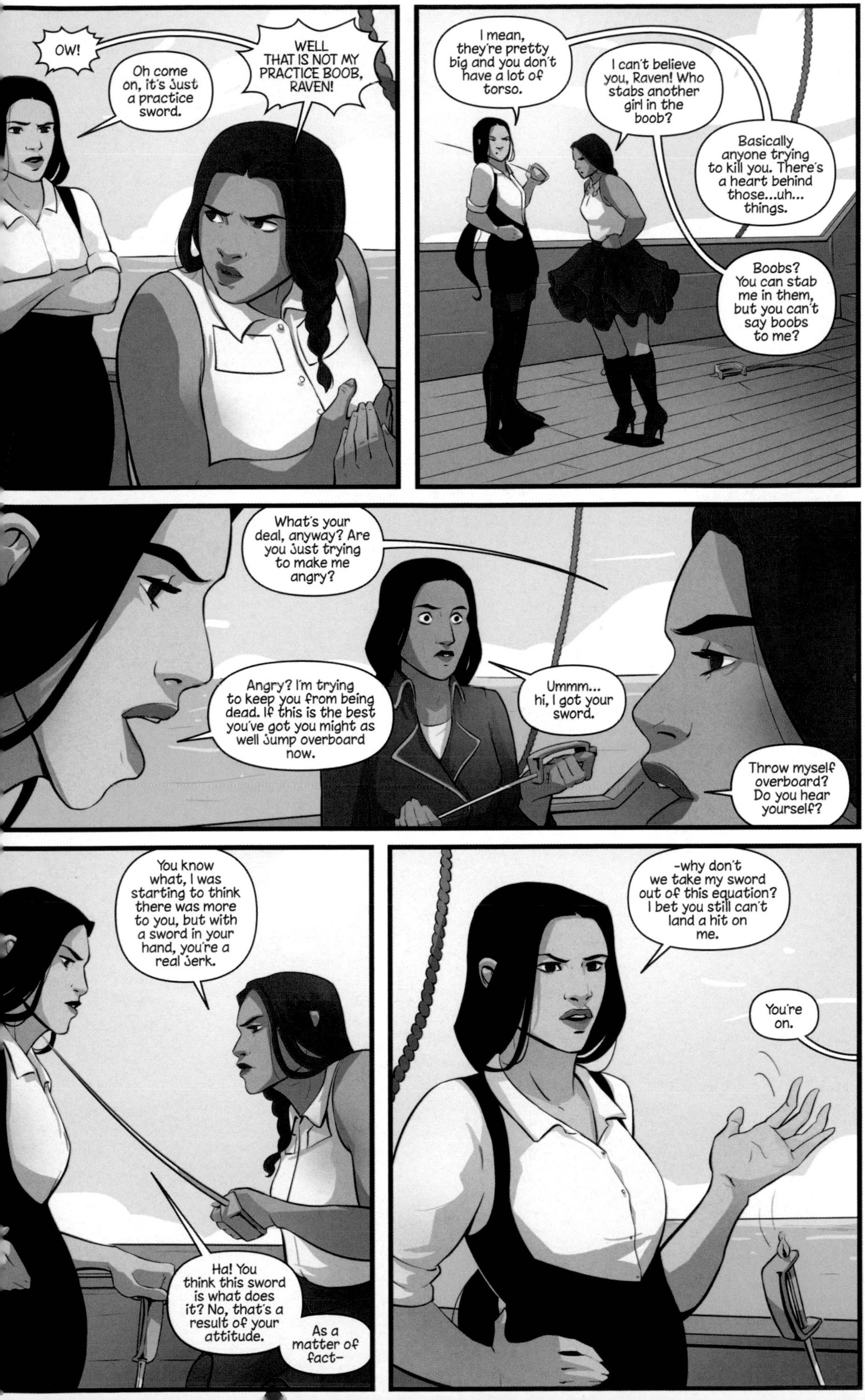
OW!
Oh come on, it's just a practice sword.
WELL THAT IS NOT MY PRACTICE BOOB, RAVEN!
I mean, they're pretty big and you don't have a lot of torso.
I can't believe you, Raven! Who stabs another girl in the boob?
Basically anyone trying to kill you. There's a heart behind those...uh... things.
Boobs? You can stab me in them, but you can't say boobs to me?
What's your deal, anyway? Are you just trying to make me angry?
Angry? I'm trying to keep you from being dead. If this is the best you've got you might as well jump overboard now.
Ummm... hi, I got your sword.
Throw myself overboard? Do you hear yourself?
You know what, I was starting to think there was more to you, but with a sword in your hand, you're a real jerk.
Ha! You think this sword is what does it? No, that's a result of your attitude.
As a matter of fact-
-why don't we take my sword out of this equation? I bet you still can't land a hit on me.
You're on.

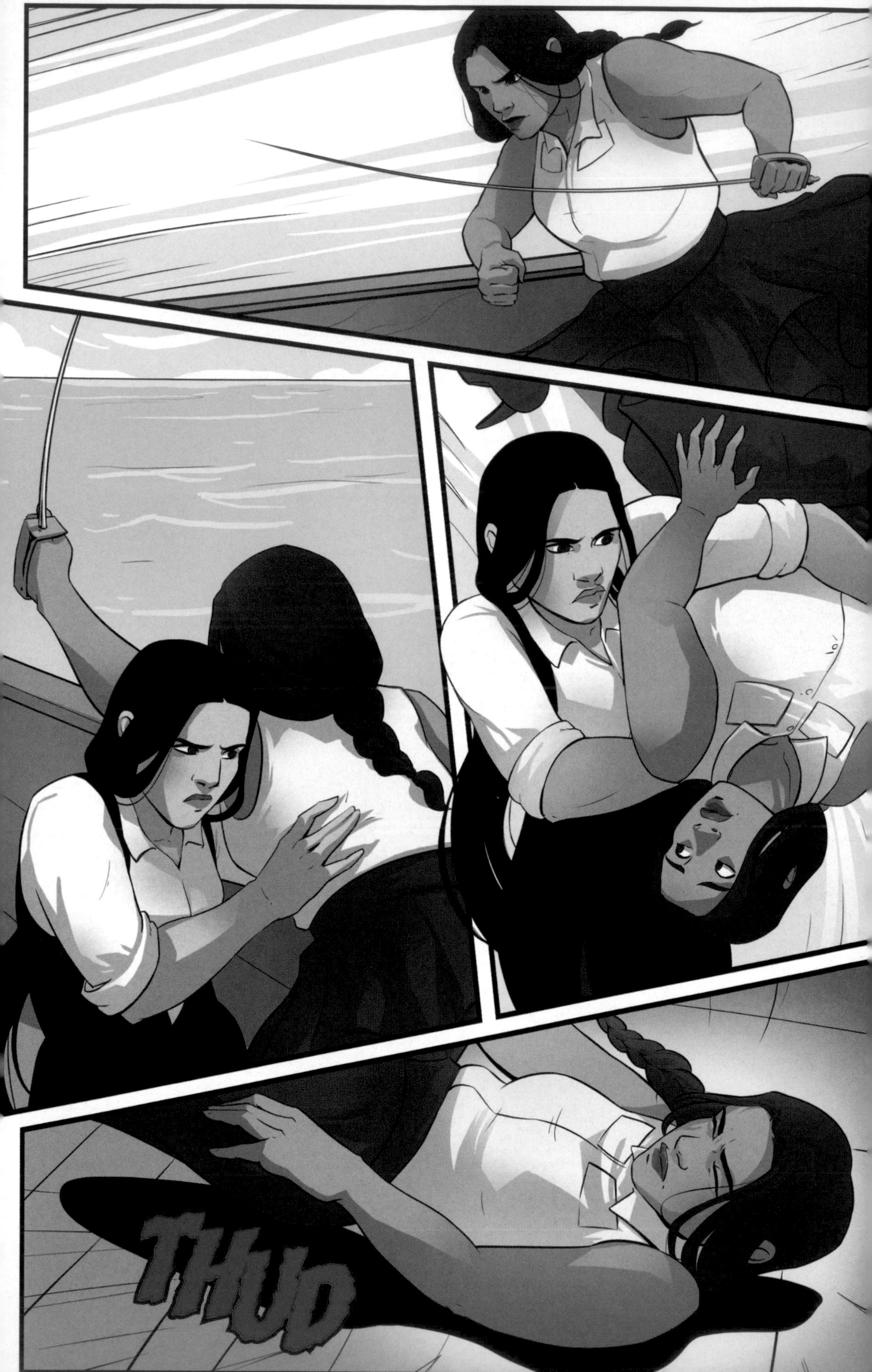
THUD

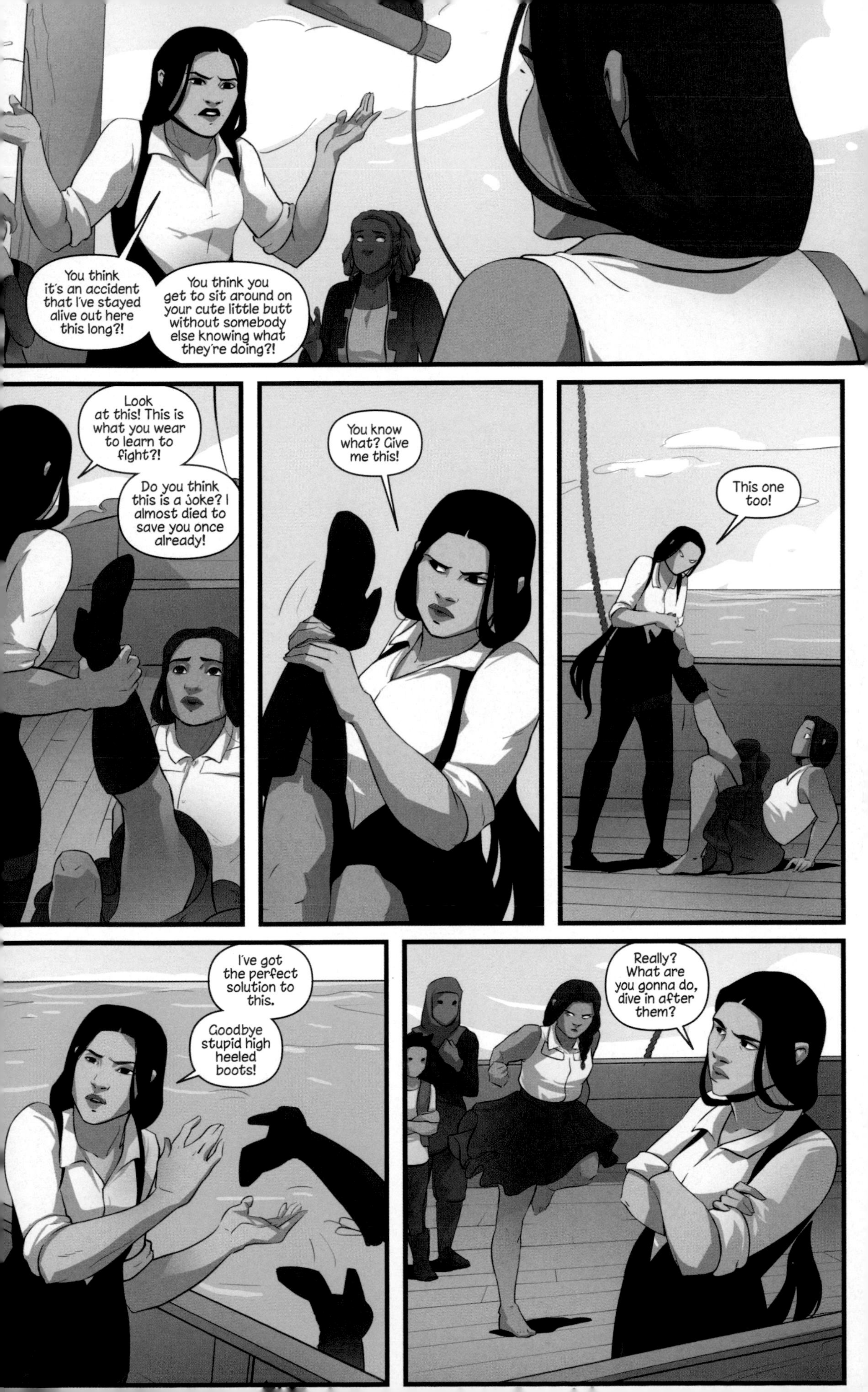
You think it's an accident that I've stayed alive out here this long?!
You think you get to sit around on your cute little butt without somebody else knowing what they're doing?!
Look at this! This is what you wear to learn to fight?!
Do you think this is a joke? I almost died to save you once already!
You know what? Give me this!
This one too!
I've got the perfect solution to this.
Goodbye stupid high heeled boots!
Really? What are you gonna do, dive in after them?

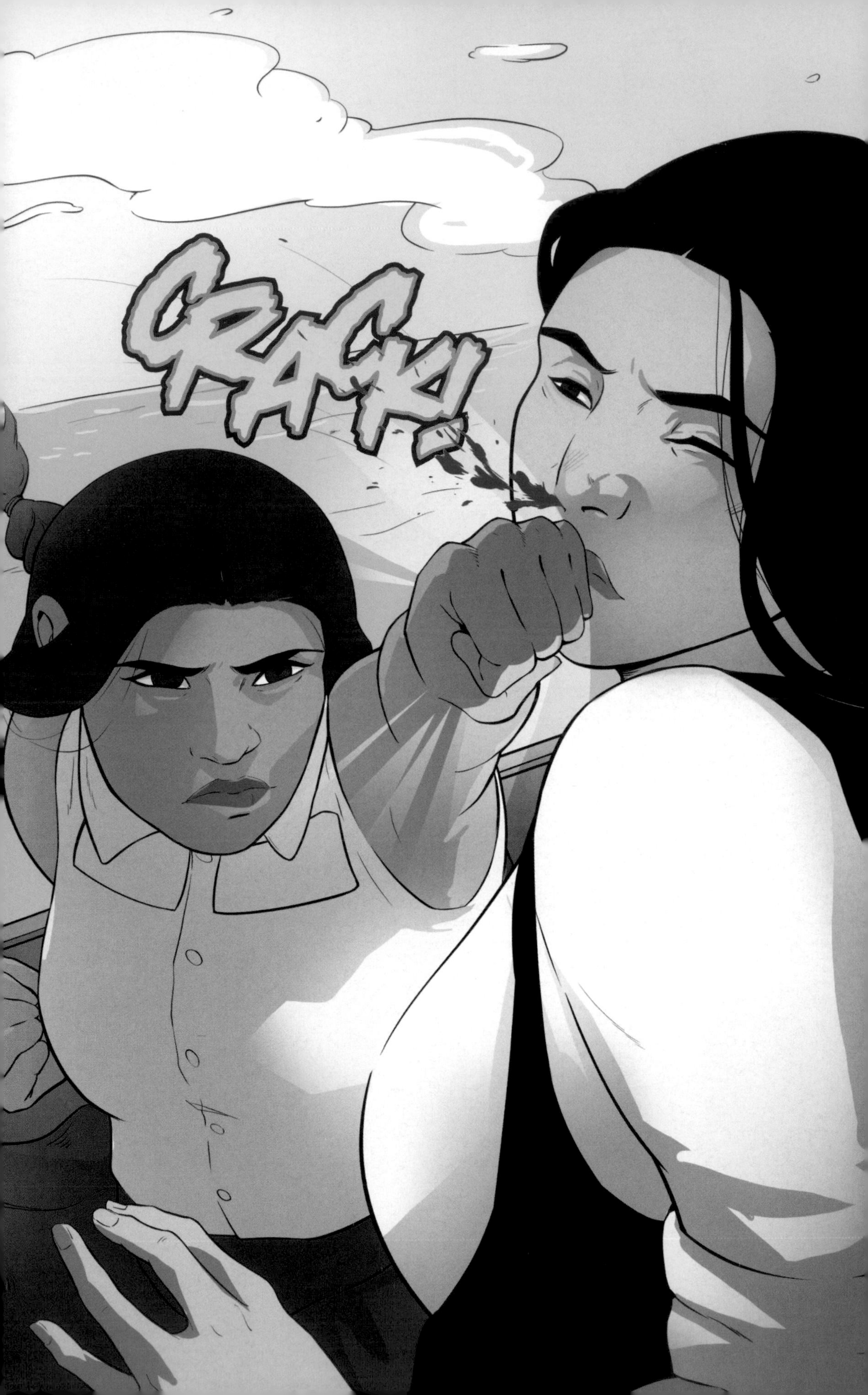
CRACK!

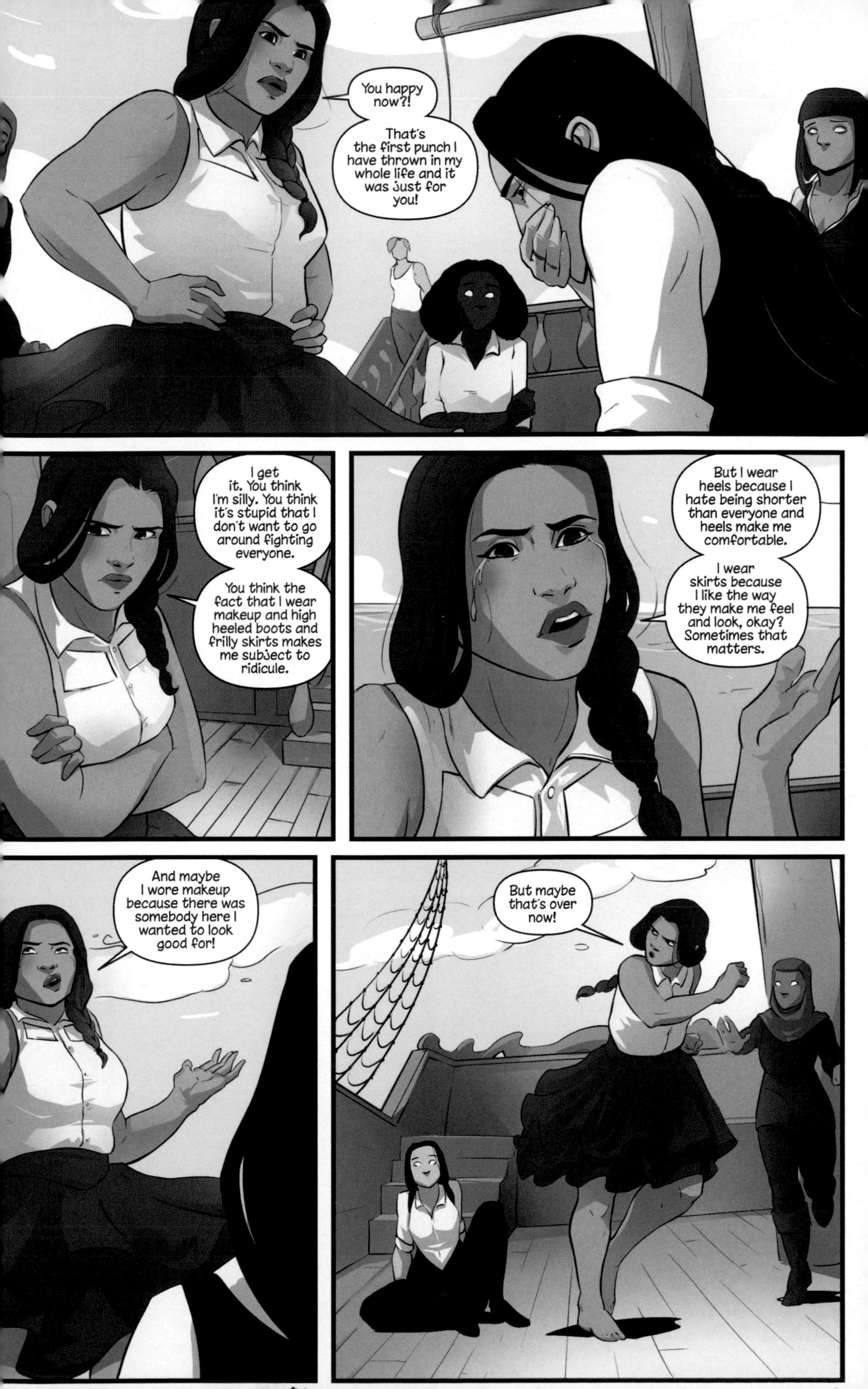
You happy now?!
That's the first punch I have thrown in my whole life and it was just for you!
I get it. You think I'm silly. You think it's stupid that I don't want to go around fighting everyone.
You think the fact that I wear makeup and high heeled boots and frilly skirts makes me subject to ridicule.
But I wear heels because I hate being shorter than everyone and heels make me comfortable.
I wear skirts because I like the way they make me feel and look, okay? Sometimes that matters.
And maybe I wore makeup because there was somebody here I wanted to look good for!
But maybe that's over now!

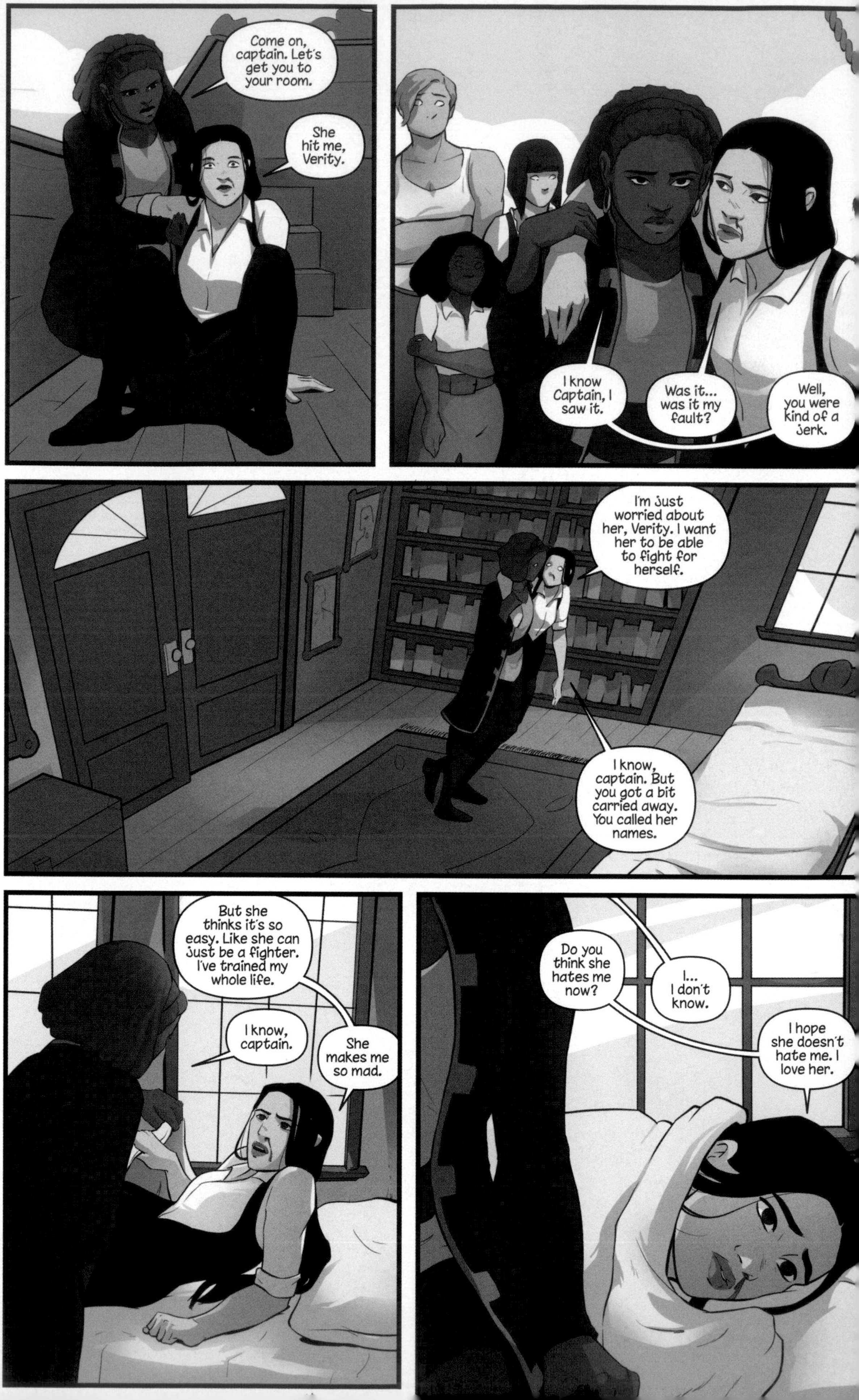
Come on, captain. Let's get you to your room.
She hit me, Verity.
I know Captain, I saw it.
Was it... was it my fault?
Well, you were kind of a jerk.
I'm just worried about her, Verity. I want her to be able to fight for herself.
I know, captain. But you got a bit carried away. You called her names.
But she thinks it's so easy. Like she can just be a fighter. I've trained my whole life.
I know, captain.
She makes me so mad.
Do you think she hates me now?
I... I don't know.
I hope she doesn't hate me. I love her.

Issue 7 Cover Progression

Issue 7 Cover Pencils

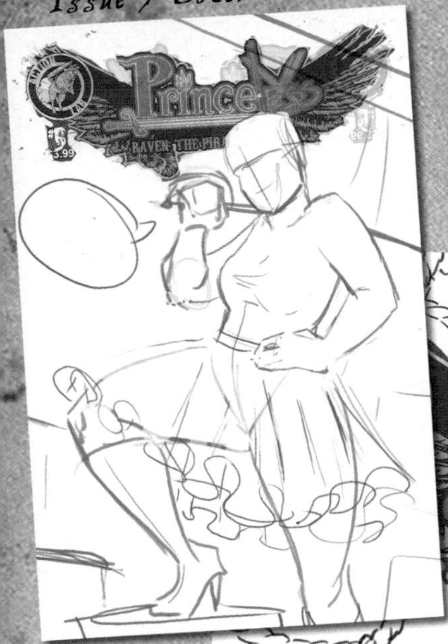
Prince
RAVEN: THE PIRA
$3.99

Issue 7 Cover Inks

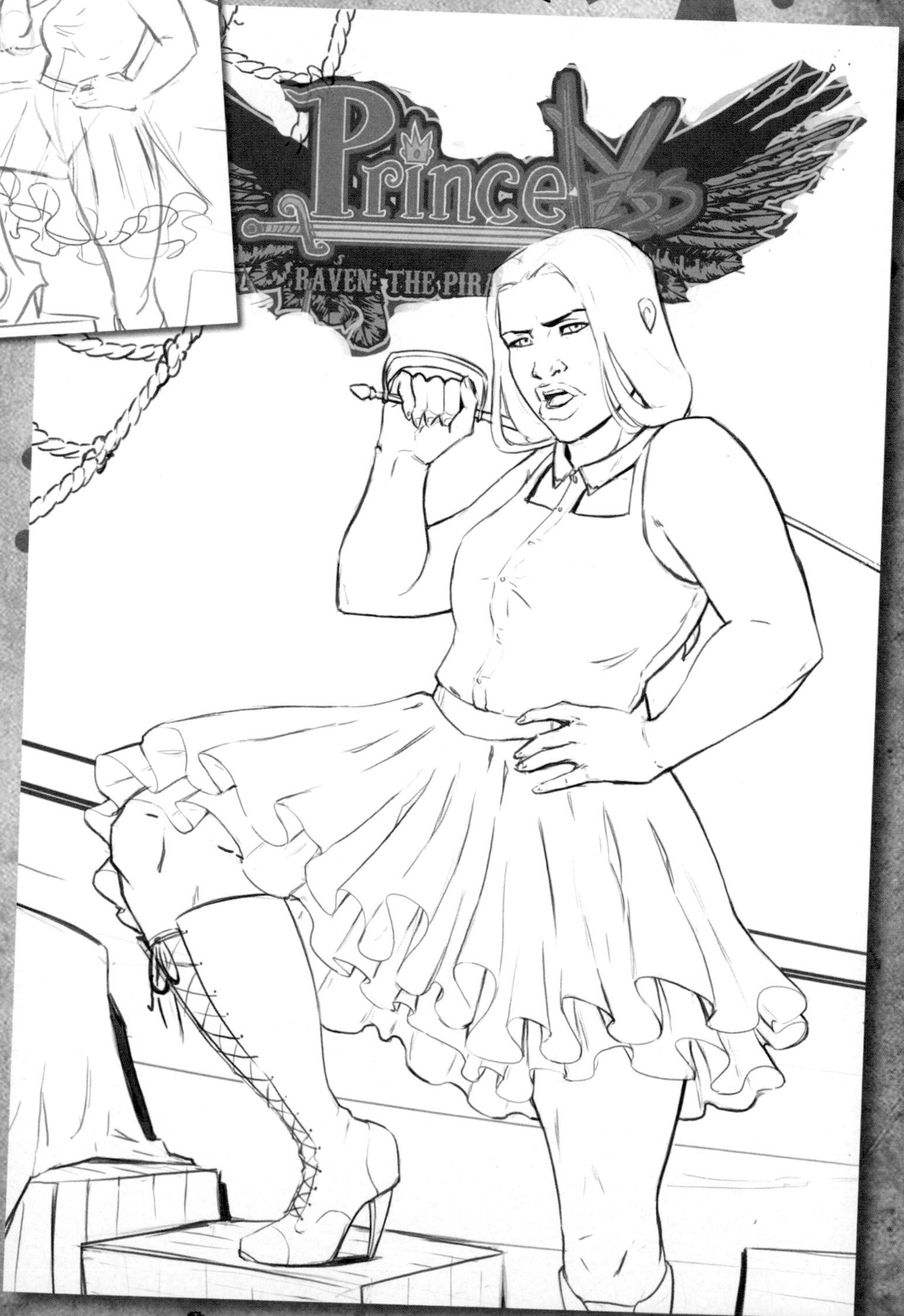
Prince
RAVEN: THE PIRA

Issue 7 Cover Progression

Issue 7 Cover Colors

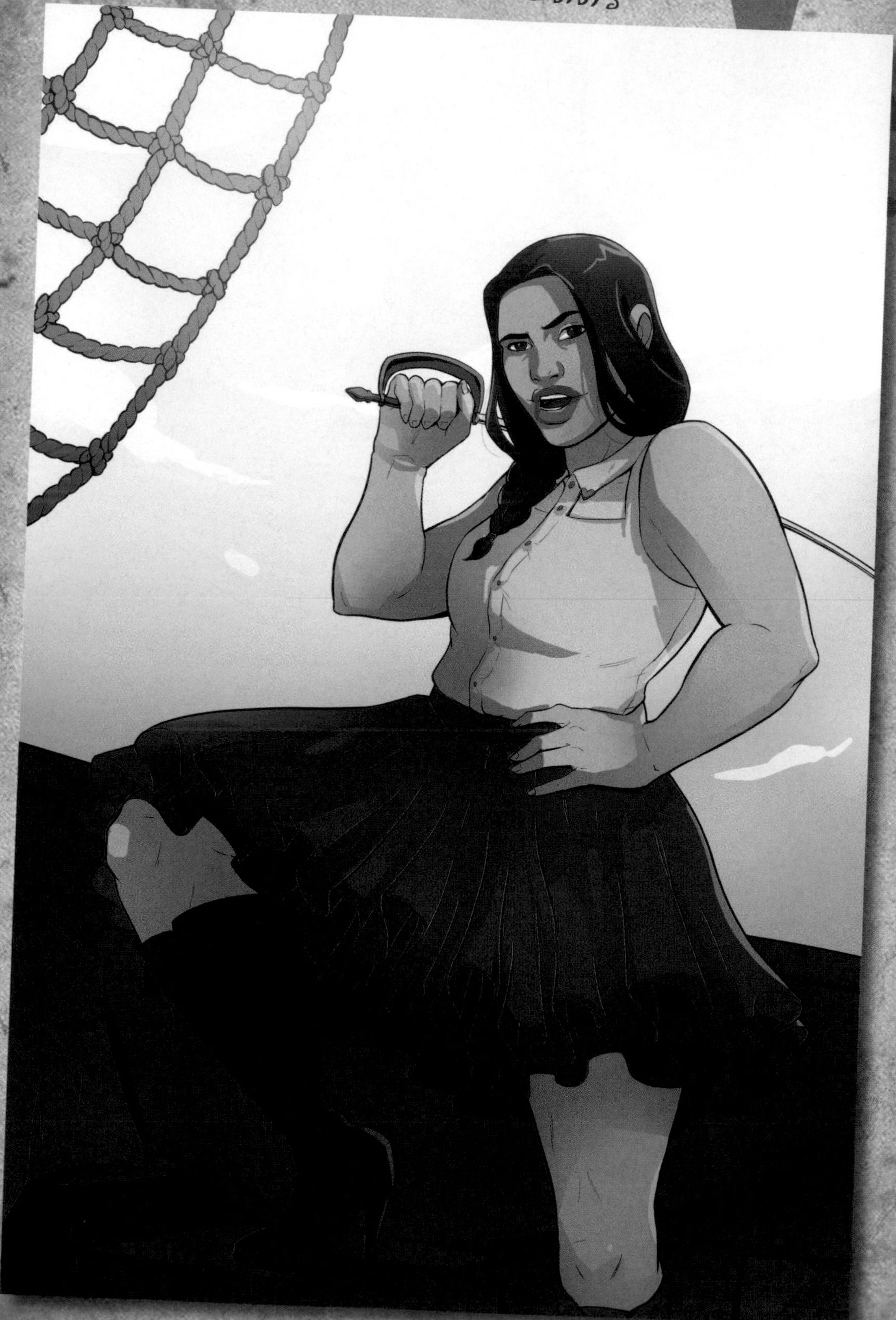

Page 10 Progression

Page 10:

Panel 1: Jayla bites her lip.

JAYLA (MUTTERED)
Here goes.

Panel 2: Jayla signs "I"

CAPTION
I

Panel 3: Jayla sings "can", her two fists out, moving down.

CAPTION
Can

Panel 4: Jayla signs "hear", tapping her ear twice.

CAPTION
Hear

Panel 5: Jayla signs "again"

CAPTION
Again.

Panel 6: Cid's face, she looks thrilled.

Panel 7: Cid signs "yay"

CAPTION
Yay!

Panel 8: Jayla smiles back.

Panel 9: Jayla signs "still"

Panel 10: Jayla signs "friends"

Panel 11: Cid squints

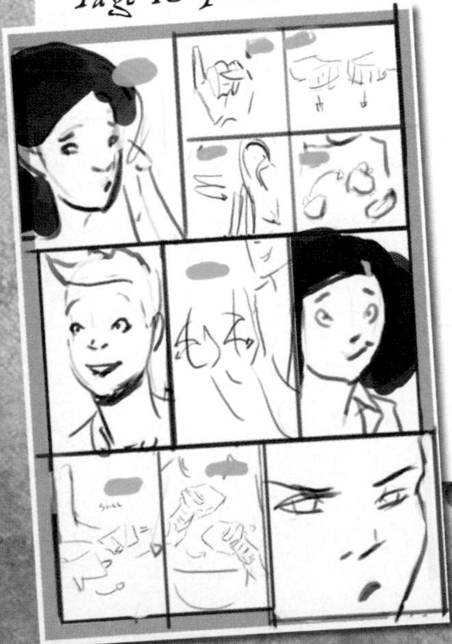

Page 10 Thumbnail

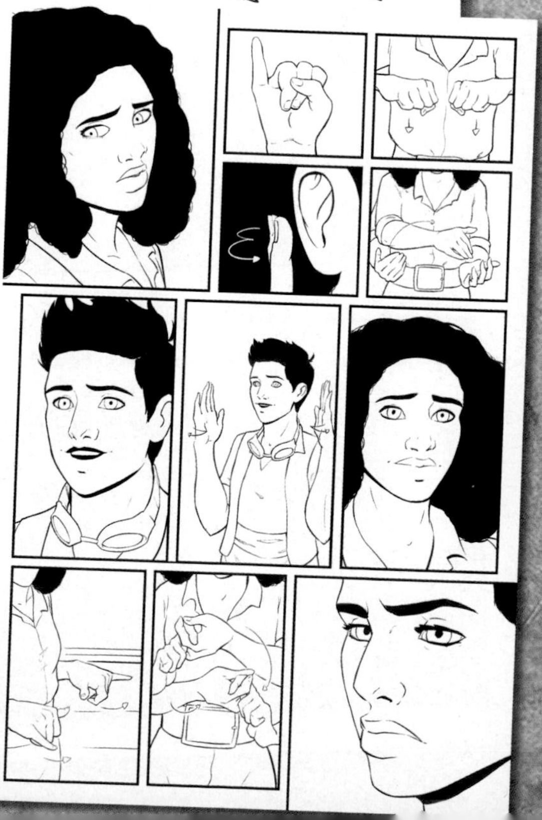

Page 10 Inks

Page 10 Progression

Page 10 Colors

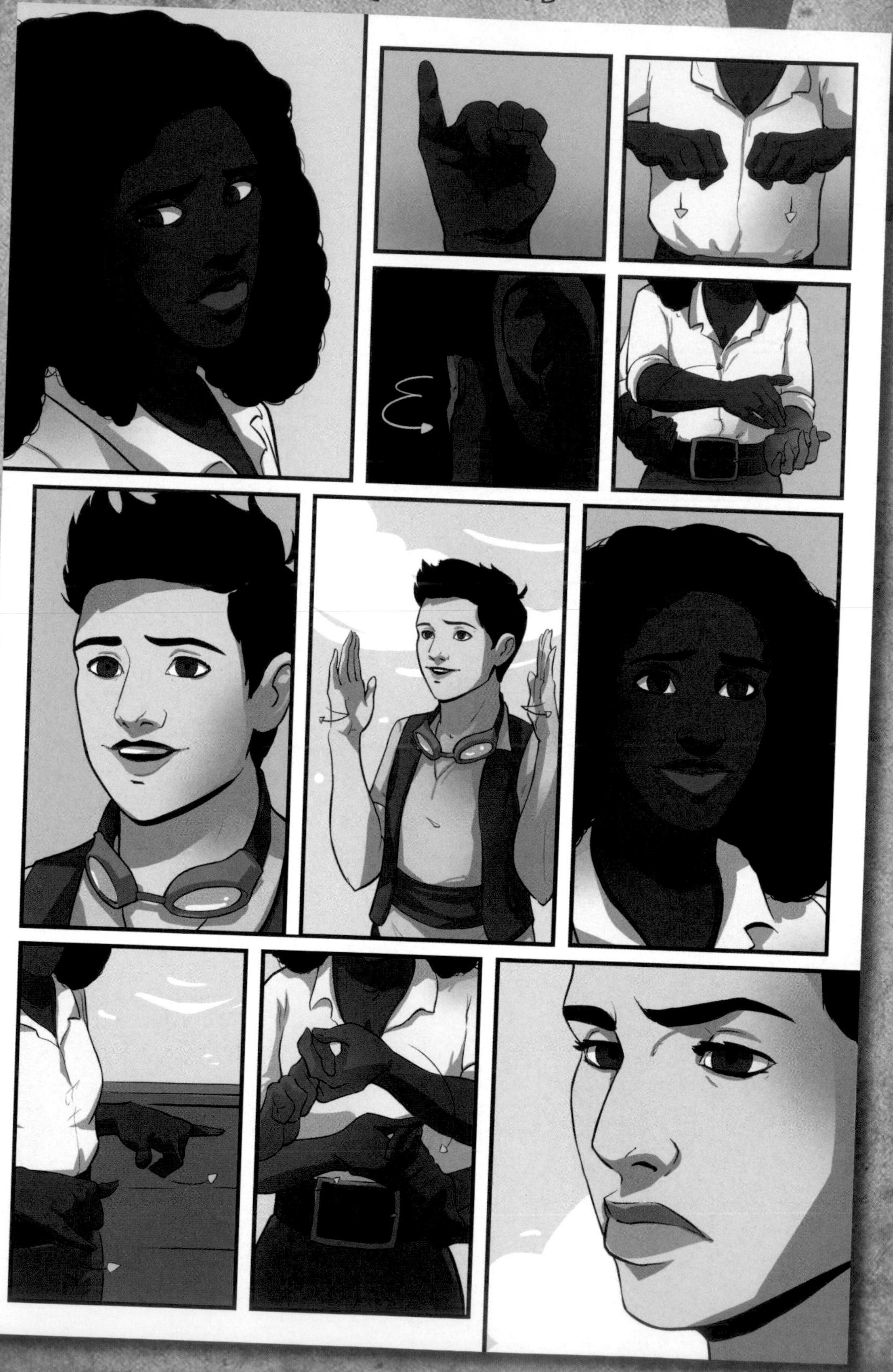

Page 11 Progression

Page 11:

Panel 1: Cid signs "Of course"

Panel 2: Cid signs "stupid"

Panel 3: Jayla almost tackles Cid with a hug.

JAYLA
Ha ha ha ha.

Panel 4: Cid smiles, returning the hug.

Page 11 Inks

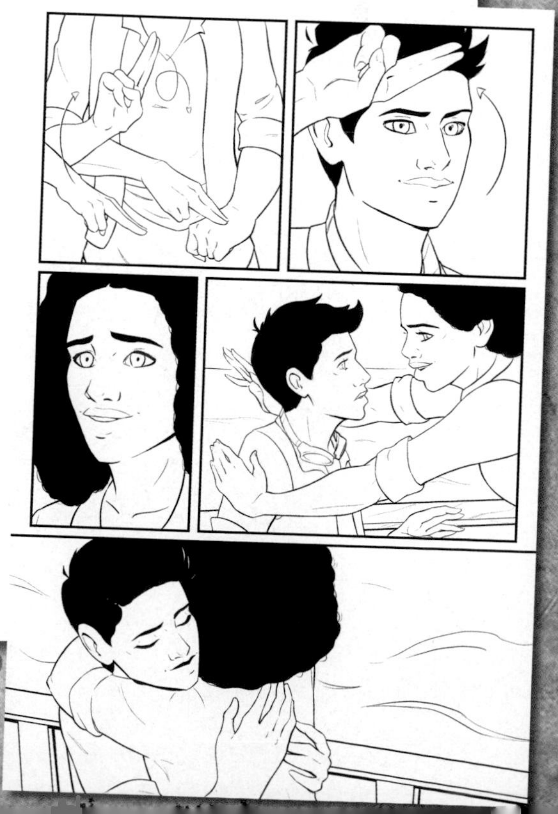

Page 11 Thumbnail

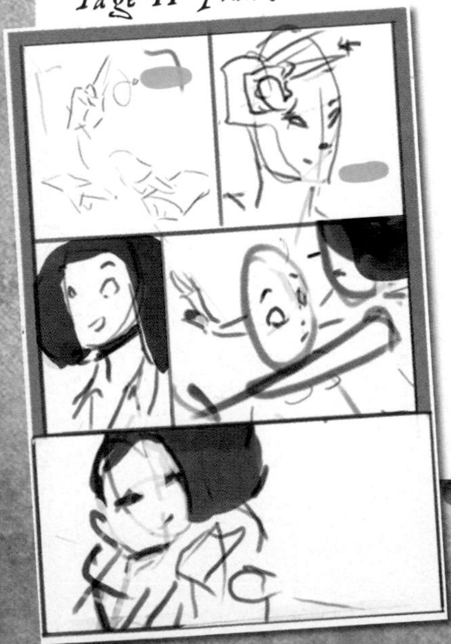

Page 11 Progression

Page 11 Colors

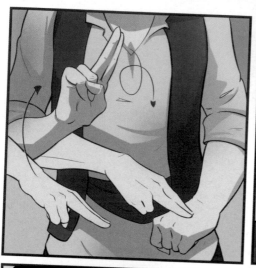

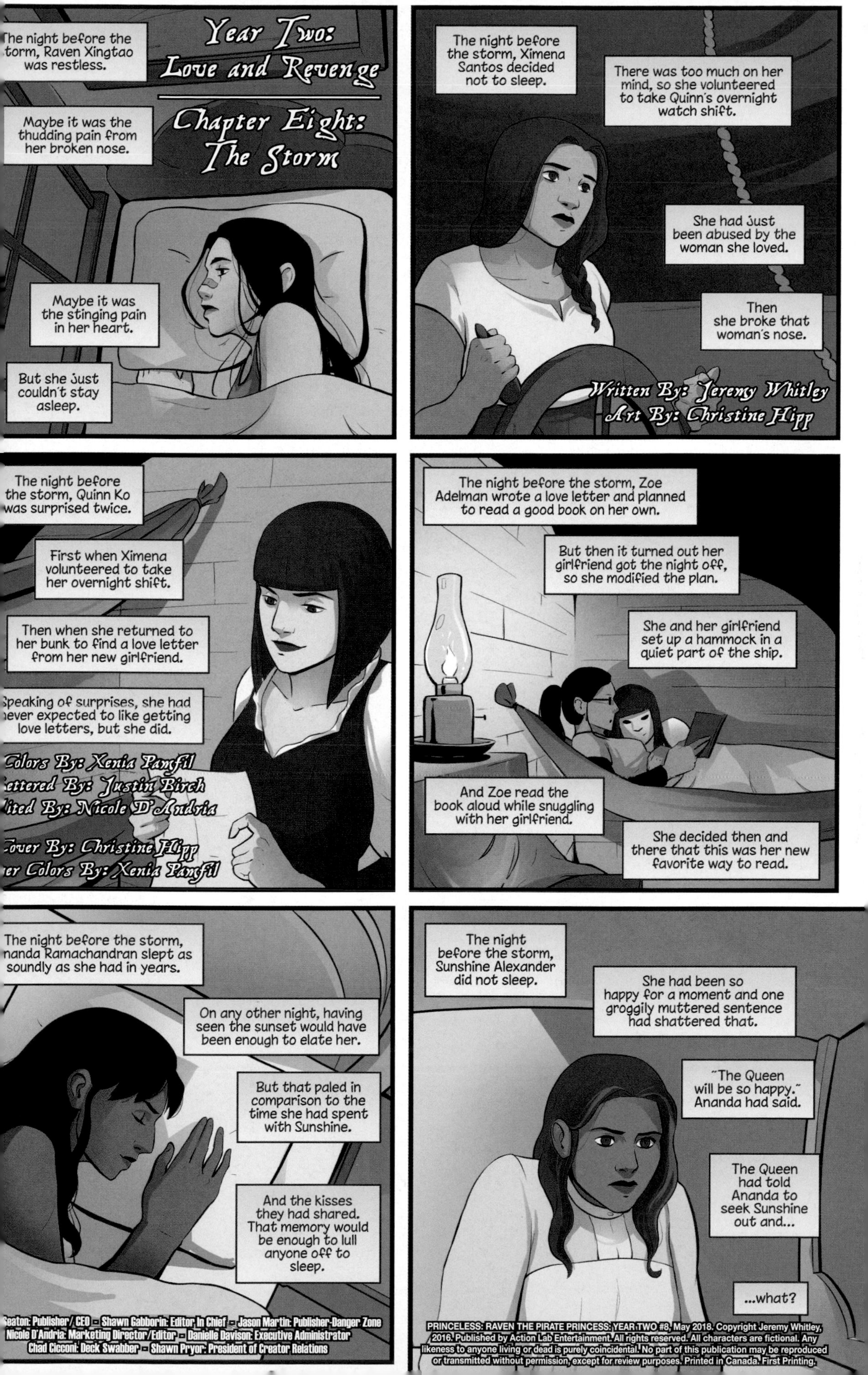

Year Two: Love and Revenge
Chapter Eight: The Storm
The night before the torm, Raven Xingtao was restless.
Maybe it was the thudding pain from her broken nose.
Maybe it was the stinging pain in her heart.
But she just couldn't stay asleep.
The night before the storm, Ximena Santos decided not to sleep.
There was too much on her mind, so she volunteered to take Quinn's overnight watch shift.
She had just been abused by the woman she loved.
Then she broke that woman's nose.
Written By: Jeremy Whitley
Art By: Christine Hipp
The night before the storm, Quinn Ko was surprised twice.
First when Ximena volunteered to take her overnight shift.
Then when she returned to her bunk to find a love letter from her new girlfriend.
Speaking of surprises, she had never expected to like getting love letters, but she did.
Colors By: Xenia Pamfil
ettered By: Justin Birch
ited By: Nicole D'Andria
over By: Christine Hipp
er Colors By: Xenia Pamfil
The night before the storm, Zoe Adelman wrote a love letter and planned to read a good book on her own.
But then it turned out her girlfriend got the night off, so she modified the plan.
She and her girlfriend set up a hammock in a quiet part of the ship.
And Zoe read the book aloud while snuggling with her girlfriend.
She decided then and there that this was her new favorite way to read.
The night before the storm, nanda Ramachandran slept as soundly as she had in years.
On any other night, having seen the sunset would have been enough to elate her.
But that paled in comparison to the time she had spent with Sunshine.
And the kisses they had shared. That memory would be enough to lull anyone off to sleep.
The night before the storm, Sunshine Alexander did not sleep.
She had been so happy for a moment and one groggily muttered sentence had shattered that.
"The Queen will be so happy." Ananda had said.
The Queen had told Ananda to seek Sunshine out and...
...what?
Seaton: Publisher/CEO - Shawn Gabborin: Editor In Chief - Jason Martin: Publisher-Danger Zone
Nicole D'Andria: Marketing Director/Editor - Danielle Davison: Executive Administrator
Chad Cicconi: Deck Swabber - Shawn Pryor: President of Creator Relations
PRINCELESS: RAVEN THE PIRATE PRINCESS: YEAR TWO #8, May 2018. Copyright Jeremy Whitley, 2016. Published by Action Lab Entertainment. All rights reserved. All characters are fictional. Any likeness to anyone living or dead is purely coincidental. No part of this publication may be reproduced or transmitted without permission, except for review purposes. Printed in Canada. First Printing.

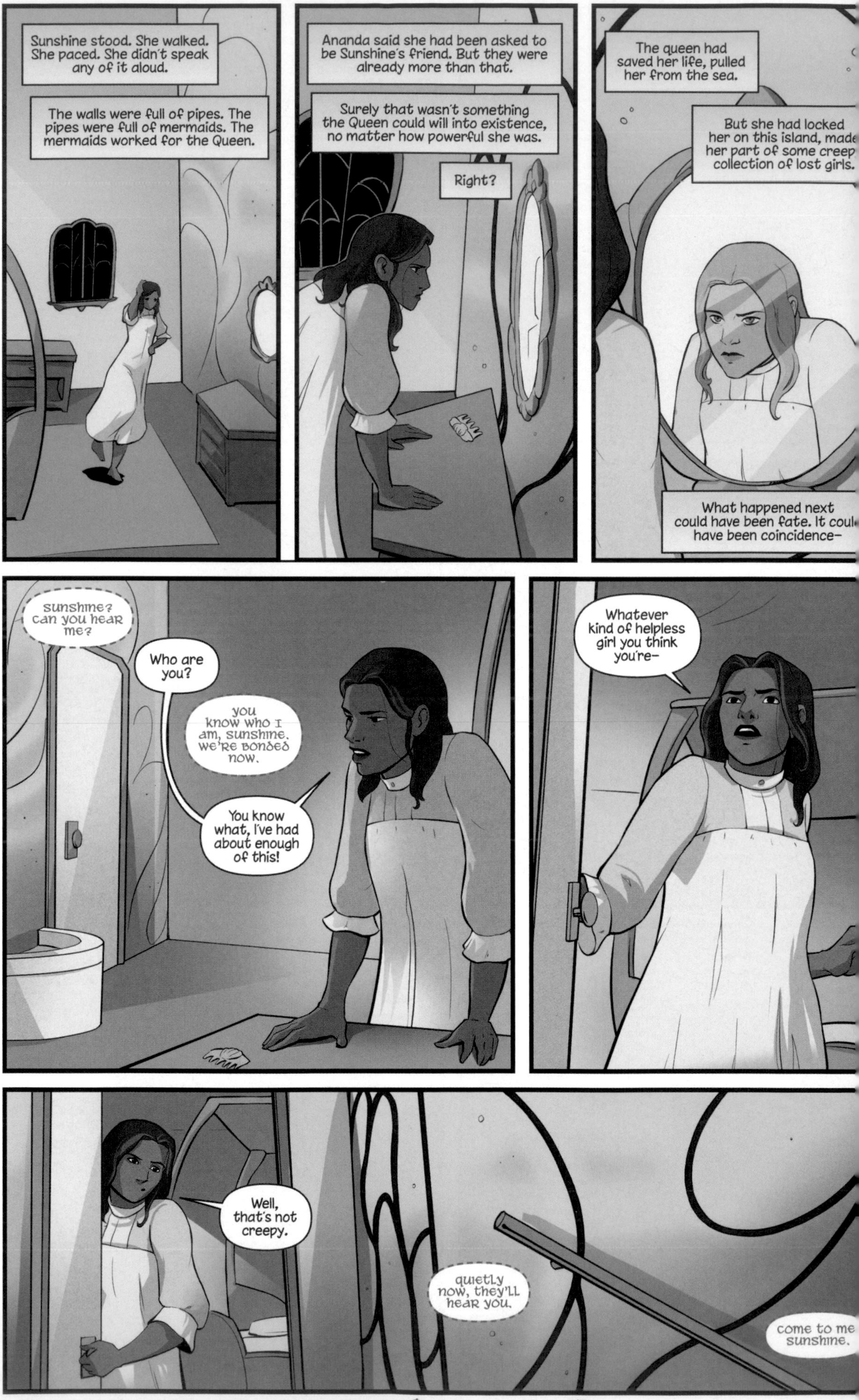

Sunshine stood. She walked. She paced. She didn't speak any of it aloud.
The walls were full of pipes. The pipes were full of mermaids. The mermaids worked for the Queen.
Ananda said she had been asked to be Sunshine's friend. But they were already more than that.
Surely that wasn't something the Queen could will into existence, no matter how powerful she was.
Right?
The queen had saved her life, pulled her from the sea.
But she had locked her on this island, made her part of some creep collection of lost girls.
What happened next could have been fate. It coul have been coincidence–
sunshine? can you hear me?
Who are you?
you know who I am, sunshine. we're bonded now.
You know what, I've had about enough of this!
Whatever kind of helpless girl you think you're–
Well, that's not creepy.
quietly now, they'll hear you.
come to me sunshine.

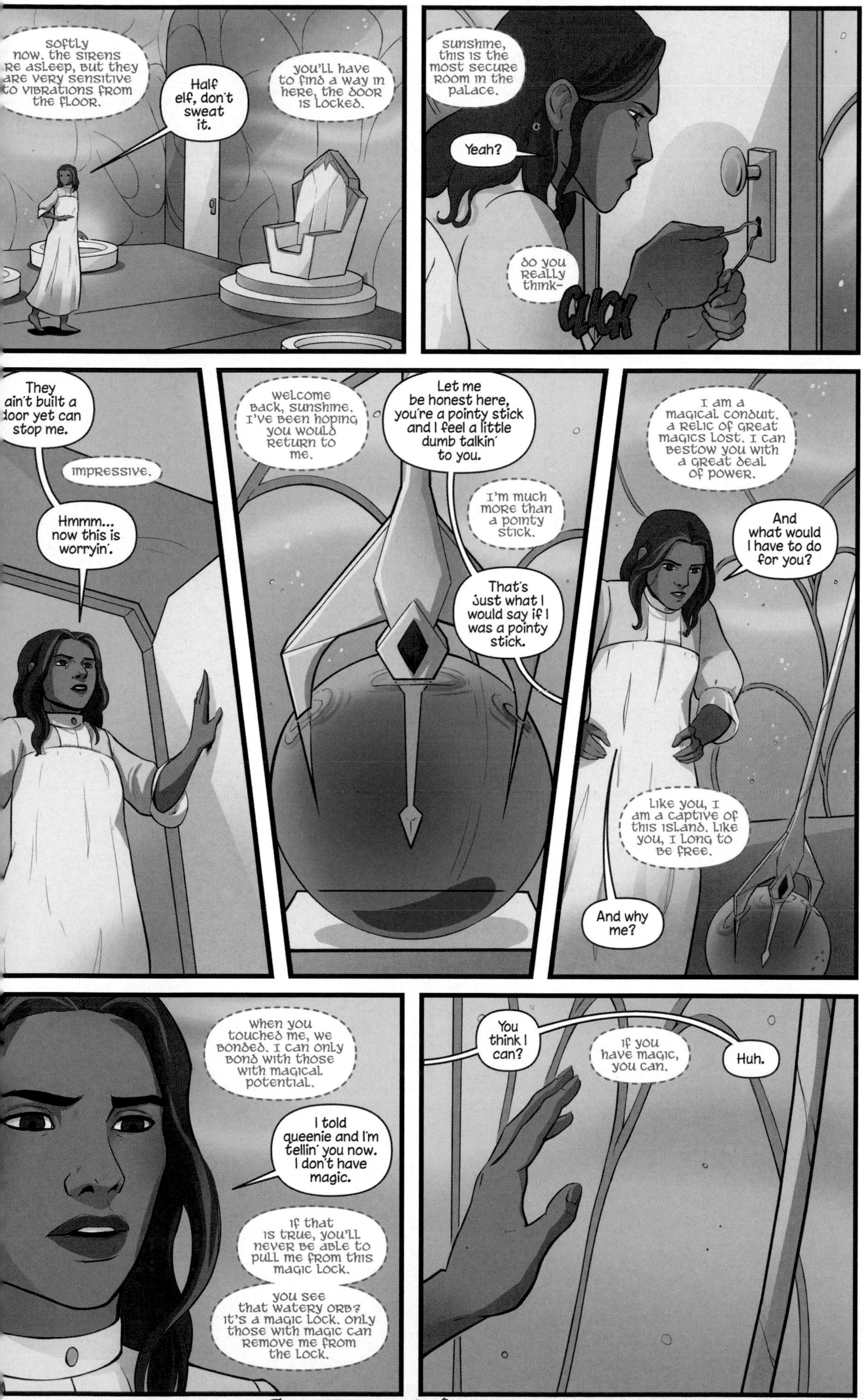
softly now, the sirens are asleep, but they are very sensitive to vibrations from the floor.
Half elf, don't sweat it.
you'll have to find a way in here, the door is locked.
sunshine, this is the most secure room in the palace.
Yeah?
do you really think-
CLICK
They ain't built a door yet can stop me.
impressive.
Hmmm... now this is worryin'.
welcome back, sunshine. I've been hoping you would return to me.
Let me be honest here, you're a pointy stick and I feel a little dumb talkin' to you.
I'm much more than a pointy stick.
That's just what I would say if I was a pointy stick.
I am a magical conduit, a relic of great magics lost. I can bestow you with a great deal of power.
And what would I have to do for you?
Like you, I am a captive of this island. Like you, I long to be free.
And why me?
when you touched me, we bonded. I can only bond with those with magical potential.
I told queenie and I'm tellin' you now. I don't have magic.
if that is true, you'll never be able to pull me from this magic lock.
you see that watery orb? it's a magic lock. only those with magic can remove me from the lock.
You think I can?
if you have magic, you can.
Huh.

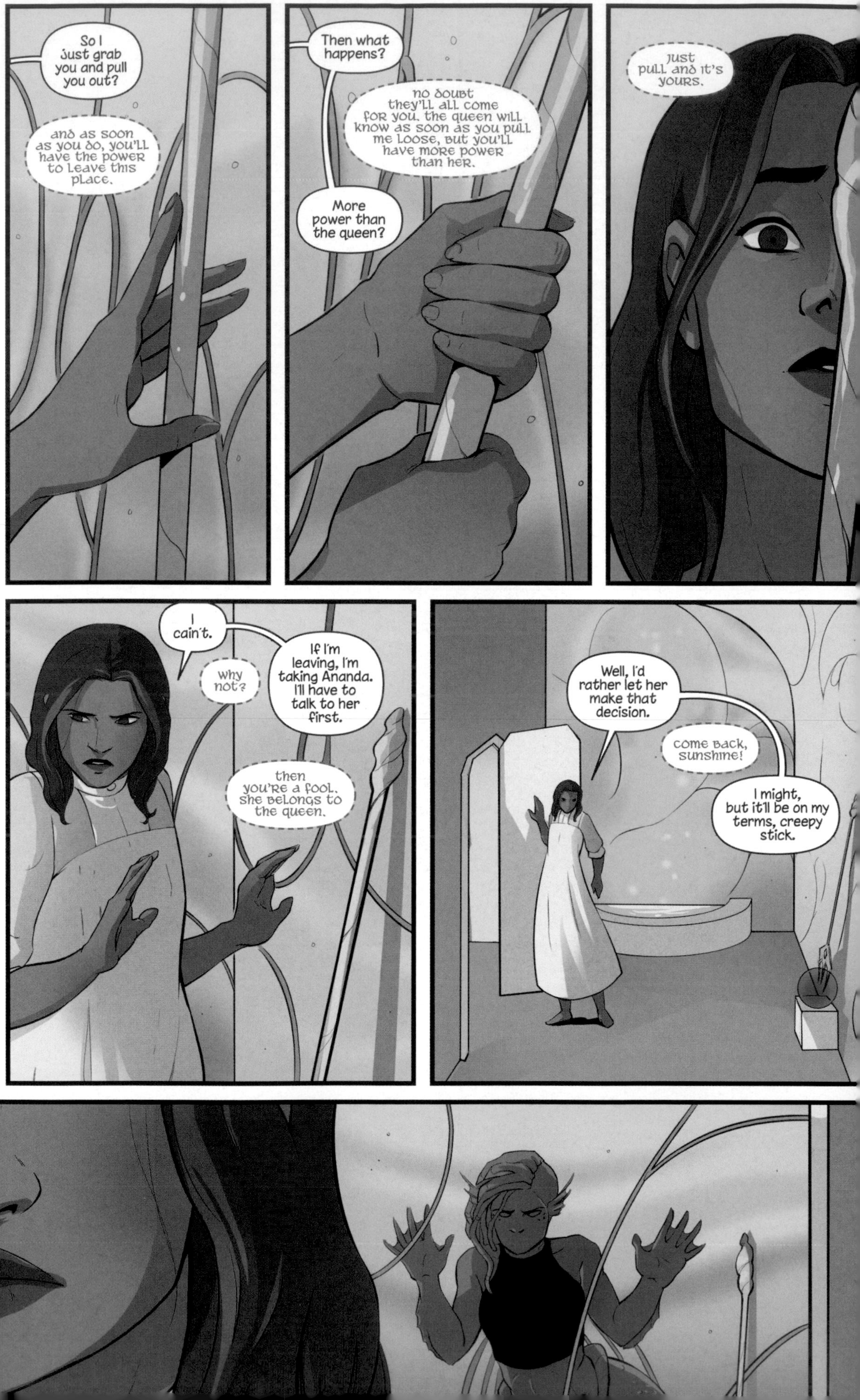
So I just grab you and pull you out?
and as soon as you do, you'll have the power to leave this place.
Then what happens?
no doubt they'll all come for you. the queen will know as soon as you pull me loose, but you'll have more power than her.
More power than the queen?
just pull and it's yours.
I cain't.
why not?
If I'm leaving, I'm taking Ananda. I'll have to talk to her first.
then you're a fool. she belongs to the queen.
Well, I'd rather let her make that decision.
come back, sunshine!
I might, but it'll be on my terms, creepy stick.

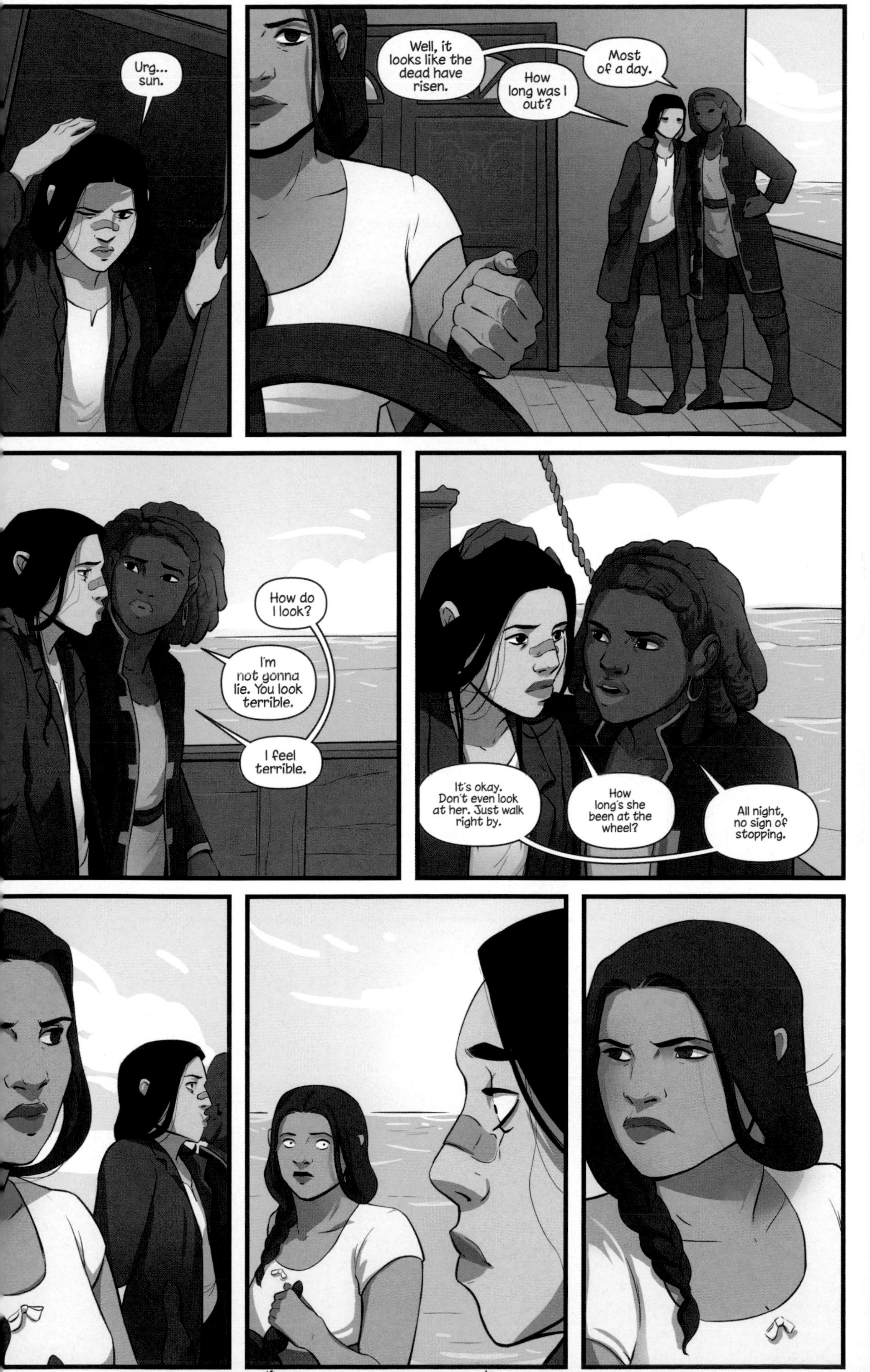
Urg... sun.
Well, it looks like the dead have risen.
How long was I out?
Most of a day.
How do I look?
I'm not gonna lie. You look terrible.
I feel terrible.
It's okay. Don't even look at her. Just walk right by.
How long's she been at the wheel?
All night, no sign of stopping.

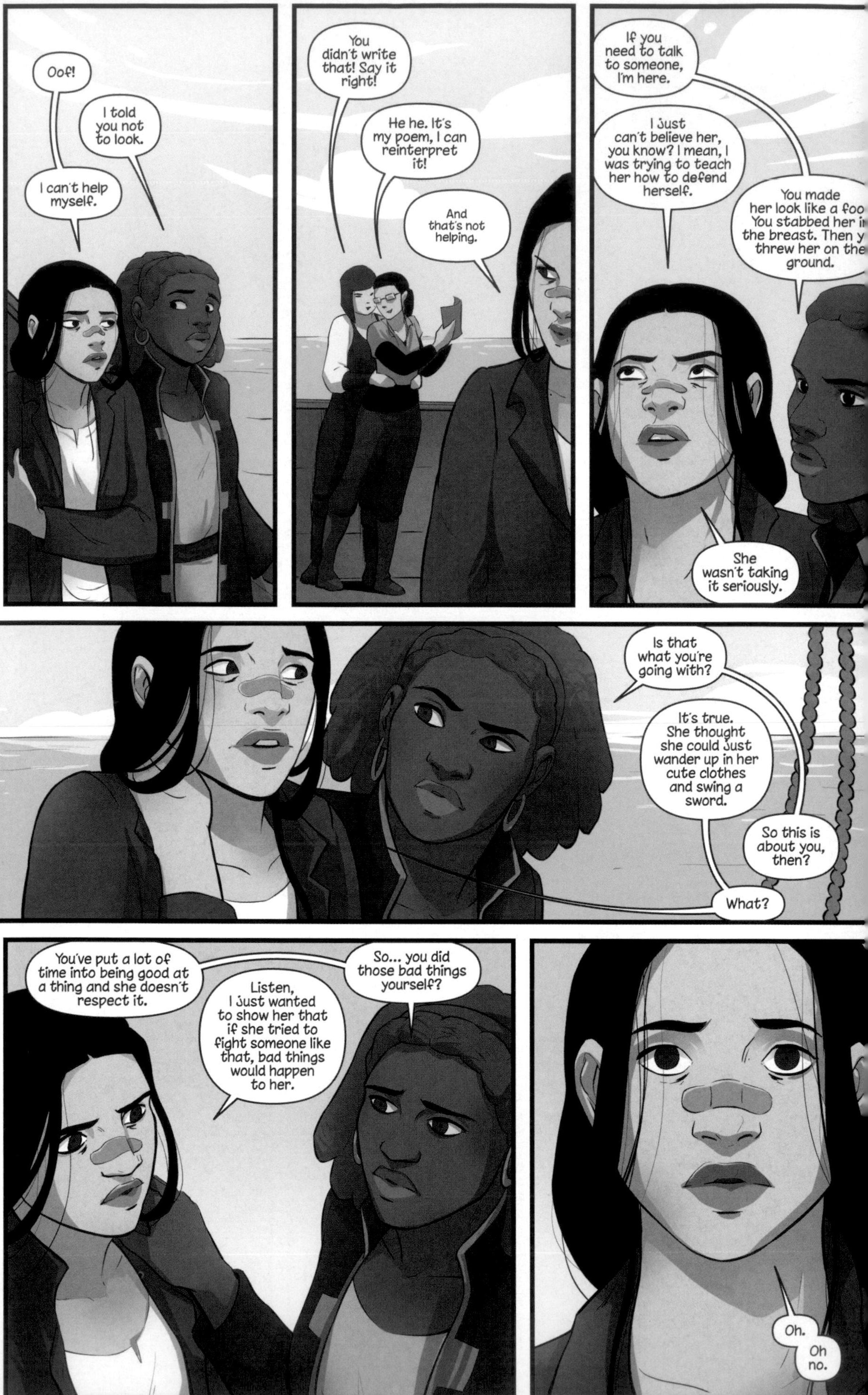
Oof!
I told you not to look.
I can't help myself.
You didn't write that! Say it right!
He he. It's my poem, I can reinterpret it!
And that's not helping.
If you need to talk to someone, I'm here.
I just can't believe her, you know? I mean, I was trying to teach her how to defend herself.
You made her look like a foo You stabbed her i the breast. Then y threw her on the ground.
She wasn't taking it seriously.
Is that what you're going with?
It's true. She thought she could just wander up in her cute clothes and swing a sword.
So this is about you, then?
What?
You've put a lot of time into being good at a thing and she doesn't respect it.
Listen, I just wanted to show her that if she tried to fight someone like that, bad things would happen to her.
So... you did those bad things yourself?
Oh.
Oh no.

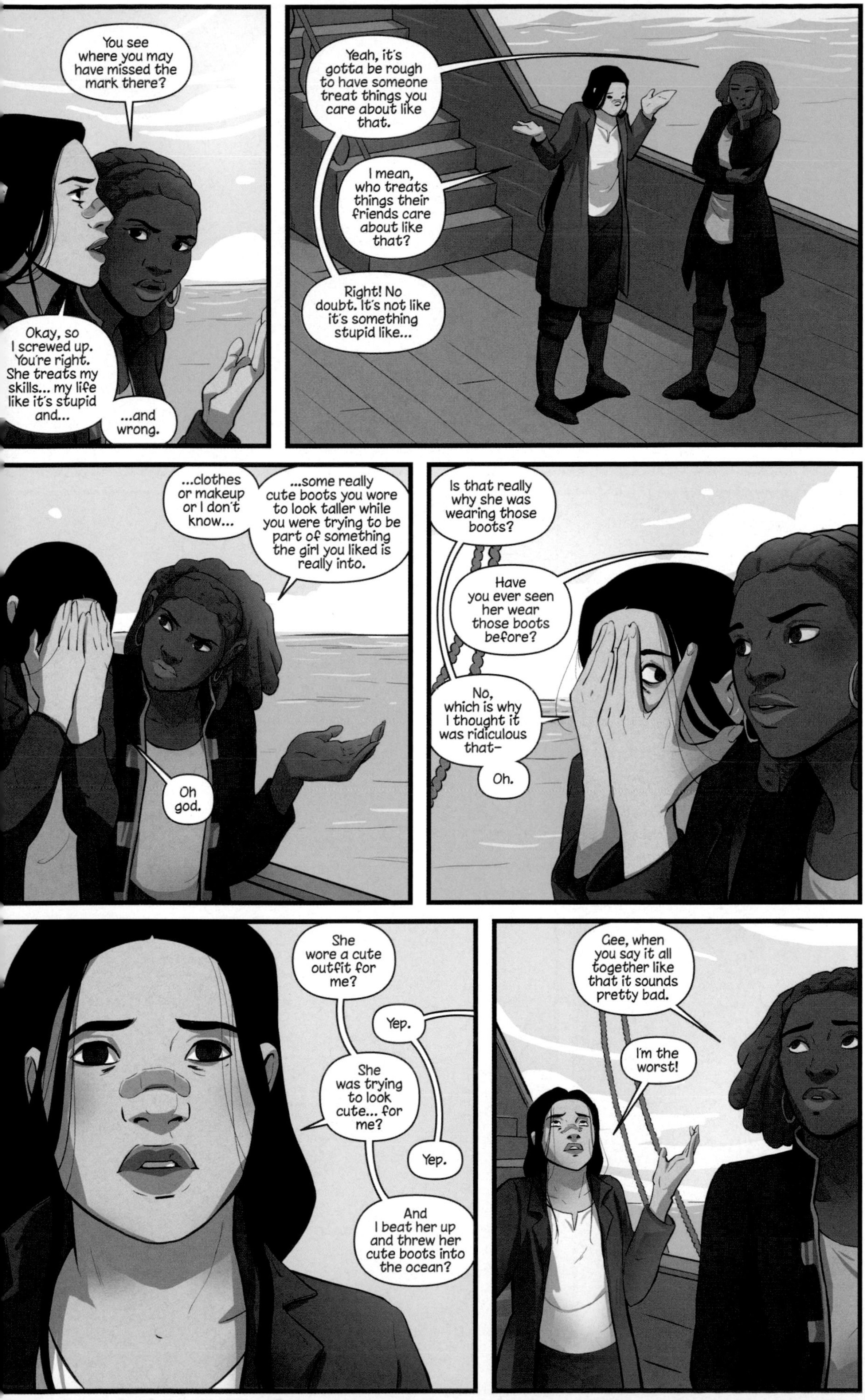
You see where you may have missed the mark there?
Okay, so I screwed up. You're right. She treats my skills... my life like it's stupid and...
...and wrong.
Yeah, it's gotta be rough to have someone treat things you care about like that.
I mean, who treats things their friends care about like that?
Right! No doubt. It's not like it's something stupid like...
...clothes or makeup or I don't know...
...some really cute boots you wore to look taller while you were trying to be part of something the girl you liked is really into.
Oh god.
Is that really why she was wearing those boots?
Have you ever seen her wear those boots before?
No, which is why I thought it was ridiculous that–
Oh.
She wore a cute outfit for me?
Yep.
She was trying to look cute... for me?
Yep.
And I beat her up and threw her cute boots into the ocean?
Gee, when you say it all together like that it sounds pretty bad.
I'm the worst!

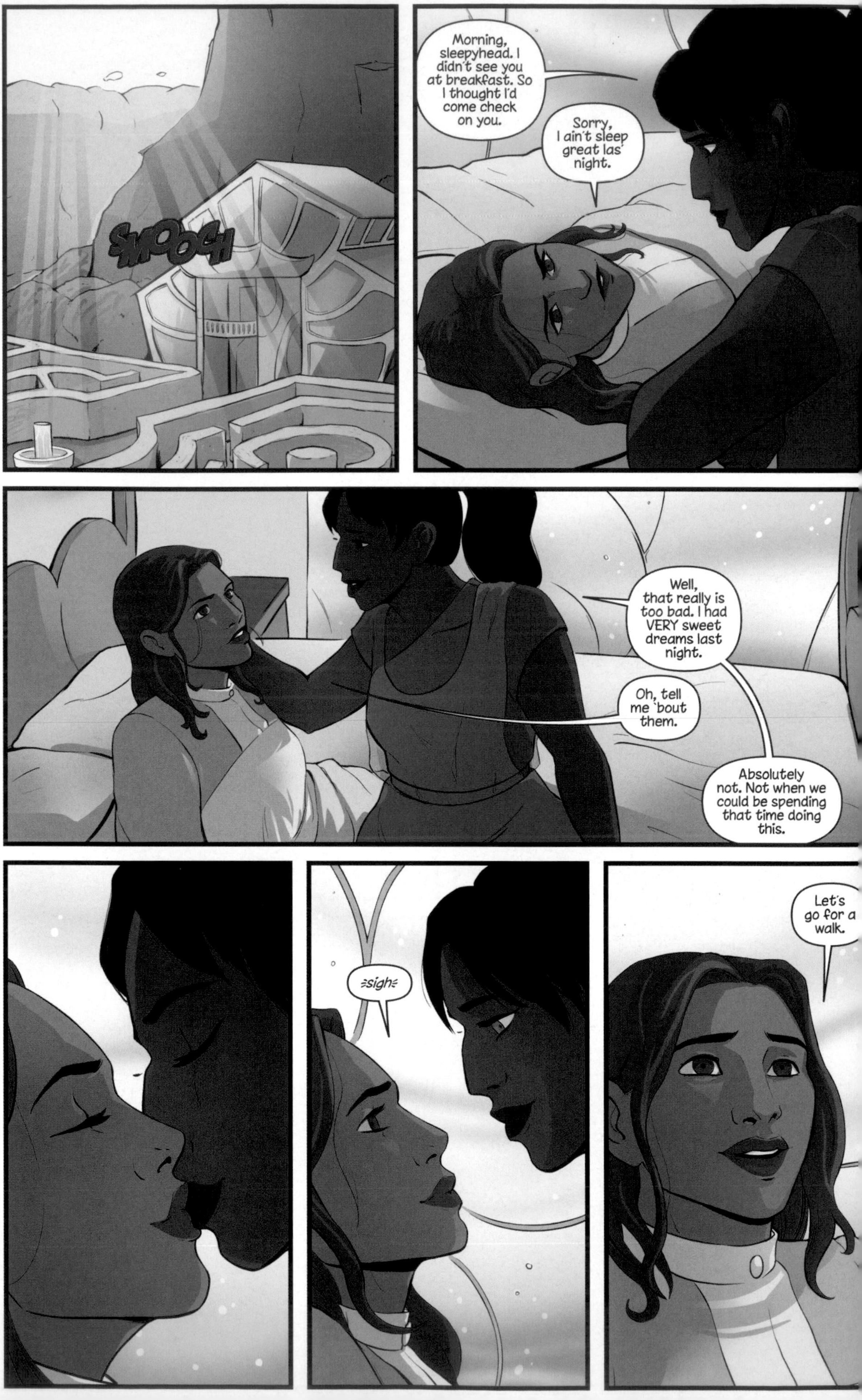
SMOOCH
Morning, sleepyhead. I didn't see you at breakfast. So I thought I'd come check on you.
Sorry, I ain't sleep great las' night.
Well, that really is too bad. I had VERY sweet dreams last night.
Oh, tell me 'bout them.
Absolutely not. Not when we could be spending that time doing this.
≈sigh≈
Let's go for a walk.

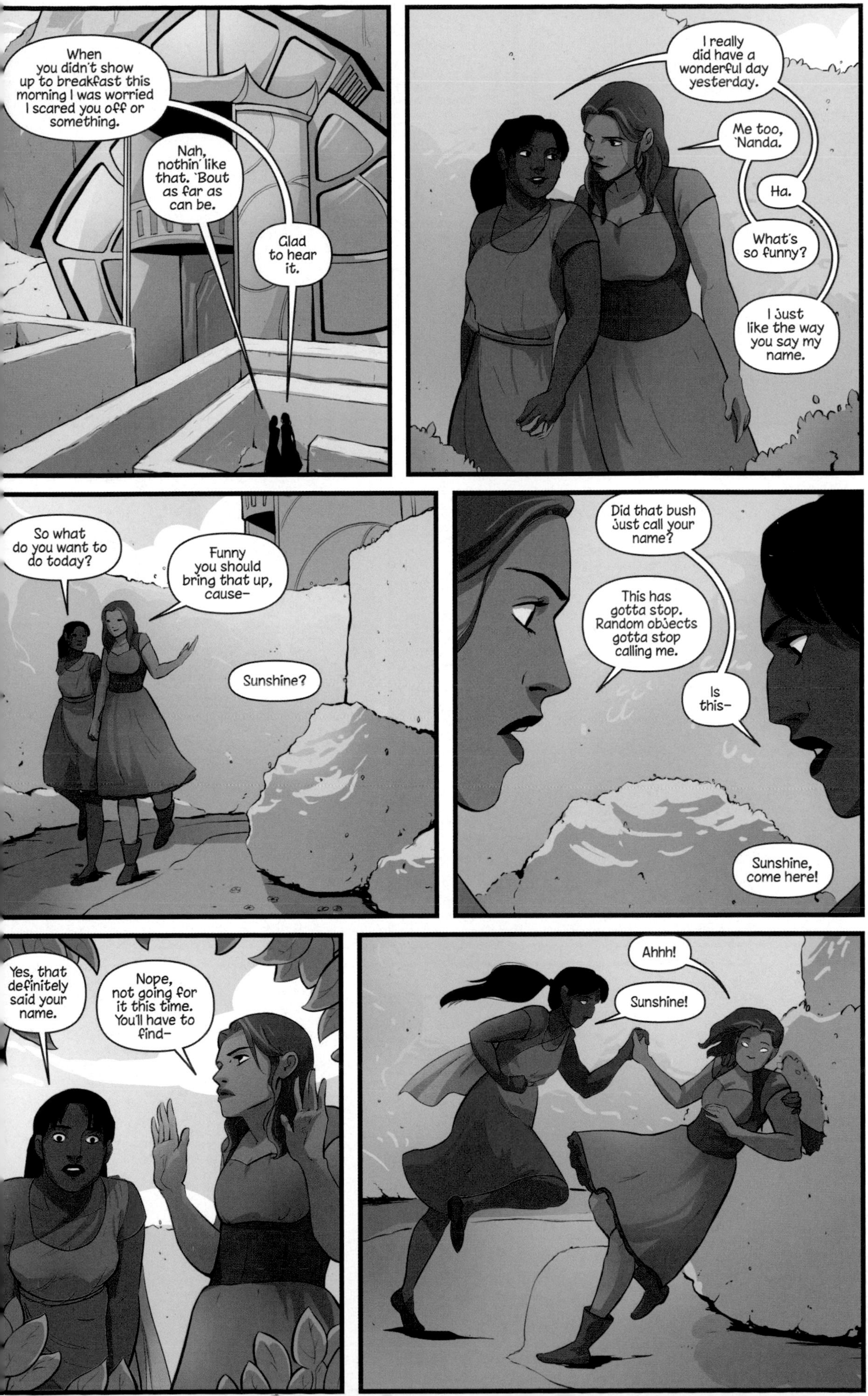
When you didn't show up to breakfast this morning I was worried I scared you off or something.
Nah, nothin' like that. 'Bout as far as can be.
Glad to hear it.
I really did have a wonderful day yesterday.
Me too, 'Nanda.
Ha.
What's so funny?
I just like the way you say my name.
So what do you want to do today?
Funny you should bring that up, cause–
Sunshine?
Did that bush just call your name?
This has gotta stop. Random objects gotta stop calling me.
Is this–
Sunshine, come here!
Yes, that definitely said your name.
Nope, not going for it this time. You'll have to find–
Ahhh!
Sunshine!

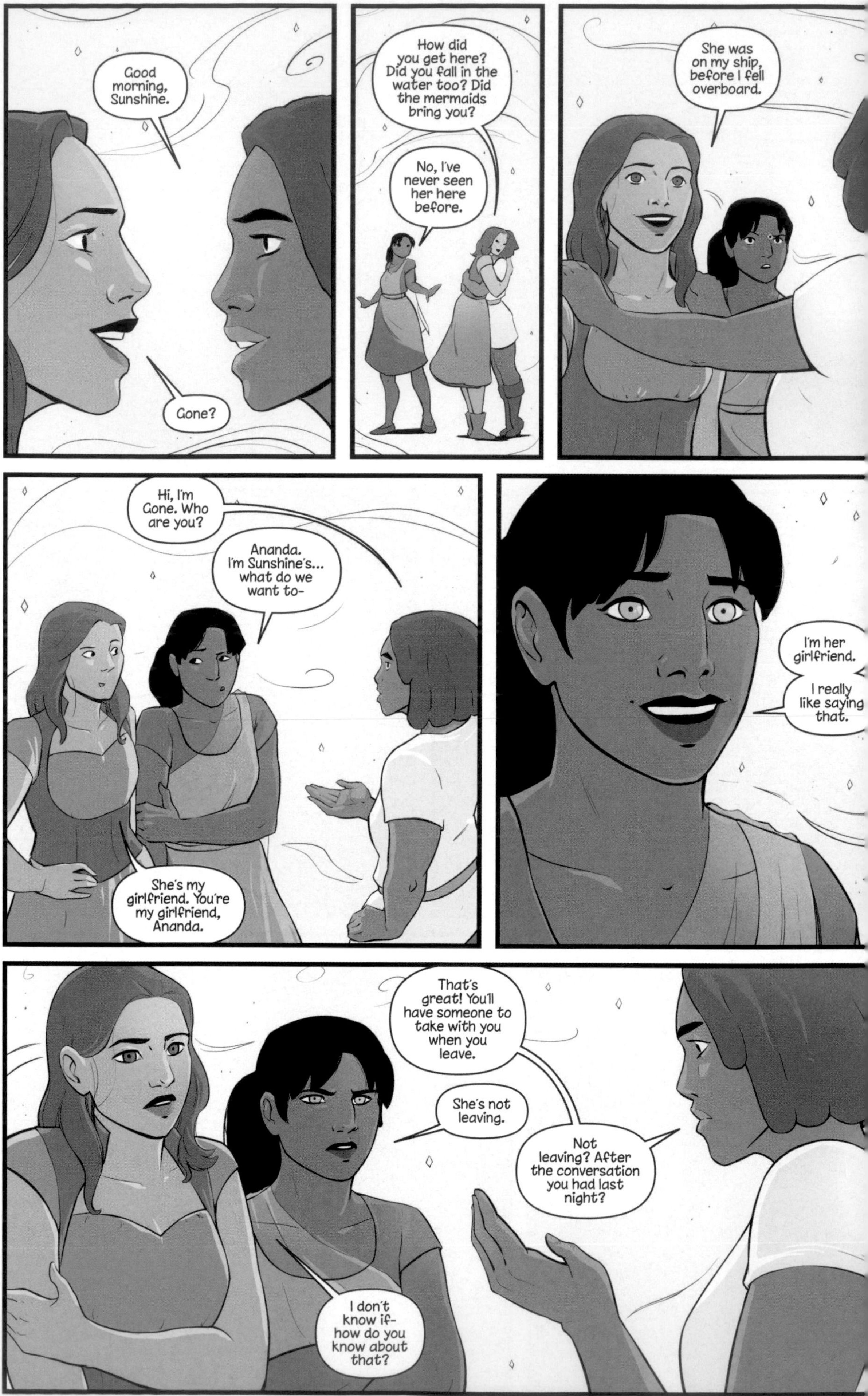

Good morning, Sunshine.
Gone?
How did you get here? Did you fall in the water too? Did the mermaids bring you?
No, I've never seen her here before.
She was on my ship, before I fell overboard.
Hi, I'm Gone. Who are you?
Ananda. I'm Sunshine's... what do we want to-
She's my girlfriend. You're my girlfriend, Ananda.
I'm her girlfriend.
I really like saying that.
That's great! You'll have someone to take with you when you leave.
She's not leaving.
Not leaving? After the conversation you had last night?
I don't know if- how do you know about that?

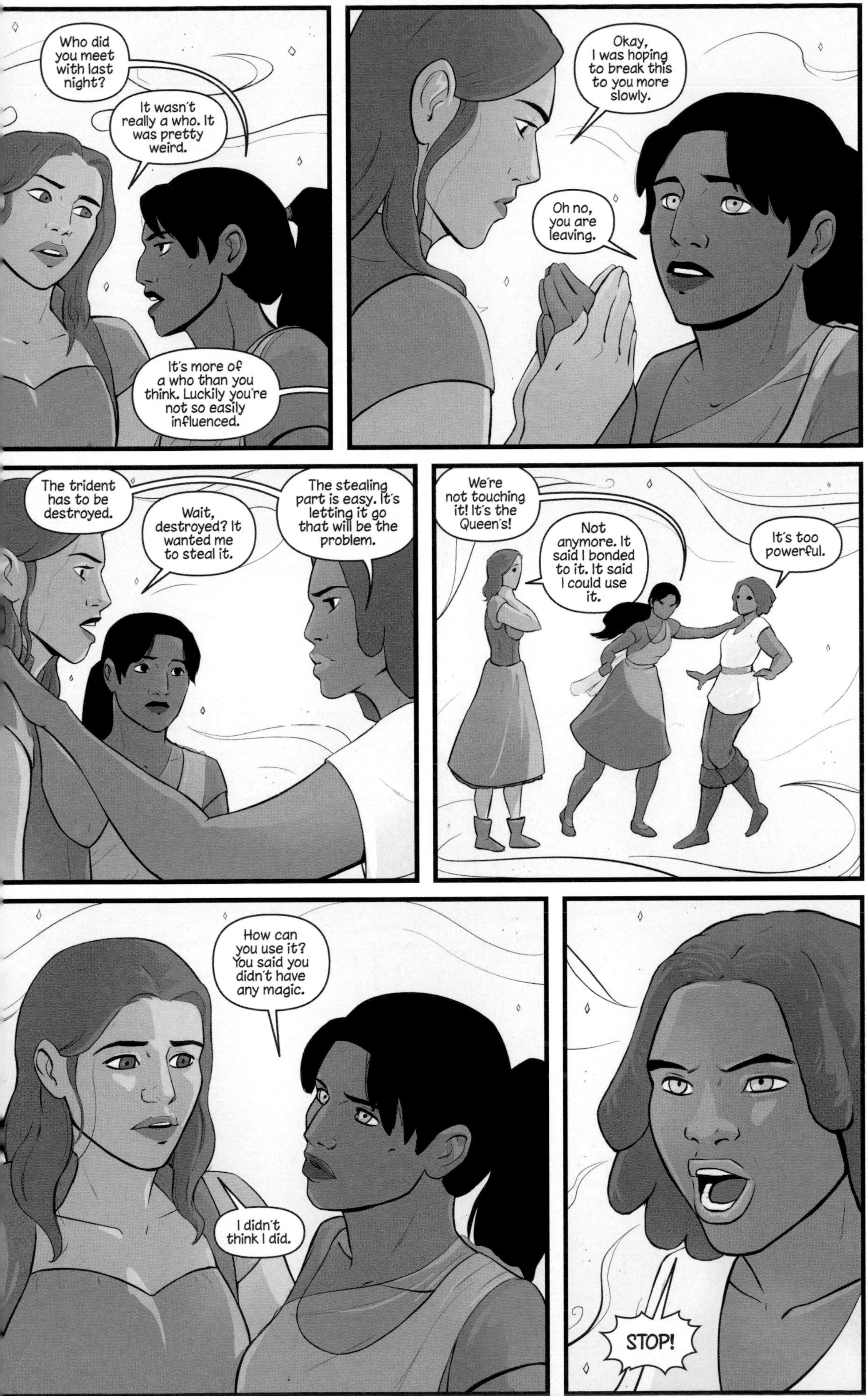

Who did you meet with last night?
It wasn't really a who. It was pretty weird.
It's more of a who than you think. Luckily you're not so easily influenced.
Okay, I was hoping to break this to you more slowly.
Oh no, you are leaving.
The trident has to be destroyed.
Wait, destroyed? It wanted me to steal it.
The stealing part is easy. It's letting it go that will be the problem.
We're not touching it! It's the Queen's!
Not anymore. It said I bonded to it. It said I could use it.
It's too powerful.
How can you use it? You said you didn't have any magic.
I didn't think I did.
STOP!

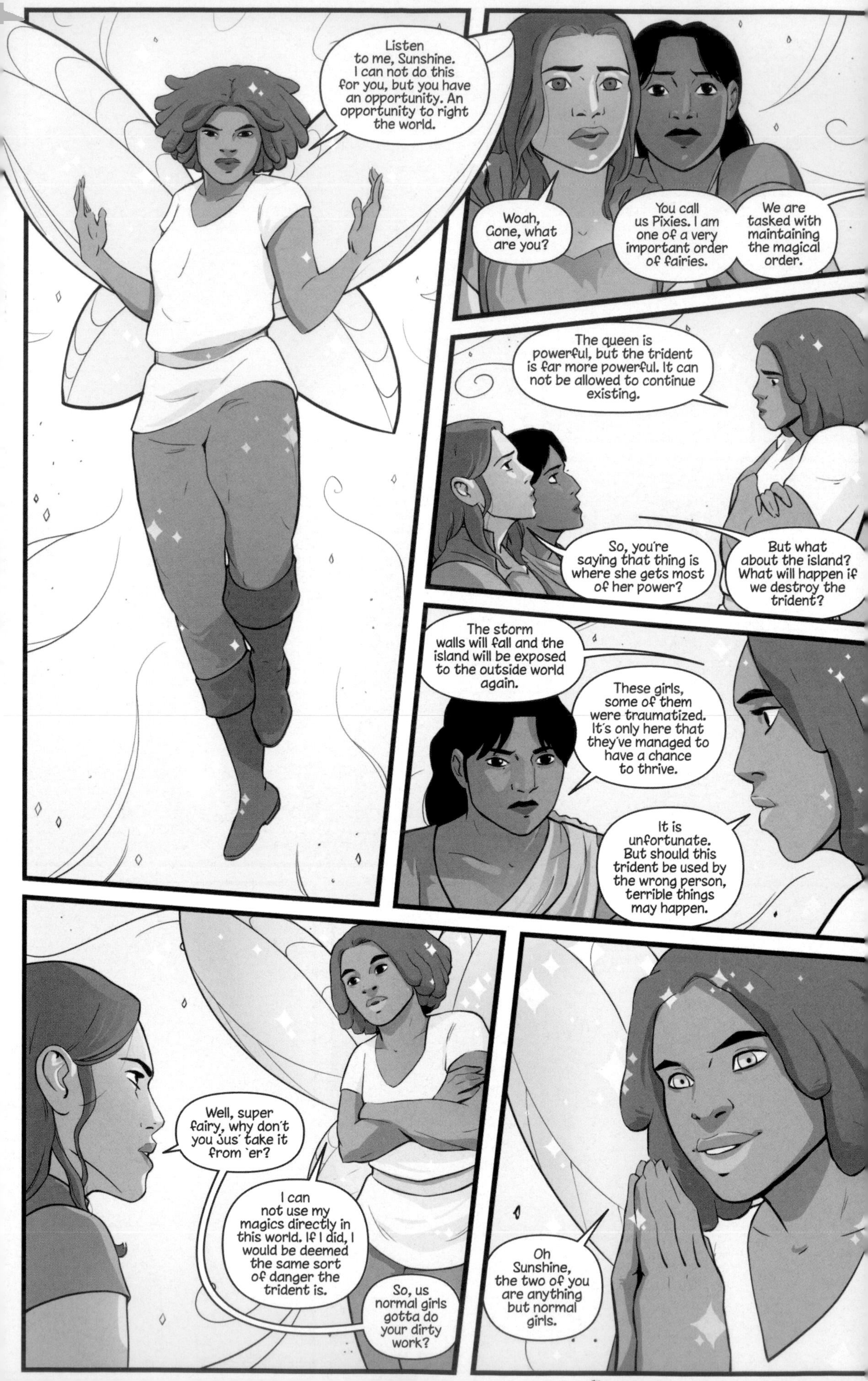
Listen to me, Sunshine. I can not do this for you, but you have an opportunity. An opportunity to right the world.
Woah, Gone, what are you?
You call us Pixies. I am one of a very important order of fairies.
We are tasked with maintaining the magical order.
The queen is powerful, but the trident is far more powerful. It can not be allowed to continue existing.
So, you're saying that thing is where she gets most of her power?
But what about the island? What will happen if we destroy the trident?
The storm walls will fall and the island will be exposed to the outside world again.
These girls, some of them were traumatized. It's only here that they've managed to have a chance to thrive.
It is unfortunate. But should this trident be used by the wrong person, terrible things may happen.
Well, super fairy, why don't you jus' take it from `er?
I can not use my magics directly in this world. If I did, I would be deemed the same sort of danger the trident is.
So, us normal girls gotta do your dirty work?
Oh Sunshine, the two of you are anything but normal girls.

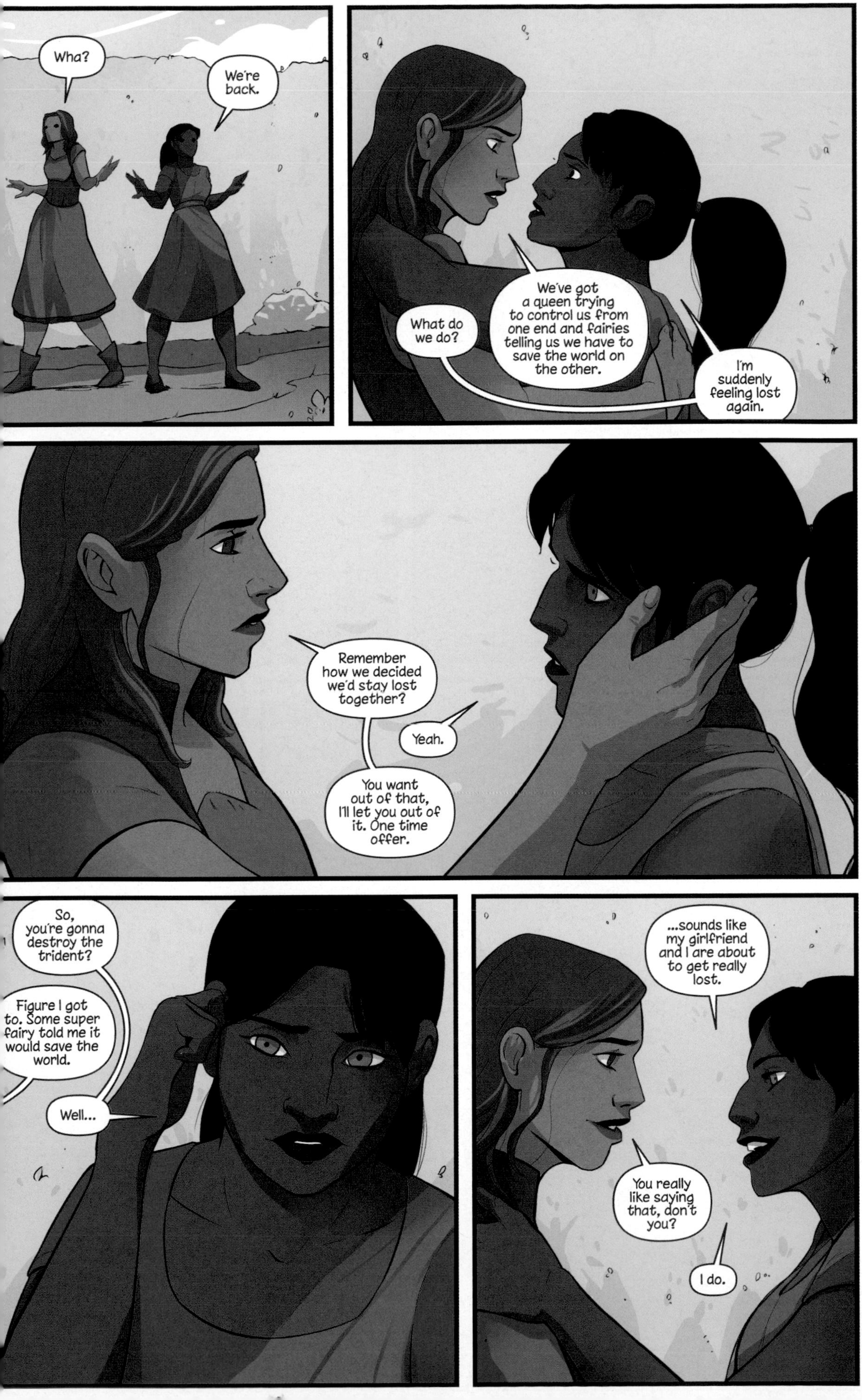
Wha?
We're back.
What do we do?
We've got a queen trying to control us from one end and fairies telling us we have to save the world on the other.
I'm suddenly feeling lost again.
Remember how we decided we'd stay lost together?
Yeah.
You want out of that, I'll let you out of it. One time offer.
So, you're gonna destroy the trident?
Figure I got to. Some super fairy told me it would save the world.
Well...
...sounds like my girlfriend and I are about to get really lost.
You really like saying that, don't you?
I do.

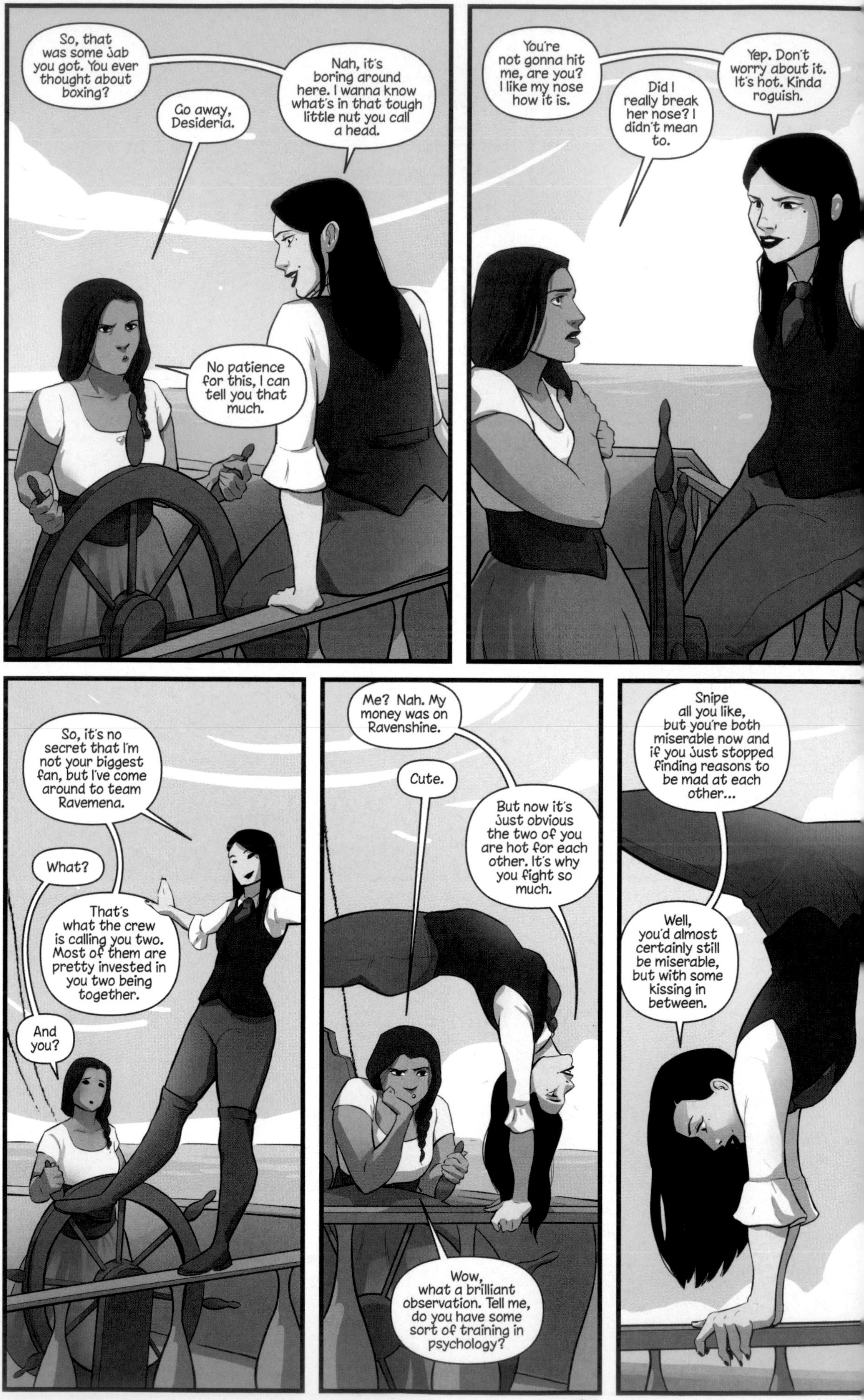
So, that was some jab you got. You ever thought about boxing?
Go away, Desideria.
Nah, it's boring around here. I wanna know what's in that tough little nut you call a head.
No patience for this, I can tell you that much.
You're not gonna hit me, are you? I like my nose how it is.
Did I really break her nose? I didn't mean to.
Yep. Don't worry about it. It's hot. Kinda roguish.
So, it's no secret that I'm not your biggest fan, but I've come around to team Ravemena.
What?
That's what the crew is calling you two. Most of them are pretty invested in you two being together.
And you?
Me? Nah. My money was on Ravenshine.
Cute.
But now it's just obvious the two of you are hot for each other. It's why you fight so much.
Wow, what a brilliant observation. Tell me, do you have some sort of training in psychology?
Snipe all you like, but you're both miserable now and if you just stopped finding reasons to be mad at each other...
Well, you'd almost certainly still be miserable, but with some kissing in between.

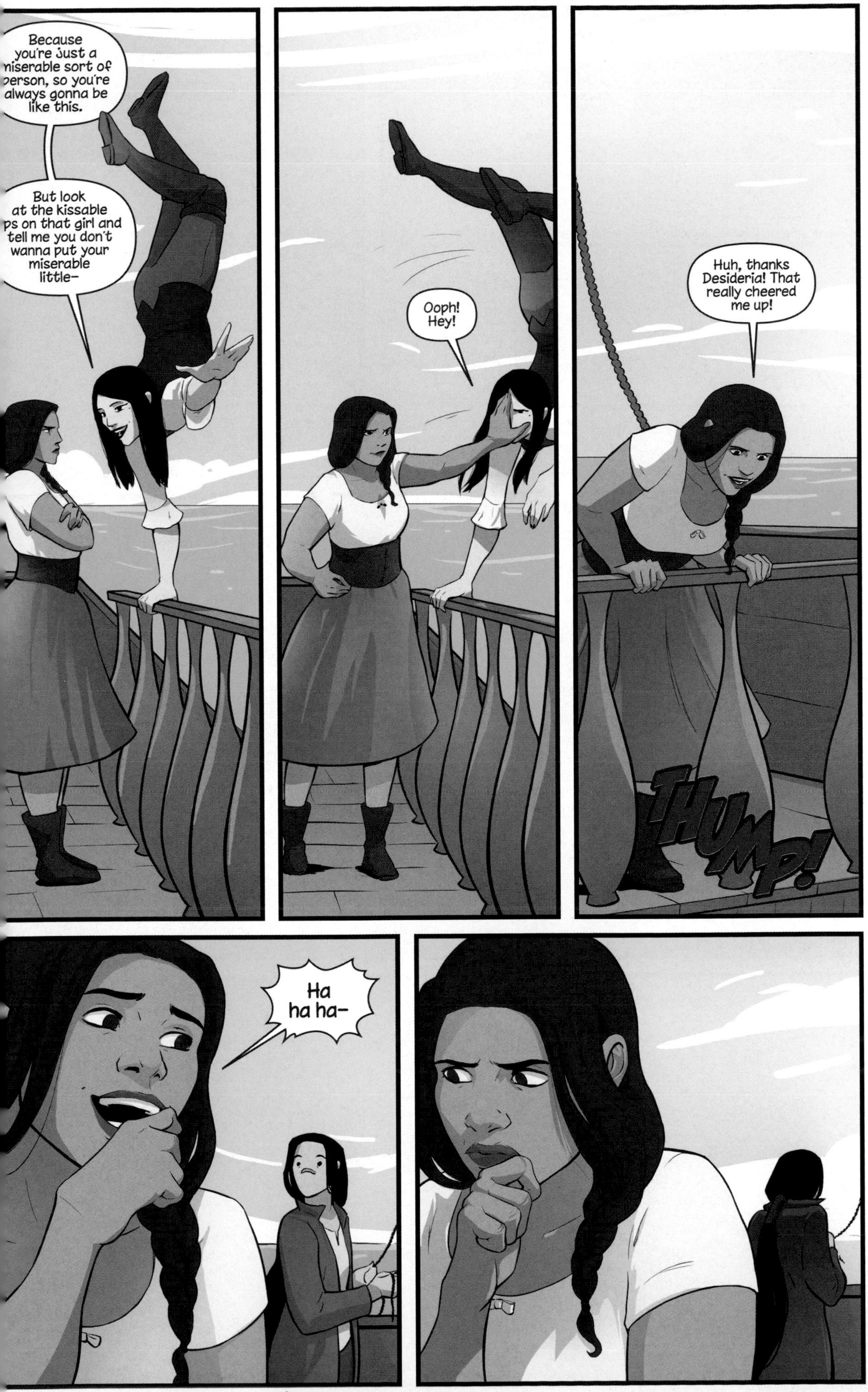

Because you're just a miserable sort of person, so you're always gonna be like this.
But look at the kissable lips on that girl and tell me you don't wanna put your miserable little-
Ooph! Hey!
Huh, thanks Desideria! That really cheered me up!
THUMP!
Ha ha ha-

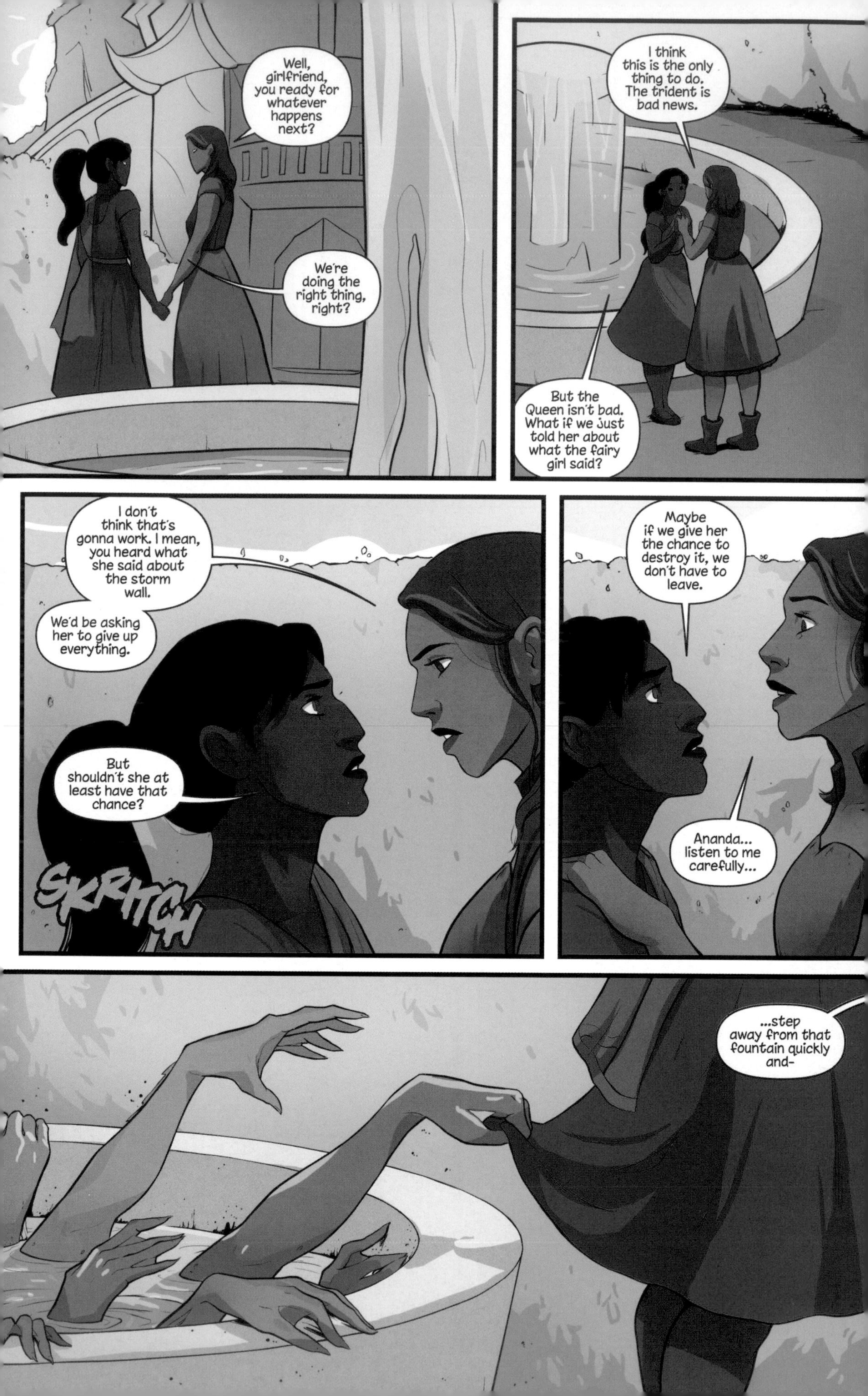
Well, girlfriend, you ready for whatever happens next?
We're doing the right thing, right?
I think this is the only thing to do. The trident is bad news.
But the Queen isn't bad. What if we just told her about what the fairy girl said?
I don't think that's gonna work. I mean, you heard what she said about the storm wall.
We'd be asking her to give up everything.
But shouldn't she at least have that chance?
SKRITCH
Maybe if we give her the chance to destroy it, we don't have to leave.
Ananda... listen to me carefully...
...step away from that fountain quickly and-

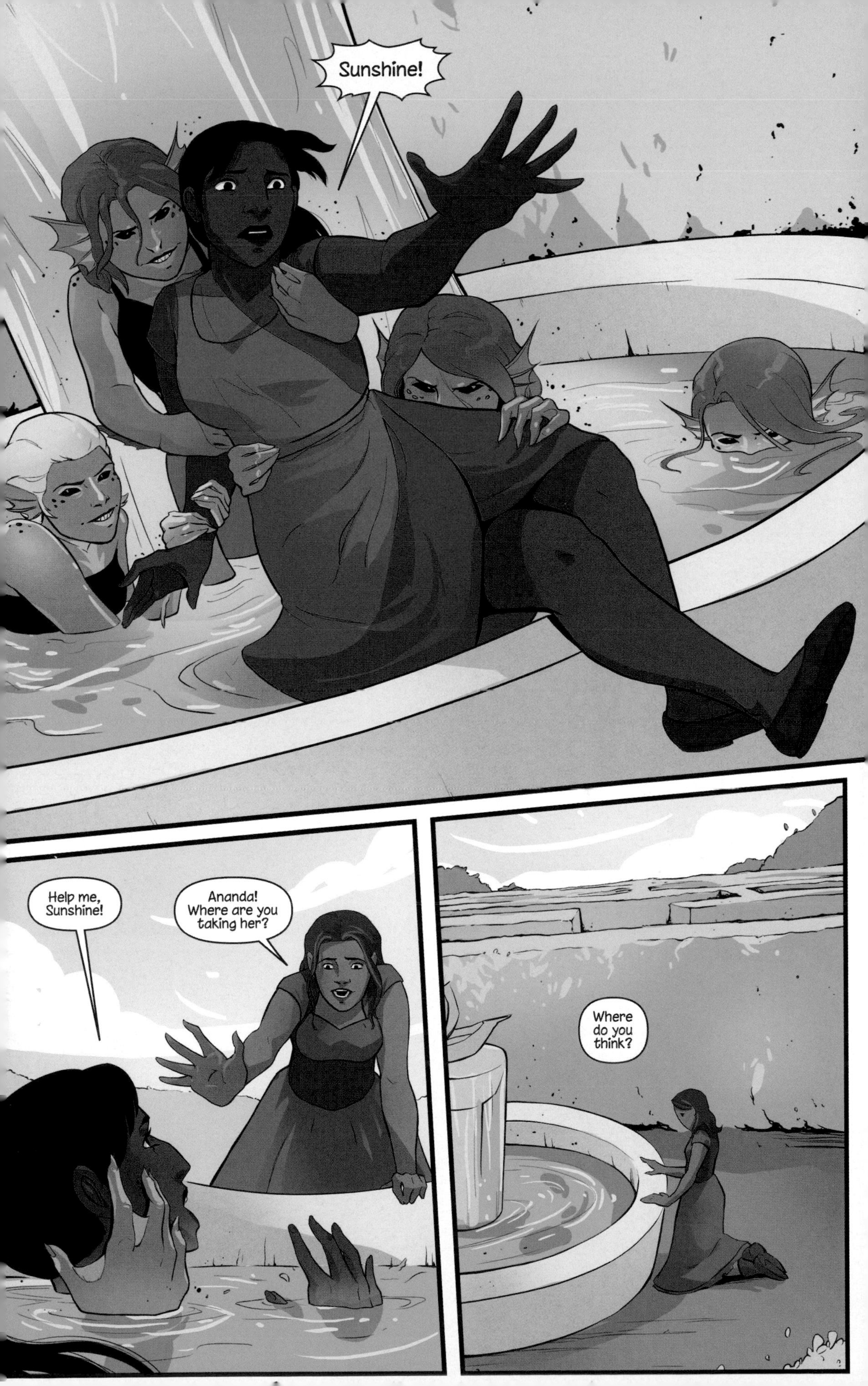
Sunshine!
Help me, Sunshine!
Ananda! Where are you taking her?
Where do you think?

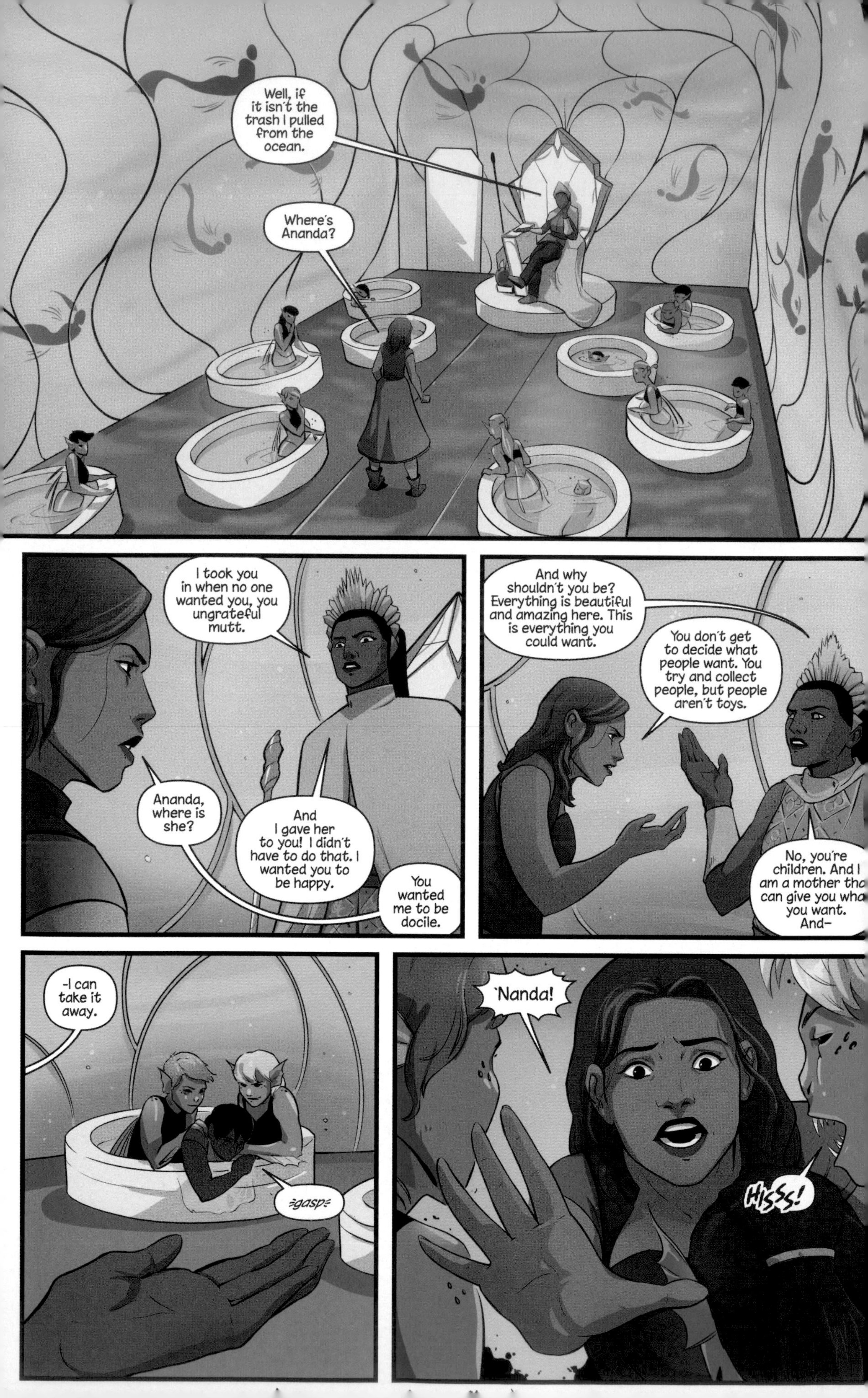
Well, if it isn't the trash I pulled from the ocean.
Where's Ananda?
I took you in when no one wanted you, you ungrateful mutt.
Ananda, where is she?
And I gave her to you! I didn't have to do that. I wanted you to be happy.
You wanted me to be docile.
And why shouldn't you be? Everything is beautiful and amazing here. This is everything you could want.
You don't get to decide what people want. You try and collect people, but people aren't toys.
No, you're children. And I am a mother tha can give you wha you want. And–
-I can take it away.
gasp
'Nanda!
HISSS!

Don't worry about me, Sunshine!

Take her back under!

Do what—

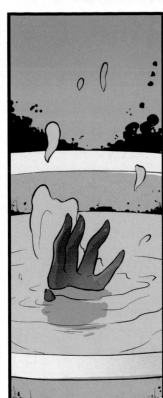

No! Let her go!

Why should I?

She was just trying to convince me to give you a chance. She said you weren't evil.

Oh?

Well, she's right. I'm not evil. I'm necessary.

And sometimes it's my job to decide who drowns and who gets saved.

Of course, in cases like yours, I make the wrong choice from time to time.

But, of course, I'm a woman who believes in correcting my mistakes.

Step into this pool with Afua. She'll return you to the sea and I'll give you my word Ananda will continue to live here unharmed.

You know that's not true.

Which is better than what's happening to her right now.

She's going to kill the girl no matter what.

What will it be, Sunshine? You or Ananda?

You've got one chance. Save ananda and save yourself. Get out of here.

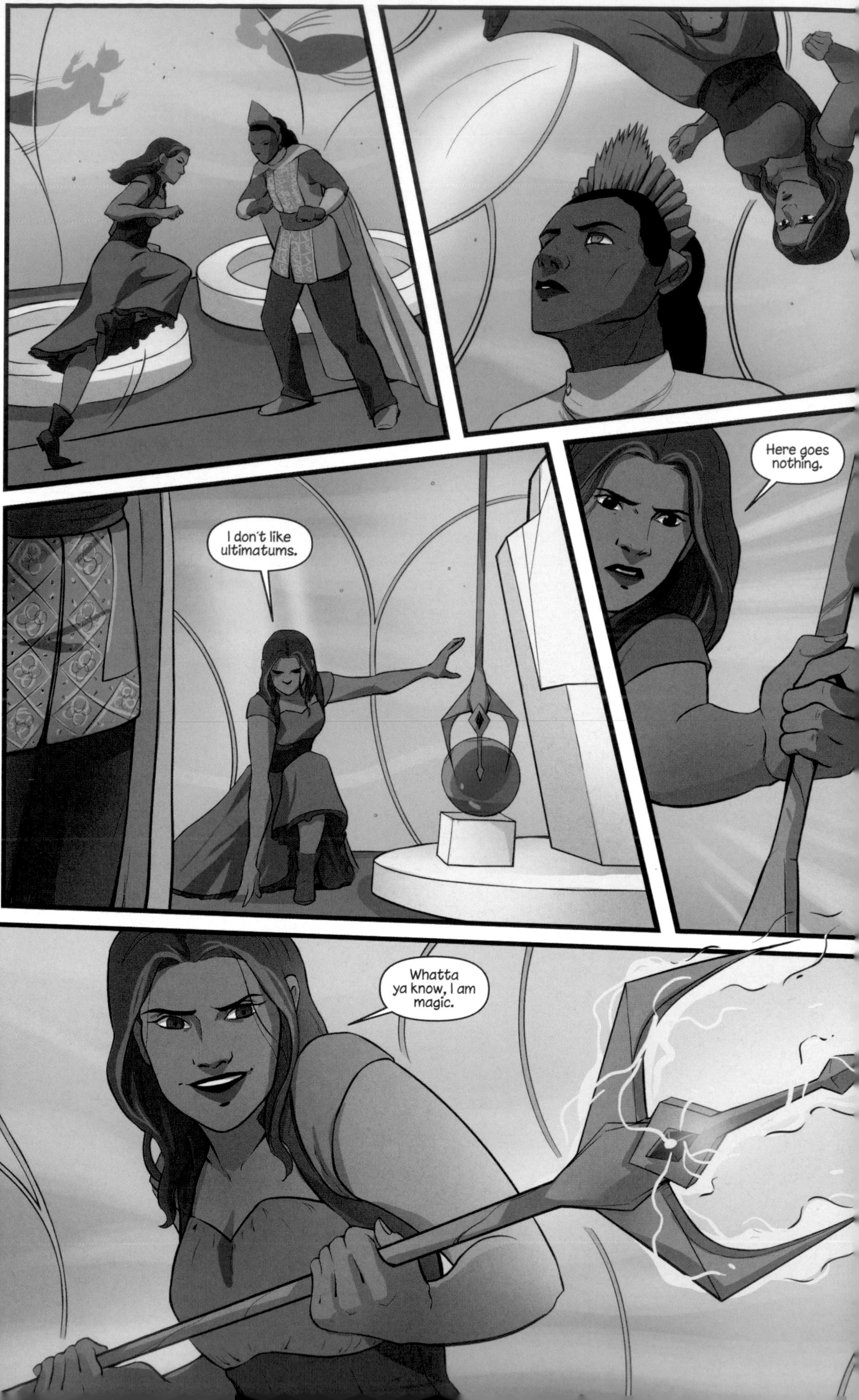
I don't like ultimatums.
Here goes nothing.
Whatta ya know, I am magic.

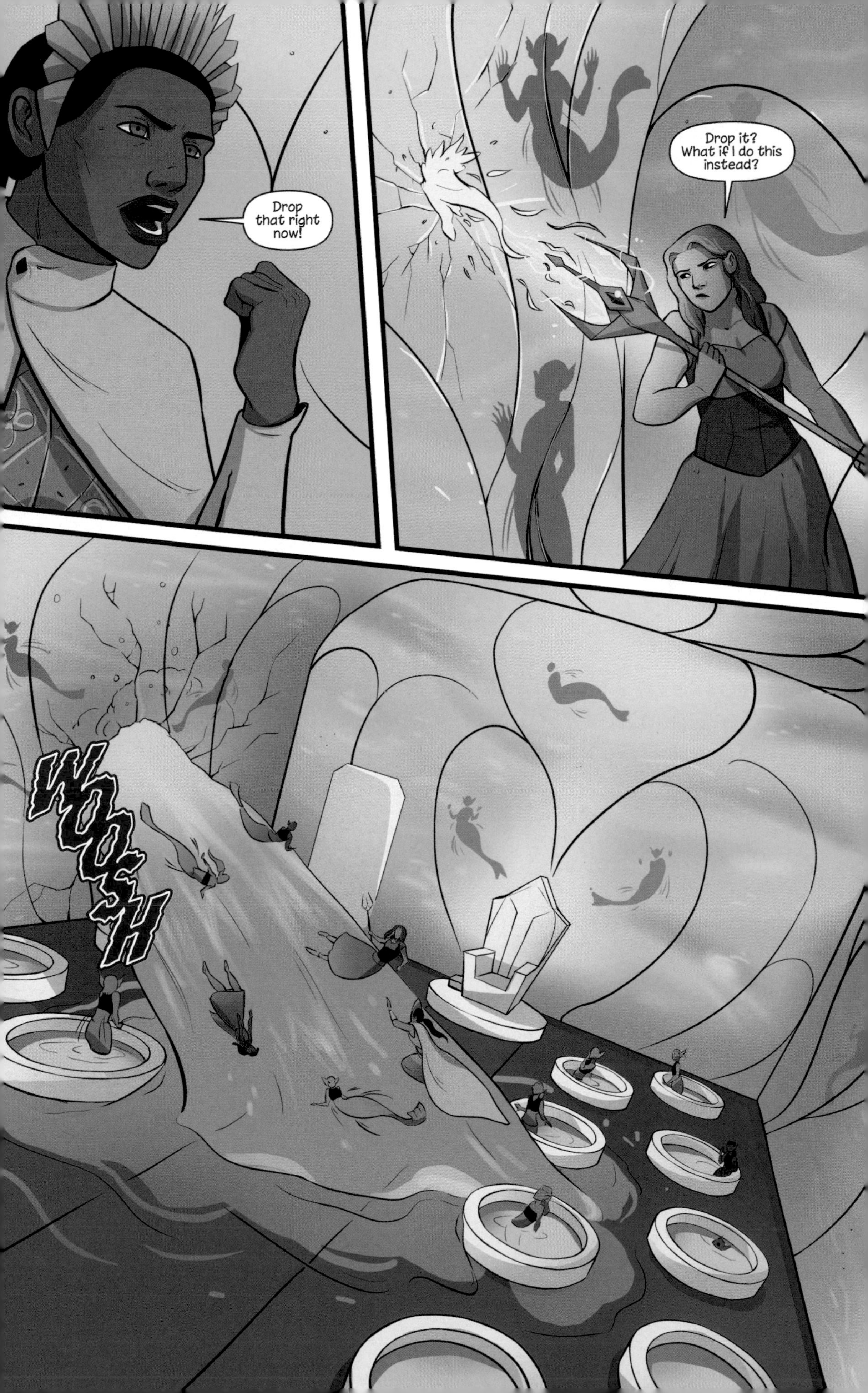
Drop that right now!
Drop it? What if I do this instead?
WOOSH

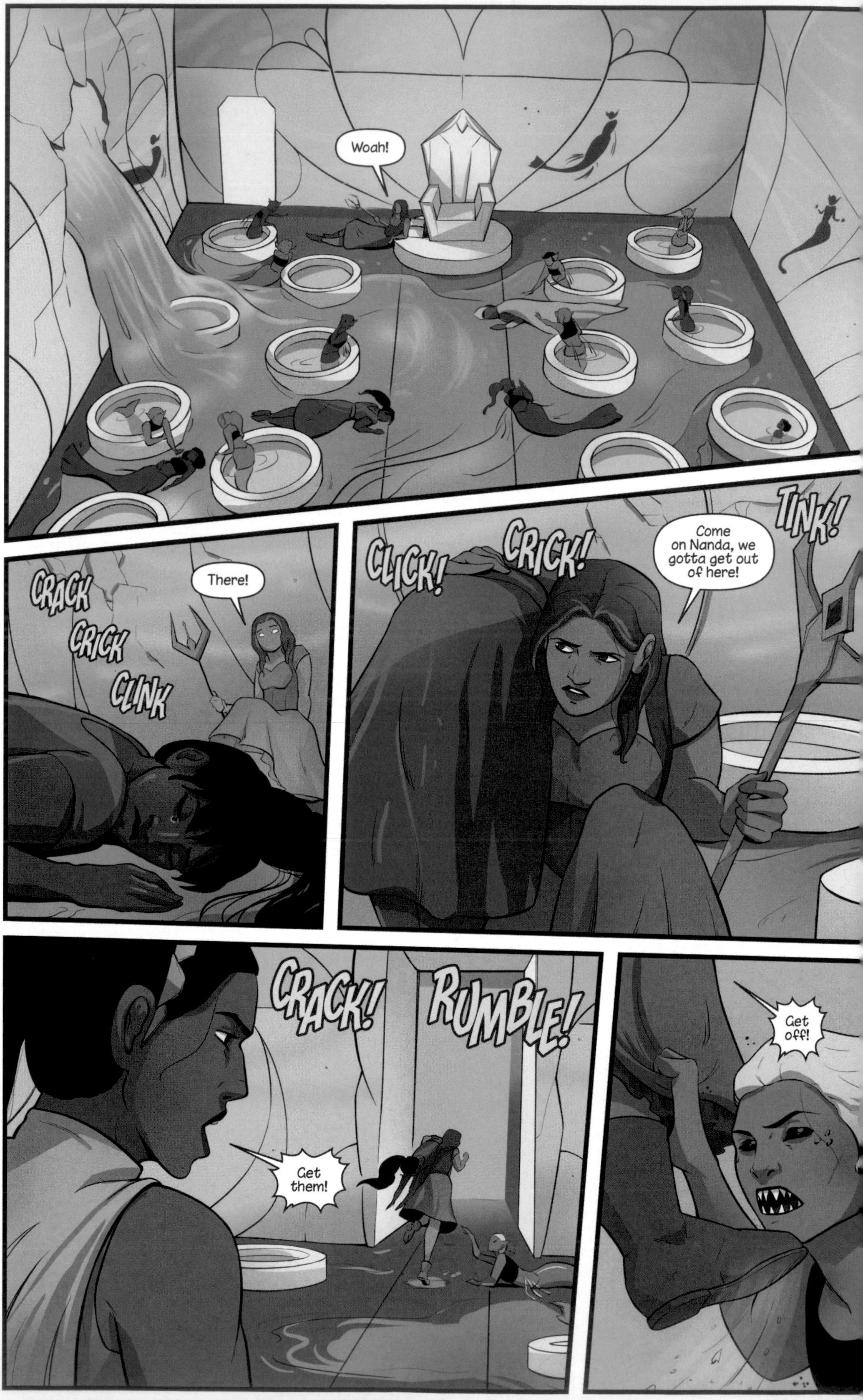
Woah!
CRACK
CRICK
CLINK
There!
CLICK!
CRICK!
Come on Nanda, we gotta get out of here!
TINK!
CRACK!
RUMBLE!
Get them!
Get off!

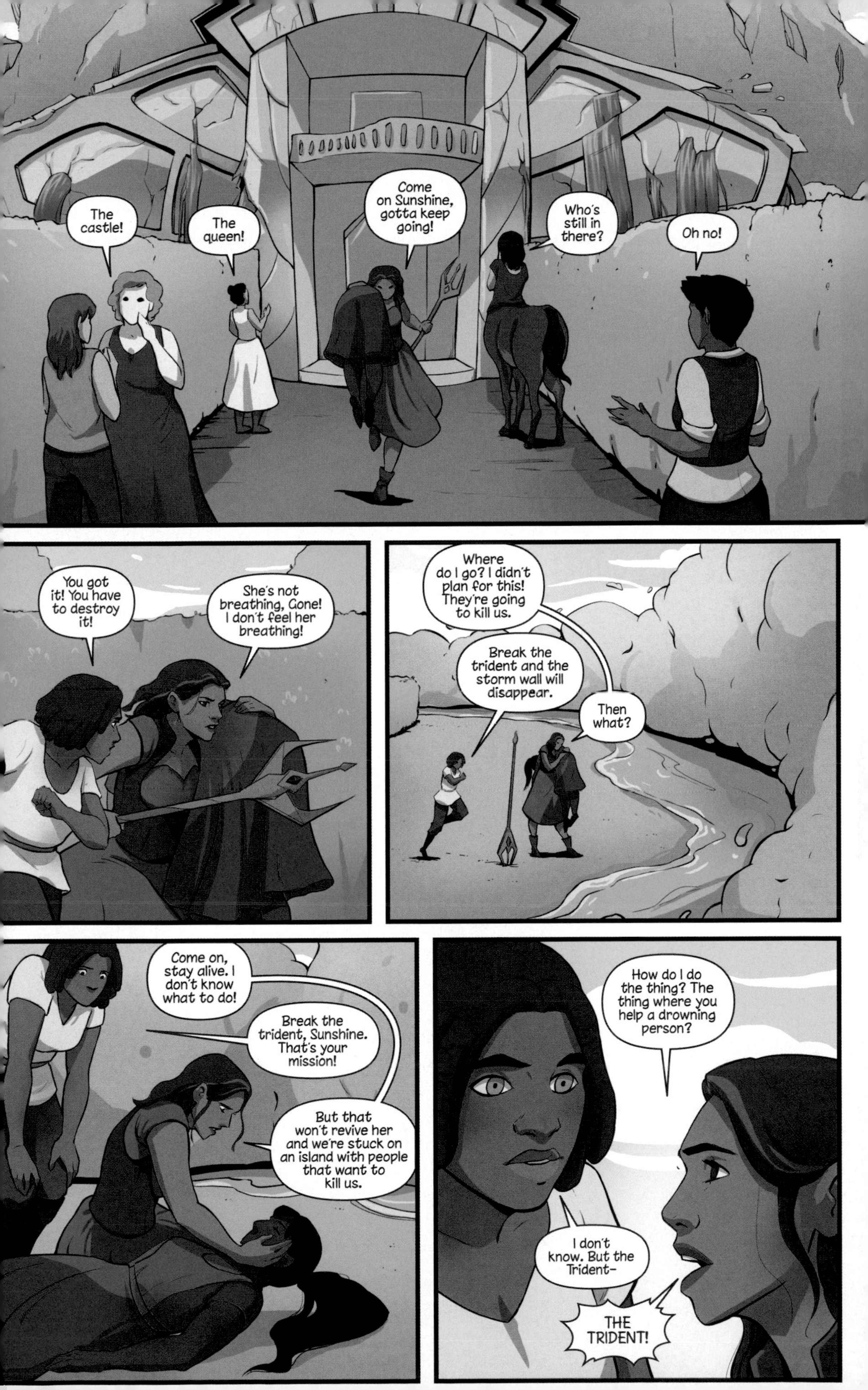
The castle!
The queen!
Come on Sunshine, gotta keep going!
Who's still in there?
Oh no!
You got it! You have to destroy it!
She's not breathing, Gone! I don't feel her breathing!
Where do I go? I didn't plan for this! They're going to kill us.
Break the trident and the storm wall will disappear.
Then what?
Come on, stay alive. I don't know what to do!
Break the trident, Sunshine. That's your mission!
But that won't revive her and we're stuck on an island with people that want to kill us.
How do I do the thing? The thing where you help a drowning person?
I don't know. But the Trident-
THE TRIDENT!

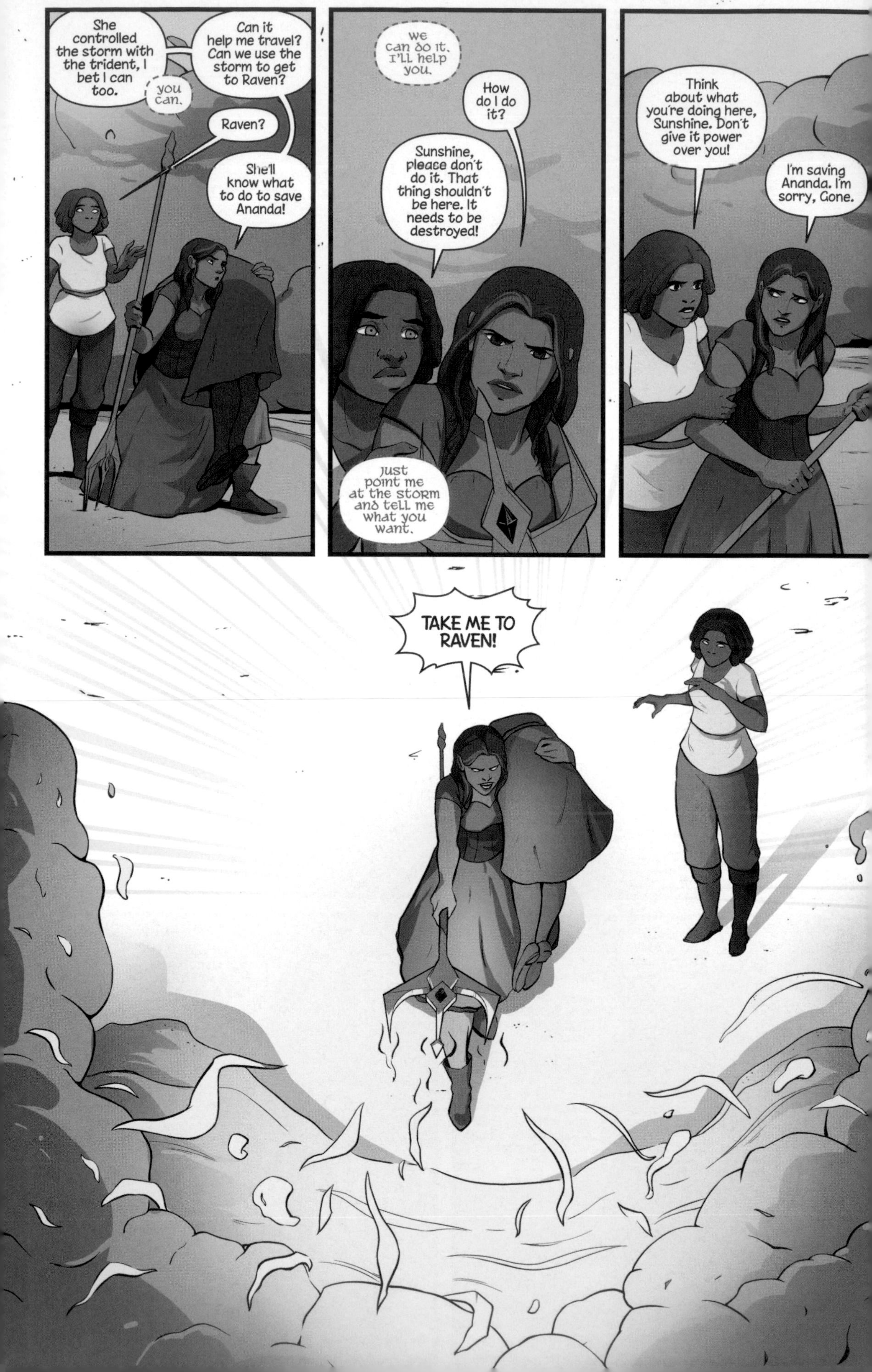
She controlled the storm with the trident, I bet I can too.
you can.
Can it help me travel? Can we use the storm to get to Raven?
Raven?
She'll know what to do to save Ananda!
we can do it. I'll help you.
How do I do it?
Sunshine, please don't do it. That thing shouldn't be here. It needs to be destroyed!
just point me at the storm and tell me what you want.
Think about what you're doing here, Sunshine. Don't give it power over you!
I'm saving Ananda. I'm sorry, Gone.
TAKE ME TO RAVEN!

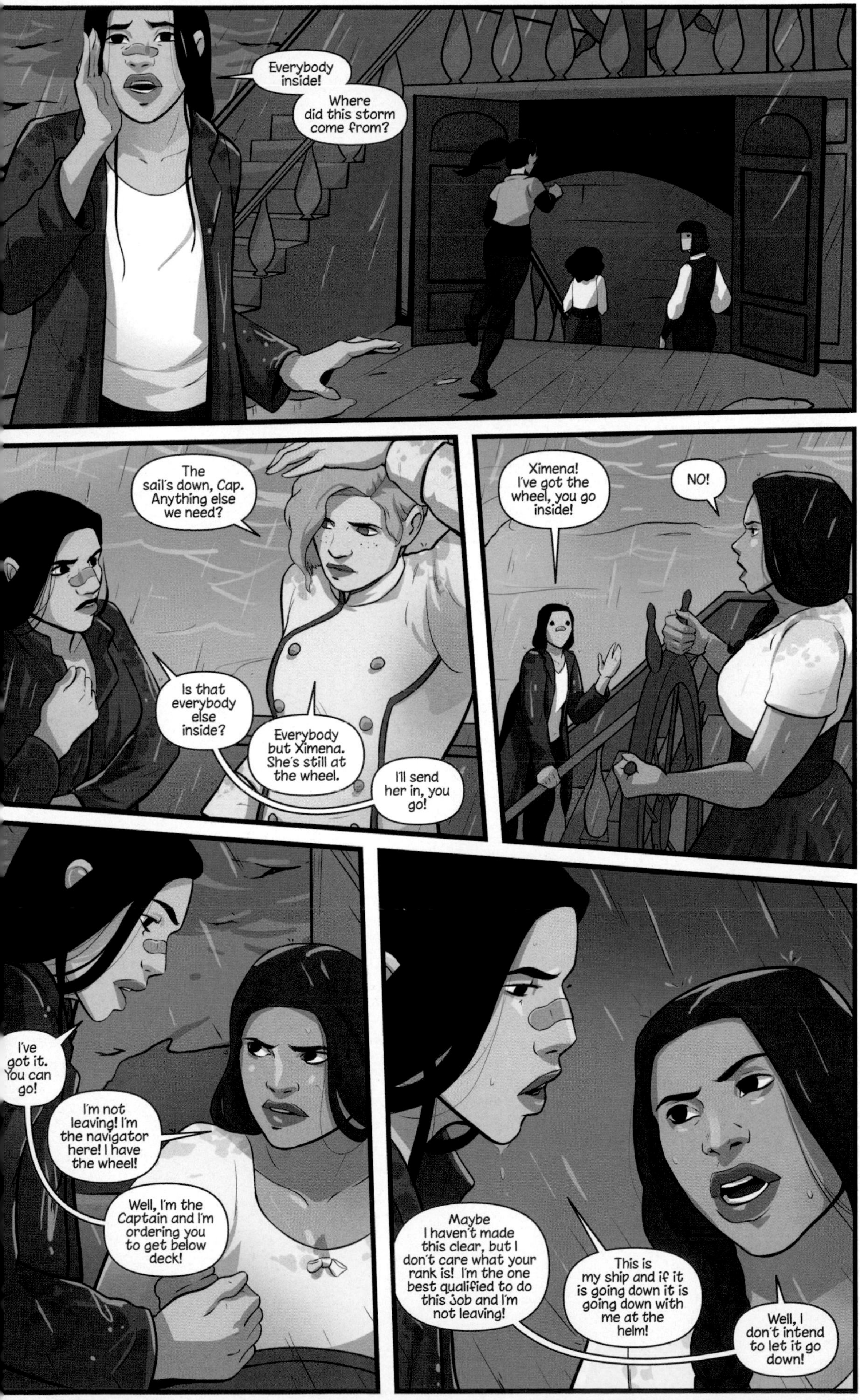

Everybody inside!
Where did this storm come from?
The sail's down, Cap. Anything else we need?
Is that everybody else inside?
Everybody but Ximena. She's still at the wheel.
I'll send her in, you go!
Ximena! I've got the wheel, you go inside!
NO!
I've got it. You can go!
I'm not leaving! I'm the navigator here! I have the wheel!
Well, I'm the Captain and I'm ordering you to get below deck!
Maybe I haven't made this clear, but I don't care what your rank is! I'm the one best qualified to do this job and I'm not leaving!
This is my ship and if it is going down it is going down with me at the helm!
Well, I don't intend to let it go down!

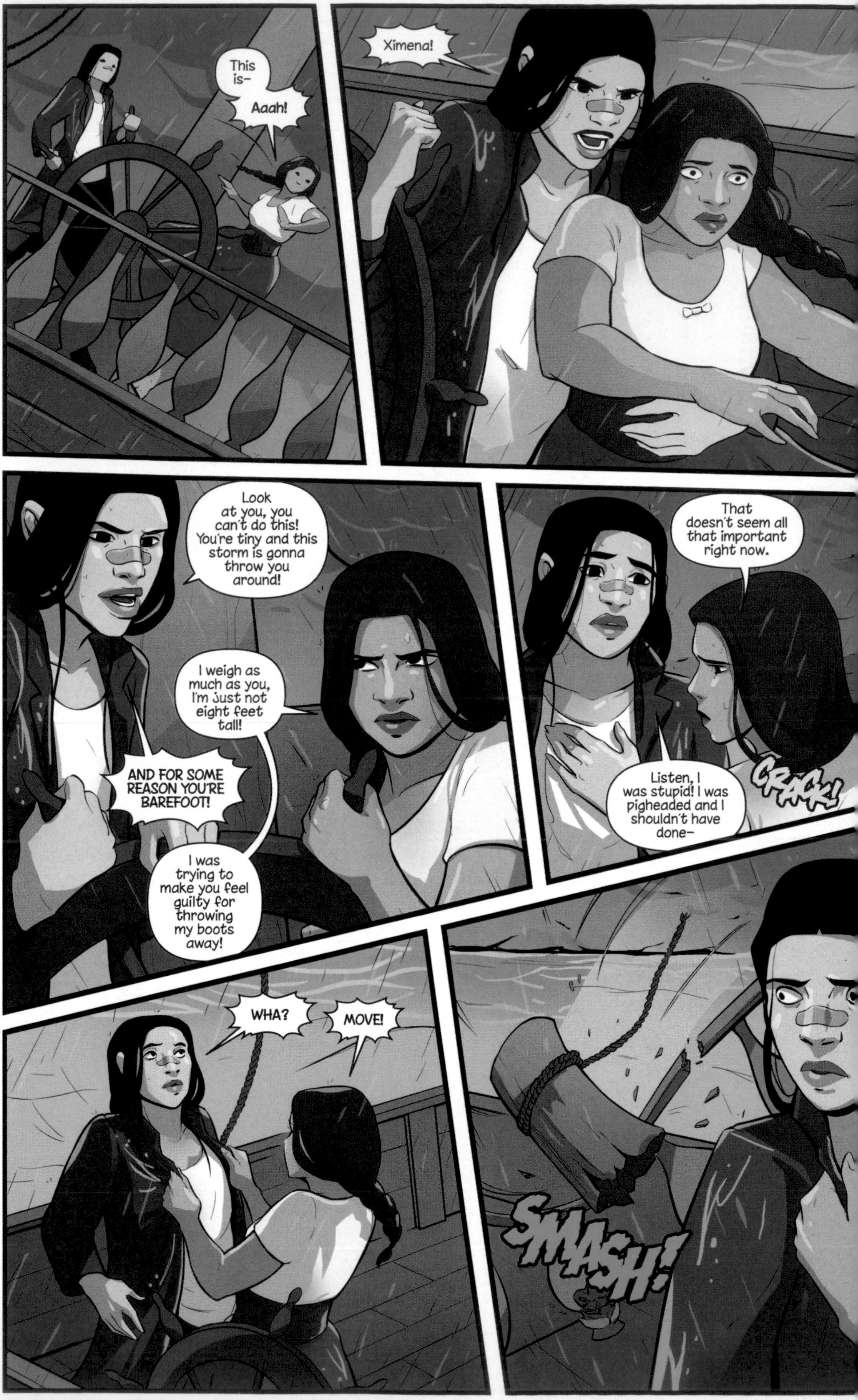
This is–
Aaah!
Ximena!
Look at you, you can't do this! You're tiny and this storm is gonna throw you around!
I weigh as much as you, I'm just not eight feet tall!
AND FOR SOME REASON YOU'RE BAREFOOT!
I was trying to make you feel guilty for throwing my boots away!
That doesn't seem all that important right now.
Listen, I was stupid! I was pigheaded and I shouldn't have done–
CRACK!
WHA?
MOVE!
SMASH!

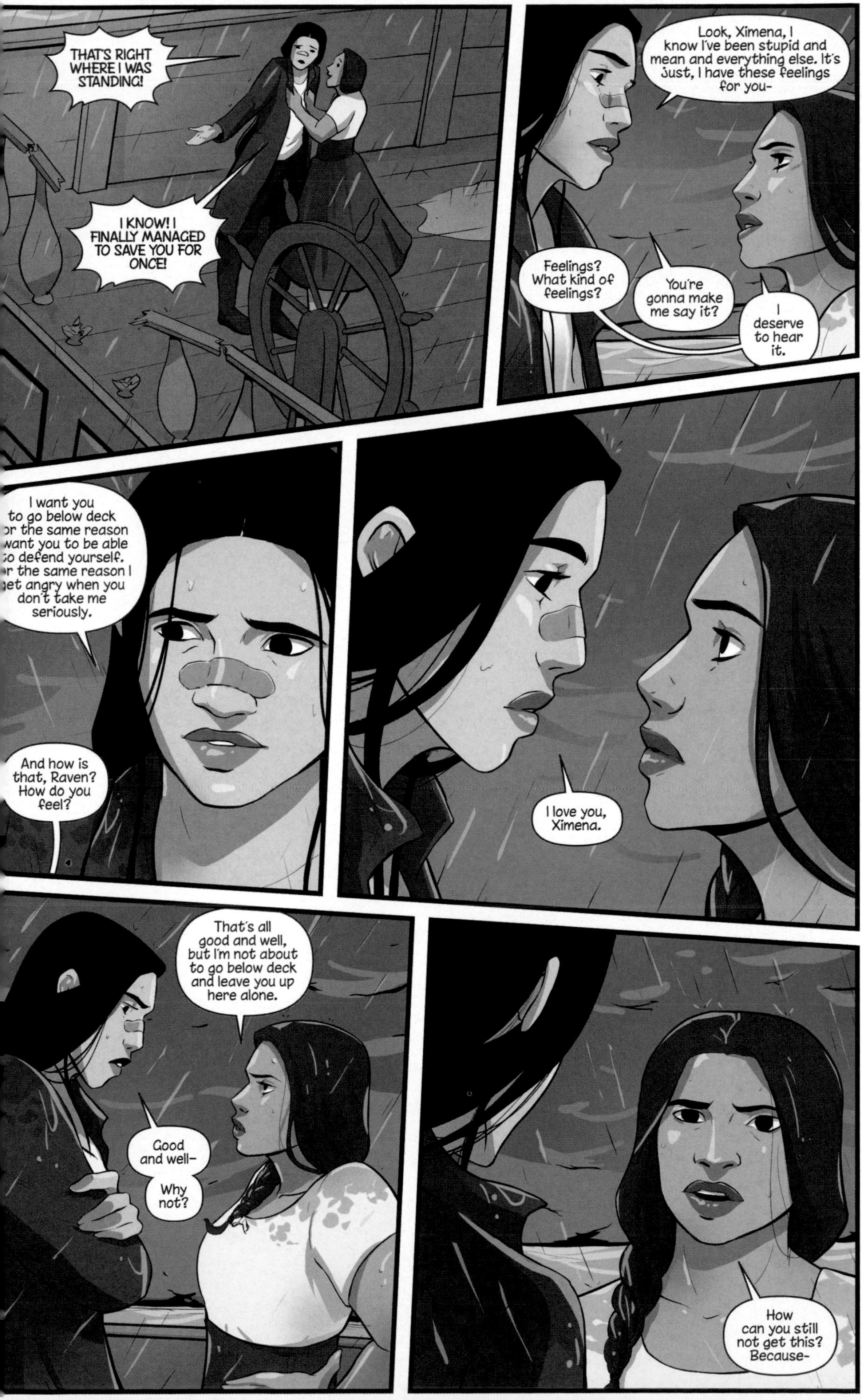
THAT'S RIGHT WHERE I WAS STANDING!
I KNOW! I FINALLY MANAGED TO SAVE YOU FOR ONCE!
Look, Ximena, I know I've been stupid and mean and everything else. It's just, I have these feelings for you-
Feelings? What kind of feelings?
You're gonna make me say it?
I deserve to hear it.
I want you to go below deck or the same reason want you to be able o defend yourself. r the same reason I et angry when you don't take me seriously.
And how is that, Raven? How do you feel?
I love you, Ximena.
That's all good and well, but I'm not about to go below deck and leave you up here alone.
Good and well-
Why not?
How can you still not get this? Because-

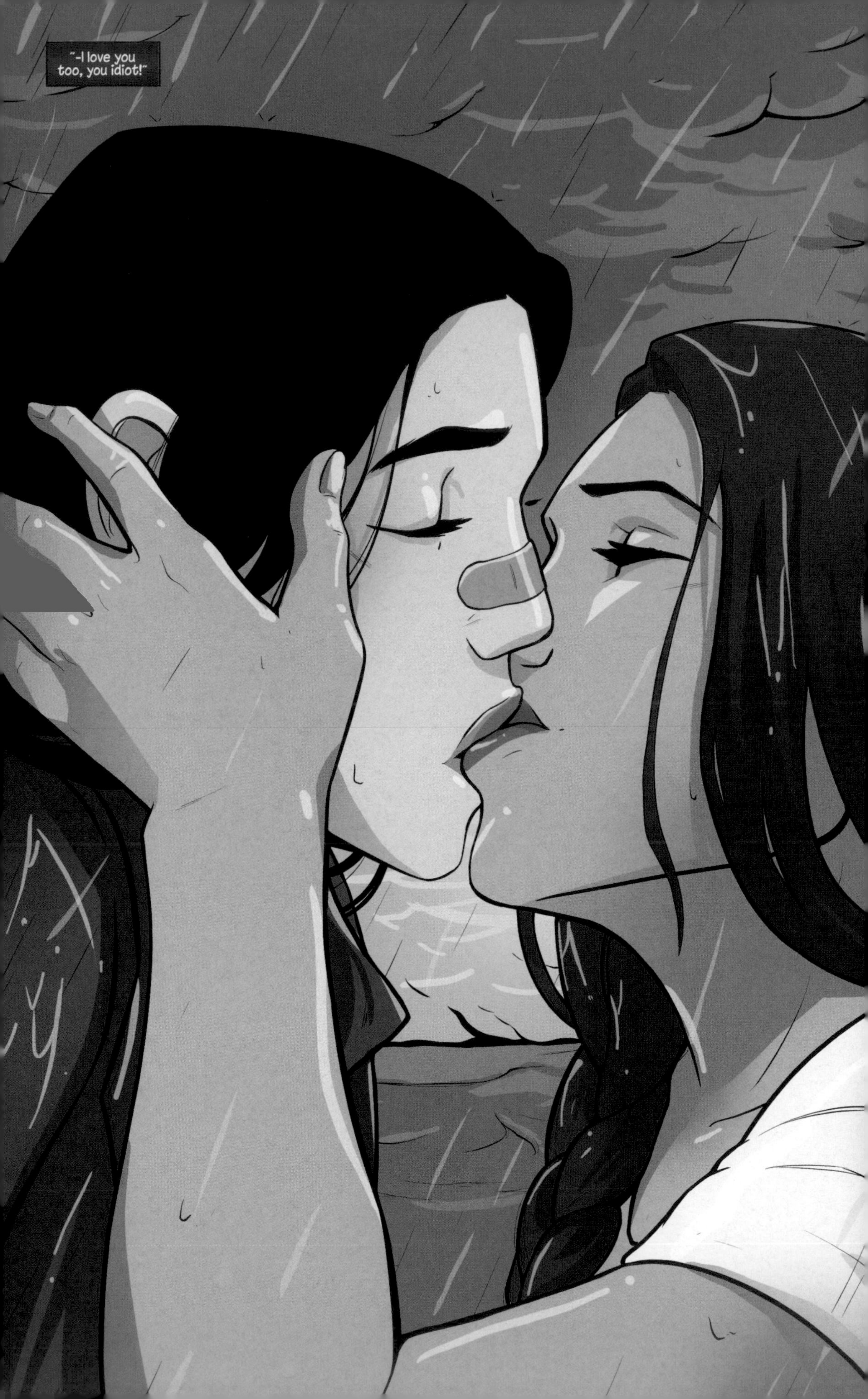
"-I love you
too, you idiot!"

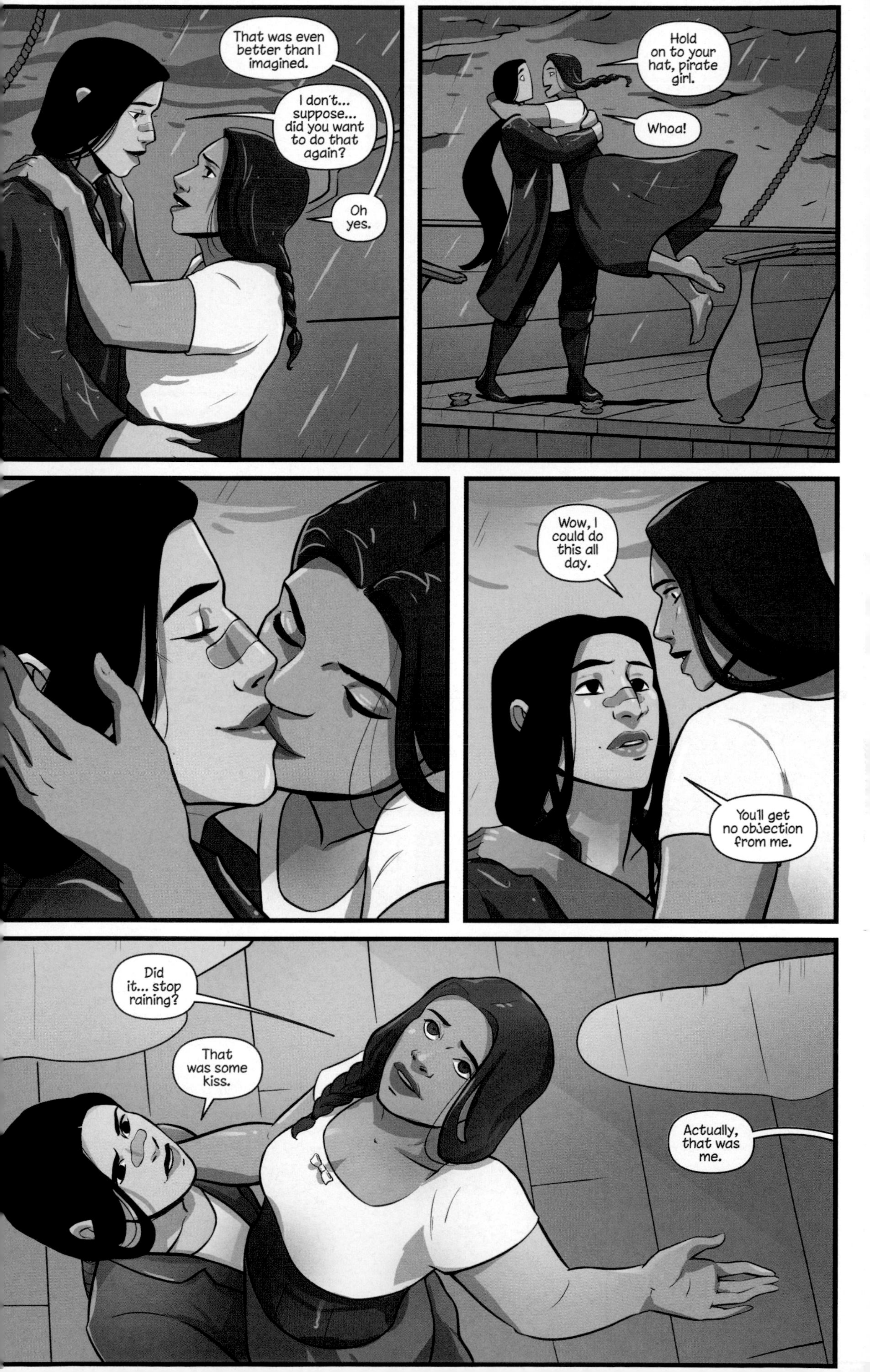
That was even better than I imagined.
I don't... suppose... did you want to do that again?
Oh yes.
Hold on to your hat, pirate girl.
Whoa!
Wow, I could do this all day.
You'll get no objection from me.
Did it... stop raining?
That was some kiss.
Actually, that was me.

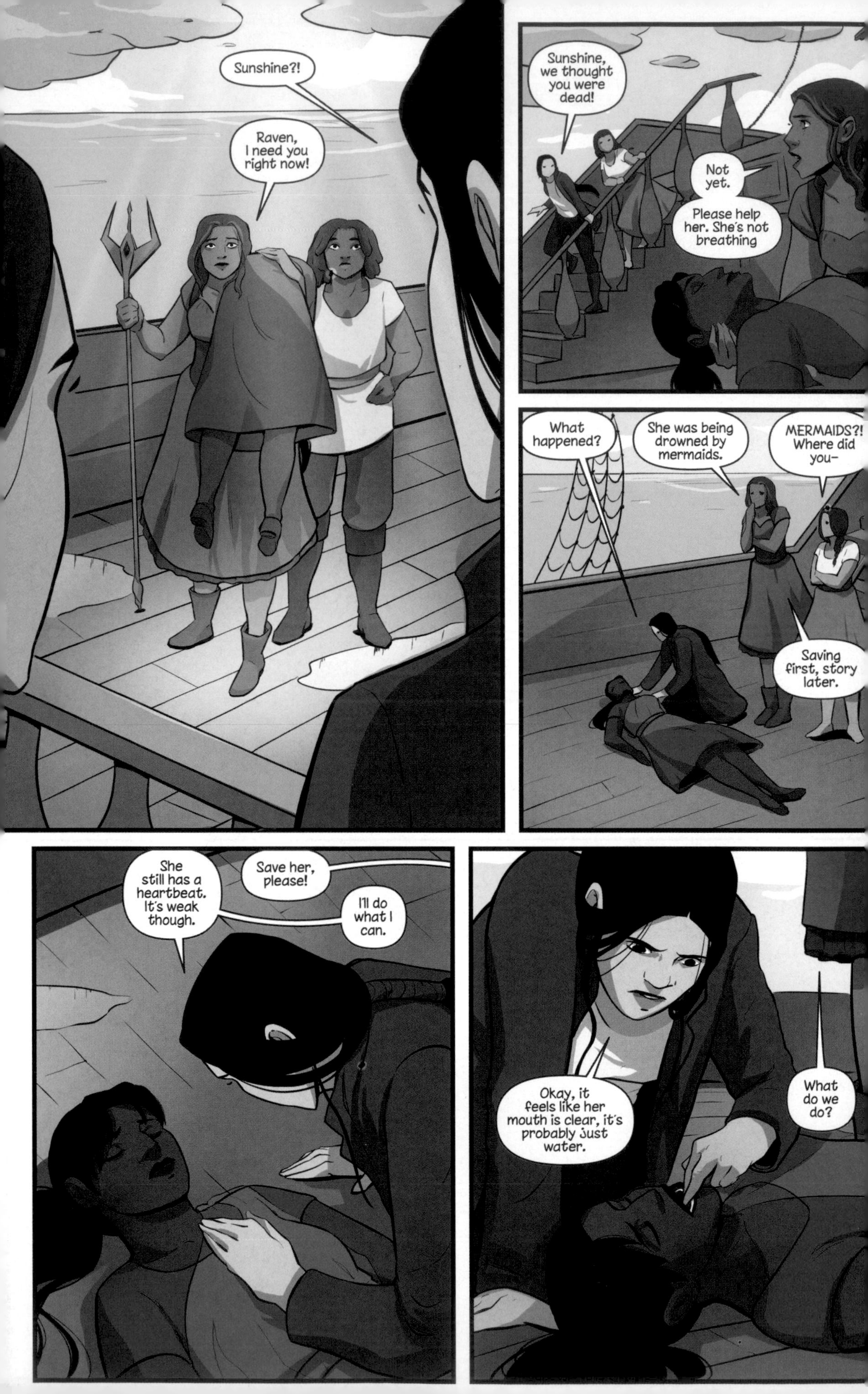
Sunshine?!
Raven, I need you right now!
Sunshine, we thought you were dead!
Not yet.
Please help her. She's not breathing
What happened?
She was being drowned by mermaids.
MERMAIDS?! Where did you-
Saving first, story later.
She still has a heartbeat. It's weak though.
Save her, please!
I'll do what I can.
Okay, it feels like her mouth is clear, it's probably just water.
What do we do?

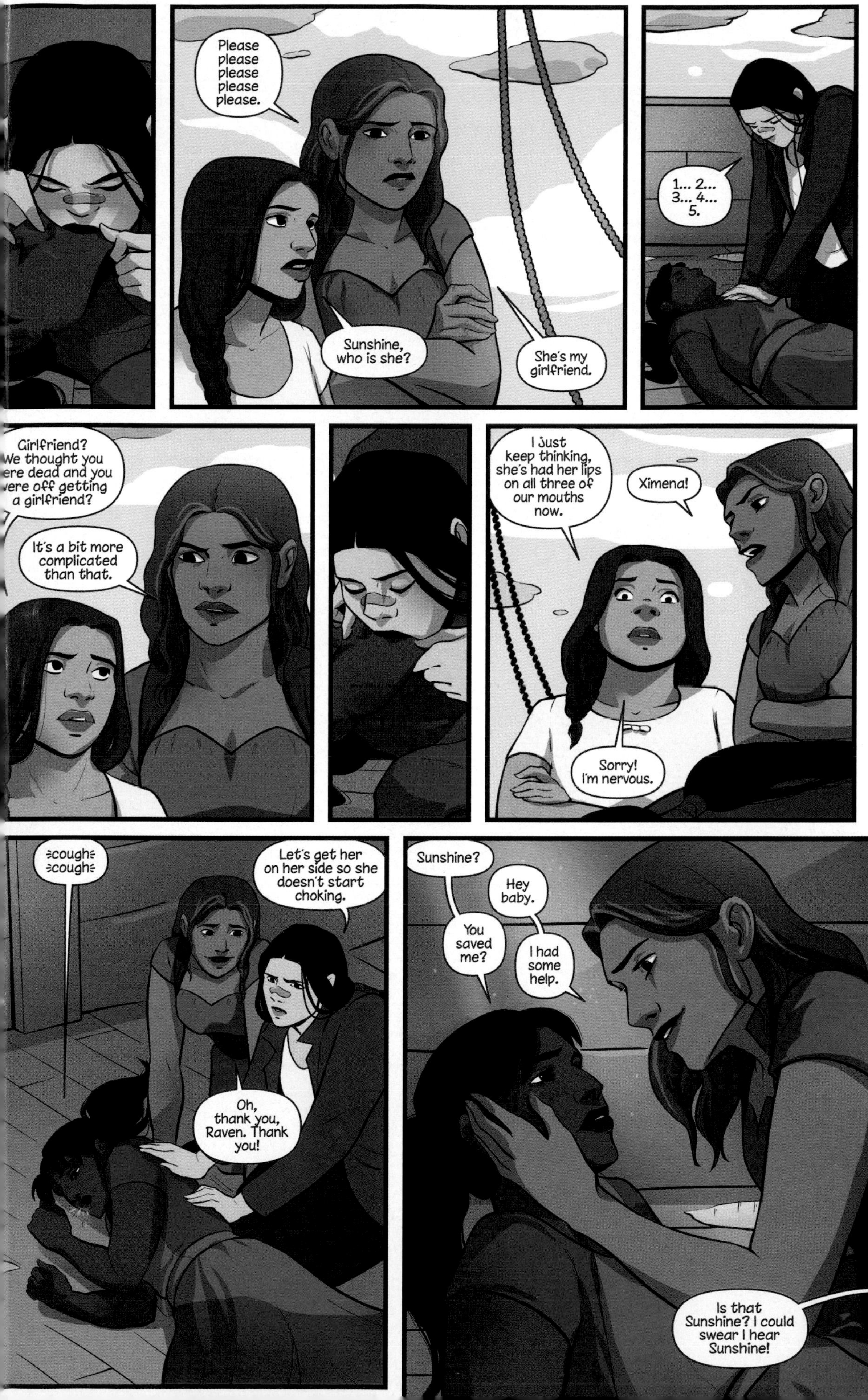
Please please please please please.
Sunshine, who is she?
She's my girlfriend.
1... 2... 3... 4... 5.
Girlfriend? We thought you ere dead and you vere off getting a girlfriend?
It's a bit more complicated than that.
I just keep thinking, she's had her lips on all three of our mouths now.
Ximena!
Sorry! I'm nervous.
cough cough
Let's get her on her side so she doesn't start choking.
Oh, thank you, Raven. Thank you!
Sunshine?
Hey baby.
You saved me?
I had some help.
Is that Sunshine? I could swear I hear Sunshine!

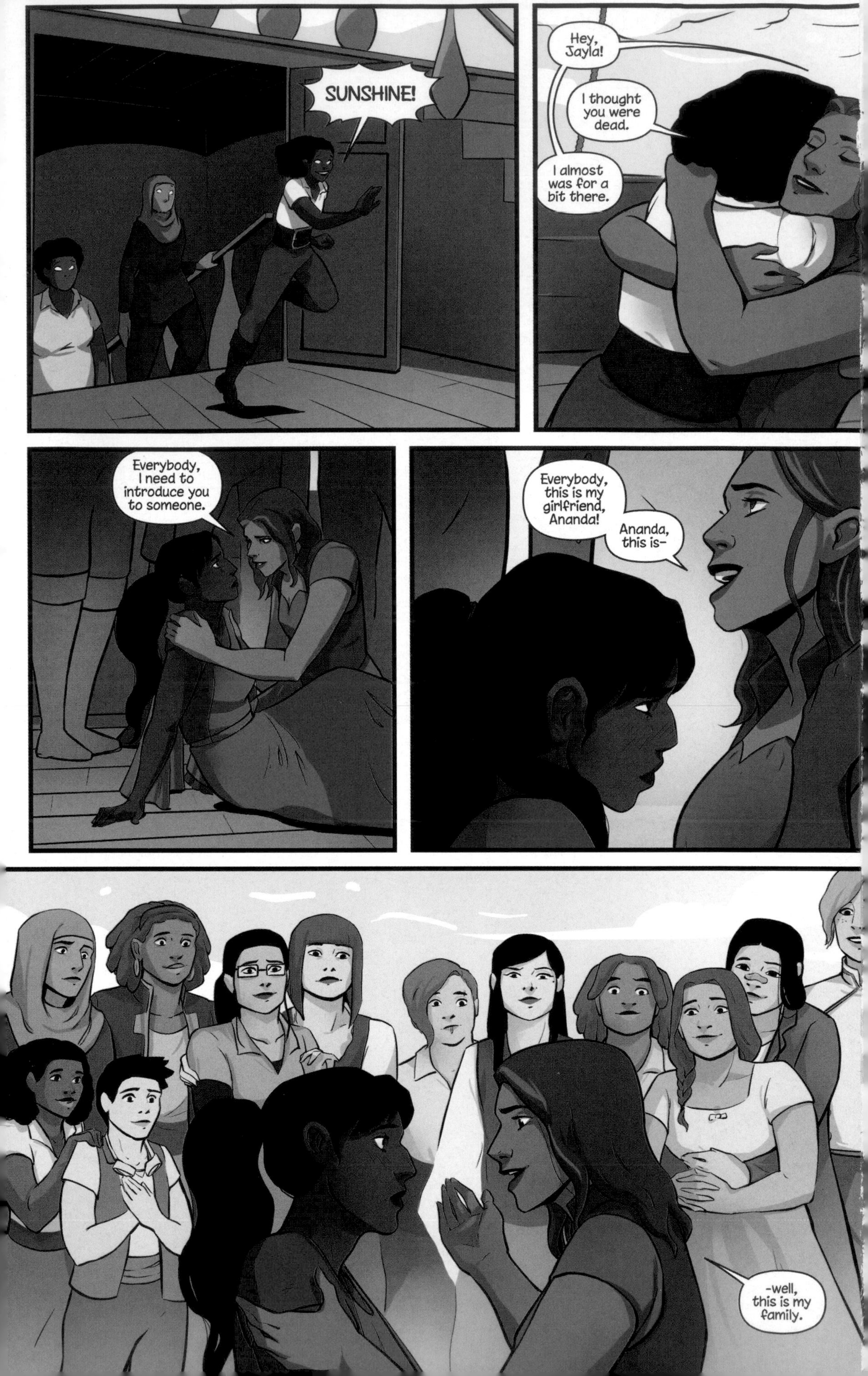
SUNSHINE!
Hey, Jayla!
I thought you were dead.
I almost was for a bit there.
Everybody, I need to introduce you to someone.
Everybody, this is my girlfriend, Ananda!
Ananda, this is-
-well, this is my family.